About the Authors

USA TODAY bestselling author **Catherine Mann** lives on a sunny Florida beach with her flyboy husband and their four children. With more than forty books in print in over twenty countries, she has also celebrated wins for both a RITA® Award and a Booksellers' Best Award. Catherine enjoys chatting with readers online—thanks to the wonders of the internet, which allows her to network with her laptop by the water! Contact Catherine through her website, catherinemann.com, find her on Facebook and Twitter (@CatherineMann1), or reach her by snail mail at PO Box 6065, Navarre, FL 32566.

Kat Cantrell read her first Mills & Boon novel in third grade and has been scribbling in notebooks since she learned to spell. What else would she write but romance? She majored in literature, officially with the intent to teach, but somehow ended up buried in middle management in corporate America, until she became a stay-at-home mum and full-time writer.

Kat, her husband and their two boys live in north Texas. Kat was the 2011 So You Think You Can Write winner and a 2012 RWA Golden Heart® Award finalist for best unpublished series contemporary manuscript.

Bestselling author **Jules Bennett** has penned nearly forty romance novels. She lives in the Midwest with her high-school-sweetheart husband and their two daughters. Sign up for her newsletter to stay up-to-date on releases and monthly contests for subscribers only. Find Jules on F julesbennett.com.

Playboys' Christmas Surprises

CATHERINE MANN

KAT CANTRELL

JULES BENNETT

MILLS & BOON

First Published in Great Britain 2018
By Mills & Boon, an imprint of HarperCollins *Publishers*
1 London Bridge Street, London, SE1 9GF

PLAYBOY'S CHRISTMAS SURPRISE © 2018 Harlequin Books S.A.

A Christmas Baby Surprise © Catherine Mann 2015
Triplets Under the Tree © Kat Cantrell 2015
Holiday Baby Scandal © Jules Bennett 2016

ISBN: 978-0-263-27013-6

9-1118

MIX
Paper from
responsible sources
FSC® C007454

This book is produced from independently certified FSC™ paper to ensure responsible forest management.

For more information visit: www.harpercollins.co.uk/green

Printed and bound in Spain
by CPI, Barcelona

A CHRISTMAS BABY SURPRISE

CATHERINE MANN

To my awesome editor Stacy Boyd!

One

Alaina Rutger was living her childhood dream—a family of her own. Her charismatic husband was driving her home from the hospital with their infant son strapped into a car seat. She had the perfect life.

If only she could remember the man who'd put the four-carat diamond wedding ring on her finger.

A man who called himself Porter Rutger. Husband. Father of her child. And a man who'd been wiped from her memory along with the past five years of her life.

She tore her eyes away from his broad shoulders and coal-dark hair as she sat in back with their baby. Her baby. Alaina tucked the monogrammed red blanket over the infant as he slept, one foot in a booty, the other in a cast that had begun the repair on his clubfoot.

Another person she didn't remember. Another heartbreak in her upside-down world. A week ago, she'd woken in the hospital with no memory of the man sitting by her bedside or of the blue bundle in the bassinet.

Waking up from a coma had felt a lot like coming to after the worst hangover ever, her head throbbing so badly she could barely move. But a quick look around showed her a hospital room rather than a bedroom.

And a hot man sleeping in the chair, his dark hair rumpled. His black pants and white button-down wrinkled.

Her own Doctor McDreamy?

"Hello," she'd croaked out, her throat raw for a sip of water.

McDreamy bolted awake quickly. "Alaina?" He blinked, scrubbed his hand across his eyes in disbelief, then shot to his feet. "Oh, God, you're awake. I need to get the nurse."

"Water," she rasped out. "Please, a drink."

He thumbed the nurses' call button. "I don't know what the doctors will want. Maybe ice chips. Your IV has been feeding you. Soon, though, I promise, whatever you want, soon."

The nurses? Doctors? He wasn't Doc McDreamy? Then ... "Who are you?"

He looked up from the control panel of buttons slowly, his eyes wide with disbelief. "Who am I?"

She pressed her fingertips to her monster headache. "I'm sorry, but I feel like hell. What happened?"

"Alaina..." He sank slowly into the chair, his voice measured, guarded. "We were in a car accident."

"We?" She knew him?

"Yes," he said, leaning closer to cover her hand carefully. "Alaina, my name's Porter and I'm your husband."

The shock of that revelation still echoed through her.

Once the nurse and doctor had checked her over Porter had further explained they'd been in a car wreck a month prior, after picking up little Thomas from the adoption agency. Her husband... Porter. Porter Rutger. God, she still struggled to remember his name. Porter told her the baby had a birth defect and had spent the past month going through surgeries while she'd been in a coma from the accident.

Too soon, before she felt ready to handle this life she'd landed in, it was time to leave the hospital. She'd been told many first moms felt that way.

But not all new mothers had amnesia.

Her throat burned with bile and fears that hadn't abated since she'd woken from the coma a week ago thinking it was November, only to find it was December.

Five years later.

Five years of memories simply gone, pushed out of her head in the course of a month. Most devastating, she'd lost the four and a half years Porter had been in her life.

How was it that four weeks asleep could steal so much of her life? That coma had left her mind missing a substantial chunk of memories and yet her body felt 100 percent normal. She'd even been attracted to her stranger husband, so attracted that the aches and lethargy left over from her coma hadn't dulled the shiver of awareness she'd felt at the brush of his hands against her as he helped her from the hospital bed and into the car.

She swallowed hard and turned to look out the window at the rolling waves as the Mercedes traveled the Florida coastal road toward what Porter had told her was their beach mansion. They also owned a home in Tallahassee but they'd been closer to the beach home when picking up the baby, then having the wreck. Traveling with their infant son so fresh from surgery and her so recently out of a coma hadn't seemed wise. The doctors had advised they stay close for the short term at least.

Porter had quickly suggested they stay at their nearby vacation home. Apparently her tall, dark and studly husband was wealthier than Midas, thanks to his construction empire that won major contracts to build corporate structures around the country. They had no financial worries as she recovered, he'd told her. Another reason to be grateful.

But instead of gratitude, she could only feel fear at the imbalance of power between her and this man who was her husband. She was adrift with only the facts he told her about her past. No family since her parents were dead. No friends, other than people she apparently hadn't seen in five years, since her breakup from an abusive boyfriend. She'd cut herself off from everyone then.

Still, she was missing the months following that breakup, the months leading up to her meeting Porter. Falling in love with him. Marrying him. He said after they married, they'd moved to southeastern Florida, away from her hometown in North Carolina. She believed what he said, but wondered what parts he might not have mentioned. Men could be so brief in their explanations, leaving out details or emotional components a woman would find crucial.

Porter glanced in the rearview mirror, his brown eyes as dark as undiluted coffee full of caffeinated energy.

Jolt.

"Alaina, is everything all right?" he said, his Southern drawl muted by some experience in another region.

Something else she didn't know about him unless he told her.

What kind of answer did he expect from her? More of the same dodgy responses they'd given each other over the past week since she woke up? Guarded words spoken in front of doctors or said out of fear her fragile world might shatter into a somnolent fog again?

Each mile closer to a vacation home she couldn't recall stretched the tension inside her tighter until she snapped softly, "Did the doctor give you any more insight as to why can't I remember the past five years? Nearly a quarter of my life is just gone."

"The doctor spoke with you. He has an obligation to be honest with you. You're his patient." The man in the front seat who called himself her husband was unfailingly polite but lacked the kind of warmth that Alaina would have envisioned in a man she'd married.

Her husband.

What had made her choose this coolly controlled male for a mate? Another question she couldn't begin to answer. In spite of the spark that seemed to arc between them amidst the questions.

"I haven't forgotten that conversation. It was more of a rhetorical question because there are so many other things I don't understand." She glanced down at her sleeping son in his impossibly cute elf pajamas. "Such as, how could anyone forget a child this precious?"

Her heart swelled to look at Thomas, his tiny nose and Cupid's-bow mouth calling to her every maternal instinct. She'd always wanted children, dreamed of having a big family after growing up an only child. If she and Porter had been married for almost four years, what had made them wait to start their family?

"You'd only known him for a couple of hours before the accident." Porter turned onto a secluded drive where mammoth houses were hidden by manicured privacy hedges on one side, although she knew the other side opened to the water.

"The length of time shouldn't matter. He's a child, my child—" she paused, brushing her fingers across the top of an impossibly small and soft hand "—our child. That's life changing. A minute. An hour. A couple of hours. That should be burned in here." She tapped the front of her head.

"Even if your marriage wasn't?" he asked wryly.

Contrition nipped. This had to be tough for him, too. "I'm sorry. This can't be easy for you, either."

"You're alive and awake, more than I ever expected to have again." He said the emotional words with a harsh rasp as he guided the car along the palm tree–lined road. "I can deal with the rest."

"You make me feel as if I shouldn't be frustrated."

"Give yourself time." He kept both hands on the wheel, the late-day sunshine glinting off his Patek Philippe wristwatch. "You've been through a lot."

How did she know the brand of his watch but not know if the band on his ring finger had an inscription? But then, she remembered studying art history when she'd got her bachelor's degree. Recalled a love of finely made things and beautiful objects. Maybe that was why the watch resonated and the ring...nothing.

"What about you? What have you been through this past month? It must have been horrible, with a child in surgery and a wife in a coma."

"That doesn't matter," he said, his voice clipped. "I'm fine now."

Her mouth twitched with amusement as the car braked at a stop sign wrapped in garland. "Are you one of those men who's too tough to be vulnerable?"

His eyes met hers solemnly in the mirror. "I'm a man who thought he'd lost everything."

And just that fast, she felt her terrified heart melt a little for this stranger husband of hers. "You still have, in a way," she said sympathetically, "because of me and how I've lost any sense of us and our memories."

At the deserted intersection, he twisted to look over the seat at her, his elbow resting along the back and tugging his button-down shirt across his muscular chest. "You and our son are alive. That truly is what's most important to me."

There had been tension between them since she'd woken up in the hospital. He still held all the answers she couldn't access. But now, with the sincerity shining in his eyes, she wanted to hug him, ached to wrap her arms around him and have him do the same to her. Most of all, to have that feel familiar. She stretched a hand out to touch his elbow lightly—

A car honked behind them and she jerked her hand back. What was she thinking? Except for the few things he'd told her, she knew nothing about him or her or what kind of life they'd built together. Or what kind of future they might have because these events had changed them. Undoubtedly.

However for Thomas, she and Porter had to try for a level of peace between them. Could the Christmas spirit work a miracle for her family?

Shifting nervously in her seat, Alaina toyed with

the reindeer baby rattle, gathering up her rapidly fraying nerve. "May I ask you questions about the past?"

"Why didn't you question more before?" He kept his eyes on the road this time.

In some ways maybe that made this conversation easier.

"Because…I was scared you wouldn't answer."

"What's changed?"

"We're not in the hospital. There are no doctors who make me do all the work thinking, insisting I should only remember what I'm ready to know. They kept asking me not to push to remember, but that's causing me even more stress, wondering." She needed to know. How could she be a real wife to Porter and a mother to Thomas if she didn't even know who she was or how they'd become a family?

"You trust me to answer truthfully?" He glanced back at her, his eyes darkening.

"What do you have to gain by lying?"

Now wasn't that a loaded question? One that called for total trust in a man she barely knew. But she had no other choice, not if she wanted to reconnect as a family. "How did we meet?"

"My firm was handling building an addition to a museum where you worked. You saw me flex my muscles and here we are."

He sure did have muscles, and if they'd enticed her half as much then as they did now she could see how he would have caught her attention. His humor made him even more appealing. "You're funny, after all, Porter."

"You think I don't have a sense of humor? You've wounded my ego."

"There hasn't been a lot of room for levity this week."

She'd been so damn scared in the hospital. Walking the halls at night when she couldn't sleep. Obsessively checking on the baby and praying she would remember something, anything from the past five years.

Most of all, wondering about the mysterious, handsome man who'd spent hours with her each day.

"True enough. Hopefully we can fix that. We have the whole holiday season to relax, settle our child and get to know each other again." Through the rearview mirror, he held her eyes with a determined intensity. "Because, make no mistake, I intend to remind you of all the reasons we fell in love in the first place."

His words made something go hot inside her, a mixture of desire and confusion and, yes, nerves. She swallowed hard. It didn't help. But even if she didn't remember it, this was her life. There was no choice but to push on. To regain her memories and her life.

And figure out just what this man—her husband— meant to her. Not just in the past. But now.

Porter Rutger had been through hell.

But for the first time in a long time he saw a way to climb back out.

His hands clenched the steering wheel as he drove his wife and son home from the hospital. The past month— worrying about how Thomas would recover from his first surgery for his clubfoot, wondering about possible hidden effects of the accident on the baby...

And all the while his wife had been in a coma.

Porter's jaw flexed as he studied the familiar beach road leading to the vacation home they'd chosen after their third in vitro failed. Before they'd adopted

Thomas, their marriage had showed signs of fraying from years of struggling with the stresses of infertility.

He and Alaina had been in hell for a long time, even before the accident. He'd thought they'd hit rock bottom when they'd contacted a divorce attorney. They'd been so close to signing the divorce papers when the call came about a baby to adopt. A special-needs baby, difficult to place, an infant who required surgeries and years of physical therapy. While foster care would have provided the basics, the search for a home would have to start all over again if they backed out, leaving the baby adrift in the system.

They hadn't made the decision to adopt on a whim. They'd started the adoption process two years ago when the reality of infertility had become clear. Then they'd faced more heartache waiting. Their already strained marriage hadn't fared well under the added stress.

To this day, he couldn't remember which of them had asked for a divorce. The words had been thrown out during an argument and then taken root, growing fast, lawyers involved. It had damn near torn him apart, but their constant arguments had made it impossible to envision a future together bringing up the family they both wanted so much. Even marriage counseling hadn't helped.

They'd reached the end—and then the call had come about Thomas.

He and Alaina had put their differences aside to adopt the baby and stay together temporarily. Her soft, open heart had welcomed the baby from the second the call had come. Thomas needed them. That had cinched the deal for Alaina.

Then the accident happened and the possibility of losing her completely had made him want to shred the documents. Maybe he could have that family he wanted after all.

And he'd had no idea how quickly that little bundle in the back would steal his heart. He would do anything for his son. Anything.

While he would also do anything to have Alaina healthy, he couldn't ignore the fact that he had a second chance to win her over—for himself and for their son. This could be a fresh start, a way to work through all the pain they'd caused each other in the past.

Yes, he'd made mistakes in their marriage, but this was a new opportunity to build the family he'd always wanted. Growing up with a single-mom lawyer who worked all the time and husband-hunted during her hours off, he'd craved stability, love.

If he could only gain Alaina's forgiveness, or convince her that he was in it for the long haul this time, that he'd changed. Hell, if he could just make Alaina realize he wasn't the man he'd been a few weeks ago, then he could have the family he'd always dreamed of. The one they'd both wanted.

He'd never been one to procrastinate or waste time. He was a man of action.

And the stakes had never been more important than now.

Porter glanced in the rearview mirror at his blonde wife, the woman he'd fallen head over heels in love with four and a half years ago. Her intelligence, confidence and artistic flair had mesmerized him. He'd seen her discussing gallery art with a visiting class of elementary school students and he'd known. She was the one. She was his every perfect fantasy—soft, openhearted. He could envision her cradling their babies. Making sand castles with toddlers. Painting with children.

And it hadn't been just the maternal images that drew him. She had a passionate nature that set him on fire. Even now, the memories turned him inside out.

But the more they'd argued, the more he'd realized how shaky their foundation had been.

"What did you want to know?"

"We didn't talk much at all in the hospital." Her blue eyes held his for an electric instant before she looked away.

"The doctor's orders. And things were hectic, with Thomas's physical therapists and your tests." He'd been pulled in two different directions even though he'd taken time off from work, passing over control of his construction firm to his second in command until he had his family in order. Seeing her so helpless in the hospital had sucker punched him. Their love for each other might have died, but they still shared a history, an attraction, and now a child. His need for the picture-perfect family had destroyed their marriage and their love for each other.

But he owed it to her to take care of her while she healed and while they figured out how to parent Thomas.

"I'm not blaming anyone," she said quickly. "I'm just trying to fill in the blanks so I can function. I felt so… limited in the hospital."

He wouldn't sabotage her recovery. The doctors had said she shouldn't push to remember, and he planned to honor that directive. He wasn't that ruthless, no matter what his competitors said. But he sure as hell wasn't going to squander this chance to convince her to stay.

He would do whatever it took to keep her in this family. He wasn't interested in being a part-time father, and had never been, even when he'd agreed to sign those damn divorce papers. He'd regretted that decision the moment he'd made it. How could he have the family he needed if he let his wife walk away? Even then, regardless of their problems, he'd wanted things to go back to the way they'd been in the beginning.

He didn't know what had gone wrong, what more she expected of him. And now that she couldn't remember their life together, he might not ever find out. "The doctor wanted to see how much you recalled on your own. We didn't want you to confuse memories with things you'd been told."

"Maybe hearing about us might help jog those memories."

He noticed she didn't mention the whole trust issue again. Did that mean she'd put it on the back burner? Or she was willing to take him at his word?

She sure as hell hadn't trusted him at the end of their marriage, before the accident. Would that distrust eek through even her thick fog of amnesia? He steered off the highway onto the access road to their security gate.

"Porter, I don't have a choice but to ask you these questions. There's no one else from my past I still have a relationship with. If I want to find out anything about these past five years, it's you or Google."

He chuckled darkly. "A ringing endorsement if ever I heard one."

A smile played with her full lips. It was almost comfortable and it caused his chest to tighten. He remembered a time when he'd been able to make her smile every day, back before their relationship had deteriorated into loud fights and long silences.

"Porter, I'm not going to apologize for speaking the truth." The smile faded. "Why didn't anyone come see me in the hospital?"

"When the accident happened, we were far from home, picking up the baby. Our friends weren't nearby." And no doubt they would have felt awkward coming to visit the couple given the impending divorce. "I saved the cards from the flowers and balloons that came at the start. I'll show you when we get home."

She chewed that full lip. "What about phone calls to quiz people? Who can I call to help me?"

He wouldn't isolate her, but he didn't want to make it easy for her to take off again, either. He just wanted a little time for them to cement their relationship again, to rediscover what they'd once had—and to parent the baby they'd always wanted. They needed this time to become the family he'd always imagined they could be.

"The doctor warned you to be careful and take it slow. You'll have to ask your physicians near the beach house. Whatever they say is good by me." It surprised him that she hadn't asked many questions publicly at the hospital, but whatever had held her back, now that they were alone, she was more relentless about getting answers. There was an urgency and an edge to her now that she hadn't possessed before the accident.

Or had she kept it hidden the way she'd hidden so many of her motives in the last months of their marriage?

"So you have no trouble giving me those phone numbers? If the doctor says it's okay." She leaned forward, resting her arms on the back of the seat as they waited at an intersection.

"No problem at all." People would be eager to hear

from her after the accident, but they'd also be busy with the holidays. And the doctor had given them no reason to think her memory would return so soon. He needed the next two weeks' Christmas holiday with her and their son to tell her his side of the story. To see if they could make this work. Maybe, just maybe they could build that family after all. For Thomas. "Whatever you want from me, just ask. We're married."

Her quick gasp brushed across his neck, and her gaze met his, her eyes wide. "Whatever I want?"

The air went hot between them. Could she see the memories in his eyes? Could she sense just how damn good they had been together? How good they could still be?

There was desire and apprehension in her eyes. Her gaze broadcast loud and clear that she might not share the same memories, but she felt their connection—and it made her nervous.

He needed to proceed carefully. He hadn't told her about their decision to divorce. He wanted the chance to convince her to stay first. He also didn't want her asking questions that would box him into lying—or telling a hard truth. Like the fact they hadn't slept together for a month before the accident. "I can promise you, I'm not about to demand husbandly rights or anything else from you until you're ready."

"That's for the best," she said a little too fast. "I'm not ready for—"

"You don't need to say anything more." He punched in the security code to open the scrolled gates that were designed like a pewter clamshell gaping wide. Christmas lights glistened on the palm trees lining the path to the yellow stucco mansion, the glimmer growing brighter with the setting sun.

"You've been very understanding the past week, Porter. I know this has been difficult for you, too, and I appreciate that you've worked to make things as easy for me as possible."

There was a time not so long ago she'd made it clear she felt just the opposite. She'd insisted he only wanted her as a place holder in the mother role. That any woman would have done, that he didn't really love her and that she was damn well tired of him hiding at the office to avoid facing their problems.

He kept his silence.

"What? Did I say something wrong?"

"You've been through a lot the past month." They both had. He steered toward the three-story mansion perched on an ocean bluff, holiday decor in full glory of wreaths, bows and draped garland as he'd ordered. "Of course you deserve understanding. I just want you to be clear that while I'm giving you time and space to remember your past, that doesn't mean I won't be trying to fill your head with happy new memories."

Her eyes went wide again. God, she was beautiful but too frail after all she'd been through. Protective urges fired to the fore. They might not be the couple they'd been before, but he needed her to make his family complete. He would do whatever it took to woo her over these next couple of weeks. And he wouldn't let anyone stand in his way.

He put the car in Park in front of the sweeping double staircase just as the groundskeeper stepped into another car to valet park…and…

Damn. Porter felt the sucker punch clear through to his spine.

He recognized that Maserati sports car well. Heaven help them all.

His mother had come to visit.

Two

Home sweet home?

Sorta.

Her eyes flitted to the sprawling house before them. Poinsettias lined the double staircase, adding Christmas spirit to the green and vibrant Florida winter. A giant wreath trimmed in gold and silver hung on the door, warm and inviting.

The warmth made her heart sink a bit. Had she picked out all of these decorations? Were they supposed to carry some sentimental value? She had been with Porter for almost five years. They owned years' worth of memories and items they had collected—and all of it was a mystery to her. Taking a deep breath, she turned her attention to Thomas and his monogrammed blanket.

As she unbuckled the baby from his car seat, Alaina couldn't miss the tension radiating from Porter. Of course he'd been under a tremendous stress, too, during this whole situation. He had just been so stalwart until now; she was surprised he let his emotions show.

Even if he'd opened up only briefly before he became the ultimate in-control guy again. Was that an act just for her? Was that how she'd preferred him to be? She'd liked seeing the emotion on his face, in his eyes. The controlled expression he wore now seemed to shut her out.

She cradled the sleeping infant in her arms, taking comfort from the scent of baby shampoo and innocence. She didn't remember becoming a wife or a mother. She didn't *feel* like a wife or a mother.

But she knew without question she would do whatever was needed to make sure this innocent life in her care felt loved and secure.

Porter opened the back door of the car, the setting sun casting a nimbus around his big body, which blocked out the rest of the world. God, he was a gorgeous hulk of man. She could see him in a painting of Atlas holding the world on those broad shoulders. He made her feel safe, protected. She could lean on him.

He propped a hand on the roof. "Are you feeling steady enough to carry the baby?"

"I'm fine, but thank you for asking." She stepped out, her hold careful on Thomas.

Porter cupped her elbow in a steadying grasp, his touch warm and gentle, sending tingles through her. She glanced at him quickly. Did he feel it, too? What was he thinking? He had to want his wife back. She wanted that for him, but even so, she couldn't shake the feeling that something was off between them. She couldn't miss how he only answered what was needed, never offering one snippet more. And his shoulders seemed so braced, tense. Where was the joy in this homecoming?

She straightened and adjusted her hold on the baby. "Thank you. I really am okay to walk on my own."

It was strange how she'd been in a coma for a month and yet her body acted as if she'd simply taken a long nap. She'd spent a week doing physical therapy and eating high-nutrient meals to regain strength in her muscles. Other than tiring quickly, she felt no ill effects from her ordeal. At least not physically. How surreal.

"I'll get the car seat and diaper bag, then." He reached to lift them out, the navy blue Burberry bag looking tiny and incongruous in his large hands. "Before we step inside, I should warn you."

Foreboding gelled in her belly. Here it came. Whatever awful thing she'd feared her amnesia had been hiding from her. "Warn me about what?"

"My mother's here," he said with a heavy sigh.

She almost laughed in hysterical relief. She walked beside him toward the towering doors, inhaling a bracing breath of salty ocean breeze. "Your mom?" If he had a mother, why hadn't she come to the hospital? That seemed strange. She hadn't thought to question him about his family in the hospital since her memories stopped just before her relationship with Porter began. "You have a mother?"

"I wasn't born under a rock," he said with a sense of humor that still surprised her.

Another intriguing element to this man.

Chewing her bottom lip, Alaina eyed the door with trepidation. The gold and silver of the wreath caught in the amber sunset. "I wish you would have mentioned her arrival before now."

"I didn't know she was coming until I saw her car as we pulled up. It's very distinctive."

"Is your father here, too?"

"If so, that would be an even bigger surprise since I've never met the man."

"Oh, um, I'm sorry." Another thing about her husband she should have known.

"Thank you, but I'm long past looking for father figures around every corner. I'm looking forward to *being* a father." He reached to lift out the infant seat. "Let's go find out what coerced my mother to drive up from Miami."

Something about the way he said that made her sad, reminding her again of all the ways this should have been a happy day for him. His family was returning home from the hospital in good health. But she again felt that their life together—whatever it was now—couldn't be summed up that easily.

She wanted to trust him.

But something deep inside her, something beyond memory and born of instinct, held her back.

Luckily for him, his mother had been settling into her suite when he and Alaina brought Thomas into the house. His wife was in the nursery with their son now, which would give him a chance to talk to his mother alone first in his study. She needed to understand that he would toss her out on Christmas Day itself if she did one thing to upset this chance he had to win back his wife and keep his family intact.

He paced restlessly, his eyes drawn to the brass clock on his desk. What the hell was taking his mother so long? This wasn't the best of times for unexpected company, damn it.

Wooing Alaina back into his life and into his bed was going to be tough enough without having his mother throw verbal land mines into the mix with no warning. Courtney Rutger was a shark in the courtroom and in life. Their relationship had been strained since he'd walked out at eighteen and put himself through college working construction rather than take her money.

There were too many strings attached to his mother's gifts. The extravagant presents had clearly made Alaina uncomfortable given her less affluent upbringing and he couldn't blame her. Still, he'd never been quite sure how to navigate the tense waters between his mother and wife.

Finally, she glided into his study in a swirl of expensive perfume and one of her favored fitted Chanel suits. She leaned toward him for an air kiss on the cheek. "Porter."

He complied, as expected, wondering if she'd ever carried him around the way Alaina cradled Thomas. Making real contact, rather than an air kiss or half hug.

"Mom," he answered, angling away and leaning against his desk. "Why are you here?"

"To celebrate Christmas, and to help you with your new baby and your *wife*."

Help now? He wasn't buying it. His mother had visited only on holidays during his marriage, and she hadn't done more than come to the hospital the day after the accident. She'd seen her grandson, brought some gifts and flowers and left. She sure as hell hadn't cooed over her grandchild, much less snapped photos on her cell phone to share with her pals. "You've never been interested in babies before."

"I've never been a grandmother before."

"Mother..." He raised an eyebrow impatiently.

"Son," she answered with overplayed innocence.

"Is that what you're about? I'm your son. I know you. And you're not going to cause mother-in-law troubles."

"I don't know what you're talking about."

"Oh, Mother, please. You've made it clear for years that you don't like Alaina." The friction between his wife and mother, which had grown over time, had added pressure to an already strained marriage. "She's working to regain her memory and the last thing she needs is you tossing in digs or telling her things she's not ready to hear. She needs to be kept calm and happy while she recovers. She should remember the happy times first."

His gaze gravitated to the framed reproduction of a map of the Florida East Coast Railway from the Flagler Museum, an anniversary gift from Alaina two years ago. She'd respected his work, complimented him on being an artist in his own right through his construction company. She'd bought the gift in commemoration of another Florida builder/entrepreneur from the past.

Some people went on cruises for vacation. He and Alaina had spent their time off touring historic sites and discussing the architectural history of the buildings.

There had been good times between them... God, he missed what they'd once had.

And now he had a second chance. He wouldn't let anything or anyone stand in his way of repairing his relationship with Alaina. Of building a family together. It was too important.

"Your wife is ill now. I understand that and will

be nice. If you're not ready for her to hear about the 'bad memories,' then okay. I'm here for all three of you." Courtney clicked her manicured nails. "I do have a heart."

She placed her hand dramatically on her chest, and gave a picture-perfect smile. It was with just such finesse that Courtney Rutger won over jury after jury—if not her son.

His mouth twitched with a smile. "That's questionable."

"And you're just like me." She winked. "Makes a mother proud."

He shook his head. "You're something else."

"That's one way to put it." She clapped her hands together. "Now where's my grandson?"

"He's getting his diaper changed."

Frowning, she smoothed back her French twist, her dark hair showing only a few threads of gray. "Then I'll wait a couple of minutes until he's through with that." She hesitated, shrugging. "What? I like to watch babies nap."

"Since when?"

"Since always. They're easier then." She grinned unrepentantly. "Now smile. It's the Christmas season. Your family is under one roof. And I certainly wouldn't have wagered a chance in hell on that happening this year."

Neither would he.

A creak of the door snapped his attention across the room. Alaina stood in the doorway frowning. Damn it. How much had she heard? Had his mother's strategic verbal land mines already blown his second chance all to hell? Courtney might have said she intended to respect his wishes, but he wasn't 100 percent certain she wouldn't try to find some way to finagle her way past on a technicality.

"Alaina?" he asked, waving her inside.

She stepped deeper into the room. "Please introduce me to your mother." She tugged a Christmas plaid burp cloth off the shoulder of her blue cotton dress that skimmed her curves. "I'm sorry I don't remember you, ma'am, but you're right. We're all lucky to be here together since I very well could have still been in that hospital bed. Or not here at all."

He exhaled hard, grateful she'd misunderstood his mother's comment. But he couldn't count on continued luck. He needed to make progress with his wife and get his family back. The sooner the better.

Two hours later, Alaina opened the closet in her bedroom. Hers and Porter's.

The space was larger than her first college studio apartment.

One side was lined with rows of Porter's clothes, suits and casual wear, each piece hung and arranged with precision, even down to sleeve length. She walked along the row, her fingers trailing the different textures. She could almost imagine the cloth still carried the heat of the man who wore them.

A half wall sectioned the male and female side of the "closet." Shoes fit into nooks, purses, too. And somehow she knew to push the button on the end—jewelry trays slid out in staggered lengths and heights. The stones that winked at her varied from semiprecious to mind-bogglingly expensive.

Who was she now? In this life? This house with an apartment-sized closet?

Even that thought gave her pause, reminding her that she hadn't grown up with finer things like the ones in this house. How comfortable had she been living here? Had she grown jaded and used to these luxuries?

Glancing back at the elegant driftwood four-poster bed, she began to seriously consider their arrangements as they became reacquainted. He'd said he wouldn't pressure her and she hoped he meant that. He couldn't possibly think they would be sharing a bed. Not yet. In spite of the attraction that still simmered between them, she wasn't ready for intimacy just now.

But someday?

She could barely envision getting through the night, much less through the next few weeks. She turned to the closet again and studied the racks of clothes and rows of shoes and purses and her clothes as if they could give her some hint about the woman she'd been in those missing five years. Certainly one who enjoyed shopping and bright patterns. Grasping at the clothes, she enjoyed the cool feel of the silks and satins. This closet was luxurious—the kind women might fantasize about. Alaina half hoped one of these garments would stir a memory, and the past five years of her life would come rushing back to her.

No such luck.

She released a floor-length gown with a jeweled bodice and glanced down at the simple cotton dress she wore, so different from the rest of her clothes. Had Porter packed this for a reason or had he simply grabbed the first item his hands fell on?

The cotton dress didn't feel like the artsy sense of

herself she remembered from five years ago. In fact, the house didn't much reflect her, either. Where was her love of Renaissance art? There were no paintings or statues she would have chosen. Everything was generic, decorator style, matching sets. Had she really spent time here? Been happy?

Where had the traces of herself gone?

The sense of being watched pulled her back into the room, where she found her husband standing by the four-poster bed with a tray of food. He wore a T-shirt and jeans now, the pants low slung on his hips as if he'd lost weight recently. Perhaps he'd been worried sick about her and Thomas. She tried to imagine what the past month had been like for him, but came up empty. It was hard enough for her to grasp her own situation, let alone empathize with his when she didn't know him beyond what the past week had shown her. But all of those interactions had been in the hospital with its sterile environment and lack of privacy. The four and a half years they'd supposedly known each other were wiped clean from her mind. Not so much as a whisper of a memory.

"I thought you might be hungry. There wasn't much of a chance to eat with the trip home, settling Thomas and my mother's surprise arrival." He set the tray on a coffee table in front of the sofa at the foot of their bed. His thick muscled arms flexed, straining against the sleeves of the cotton tee. She tried not to notice, but then felt slightly absurd. He was her husband and yet a stranger all at once.

"That's thoughtful, thank you." She watched him pour the tea, the scent of warm apples and cinnamon wafting upward. "Between a night nanny for the baby and a full-time cook-maid, I'm not sure what I'm going to do to keep myself occupied."

"You've been through a lot. You need your sleep so you can fully recover. I'm here, too. He's my child."

"Our child."

"Right." Porter's eyes held hers as he passed over the china cup of tea with a cookie tucked on the saucer. "He needs you to be well. We both do."

The warmth of the cup and his words seeped into her and she asked softly, "Where are you planning to sleep?"

He studied her for a slow, sexy blink before responding, "We discussed that in the car."

"Did we?" She wasn't certain about anything right now.

"We did." He sat on the camelback sofa, the four-poster bed big and empty behind him as he cradled a cup of tea for himself in one hand. "But just to be clear, nothing will happen until you're ready. You're recovering on more than one level. I understand that and I respect that. I respect you."

His sensitivity touched her. She should be relieved.

She *was* relieved.

And yet she was also irritated. She couldn't help but notice he still hadn't said he loved her, that he wanted her. He wasn't pushing the physical connection that obviously still hummed between them. Was he giving her space? Was he holding back because she couldn't possibly love a man she didn't know? She kept hoping for some kind of wave of love at first sight. But they were fast approaching more than a few hundred sights and still that wave hadn't hit.

Attraction? Yes. Intrigue? Definitely. But she was

also very overwhelmed and still afraid of what those memories might hold. She wasn't able to shake the sense that she couldn't fully trust him. If only he would say the right words to reassure her and calm the nerves in the pit of her belly.

She looked around the room, everything so pristine and new looking, a beach decor of sea-foam greens, tans and white. More of the matched set style that, while tasteful, didn't reflect her preferences in the least. "How often did we come here?"

"I have a work office in the house. So whenever we needed to."

She set aside the tea untouched. "You're so good at avoiding answering my questions with solid information."

A flicker of something—frustration?—flexed his jaw. "We spent holidays here and you spent most of your summers here."

"Then how do I not have any friends in this area?" Where were the casseroles? The welcome home cookies? Or did the überwealthy with maids and night nannies not do that for each other?

"Many people around here are vacationers. Sometimes we invited friends or business acquaintances to stay with us, but they're back home in Tallahassee or at their own holiday vacation houses. We also traveled quite a bit, depending on my work projects."

"So I just followed you around from construction job to job?"

"You make that sound passive. You're anything but that. You worked on your master's degree in art history for two years. One of your professors had connections in the consulting world and our travels enabled you to freelance, assisting museums and private individuals in artwork purchases. You did most from a distance and we flew in for the event proper when artwork arrived."

That was the most he'd said to her at once since she'd woken from her coma. And also very revealing words. "We sound attached at the hip."

He rested his elbows on his knees, staring into his empty teacup. "We were trying to make a baby."

His quiet explanation took the wind right out of her sails. She'd guessed as much since they were adopting and had no other children, but hearing him say it, hearing that hint of pain in his words, made her wonder how much disappointment and grief they'd shared over the years while waiting for their son. Then to have that joy taken from them both because she couldn't remember even the huge landmarks in their relationship that should be ingrained in her mind—when she'd met him, their first kiss, the first time they'd made love...

"And starting our family didn't work the way we planned."

He looked up at her again. "In case you're wondering, the doctors pinpointed it to a number of reasons, part me, part you, neither issue insurmountable on its own, but combined..." He shrugged. "No treatment worked for us, so we decided to adopt."

Thomas. Their child. Her mind filled with the sweet image of his chubby cheeks and dusting of blond hair. "I'm glad we did."

"Me, too," he said with unmistakable love.

The emotion in his voice drew her in as nothing else could have. She sat beside Porter, their shoulders brushing. It was almost comfortable. Or did she want it to be that way? So many emotions tapped at her, dancing in her veins. "He's so beautiful. I hate that I don't remember the first instant I laid eyes on him, the moment I became his mother."

"You cried when the social worker at the hospital placed him in your arms. I'm not ashamed to say I did, too."

Oh, God, this man who'd not once mentioned love could make a serious dent in her heart with only a few words. It was enough to make her want to try harder to fit into this life she didn't remember. To be more patient and let the answers come.

She touched his elbow lightly, wanting the feel of him to be familiar, wanting more than chemistry to connect them. "This isn't the way Christmas was supposed to be for us."

"There was no way to foresee the accident." He placed his hand over hers, the calluses rasping against her skin, another dichotomy in this man who could pay others to do anything for him yet still chose to roll up his sleeves.

"I never did ask how it happened. There have been so many questions I keep realizing I've forgotten to ask the obvious ones."

"We picked up Thomas at the hospital. Since it was so close to our beach house, we considered staying here for the night, but instead opted to drive back home to Tallahassee. A half an hour later, a drunk driver hit us head-on."

"We wanted our son in our own house, in his nursery."

"Something like that."

"What does his nursery look like at our house in Tallahassee?"

"The same as here, countryside with farm animals. You said you wanted Thomas to feel at home wherever he went. Even his travel crib is the same pattern. You even painted the same mural on the wall here."

She remembered admiring the artwork when she'd laid the baby in his crib, enjoying the quiet farm scene with grazing cows and a full blue moon.

"I painted it?" Finally, something of herself in this house of theirs. Her eyes filled with tears. Such a simple thing. A mural for their son in their two homes—or did they have more?—and yet she couldn't remember painting the pastoral scene. She couldn't remember the shared joy over planning for their first child, or the shared tears.

And right now she was seconds away from shedding more tears all over the comfort of Porter's broad chest.

When would she feel she belonged in this life?

Three

Porter woke from a restless sleep. He would have blamed it on staying in the guest room, but he'd bunked here more than once as his marriage frayed. He knew that wasn't the reason he couldn't sleep. Sitting up with the sheets tangled around his waist, he listened closer and heard it again. Someone was awake.

The baby?

He swept the bedding away and tugged on a pair of sweatpants. Even having a night nanny, he couldn't turn off the parenting switch. Over the past few weeks, the accident and time in the hospital had kept him on high alert, fearing the worst 24/7.

A few steps later, he'd padded to the nursery, determined to relieve the night nanny and watch Thomas himself. He'd worked with minimum sleep before. Actually, this past month had made him quite good at operating on only a few hours of rest. He was still so glad his son was okay that being with him was reassuring, even in the middle of the night. Those quiet hours also offered the uninterrupted chance to connect with his child.

Stepping into the doorway, he stopped short. Instead of the matronly granny figure he'd hired to help out, he found his wife feeding their son a bottle in a rocker by the crib.

"Hey, little man," she said softly, propping the bottle on her arm, "I'm your mommy. Forever. And I do want to be your mother. Who wouldn't love that precious face of yours? I wish we could have had the past month together, but that wasn't my choice."

Alaina took his breath away.

Though her pale pink T-shirt was crumpled from sleep, it still hinted at the shape of her curves and the matching pale, striped shorts exposed her beautiful legs.

But Porter couldn't see her face. Like any new mother, she was focused, homed in on her child. Her head was tilted down toward Thomas, blond hair spilling over her right cheek and shoulder.

She was beautiful and the warmth of her love for Thomas pulled at him. For the first time since she had woken up from the coma, she looked at ease. She looked almost happy. If he were being honest with himself, it was the first time she had looked truly happy in months.

A pang of guilt welled in his chest. Porter wanted to do anything—give anything—for her to stay like that. For her to be happy with him again. And she deserved it. Relationships hadn't always been kind to her.

When they'd first started dating four and a half years ago, she had recently left an emotionally abusive boyfriend. He had controlled all aspects of her life, telling her who she could and couldn't see. He'd shown up to check in on her. Slowly isolating her so she would have no one to turn to for help.

That was one of the reasons she didn't have friends around to help now. She'd told him it had been hard to make friends after that experience. Possibly that was why she was struggling so much to trust him now.

He couldn't blame her for feeling that way.

Five years ago, she'd tried to take charge of her life when she'd left the boyfriend. But the abuse hadn't stopped. He'd stalked her. Only the restraining order had given Alaina her life back.

And even after all she'd been through, Porter admired the hell out of that. Her capacity to still love, to still believe in people. It was one of the things that had drawn him to her.

And tonight, he saw that spirit, that beautiful resilient spirit fill the room. A pang of guilt flooded him for not telling her about their marital struggles, but damn it, he couldn't shake the sense he would lose her altogether if he did that. He would do whatever it took to get his family back. He would make sure she had no wants or desires not satisfied.

How had it taken such a terrible accident for him to appreciate how important his family was to him? Shouldn't he have realized all of this on his own, without the fear of almost losing this chance to have a family he of his own?

She must have felt his eyes on her, because she abruptly looked up and met his stare, and the relaxed expression on her face faded. "Porter?"

He quirked an eyebrow. "What good is a night nanny if you don't let her work?"

"I've already missed out on a month of his life. I want him to bond with me."

"You shouldn't push yourself."

"I'm an adult. I know my limits," she said with a tight, bristly tone. Thomas squirmed and whined. She brought him to her shoulder like a natural, patting his back and tapping the rocking chair into motion. "Do you?"

He chuckled drily. "Now that sounds like the wife *I* remember. Yes, I'm a workaholic." He gave her a sideways smile. "But you taught me to slow down and admire art."

"That's a nice thing to say." She patted Thomas's back faster, and still he fussed and squirmed, kicking his casted foot.

"Here, pass him to me." Porter walked deeper into the room, his arms outstretched.

Hurt and irritation flashed in her blue eyes, but she handed over the baby, anyway. "Sure. I want him to be comfortable."

"Alaina," he said, taking the baby and cradling him like a football, while massaging his little leg above the cast, "you aren't expected to know everything any more than I am. We're a team here and together we'll get it all covered."

She nodded once, shoving up from the rocker. "I know. It's just difficult feeling like I bring so little to the table right now."

"You told me once that marriage isn't always fifty-fifty. The pendulum swings back and forth." His mind drifted back to when she'd spoken those words.

She'd been so angry. He'd come home with a cast on his wrist, fresh out of the emergency room because he'd fallen off a scaffold while inspecting a work site. He'd broken his wrist, but he hadn't wanted to worry her. She'd made it clear she should have been called and included, allowed to help him and drive him home. She'd wanted to tend him and he'd wanted to get to change clothes to go back to work…

He damn well wouldn't let his job interfere with repairing his family now.

Porter felt Thomas drift off to sleep again, his body relaxing. Later he would tell Alaina the baby hadn't been hungry. His leg had been aching from the weight of the cast and the surgery. Alaina felt insecure enough right now. "Let's pass over the nursery monitor to the woman paid to stay awake."

"Sure, but I'm not tired. Maybe it has something to do with that month-long nap I took."

He stifled a laugh to keep from waking the baby, glad that she could joke about their ordeal. He set Thomas in his crib again, stroking the baby's head for a few seconds before turning the monitor back on. Porter nodded to the door and walked into the hall. The night nanny, Mrs. Marks, poked her head out of her bedroom, waved with her puzzle book and ducked into the nursery.

Porter held out a hand to his wife. "Want to see the beach view from the balcony? It was too foggy at supper time to enjoy much. The Christmas lights along the yachts will be more visible now."

"Yachts?"

He winced. From the beginning, she hadn't been comfortable with some parts of their wealthy lifestyle. She'd grown up with hardworking parents who ran a beach food cart in North Carolina's Outer Banks. Their business had paid the bills, but hadn't provided much in the way of extras. What would she say when he told her one of those yachts anchored off the shore was theirs?

"Forget it. You should rest even if you can't sleep."

"I can make decisions for myself," she said with blue fire in her eyes. "Show me the lights."

"Right this way," he said, once again extending his hand to her. Gingerly, she took it, but her grip was loose, as if she was ready to tear away from him at any moment.

Porter led them down the stairs, guided by the muted twinkle of Christmas lights that were twined with garland and wrapped around the banister.

There was an audible silence that followed them, but Porter tried to focus on the fact that she had chosen to come with him instead of retreating to the privacy of her room. It was a good sign.

They reached the stairway landing where the sleek black baby grand piano stood beneath one of Porter's favorite portraits: Alaina in her wedding gown. Her hair had been curled in loose waves that framed her face and the lace wedding gown accentuated her slender figure. She had looked like a princess that day. And it was Porter's renewed intention to make sure he treated her like royalty so she would want to stay once her memory came back. So the good now would overshadow the bad then. That she could forgive and move forward with him and Thomas, building a future.

And if her memory didn't return? He still needed to convince her to stay and build that life with him and their son. Family was everything and he refused to lose his.

Alaina squeezed his hand as they passed in front of the portrait. He watched her gaze lock on the photograph. She didn't say anything for several minutes, and he didn't push her as they strode out onto the patio that overlooked the Atlantic.

Rebuilding his family was a game of growing trust. And she deserved to raise questions without him dumping information on her. He wanted to give her the space she needed to realize she belonged here.

"Tell me about our wedding." The words came out almost like a prayer. Soft. Earnest.

"There's a photo album around the house somewhere. And plenty of extra pictures on the computer."

"But here's the bridal portrait, and it doesn't tell me anything. Not really. I feel a disconnect with the person in the pictures you've already shown me. Maybe if you tell me, then I will recognize the emotions of the moment."

"Maybe?" His heart hammered.

"Men don't get all emotional about weddings."

He considered her for a moment. She dropped his hand and moved to the piano bench. She sat with her back against the keys, eyes fixed across the room and on the ocean. The Christmas lights from the yachts illuminated the edges of her face, framing her in an otherworldly glow. Damn. She was gorgeous, even when she was stormy. He wanted her in his bed now as much as he ever had. But he wanted to put his family back together even more, and he had to remain focused on the end goal.

Quietly he offered, "I was happy the day we married."

It was true. He had been so entranced by her sense of the world, by the family they could make together, that he hadn't been able to marry her quickly enough. They'd started trying for children right away. His mother had told him that he and Alaina should take time to cement their relationship. He hadn't given much thought to that—until now.

"How long had we known each other?" Her eyes searched his. He could feel her trying to grasp hold of the past. Of who *they* were.

"We met a year prior. We were engaged for four months of that."

She slid over on the bench and motioned for him to sit next to her. He sat sideways so he could look at her directly.

"Why the rush?"

"We loved each other, knew it was right. Why wait?"

"I wasn't pregnant?"

"No, you weren't. We were never able to conceive."

It had been no one's fault. And they had Thomas now. They had taken in a child who desperately needed a home and stability. And somehow, that seemed to soften the animosity they had felt. They'd agreed to a temporary truce and now he planned to make them a permanent family.

"I hate being dependent on you for all my memories." Her eyes were shining with frustration. But, Porter realized, the frustration wasn't entirely directed at him.

He gently lifted a wisp of hair out of her face and tucked it behind her ear. "Then tell me what your dream wedding day would be like and that will be our wedding memory."

Her eyes went whimsical, a smile pushing dimples into her cheeks. "I would want to get married at a museum, or some historic site on the grounds, but with a preacher there."

Porter nodded to encourage her. "What else?"

"I think I would want a vintage gown and you in an old-school tuxedo, tails perhaps. And if I could dream big—sky's the limit—I would want flowers, so many flowers, all different colors. Southern flowers, magnolias and azaleas, too."

A long sigh escaped her lips, and she turned in her seat to face him.

"And the reception?"

"A band, so people could enjoy themselves. A buffet meal so people could eat or dance or talk, whatever they wish. I would want there to be children there, activities and a tent where they could play, sitters on hand. How does all of that sound?"

"Very close to the wedding we planned." He took her hand in his and ran his thumb over her silk-smooth palm.

"Planned?"

He shrugged. "My mother put in her two cents, your friends put in theirs. Weddings get complicated and we both let them have their way to get things moving so we could start our life together. To be truthful, I just remember you and how beautiful you looked and how damn lucky I was to have convinced you to marry me."

More memories hit him, about how later she'd come to resent not having stood her ground to have the wedding of her dreams. Her insistence that her style and wishes got pushed aside by his mother and wedding planners.

She inched toward him on the bench, resting a hand on his knee. Her touch made his blood surge hot beneath his skin. Damn. He wanted to take her in his arms. Wanted to taste her kiss. To taste *her*—over and over until they both stopped thinking and remembering.

"That's lovely, what you just said and the way you described the feelings. I wish I recalled even a part of that." The murmur leaped from her lips as her eyes searched his face. There was intrigue there, sure. Attraction, definitely.

"You will. Someday."

Another deep sigh. "And if I don't?"

"Then we'll keep taking things a day at a time and looking to the future. Marriage isn't perfect, Alaina. You've forgotten the arguments and disagreements, too. So perhaps it's a trade-off, getting to start over with a clean slate."

Alaina shook her head, but didn't pull away. Her fingers continued to trace light circles on his knee. "Amnesia is a horrible illness, not some trade-off. I would gratefully welcome one bad memory now from those years, just to open the door. To see our life together."

"What if that one memory made you stop loving me because you couldn't recall the rest?"

He wanted this fresh start for their family so badly. He needed it down to his core. And he was afraid that if she recalled any of the past year, she'd pack up and be out of his life the way she'd intended to do before the accident.

"I don't mean to be harsh, but I can't remember falling in love with you. So how is that a point?"

He threw her a playful wink. "I guess I'll just have to help you fall in love with me again."

She didn't smile back, her gaze narrowing with intensity. "So do you still love me?"

"Of course I do," he said automatically because that's what she needed to hear.

But from the look in her eyes, he could tell that on some level, behind the amnesia, she sensed the truth.

This wasn't about loving or not loving each other. After all, they hadn't spoken those words to each other in over a year. This second chance was about finally building the family he'd always wanted and doing whatever it took to make that happen.

Alaina leaned against the door frame of Porter's home office, making the most of the moment to study him unobserved. Much like as he'd watched her last night in the nursery. She'd been more moved by the way he'd looked at her, almost as if he was thinking the words he never spoke. Words about loving her.

Why was it so important to hear that from him when she didn't know how she felt about him? When she couldn't remember meeting him, marrying him— falling for him? And some men weren't overly demonstrative.

What about him?

She searched for clues as she watched him work at his computer, seated behind an oversize desk. He wore casual clothes, jeans and a polo shirt, his watch the only cue to his wealth. She liked that about him, how if she'd met him on the street she wouldn't have guessed he had all these houses—and a closet as big as some apartments.

She also liked the artwork on the wall behind him. Nice choice. It fit him more than a lot of things in this elaborate vacation place. She wondered if she'd picked it out for him.

He wore thick black-framed glasses as he typed, something she hadn't noticed before. There was so much about him she didn't know. So much to learn and on the one hand, some would say she had all the time in the world. But she felt an urgency to settle her life, for Thomas's sake.

And she couldn't ignore how much it touched her heart to see her son snoozing in a bassinet beside Porter's leather office chair. That he'd made arrangements to watch the baby while working spoke volumes. She could see that Porter wanted to be a good father, that he wanted to be active in his son's upbringing. She wanted to trust her impressions of him and accept that she had an amazing life. She wanted to quit worrying about the past she couldn't remember.

And yet she couldn't dismiss the sense that she should be wary of assuming everything was as it seemed.

Porter glanced up, as if sensing her gaze. He tucked his reading glasses on top of his head, his eyes were full of awareness from their almost kiss earlier.

Even if she couldn't remember what they'd had, she could swear she felt all those shared kisses in their past on some level. Did he have regrets about them as a couple? Was that the unsettled feeling she sensed in him?

Had he appreciated what they had?

"Alaina," he said softly, rocking back in his chair. "I've got this. Easy. He's sleeping. Go relax. Take a walk on the beach. Read a book."

Or stay with Porter and be tempted even more? How long would she be able to resist?

Not long.

She backed out of the door. "Sure, thanks. I'll have my cell phone with me. Don't hesitate to call if you need me to come back for him. I want to be with him whenever he's awake."

She'd missed so much already. Oh, God, she was going to start crying if she kept thinking about it.

Her emotions were swinging from desire for her stranger of a husband to grief over all she'd lost. She needed to get herself under control or she would be a nervous wreck. Thomas didn't need to have all those negative feelings around him. Maybe Porter was right about her taking time to decompress for a while.

With determined strides she moved toward the kitchen, scarfed down some toast and tea, and contemplated the events of her past twenty-four hours.

A whirlwind didn't even begin to cover it.

Glancing around the open space, she couldn't help but feel the decor looked as if it had been directly lifted from a catalog. Everything was gorgeous—stainless steel appliances with rustic wooden accent bowls—but it all felt too...put together.

Was this the kind of woman she had become over the past five years?

Unable to suppress her need for more answers, Alaina began to explore the house. Their house, she reminded herself. This was supposedly all hers, too, even if it felt alien in comparison to her more Spartan upbringing. She needed to learn to be comfortable here again.

Porter had made it clear that he wanted her to relax. To take time for herself. And while that was sweet, she wasn't entirely sure she enjoyed being forced into downtime. She had lost so much of her life that downtime intimidated her.

But she had to admit she admired Porter's dedication

to Thomas. It was endearing. He had found a way to integrate work and family. And that trait was sexy as hell.

She searched for more signs of encouragement regarding their life, but the rest of the house mirrored the kitchen. It was also well put together. So manicured and manufactured. She couldn't seem to find a trace of her artistic side at all.

Alaina thought back to the last apartment she could remember, the one she'd had five years ago. It had been modest, but hanging above her bed, she had placed a Renaissance-style painting. The myths drew her in. She loved that each painting captured a Greek tragedy or legend.

There wasn't one painting like that in this whole place.

Did Porter hate that sort of thing? Had she given up her taste in favor of his? And should she just start changing things now?

The bramble of her thoughts was interrupted as she came to the staircase and practically walked into her mother-in-law.

Courtney's hair was swept into a tight but elegant topknot. Polished. Her green dress swished as she moved toward Alaina. Jimmy Choo heels clicked with each step.

The poised, older woman waved with long, manicured nails. "Come with me. I need coffee. Or a mimosa. Unless you would rather some time by yourself?"

"Of course not." Alaina had too much time to spend with a jumble of questions about her missing thoughts. "I would love the chance to visit with you."

Her mother-in-law cast her a sidelong glance. "Dear,

it's all right. You don't have to tiptoe around my feelings."

"I welcome the chance to get to know you. You're Porter's mom." She extended her arm for Courtney to take. It was time to start to get to know her family. Her old life.

Had they got along before?

Courtney linked her arm with Alaina's. "I'm also your mother-in-law. Thomas's grandmother. I'm here to help however I can. Not that you really need it. You're very good with Thomas."

Was she? God, she hoped so. "I don't know anything about babies."

"Maybe not before you got married, but since I've known you? You've learned a lot about infants. You volunteered in the NICU three times a week, holding the newborns or just talking to the ones too tiny and fragile to be held." Her mother-in-law guided her back toward the kitchen.

Back toward Porter.

"I did that?" Another thing to add to the list of things she was learning about her life during these missing years. Fancy art exhibits. A postgraduate degree. NICU babies. She had certainly filled her time while married to Porter.

"It was hard for you, wanting to be a mother so desperately." Courtney patted her hand. Sympathy radiated from her touch.

There was a certain calm that settled between them. An understanding Alaina seemed to be close to grasping, but couldn't quite settle. Not yet. Although it wouldn't hurt to ask a few questions.

"What about Porter? Does he want to be a father?"

"Of course he does. You've seen how he is with Thomas."

Alaina thought back to the way he had massaged Thomas's hurt leg last night. About how he had insisted on watching him as he worked. He was taking his fatherly duties seriously. And it made her heart melt.

"Whose idea was it to adopt?"

Her mother-in-law hesitated midstep before walking again, heels clicking on travertine tiles. "You would have to ask him that question."

Did Courtney not know or was there something deeper here? An argument within the family? "I'm so tired of asking him about every single detail of our lives together. I was hoping you could help fill in some details."

"I'm sorry about the amnesia, dear." She squeezed Alaina's hand, her touch lotiony soft. "That has to be so frustrating, but maybe you can focus on the good things, like your child, your marriage, your home. Not everyone has all of that."

The woman was such a mix of coolness and warmth. One minute Alaina was certain her mother-in-law disapproved of her, and the next Courtney was offering genuine comfort. Navigating life lately was like walking through a maze with a blindfold on.

"I hear what you're saying and I appreciate your trying to help. Really." They were practically at Porter's office now. Alaina glanced at the wall that housed photographs in handsome frames. Not one photograph had Alaina side by side with Courtney.

Glancing at her mother-in-law, Alaina chewed on her lip. What had their relationship been like? Judging by the photo albums she'd pored over, there wasn't much of a relationship between them. She forced herself to ask the question that had weighed on her mind since Porter announced that Courtney was at their vacation house. "Did you and I like each other?"

Arched eyebrows lifted. "Honestly? Not very much. We don't have a lot in common."

Finally, what felt like an honest answer from someone. "I think I like you now."

"That's probably because you don't feel married to my son."

True as it was, the declaration stung. Alaina spun her wedding ring around on her finger. "And could it also be that you don't see me as Porter's wife anymore?"

"Maybe…" Courtney paused, worrying one fingernail with another. "I made my mistakes—you made yours. But lucky for us, we get a fresh start."

There was a lot of fresh-starting going around. A lot of work going into creating a second chance at her life. If only she knew how long it would be until her memories came back. If they ever would. Was the effort to start over wasted—or vitally necessary?

Either way, right now, Alaina had no choice but to press on. "Courtney, will I dislike you again if I remember? Was it that bad?"

And if she remembered, what would she think of her marriage? That was a question she couldn't bring herself to ask.

"Somehow, I think we've found a middle ground that will stick regardless of what you remember."

"Good. I need a friend I can trust." And she meant it. Whatever had been in the past between them—well, it didn't matter right now. Alaina wasn't that person anymore. While it hadn't been long ago since she'd woken up in that hospital, the accident and the amnesia had changed her irrevocably. "So? Can we be friends?"

"Friends. I like that. No mother-daughter mess. I'm not your mother. Hell, I'm having enough trouble getting used to being a grandmother. And just so we're clear, I don't change diapers. But I excel at watching while a baby naps and I'm superb at holiday shopping." Courtney winked a perfect smoky eye.

"I'm not going to be ready for that anytime soon." The idea of going out in public was absolutely overwhelming. And venturing out in public at Christmastime? That sounded dreadful.

Claustrophobic.

"That's why we're going to shop online. Later, of course, once you've had time to settle in and recover." Courtney stopped outside her son's office door and tapped lightly until Porter glanced up. "Since the baby is napping, that's my call to be a grandmother. Son, take your wife out and romance the socks off her."

Four

His mom walked away from the office door, heels click-clacking in time with her singsong voice as she spoke to Thomas. He hadn't expected his mom to embrace the grandmother gig so wholeheartedly, but then his life was anything but predictable these days.

Porter searched Alaina's expression. The tension in her jaw. The way her brow furrowed as she subconsciously drew one arm across her midsection to grasp the opposite upper arm.

She gave him a good-natured grin, but it was clear she was still unsure of how to act around him. He couldn't blame her for that.

But she also looked ready to bolt and that's the last thing he wanted, so he took the time to take her in. Alive. Vibrant. Here, with him and Thomas. Thank God.

On top of her head, she'd piled her hair in a loose,

messy bun. Wavy blond strands fell out of the bun, framing her slender face.

Her white dress hugged her breasts, drawing his eyes. Tempting him. Reminding him of the heat they'd always found in bed. The passion that still simmered between them, that they could find again if he could make the most of this time. His hands ached to stroke the fabric along her skin, to caress her along the length of the dress that fell in rolling pleats from her waist, to trace the red flower embroidery snaking around at midthigh.

To press his mouth behind her knee and tunnel his way up her skirt.

She looked like a vision right out of *The Nutcracker*. Clara, as she ran away with the Nutcracker Prince. The only question was, could he be that prince again? Could he charm her, show her how damn great they were together? Somewhere along the years the fantasy had given way to a reality that neither of them had anticipated.

And he hated that.

And he hated that the reality had broken their family, nearly ending the life he'd dreamed of as a boy.

Though she lacked memories, every item she'd added to the house screamed its sentimentality. It was like alarms blaring. The dress she wore was no different.

It was the same dress she had worn two years ago, on their vacation to St. Augustine. They were only supposed to be in town for the night. He had surprised her after a major art opening by booking a charming bed-and-breakfast room for the weekend. They'd spent the whole time laughing, drinking local wine. Back when things were simpler. When they still sparkled and sizzled together.

It could be that way again.

It would be that way again. He refused to accept any other outcome.

"Don't let my mother get to you or put pressure on you when it comes to our marriage."

It was the best he had to offer. Wooing her back into this family was a delicate task requiring finesse.

"There's not much you could do to romance a new mom who's recovering from amnesia." She tapped her forehead in jest.

"That sounds like a challenge." He thrived on a challenge.

"Okay—" she spread her arms wide "—give it your best shot."

"Really? You want me to sweep you off your feet?" He cocked his head to the side, a thrill zipping through him.

"Sure, what woman wouldn't want to be swept off her feet?" Inclining her head, she dramatically twirled. The fabric of her skirt tightened and loosed as she turned. She was so damn sexy.

And he wanted her for his own.

"Challenge accepted." Progress. He could practically taste it.

She stopped midspin. "Wait, never mind. This shouldn't be a game."

"Believe me—I understand that all too well." Closing the gap between them, he rested his hands on her shoulders. "So relax. I've got this under control. Let me pamper you, and you focus on recuperating."

"You're right. The best thing I can do for my family is to regain my memory so we can move forward with our future rather than staying here in limbo with you working from home at a vacation house." She twisted her hands nervously, glancing out the window. "Honestly, I believe it's too soon for us to go on some extravagant outing."

So large gestures were out of the question. It was time for a game plan. He knew he had to be quick. They couldn't hole up in this house forever. Her memory would slowly come back into focus. It was time for action. Now.

Still, he said, "Of course. I agree and I have a few ideas, but I'll need a half hour to pull things together. There's a hammock past the pool, by the shore. I'll meet you there."

Her smile was hopeful. Beautiful. "Sounds perfect."

Alaina inhaled deep breaths of ocean air, one after the other, a foot draped over the side of the hammock, toe tapping to keep the steady swaying motion. The hammock was attached to two fat palm trees, branches and fronds rustling overhead.

Could Porter really find a way to put her fears to rest? Could regaining her memory be as simple as relaxing and enjoying time with the man she'd married?

She wanted to believe that. It had only been a week since she'd woken up after all. Yet, every hour that passed with no breakthroughs knotted the anxiety tighter within her.

Answers. That was what she needed. She was desperate for them. She kept hoping the scenery would jog her memory. Bestow the memories that were locked away somewhere in her mind.

Glancing at the harbor, she tried to imagine what sort of person she had grown into. A twenty-eight-year-old woman with a husband rich enough to bump elbows with the incredibly wealthy. And, judging by the sheer size of the yachts before her, incredibly wealthy didn't even begin to cover it.

Yachts spotted the water with the same frequency as white caps in a storm. A few of them looked like personal cruise ships.

Had she been out on any of these? Did she move comfortably in a world like this? Knowing what her life had been like before, she couldn't imagine it.

Her thoughts were cut short as a sun-bronzed woman approached. Alaina guessed the woman was probably a decade older than her. Maybe more. But older, Alaina realized, was a matter of perspective. She still felt as if she was looking through the eyes of a twenty-three-year-old.

The woman bustled toward Alaina, brunette hair flapping beneath an oversize white floppy hat. Cat-eyed sunglasses shielded the majority of her face, concealing her eyes from view. The gust of wind tugged at her bright pink-and-peach shift dress.

Alaina stood with mixed feelings. On the one hand, she was glad to have someone else to talk to, but on the other, she was nervous. It was too soon. What if the woman asked something Alaina couldn't answer?

But then hadn't she just thought how she needed to push ahead? She had to be strong, brave, for Thomas.

And Porter.

The woman jogged the last few steps and hugged Alaina hard before stepping back, her hands clasped to her chest. "Oh my God, Alaina, I thought that was you." The woman scrunched her nose, crinkling zinc oxide into the creases. "I forgot for a minute you can't remember all of us. I'm Sage Harding. Your neighbor. I like to think I'm your friend, even if we only see each other a couple of times a year for holidays."

A couple of times a year? But Porter had said they came here often. Perhaps Sage didn't come as often and so their paths only crossed a couple of times a year. Alaina wanted to believe that. Porter had no reason to lie.

She didn't understand her need to believe the worst in him, to be so suspicious of his every word.

They were married. There was ample proof. And they'd adopted a child together. They had a beautiful life—if she could just bring herself to accept it.

"Thank you for coming over to speak to me, Sage. That makes me feel less like an amnesia freak or a patient."

"Honey, you can't help what happened to you." Sage sat on a teal Adirondack chair next to the hammock. "You were in a car accident."

"I understand the facts in my mind, but it's difficult to trust my mind these days." She rolled her eyes at her own lame joke. "But enough about my medical woes. Tell me about yourself. Where are you from? Are you here with your family? How did we become friends?"

"Wow, that's a lot of questions." Sage held up her fingers, holiday-green glitter polish on short nails. "I'm from the D.C. area. My husband's in the House of Representatives, so we keep this house to stay Florida residents. Our two kids go to boarding school. And you and I became friends at an art gallery fund-raiser for the homeless."

That all rang true and fit with everything Porter had been telling her. "What type of art do you enjoy?"

"Oh, I don't know jack about art." Sage waved a self-deprecating hand. "I was there for the canapés, champagne and movie-star company. And helping the homeless. I like being a part of charity work. It's a rewarding way to spend my time."

"That's nice." Alaina wasn't sure what else to say to this refreshingly honest woman.

Sage leaned closer, her elbows on her knees. "Are you okay, really okay? I've been so worried. I came by the hospital when I heard and left flowers. But you weren't allowed to have visitors. I would have a baby shower for you, but that might be awkward just now. Maybe we'll wait until you get your memory back."

"I think that's best. And I'm still…resting."

"Oh, right. Silly me. I didn't mean to intrude. I was just so glad to see you and wanted to make sure you and Porter are doing okay."

Now that was a loaded statement. Alaina opted for an answer that wouldn't land her in hot water. "We're enjoying being parents."

"How is your little guy's foot?"

"Healing."

"I'm so relieved." Sage studied her matching Christmas-green toenails for three crashes of the waves. "I wasn't sure you would be back this year after, well, your male visitor last Christmas."

Alaina forced herself to stay still. There was no answer to that revelation and she sure as hell wasn't going to quiz a virtual stranger. "Thank you for stopping by."

"I shouldn't have said anything. I thought maybe he'd contacted you and I wanted to be sure you knew. I mean well." She pushed to her feet and dusted sand off her legs. "Please accept my apology."

"Accepted. It's tough to know the right thing to say. Amnesia isn't an everyday occurrence and it's difficult to know how to handle it." Alaina stood and saw Porter walking down the bluff carrying a picnic basket and an insulated bag. "There's my husband."

Sage crinkled her nose again. "That's my cue to leave."

"Merry Christmas to you and your family."

"To you and yours, too, honey." Sage squeezed Alaina's hand quickly. "Enjoy your baby's first visit from Santa Claus."

Santa Claus?

Of course. She should be focusing on Thomas's first Christmas. On doing normal family things like picking out toys for him to enjoy over the next year. Or making Christmas cookies, as her mother had always done as far back as Alaina could remember. Starting her own family traditions with Porter.

Or had they had traditions? Tough to tell in this generic-looking house without her own personal stamp.

She wanted that homey holiday life so desperately. Wanted to be normal again. To be herself again. Whatever that meant and whoever that was.

If things were normal, she and Porter might be standing in line somewhere, debating how to spoil their beautiful new son.

Anxiety ebbed back into her chest. Not that it was ever far away.

The thought of melting away into a crowd sounded a lot more appealing now than it had earlier.

A quick glance back down the sandy path toward the vacation home revealed that Porter had already started to make his way toward her. He was only about ten feet away and just the sight of him took her breath away all over again.

She allowed herself to examine him fully as he approached, basket in hand. His broad shoulders and chest, the clear suggestion of muscles beneath his casual light blue button-down. The way his jawline appeared to be chiseled out of marble. Strong. Defined. Like some of the statues she used to have in her old apartment.

But it was the lightness in his demeanor, the force of his smile that made her heart hammer. While he was made up of hard angles, his smile made him seem approachable. Understanding. Maybe even affectionate.

Was that what she'd seen in him from the first?

She wanted to kiss him. To know what they were like together. In bed. Or in the shower. Or in the dozens of other places her imagination wandered with fantasies.

Or were those memories? She couldn't be sure. There had been an undeniable physical connection between them from the moment she'd seen him in the hospital. It had laced each of their conversations so far. Amnesia or not, that much of a connection had persisted.

How could she have looked at another man as Sage had not too subtly insinuated?

Alaina had wondered more than once if Porter had been hiding something from her. She just hadn't considered that whatever he might be hiding was her fault.

Sunglasses shielding his eyes from the late-morning sun, Porter jogged down the last step cut into the bluff, his deck shoes hitting sand. He'd expected to find his wife napping in the hammock. Not chatting with their gossipy neighbor. Hell, he'd even checked with the staff to make sure the Hardings wouldn't be here for Christmas.

Apparently, staff intel was wrong.

Sage Harding fanned a wave at him as she slid her own sunglasses back on her face and sashayed through the sea oats and around a bluff back to her white mansion on stilts.

Between his mother and Sage, he couldn't catch a break. Although a voice in the back of his mind persisted that he didn't deserve one. He was deliberately keeping parts of their past from his wife. He tamped down that voice, not just for his own reasons but for her sake, as well. The doctor had said not to push her, but rather to let her recover the missing years on her own.

All the CT scans and MRI scans hadn't shown any brain damage, and yet her coma had persisted. The doc had said her mind was most likely protecting herself from something she wasn't ready to deal with. Again that voice piped up that maybe she didn't want to recall how close they'd been to signing the divorce papers their lawyers had drawn up. That she wanted this second chance at creating a family every bit as much as he did.

His pace quickened as he approached. He could see that there was something sparking beneath the surface of her eyes. It was in the way she cocked her head to the side and studied him up and down. A question in her expression. A curiosity. One he wanted to answer.

Time was limited now as their son napped—and the holidays were a brief interlude, too. Soon, they would have to return home. She would find out all that he'd been keeping from her and all hell could break loose. He intended to use this time with her, away from all that, wisely.

Porter placed the picnic basket and insulated bag

on the Adirondack chair so there would be nowhere to sit except beside his wife. "You'll want to stay clear of Sage Harding."

"Sage?" Alaina shifted, the roped hammock swaying beneath her. "Why on earth should I avoid her?"

"Because she's not as genuine as she tries to appear. She's cultivating wealthy friends to fund her husband's run for the US Senate. Plain and simple, she uses people."

Alaina slowly nodded as if she was unsure how to respond. As if she didn't trust his word. Ouch.

"Okay. That's sad to hear, that someone's using others."

"You're not sure if you believe me about Sage's motivations for coming over?"

She shook her head. "It's not that. But people can have different impressions of someone."

A diplomatic answer. But one that reminded him he still had to earn her trust. Well, re-earn. "Fair enough. It's your judgment call to make. Just promise me you'll be careful around her."

"I will." She chewed her bottom lip. "Maybe I was too eager to believe what she said about being friends because I feel so isolated. There's no one I know outside of our family."

"You asked for phone numbers. I looked up ones for your old friends." He held out a sheet of paper with scribbled names and numbers. It was a small gesture, but he hoped it would matter to her. Show her that he was committed to making their family work.

"*Old* friends? We're not friends anymore?"

"You moved away from North Carolina years ago. They got married, too, and many of them relocated, as well." He shrugged. "People lose touch with each other. It happens."

She pressed her forehead. "Not that it really matters anyway, I guess. They would only know what I already recall. They won't have much of anything to offer about the past five years other than maybe one of those 'the world is rosy' Christmas letters I must have sent out." The hurt and frustration in her voice filled each syllable.

"Maybe there's something they can offer. I want you to be happy. I'm trying to help you, Alaina."

"And I'm not trying?" she snapped. "This is so very hard, not remembering even meeting you, yet trying to be a wife and a mother in a completely alien world."

This wasn't going the way he'd planned. He didn't want her to feel more isolated, more alone. "I'm sorry. I know this is a million times tougher on you, and I want to help you." He smoothed back her hair, his hand resting lightly on her shoulder. "I didn't mean to upset you. Can we start over? I've ordered brunch. You barely touched breakfast. Okay?"

"Sure, Porter, that's probably a good idea. I'm sorry for lashing out at you like that. I know this has to be difficult for you, too. And I can see you're truly trying to make things easier for me." She pressed her fingers to her temple again as if her head was throbbing. "Did we used to argue like that a lot?"

Arguments?

He needed to tread warily as hell on this topic.

It was such a loaded question she'd asked. And a difficult one to answer.

Porter reached into the basket to give himself time to think, and hefted out an impressive spread. Brie. Herbed crackers. Fresh fruit, cut and quartered. Dark chocolate–covered nuts. All of her absolute favorites. Years ago, when things were easier between them, they had made brunches on the beach a ritual. It was also how they had spent their first date. A picnic on the beach.

"We exchanged words, and yes, we argued." He glanced back at her, looking over the top of his sunglasses. "Our reconciliations were incredible." He handed her a piece of chocolate.

She eyed him pensively for a few seconds before her shoulders relaxed and she took the truffle with a playful smile, blue eyes twinkling like the ocean reflecting the sun. "It's not sexy to hit on a woman who just came out of a coma."

"Why?" He pivoted on one knee, cupping the side of her face in one hand. "You're beautiful."

She didn't pull away. "I'm pasty and exhausted."

"That's why this is the perfect place to rest." He pulled a slice of cheese from the cutting board and popped it into her mouth before she could respond. "Now eat. You need to put back on the weight you lost."

Her throat moved in a swallow before she said, "Was that an insult?"

"I just told you. You've always been beautiful to me." He traced her bottom lip with his thumb. "I'm more than willing to practice our reconciliation skills whenever you're ready."

She nipped the pad of his thumb and sent a jolt of arousal clean through him.

"Porter, I would be lying if I said I wasn't tempted. So much." She pressed a kiss into his work-roughened palm before moving his hand away. "But you're right about me lacking energy and needing to refuel. And you were right about me needing to decompress. My emotions seem to swing from high to low without warning."

"Damned by my own words," he said, but glad for the reminder to put her needs first.

"And we should go back soon. The baby..."

"Is sleeping. With my mother watching and a nanny as backup." He frowned, shaking his head. "Because I would never trust my mother as the sole caregiver of a child. Our child."

"That's sad."

"I meant it as a joke." Sorta.

"Really? Because I don't think it's funny. Is that why you have the nanny? Because you don't trust me?"

He could hear her winding up again.

"I trust you with our child, unequivocally. Truly, I only want you to rest." They needed the extra help right now until things returned to a normal routine. Because it had to return to normal. He refused to accept the possibility he could lose the family they had created for their son.

"You're maxed out, as well."

He rubbed the back of his neck and didn't answer. Didn't quite look at her.

She ran her hand slowly along his shoulders. Her fingers lightly tracing circles down his back, reigniting his desire. She inched closer, so her head was inches from his. Her voice lowered, filling with concern. With understanding.

"And having your mother here stresses you more."

He reached out, closing the distance between them. Hand to her cheek, he stroked her skin with his thumb. She sighed into his hand, her breath warm against him. Sexy and moist. He wanted her so damn much.

"Damn it, Alaina, you always did read me well, right from the start."

Unable to resist a taste, just this one moment to connect with his wife again, Porter leaned in to kiss her.

Five

The warmth of his lips sent an electric pulse through her, and she hungered for more. His hand wound into her hair. Alaina's own body melted into his as she pressed herself against his hard, muscled chest.

The kiss deepened, mouths opening, hands stroking. Alaina's desire became more urgent as she tasted a hint of raspberries on his tongue. He angled her closer, tongue exploring. Testing. Her fingers curled into the fine texture of his shirt. Everything about him drew her, from the way he looked at her to the way he made her smile. From the way he touched her to the care he gave their child.

Right now, she could easily envision how she'd fallen in love with this man and married him. She ached to remember the passionate experiences they'd shared, words they'd exchanged. Anything. And she hated that he had it all and she had nothing.

But she reveled in how hard he was working to win her over. That thrilled her and excited her—

From somewhere outside of this wonderful moment, she heard the distinctive hum of a speedboat skidding across the water. It snapped her to her senses. Reminded her of the fact she was kissing a man she didn't really know, a man she didn't fully trust, which complicated her feelings even more.

She pushed against his chest. Broke the kiss and connection before looking shyly at him.

She laughed self-consciously. "I shouldn't have done that. You have an amnesiac wife and a new baby and here I am making a move on you."

He burst out laughing, the sound rolling out on the ocean breeze. He laughed again, his head falling and broad shoulders shaking. Pinching the bridge of his nose, he said, "God, woman, you turn me inside out. You always have."

The words sent a shiver through her every bit as arousing as his kiss had been. There was emotion behind the words.

Had there been emotion in his touch, as well? She didn't trust her judgment yet.

The wind blew her hair across her face and she swept it away again. "I'm sorry. I, um, didn't mean to send mixed signals and mislead you—"

He traced her lips. "You turning me inside out has always been a good thing. We may have argued about a lot of issues, but we always connected on a physical level." He tapped her lips a final time. "But I meant it when I said I wouldn't pressure you to take this faster than you want to take it."

"That's good to know." She shot to her feet restlessly,

gathering up their lunch and putting it back in the basket. "The attraction between us is…problematic."

An urgency to move filled her. They needed to get back to the baby, anyway. She gathered more remnants of the picnic, sliding the lids onto the various containers. But not before she snagged another piece of brie and popped it into her mouth. She reveled in the creamy texture, using the food-induced silence to steady herself.

"We were married for years," he said into the silence. "Even if your brain doesn't remember, I believe that on some level your body does. We'll take things slowly until your mind catches up." He offered her another piece of dark chocolate. Her fingertips gingerly brushed his as she took it. Another confusing jolt of desire burst through her.

"What if my mind doesn't ever catch up?"

A devilish smile spread across his lips. "Then we'll start over."

"And what if I'm not the same woman I was?" In her chest, her heart pounded. Tension rose again, unmistakable.

"You are the woman I met five years ago."

She left the hammock, placing the basket on the chair and stacking the containers inside. "But I'm not. I recall what I was like then. It feels like it just happened. But the past week, waking up and finding out that I'm married and a mother and I have this whole chunk of life I lived? That was a surprise. That's changed me. Immeasurably."

"Sure, of course it did."

"You say that. But I don't think you're hearing me. Not really. You seem to want to pick up where we left off."

On a certain level, she could understand that desire. On the logical level. But the emotional one—that was an entirely different scenario. How could she make him understand how overwhelming all of this was?

His jaw flexed and he left the hammock, helping her pack their meal, kneeling beside her. "I'm trying to help you remember, like you asked."

"I don't believe that. You want me to be the woman you married. To have our lives back the way they were."

He snorted on a dark laugh. "You couldn't be further from the truth."

She went still, sagging back to sit on her butt in the sand. A chill settled in her stomach. "So things weren't great between us."

"I didn't say that."

"When I asked you if we argued a lot, you answered that we exchanged words and had great make-up sex."

"We did."

"But we argued. A lot." She packed up the last few items into the basket. And shut it hard.

"Married couples do that."

"We did."

"Yes, Alaina, we did." He clasped her shoulders. "We weren't perfect. We still aren't. But we have a chance here to build our family. We've been wanting this for a long time. Can you believe that much at least?"

He searched her face, scrutinized her expression. Cheeks ablaze, she tried to work out the harrowing emotions that knocked against each other inside of her like kids in bumper cars. He was asking for her trust. And she *should* trust him. They were married after all—but she had been close to having an affair, if Sage Harding was to be believed. What did all of that add up to?

Porter was practically a stranger to her. And his desire to have her put her faith in him frayed her nerves more. It didn't make sense. The Porter she was meeting now had never given her a reason not to trust him. But deep down, something stopped her from giving herself over to him completely.

"Sure," she said, knowing her answer was a brushoff and not able to come up with more than, "I believe you want to build a family."

Dizziness hit. Her chest tightened. She felt a moment of panic over being confined even though he was just holding her. She knew the fear was unreasonable, but still, given what had happened in that past abusive relationship. she couldn't help but feel nervous over how isolated she'd allowed herself to become. And how some might say Porter had taken away her resources by bringing her here where she wasn't close to anyone, just as her old boyfriend had done before.

What did she really know about this man beyond that he was gentle with Thomas?

Her arms began to tingle. Alaina felt so boxed in by the weight of the past she remembered and the past she didn't. Space. That's what she needed. She shot up from their beach picnic, turned on her heel...

And ran.

The pounding of her feet hitting the ground reverberated in her mind. She hadn't even noticed she had balled her hands into fists until she made it to the kitchen. The sticky sweet remains of a raspberry fell into the sink as she unclenched her fingers.

One deep breath. And then another.

There was no one to call. It was times like these that she desperately wished she could talk to her mother or father. They had always known what to say, how to help her parse out a situation. But they had died during her junior year of college. The memory of that moment, of that horrible phone call, was still fresh in her mind.

She'd give anything for her family to be intact.

Didn't Thomas deserve the same? An intact, functional family? Parents who adored him? She already loved her son so much. And if she were being honest with herself, she wanted a family just as much as Porter seemed to. She wanted them to be a complete and intact unit.

More than her own happiness was at stake now.

And for the first time, she was more afraid of what might happen to her marriage if she remembered, than if she left those five years buried.

Relieved Thomas's checkup had gone so well, Porter shut the door of the car behind his wife in the parking lot of the pediatrician's office. This had been their first joint trip off the property since the family had left the hospital together last week. He glanced in the backseat, where Thomas smiled at him in his "Santa's Little Helper" onesie.

The doctor had confirmed that Thomas was healing well. It would just take time. That seemed to be the theme of his life recently. Wait. Be patient.

It was damn hard to do sometimes. Porter strode around the car and positioned himself in the driver's seat. On the one hand, he was grateful they were all still together. On the other hand, he felt as if things had stalled since their beach picnic. She had built a wall around herself and he didn't understand why. Since that kiss, she'd been antsy, jumpy over being touched. Only when they were with Thomas were they both at ease. He didn't doubt for an instant—she loved their son every bit as much as he did. That baby boy had them wrapped around his finger.

Porter had built multimillion-dollar homes around the country. He'd built a billion-dollar corporation on his own, with no help from his wealthy mother. And yet those accomplishments didn't mean as much to him as coaxing a big belch from Thomas or laughing with Alaina as they struggled to work a tiny flying fist into a sleeper.

He wanted a family no matter what. People accused him of being determined at work, but that was nothing compared to how hard he would devote himself to making this come together. He wouldn't give up what he was building in his life. It was a helluva lot more important than any structure put up by his corporation.

Porter started the car and adjusted the radio. "Would you like to pick up carryout on our way home or stop by a deli? The weather's perfect to eat on the deck."

Would she be interested in unwinding later in the hot tub? He didn't know what to expect from her after she'd welcomed his kiss on the beach, and then proceeded to push him away.

"Porter, do you mind if we do something away from the beach house? I don't want to be cooped up all day. It's too nice of an afternoon to spend inside." Alaina stared out the window as they drove past a team of reindeer made of bent willow branches in the courtyard of the doctor's office.

A smile pulled at his lips. Perhaps this patience thing was paying off. Alaina hadn't wanted to do anything outside of the house since they'd arrived there. This was a good sign. Maybe she was beginning to trust him.

"Of course. I have to swing by a job site for a final walk-through. Then the rest of the day is ours." He reached for her hand and gave it a gentle squeeze.

"I don't mind that at all. Besides, I'd like to see you in action."

She flashed him a quick smile as she turned the radio to a Christmas station. Her head bopped along to a jazzy rendition of an old classic as they drove through town, where lighted white snowflakes hung from palm trees lining the village's main thoroughfare.

It didn't take long to reach the job site. This was an up-and-coming section of town. The beach stretched and wound lazily in front of them, beyond the Spanish-influenced mansion Porter needed to inspect.

"Porter, this place is beautiful. It's so exotic looking." Her eyes darted to the lattice that was pressed against the side of the house between the garage and door. Scores of plants were strategically placed around the yard.

He slowed the car to a stop. "It is. It's been my favorite recent project. Do you want to stay in the car or come with me?" He searched her eyes for a clue as to what she was thinking. She glanced behind him, over his shoulder to the two men who were talking to each other by the large arched doorway.

"I want to come. But first, can you tell me who they are?" She gestured toward the men.

"The taller man with the buzz cut is my second-in-command. His name is Oliver Flournoy. He's a smooth-talking guy, but he's still single. The man he is talking to is Micah Segal, our CFO. Sometimes we go out with him and his wife, Brianna. They have a toddler, Danny. He adores you. Like all kids do."

"Okay. Oliver and Micah. Got it in here." She tapped her temple and let out a shaky laugh. She unclipped her seat belt and pushed herself out of the car so she could unbuckle Thomas.

Alaina really was something else. This was a huge step for her and seeing her step back into the world so fearlessly even in the face of her amnesia impressed him in a major way. She was an amazing woman, more than just beautiful. She had an inner strength that shone— and drew him. How had he lost sight of this side of her?

What a helluva time to want to tuck her away from prying eyes and kiss her until she sighed, and more.

He cleared his throat and his thoughts, narrowing his focus back on the moment at hand. By the time Thomas was out of his seat, Micah and Oliver were over at the car. Palpable silence descended on the group. Alaina rocked Thomas back and forth, eyes flicking from Oliver to Micah and back to Porter.

Oliver, a slim man with deep brown hair, cleared his throat to break the silence.

"How are you feeling, Alaina?" he asked, clearly feeling awkward as hell with her amnesia.

"Well. All things considered… And how are you, Oliver?"

"Doing well, doing well," he answered, repeating her polite words, bobbing his head. "Just gearing up for Christmas at my sister's."

"That's…good." She rocked Thomas, turning her attention to the shorter man with auburn hair. "And how are things with you, Micah?"

"No reason to complain, ma'am." He blinked fast

as if forcing himself to make eye contact. "All's quiet and well at home."

More awkward silence descended. Damn. This was not going the way he'd thought it might.

"We are glad you are feeling better," Micah added. Blink, blink. Blink, blink.

"We are, too," Porter said, wishing he could say something to smooth things over. "Alaina, why don't you let me hold Thomas and you can go explore the grounds. The view from the back deck is stunning. Oliver, would you unlock the door for her?"

Alaina nodded, visibly relieved at the opportunity to escape. Brushing his hands along her arms, Porter took Thomas from her.

"Of course." Oliver unlocked the door and strode inside, flipping on lights. Alaina walked through the door frame, her movements quick and brisk. She was taking everything in. Seemed to love the driftwood-colored hardwood floors, the crisp white trim. She flashed Porter a quick smile over her shoulder before walking across the rooms to the patio door.

His eyes stayed on her a moment longer. He was struck by her bravery in facing this amnesia head-on, even when it wasn't easy. In the old days, he might have asked her about artwork for the place. Her expertise was always coveted by home buyers. He missed seeing the way her artist's mind worked. It had been one part of their marriage where they shared an easy accord.

"How are you handling the new kid? This father-hood gig is something else." Micah made small talk with Porter as they moved through the house.

"It's everything I wanted and nothing I imagined." He would do anything for his son. Anything. He'd never expected to feel this much for another living being—the love, the protectiveness, the pride. "He's fun."

"And cute as hell." Micah tugged Thomas's healthy foot lightly. "How's his clubfoot healing? Gotta confess, I don't know a lot about this type of issue."

"He'll need two more surgeries and physical therapy, but the doctor expects a full recovery. I just hate that he has to hurt."

Micah nodded sympathetically. "He smiles when he sees you. That rocks."

"Truth." At least he had that going for him. The bond he was already creating with his son made his heart swell. It made the dream of a family of his own more real—and more important.

"And Alaina?"

"She's a natural mother. No amnesia could steal that from her."

"I'm sorry, man. I wish I could say it's for the best, since y'all— Hell, that sounds insensitive."

Micah's features tensed. But Porter knew he didn't mean anything by the comment. Things had been so difficult before the accident. So rocky. It wasn't something they could keep hidden.

"Don't worry. I know you mean well." Their voices bounced around the skeleton of the house.

"Come have dinner with us. Let's hang out like old married couples." Micah's face showed genuine concern and interest. He was a good guy. The type Porter could always count on.

"I'll talk to Alaina. We'll see if she's up to it. She wants to talk to people from our past, and I want to give her whatever she needs. We just have to tread carefully and follow the doctor's instructions." Porter explained a little of the situation to Micah, but his gaze moved to the side. Toward Alaina.

She was walking around the property, taking in the features of this house. She seemed to belong in the place. The softer, more classical lines and arches fit her better than the angles and modernism of their beach home.

Why hadn't he perceived this before? His mind filled with all the times she'd catered to his tastes and desires. He couldn't escape the realization that he needed to appreciate her for who she was, not just how she fit into his vision of the perfect family.

"Of course. Let's talk more and pick a time. Dinner at our place. Or a restaurant." Micah clapped him on the shoulder. "Or even go to the ballet."

"Seriously? The ballet?" Head cocking to the side, Porter snapped his attention back to the conversation.

"Just checking to be sure you're still listening. You were so busy staring at your wife."

It was hard not to stare at her. Alaina captivated his attention, his thoughts.

Seeing her in this house he wondered if surprising her with the beach house after finding out they would need fertility treatments a few years ago had been the right call. Should he have had her pick out a house with him instead? He'd cut her out of the decisions sometimes, telling himself he was surprising her. Yet then she was stuck pretending to be pleased.

He needed to set his mind on ways to fix that in the future, when he was considering major changes like remodeling or even relocation. Big changes he couldn't tackle right this second. But he could—and wanted—

to do something special for her now, something she would like.

After they were back in the car, Porter started to drive toward a place they hadn't been to in ages. Fishin' Franks—her favorite restaurant. He wanted today to be special.

Lunch was absolutely delicious. Cajun fish tacos. Fresh avocados. Live music.

All things considered, Alaina was having a decent time being out of the beach house today. Porter was as charming as ever, completely sensitive to her every whim and desire. And to Thomas. Seeing them together made her heart surge. Porter was dedicated to the boy. Completely devoted to becoming a family.

For a moment, she considered what it would be like if her memories never came back.

Maybe this was all they needed. A completely fresh start. A new house for a new family. A house like the one at the job site. One that fed into her eclectic sensibilities and symbolized their new life together.

She could practically picture Thomas taking his first steps on the driftwood-colored hardwood floors. And art hanging all over the living room.

As they walked into the Baby Supplies Galore store, she scanned the faces of the other shoppers. In true Florida Christmas fashion, babies were dressed in shorts and tanks that sported flamingos in Santa hats.

The aisles were packed with late-December holiday shoppers. Christmas music mingled with the rush of families debating gifts.

Porter kept stride next to her as she pushed the cart down the least crowded aisle. His hand went almost instinctively to the small of her back. The warmth of his touch begged her to recall their past again. It clouded her sense of the present. Even knowing that they could be a family with a fresh start, she yearned to remember what they'd shared.

"What was the best present you ever received from me for Christmas?" she asked, looking at the blanket sets.

Glancing at the prices, Alaina quickly realized this was a high-end baby store. Just one item probably cost as much as five of her childhood Christmases altogether. This was a completely different level of shopping.

"Hmm. There was one year that you did a painting based on the blueprint of the building project that launched my career. I loved that. It's hanging above my desk in my office."

"I'd like to look at that more closely. Get an idea of the direction of my art. And what was my favorite Christmas present from you?"

"I think the best gift I ever gave you may have been the surprise trip to Paris. We spent a week in art galleries eating brie and bread."

"Ah, bread and cheese. Such a solid combination." She laughed to cover her regret that she couldn't remember what sounded like a beautiful trip. "What about your Christmases as a child?"

She slowed down beside a tower of holiday-themed baby rattles—penguins with red-and-green scarves, polar bears with fuzzy hats and deer with jingle bells.

"My mom went all out. Good God, she went all out. Mom's a lawyer. Did I tell you that?" He plucked a snowy owl out of a bin and waggled it in front of the baby, who rewarded him with a gummy grin.

"I don't believe anyone thought to tell me that detail, actually." She'd taken in so much information in such a short time it was hard to keep the facts straight. "I assumed she was independently wealthy. She took time off to be here? That's really sweet."

He waggled his hand. "Taking time off work is a way to put it, I guess. My mother sneaks off to work just like I do. Neither of us has ever been big on sleep."

"That's funny, given the impression she relays, snoozing in, preferring the baby be asleep."

"That's my mom. Contrary."

Alaina hugged a stuffed bear against the ache in her chest. "I wish my mother could be here to meet Thomas. She would love him."

His forehead furrowed with deep creases of concern. "I wish she could be here for you."

She set the bear back on the shelf, arranging him precisely. "Your mother's been surprisingly easy to get along with. This fresh start has been helpful perhaps. We don't feel threatened."

"You have no reason to feel threatened by my mother."

"She's certainly got it all together."

And what about her own life? Nothing about it felt together. A whole degree and career she couldn't remember participating in. What kind of exhibits had she been a part of?

There was no sense dwelling on it, though. Instead, she would put all of her energy into the present moment. Focusing on the past wasn't doing anyone any good.

For now, she would worry about making Thomas's first Christmas something special.

Porter picked a reindeer and snowman ornament that read Baby's first Christmas. He flipped it over in his hand before handing it to Alaina. "What do you think of this one?"

She traced the ceramic ornament. "It's perfect. And speaking of firsts, since I haven't remembered anything, let's choose some new traditions to start today."

The fresh start she'd been daydreaming about could begin now.

"Such as?" he asked.

So many traditions to pick from. She opted for the simplest, one that connected so many families at the holidays. "Let's start with meals. What do we usually eat for Christmas?"

"Traditional turkey and a duck with all the trimmings. You like oyster stuffing so we have that. I like cranberry pie."

"While that sounds delicious, let's do away with it or eat it all on another day. For Christmas let's serve something totally different this year. A standing rib roast…" She snapped her fingers. "Or I know—how about we have a shrimp boil?"

"A shrimp boil? For Christmas?"

"Yes," she said, warming to the idea, feeling in control of the holiday and her new life for the first time. "In the Carolinas we call it frogmore stew, but down here it would be a shrimp boil. Shrimp, corn, new potatoes, maybe crawfish or crab or sausage in it, as well. We could have corn-bread stuffing, or crab and corn bread stuffing. What do you think?"

He held up a Santa hat and plopped it on her head.

"I think you're so excited I'll eat anything if it makes you smile like that." His hand slid down to cup her face. "I've missed your smile."

Again, she thought about how he must feel in this situation. He'd lost his wife, for all intents and purposes. First to the coma and now to her inability to remember what they'd been to each other. And this certainly couldn't have been how he'd envisioned their first Christmas with their child. "I'm sorry for all the pain this is causing you."

"I'm not in pain right now. I'm happy. Really happy."

His eyes shone with sincerity that sent tingles into her stomach.

"Let's shop. This is one time I won't complain about all that money you have. Let's be Santa."

She pushed the cart forward to the next line of plush toys.

"I like the way you think. And I'm a sucker for stuffed animals." He tossed a giant polar bear at her. She caught it easily.

She waved it in front of Thomas, and even gave the bear a voice. Porter pulled down a small duck and started to play along with her.

It felt so natural. As if they were a normal family. As if they all belonged together. The baby giggled at the impromptu theater provided by his parents.

An elderly lady walked up to them. "If all parents were like you two, the world would be a wonderful place. You're giving that child the gift of imagination. It's lovely. What a beautiful family." The elderly lady grabbed a small teddy from the shelf.

"Thank you, ma'am." Porter rubbed his hand over Alaina's shoulder.

His hand sent her senses tingling. It had felt so natural. So perfect. Maybe there was a shot for them all after all.

"Merry Christmas. Y'all enjoy him while he's that small and adorable. Before you know it, he'll be a teenager asking for a car." She smiled at them and continued farther into the store.

"A car?" Porter chuckled, plucking up a rattle shaped like a race car. "Easy enough for now. And clearly the polar bear and duck have to come home. They have Thomas's stamp of approval."

"I think you are right. I really like this elephant, too, though." She scooped the blue elephant off the shelf and her hand tightened.

The inky tendrils of a memory pushed into her mind. It felt as if she was underwater without goggles. It was unfocused at first. She and Porter at a friend's baby shower around the holidays. Laughing at the party. Overwhelmed with joy for their friends, for the baby that was about to come into their lives.

But knowing all the while that a baby wasn't about to enter her and Porter's life. How hard it was for them to go back home to their house on Christmas knowing they couldn't conceive. How much pain welled in her chest even now at the thought of that Christmas.

"What is it? What's wrong?" Porter asked, concern flooding his voice as he took the elephant from her.

The memory evaporated and she sank down, sitting on the edge of a display platform. "I just remembered something. From before. From a Christmas a few years ago, I'm not sure exactly when."

"Tell me," he insisted, kneeling beside her while keeping his hand securely on Thomas.

She struggled to remember every detail as if that might pry out more. "We went to a baby shower after finding out we couldn't conceive… I just…" Her voice trailed off. The words faded and closed in her throat.

"Shhh. It's okay." He wrapped an arm around her. Drew her close as ragged breaths escaped her throat. His embrace was somehow more familiar than the kiss, more real.

He stroked her back, murmured into her hair. This moment felt like the first thing she'd really shared with Porter since waking from the coma. And she sank into that feeling.

Would she be able to hang on to that once they returned home? Or would it evaporate like that ethereal memory?

Six

Porter had a knack for presentation and plans. It was a skill he'd picked up as he grew his construction empire. And it was something easily transferred to romance. He was a big-picture kind of guy.

And if any of his visions needed to pan out, it was this one.

The day after their shopping outing, he led Alaina through the house, hands covering her eyes.

"You swear you can't see?" His body pressed against hers as they shuffled forward. The light scent of her coconut shampoo wafted in the inches between them, making him remember the countless nights they'd spent together. How he wanted that now. Wanted her now.

But he had to put recovering their family first. Taking her to bed would jeopardize his plans since she didn't trust him yet.

"I swear. But what is all this about?"

"It's a surprise. You'll just have to trust me."

Damn. If that wasn't the statement of the moment. Trust him that the surprise was worth it. And that he was, too.

He spun her around the room, turning in circles until there was no doubt in his mind that she was completely disoriented.

Two turns later, and they were in the family room. Dropping his hands, he waited while she surveyed the room and the additions he'd purchased just for her.

A ten-foot-tall live Christmas tree stood centered in the three bay windows. It was already lit, the white lights bathing the room in a warm glow.

Two boxes of decorations—special ordered and newly delivered—were stacked on the white-and-tan-striped couch, pushed up against the blue pillows of embroidered crabs and starfish. The shelving unit behind the couch had been emptied of the normal knick-knacks of lighthouses, shells and boats.

A blank canvas. Perfect for making new memories. And maybe uncovering other old ones that would bring them closer together. Of course there was also the risk that she would remember the wrong ones. That she would realize how close they'd come to divorcing and wonder why he hadn't told her.

This was how they would build a family together. She had been right earlier. It was time to start creating family traditions. Ones Thomas would grow into.

Traditions grounded a person, gave them a firm foundation to build a life upon, and clearly Alaina had a gift for that he hadn't recognized before. Maybe because he'd been too busy trying to wedge her into his preconceived notions of a family portrait rather than letting them make it together.

He wanted to create the family he'd never had as a kid. It was always just him, his mom and whatever guy she was pursuing at the time. There had been no long-standing traditions on Christmas or any other time. He loved his mother, of course, but they were distant. And he wanted better for his son.

He'd always wanted this. It was why he'd grabbed this second chance. But he was starting to see he'd sacrificed some of Alaina's preferences to reach his goal.

"How did you get this here so quickly?" Gesturing to the boxes and the tree. Blue eyes dancing in the muted light.

"The idea came to me while we were shopping and I had it all delivered."

"But you already had the decorations in place for when we arrived."

"Those were the ones here before, the ones outside and in the living room. It struck me today we didn't have anything less formal, for us as a family here, to open gifts with Thomas."

She hugged him hard. "Thank you, it's perfect." Then she froze, stepping back and turning away fast to dig around in the box closest to them. She lifted the decorations out and stacked them on the coffee table in front of the couch.

"Did I choose those others in the main living room? They don't seem like me." She shot him a look. "They're so…matchy…modern art deco rather than the smoother Renaissance palettes I gravitate toward."

"You're right." And he was seeing how he'd missed the mark and wished that he'd paid more attention.

"Most of the decorations came with the house. I bought the place as a gift to you."

"You didn't build this?" Surprise cut into her voice as she lifted the palm tree crèche out of the box. Leaning against the space between the boxes on the couch, she placed the crèche on the center shelf.

"Oh, I did. But for another family. They had everything in place, ready to move in and then they split up. I picked up the place for a song…um…not that I wouldn't have spent a fortune for you." A sheepish grin pulled on his cheeks. He placed a running silver reindeer on the lowest shelf behind the couch.

"I know that. Clearly."

Was that a dig? Was she complaining about their lifestyle? He shook off the defensiveness and thought about her, her wants and preferences, and recalled how uncomfortable she'd always been with his wealth. "We always planned to redecorate and never got around to it. I should have insisted."

"Or I should have insisted. I'm an adult. I take responsibility for decisions I made, even if I can't remember them." She rolled her eyes.

"Would you like to redo the whole place? Or our primary residence?"

"Primary residence? Hmmm. That still feels so… surreal. Like everything else in my life." She toyed with a red satin bow. "I haven't even seen our regular house in Tallahassee yet. Is it like this?"

"No, you had carte blanche there."

"How long have we lived in that house?" She sat on the tile floor between the couch and the coffee table with the box of new tree ornaments in front of her. Each one unique and made by a local artisan. Reaching into the box she began to remove all kinds of ornaments. It was a mismatched set. She set them down, one by one, on the coffee table, eyes sharp with obvious approval.

He thought back to those early days when they'd had so much hope for their future, planning a big family, children, grandchildren, growing old together. "We had it built when we got married."

"So we made those decisions together."

"We did." Kneeling, he helped her take the remaining ornaments out of the box. He lifted the first ornament they'd ever got together as newlyweds: two penguins on a snowbank holding hands. Gently, he set it next to the ornament that sported a snowman made of sand.

"I wish we'd gone to our house first." Her fingers roved gently over top of all the decorations. It was as if she was trying to gain memories by osmosis. She stopped over a Santa Claus ornament. He was posed in a Hawaiian shirt and board shorts, and he had a pink flamingo beneath his hands. A small laugh escaped her lips and she brought the Santa to the tree and hung it on a bough.

"We still can." He brought a snowflake ornament with him and hung it slightly below hers.

"But we're settled for now and have the follow-up appointments with Thomas's doctor. After Christmas we can settle into a new routine."

"It's a lot to take in at once, both places."

"That's perceptive of you."

They kept bringing ornaments to the tree, filling the boughs until they grew heavy with their collective past. He enjoyed the way that she laughed over the ornaments. The way each one was an act of discovery for her.

The evening was too good to be true.

Just as they were getting ready to put the angel on top of the tree, his mother's laughter floated into the room a second before she entered, hanging on the arm of a man with salt-and-pepper hair.

She waved her son over. "Come here, darling. You too, Alaina."

What the hell? Porter pushed to his feet and silently fumed. Who was this man? Didn't his mother realize they needed a calm and quiet family holiday? Her surprise visit had already added enough additional chaos to the equation.

"Mom, what's going on?"

"I want you to meet my new friend Barry. He's a tax attorney."

Now that seemed right. He was as polished as she was.

Barry thrust out his hand. "Nice to meet you both. Your mom has been telling me a lot about you." His grip was tight as he shook Porter's hand. "Oh, you're putting up another tree? Best part of the whole Christmas season if you ask me."

The guy was nice enough. Smooth. But so were most attorneys. They knew how to read people and work a room. This guy was no exception.

"I feel the same way, Barry." Alaina's voice cut his thoughts in half.

Courtney hugged Barry's arm closer. "I'm so glad he's joining us for dinner tonight. It'll be a little party."

"Mother, I need to talk to you. Mind if I show you something?" And with that he hooked Courtney's arm in his. Smiling tightly, he led her out of the family room and into the hallway.

He glanced back into the room to see his mother's newest suit-of-a-boyfriend helping Alaina put the angel on the tree. Something he had wanted to do with her. Damn it. Who pushed in on someone else's Christmas decorating?

"Mom," he hissed softly, "did you have to bring your boyfriend over now? Alaina's condition is delicate and we have a new baby."

"First—" she held up a slim finger "—Alaina is stronger than you give her credit for. Second, your child is asleep. And third, he's not my boyfriend. We just met at a local fund-raiser I was attending at the invitation of your neighbor Sage."

How freaking perfect. Sage was up to her usual tricks. She'd probably invited his mother to glean some information about what was going on with Alaina. She'd use their struggle as gossip at the next society function.

"There's a helluva lot going on here without adding strangers to the mix. You should have spoken to me."

"Let me get this straight." His mother folded her arms. "I showed up uninvited and brought my uninvited pickup. That makes you uncomfortable."

Always the lawyer. Even out of the courtroom.

"You're leading the witness, Mother."

"Fair enough." She held up both hands. "Barry and I will go out."

He gave an exasperated sigh as he put his hand to the back of his neck. "No, stay. It'll only be more awkward if you haul him back out after announcing he's staying for dinner."

She clacked away from him, back into the great room, heading to the last box of Christmas decorations.

So much for creating stable traditions and experiences like a normal family. Tonight was supposed to have been calm. Relaxing. A night for him and Alaina to grow closer. To move toward becoming a family. Turns out that was just as difficult for him as it was for her.

Alaina cut through her petite filet with ease. Shoveling a forkful into her mouth, she watched the verbal volleyball tournament between her mother-in-law and Porter. The tension in the room rolled in waves.

"I'm just saying, sweetie, that if you move the Christmas tree closer to the fireplace in the family room, there will be enough room for us to sit comfortably and display all of Thomas's gifts." Courtney used her fork to slice up the asparagus before continuing. "Think of how visually appealing that will be. Think of the pictures of Thomas's first Christmas. You only get one first Christmas, you know."

Porter set down his crystal water goblet. "Yes, Mother, that is true, but—"

"But what? You're not worried about the pictures. Believe me, you'll regret that in a few years."

Porter let out a deep sigh, and speared a piece of his medium rare steak with his silver fork. His face remained calm, but Alaina noticed the way his jaw flexed. It was a small movement but it was there and had nothing to do with eating his meal.

"So, Barry—" Alaina broke into the conversation in an attempt to let the heat fade "—have you always lived in Florida?"

"No, no. Though I have been here for forty years, so it seems funny to claim another state when I've acquired the Florida tan we all get from simply walking around. I'm actually from Colorado originally. Just outside of

Denver. Have you ever been there?" Barry sipped his wine, eyes as keen as the cut crystal.

Such a simple question. Yet panic filled her. Had she been to Colorado? That was the tricky part about conversations with strangers.

"Oh, Barry, you can't put Alaina on the spot like that right now." Courtney chimed in, touching his arm. "She was a victim of a terrible car accident. She's got a mild case of amnesia."

Porter pinned Courtney with a glare. She merely blinked in response. Alaina's eyes slid from Courtney to Porter. While it was true, she didn't like the ill effects of her accident being casually brought into conversation. So she decided to take charge of this conversation.

"By mild amnesia, my mother-in-law means I've forgotten the past five years." Alaina tapped her fingernail on her water glass. "Other than that, I'm fine and prefer people not treat me with kid gloves."

"All right, then," Barry agreed. "I can understand that—"

Courtney stopped him with another touch to the arm. "It's just easier if people know what they are dealing with up front. They get a fact pattern and suddenly, they understand how to handle a situation."

"Spoken like a true lawyer. Give me the facts." Barry wheezed out a laugh.

Porter's jaw flexed again. His disapproval of the way his mother had introduced the life-changing accident was more than apparent. Alaina could tell that any second now, he might explode, and that was the last thing she wanted or needed. Not to mention their reactions confused her. What was with all this tension? What was she missing—well, other than five years. So much of her life was confusing.

But right now wasn't about her. It was about her husband, who was clearly upset. She reached under the table to touch his knee, squeezing lightly until he looked at her. She pleaded with her eyes and somehow he seemed to understand.

Was this what it was like to be married? Was this an almost memory, the way they could communicate without words? It felt good.

"Amnesia, huh," Barry said between bites of his dinner. "That's rotten luck, Alaina. I wish you a speedy recovery."

"Thanks. I'm lucky to have such a great support system here." It was the most diplomatic answer she could manage. She gave Porter's knee another quick squeeze of thanks. And then returned her attention to her filet.

From the other end of the room, Thomas erupted in a gut-wrenching cry.

Alaina and Porter both sprang to their feet and rushed to the jungle-themed baby swing. She eased Thomas out and up, cradling him in her arms, rocking him back and forth. He still fussed.

"He's hungry," she said, glancing down at her watch. It was definitely dinnertime.

"I've got it." Porter's murmur was low, almost too soft to hear. Porter left the dining room and jogged into the kitchen. Moments later, he reemerged with a burp cloth and bottle, already a seasoned pro at this dad thing.

How long had they wanted this?

A whispery memory rippled through her mind of her looking at Porter as he held an infant swaddled in blue. But the baby boy wasn't Thomas—somehow she knew it was the son of Porter's CFO, the boy who was now a toddler.

Her heart ached to see the longing in his face, and then the memory faded, the rest gone. She swallowed down the lump in her throat and looked at her husband, the man still so new to her now but who had felt so familiar in the memory.

Courtney set her Waterford wineglass down on the table, half rising from her chair to get a better look at them. "Don't you have a live-in nurse to take care of him, Porter?"

"I just want to make sure I'm there for my son and that he knows who I am." He tested the milk on his wrist, then handed it to Alaina.

"And you are, Porter." Courtney dabbed at the corners of her mouth. "But you hired help. So let them help. You don't need to hover. I certainly never hovered over you and I was a single parent. I wouldn't steer you wrong. Not when it comes to my grandson."

"I appreciate that, Mother." Porter's tone was level as if he knew to keep it calm for his son, although the set of his broad shoulders made it clear his patience with his mother was nearing an end. "But I think a mix of help and hands-on work is best. Besides, we won't use the help forever. That's just until we've settled back into a routine."

So he had been serious when he'd said the night nurse was a component of her recovery. He was sincere about being a fully involved parent. She admired that. Wanted to be part of that unit. Thomas deserved that dedication from both of them.

His mom's counter came within seconds. "That's

where I think you might be wrong. I think the full-time help is wonderful. It really expands what you can do at the company. You know he's in good hands. And you can work more, grow the empire and make sure he has whatever he wants in his life."

Alaina assumed her mother-in-law's advice was coming from a good place. But it seemed more than a tad controlling. She admired Porter's restraint in not calling out his mom on that and wondered if he was holding back to keep things peaceful, not just for Thomas, but for Alaina, too.

Maybe this had been why she and her mother-in-law hadn't gotten along before the amnesia. She didn't need her memories to clue her in on *that*.

She just resented the way Porter's and his mother's issues were intruding on what had been the best day Alaina could remember having with her husband, when there were precious few to remember.

In spite of knowing there was so much of her life left to uncover, she found herself wanting more of those new memories.

He closed the door behind his mother. Finally. And not soon enough.

He'd known this was a bad idea, having his mom here for Christmas. She hadn't ever been the home and hearth for the holidays sort, and she certainly hadn't got along with Alaina. This wasn't the joyous, peaceful atmosphere he'd been attempting to create with his wife. This evening was a prime example. His day with Alaina had been derailed by that damn awkward dinner.

At least Courtney was out for the evening with Barry the tax attorney. Just like that, she'd become the mother of his youth. The one who was interested in men more than family. The one who put boyfriends first.

Alaina's misfortune was that she couldn't remember a thing. His great curse was that he couldn't forget a single damn moment. What a pair they made.

Cricking his neck to the side, he strode to his office computer and uploaded some videos of their Tallahassee house onto a disc for Alaina so she could see where they'd lived. Maybe that would jostle a memory. And maybe she would see her own stamp on their life in a way she hadn't here.

He was struck by the irony. Even with streaming music, some people still made music mixes on CDs as a gift, full of "their songs." Not him. But then he wasn't sure she would even like the same music anymore. His whole life felt upside down lately.

He thought all he'd wanted was the family he'd dreamed of having, but in getting to know Alaina again, seeing her in a new way after the accident, his feelings were mixed up.

Even his mother's behavior tonight had rocked him. It's not that he minded that she had a new beau. She was a grown-up, after all. But it brought the weight of his past crashing down on him.

Needing to calm himself, Porter made his way to Thomas's nursery. Seeing his son was a way to remind himself that this was not the past. That he was going to be an active part of his son's life. That he was making the family he'd always wanted.

Porter had never lacked material objects as a child. His mother was a brilliant attorney and made a decent salary.

But he had been profoundly lonely. And he never

wanted Thomas to experience that. Never wanted him to feel as if he wasn't welcome, as if he wasn't wanted.

Courtney had chased love for Porter's whole life. Moving from man to man. Men who seldom bothered to learn Porter's name, always settling on the generic "sport" or "son." Nameless. Invisible.

He'd attended an elite boarding school from middle school through high school. He was home for three weeks over Christmas and two months over the summer.

It was common for his mother to promise to spend time with him only to bail in favor of a date and time at the bar. She'd always promised to take him to movie releases, or ice-skating or bowling. But more often than not, Porter did all those things with a nanny instead of with his mother. He was frequently sent to his room so his mother and her current boyfriend could have the run of the house, child-free.

But there had been one Christmas break when he was in seventh grade that completely changed their relationship forever. It was part of the reason he still felt so distant from his mother. The experience left him feeling like a part-time son in a part-time family.

Alaina might not have ever gone to Colorado, but he sure as hell had.

He had come home from break, excited for the plans he had made with his mother over the school year. They were supposed to go skiing in Colorado. It was going to be a winter wonderland filled with snow, hot chocolate and sports.

They had gone to Colorado. But Courtney had brought a nanny along for the ride. As well as her boyfriend. She'd enrolled Porter in a snow camp for the day and the nanny entertained him at night while Courtney wined and dined. He'd even discovered she planned the whole trip around her meet-up with the guy. Porter had felt completely let down. He'd wanted to spend time with his mother. Even as a teen, he'd been seeking that connection. But it was on that trip that he'd realized it would never happen. If he wanted a family of his own, he would have to create it himself.

Shoving the memory aside, Porter stood over the crib. Thomas snoozed, breathing light little breaths. He was so peaceful.

It would be different for Thomas. Porter and Alaina would figure out how to be around each other. They would move past the temporary truce they'd erected before the accident and live as a family. Alaina seemed to feel their connection as much as he did. Even if she regained her memories, surely she would forgive the past and stay this time. And they both already felt so bonded to their son.

A muted knock sounded from behind him. Porter wheeled around to see Alaina standing in the doorway. She'd already changed for bed. She was in a racerback tank top that showed off her ample curves. The black shorts hugged her legs, inching up her strong thighs. His gaze lingered on her smiling face.

"Hey. You know, today was pretty amazing. Maybe you're not so terrible at that romance thing." Her voice was low, but playful. Almost like the Alaina he had first fallen in love with. He ached to grab her, to draw her into his arms.

"Well, I only know how to go big or go home."

"Today was great. All the things we found for Thomas. You bringing the decorations out for us tonight. Trying to get our own holiday traditions started. It was sweet and it meant a lot to me." She stepped close to him. Just barely out of reach.

Close enough that the coconut scent of her shampoo teased his senses. Close enough that he ached to pull her to him and take her to bed. Patience be damned. But there was too much at stake. Keeping them together. Keeping her happy. Keeping her.

He forced himself to measure his words.

"I want us to be a family." He stuffed his hands into his pockets to keep from grabbing her and saying to hell with talking. "And I think your idea of a shrimp boil is a great follow-up to what we did tonight. We are a team. Input from both of us matters."

"I think so, too. The time we're spending here is helping." She paused, her beautiful blue eyes glazing over with her attempt at looking inward. "I also vaguely recall making the painting I gave you. I can see it in my mind. It's a bit fuzzy, but I can remember the colors I used, the brushes…"

Memories. He should be rejoicing. And he *was* glad for her, but he couldn't stop the impending sense of doom. What would happen when she remembered all the mistakes he'd made? When she realized those were the questions he had avoided answering?

"It's great that you're starting to remember. I love your paintings. Your colors. I can't wait for you to re-see our house in Tallahassee."

He just prayed they could mend their marriage— their family—before the rest came rolling in. The bad parts. The possible divorce.

And God—that sucker punched him. The stakes

were higher than ever. They had a child now and Porter felt he was getting to know Alaina all over again.

"What other kinds of things did you give me over the years? You know, aside from a beautiful beach house?" Leaning over the crib, she rearranged the baby blanket.

"The humanities, art specifically, is clearly important to you. In Tallahassee, you're extremely active in the Art Association. And you wanted elementary school kids to be exposed to art. So I started a scholarship program in your name that brings artists into the classroom."

"Porter, that's so generous of you. I don't know what to say."

Her face flushed with such gratitude he felt guilty for keeping other facts from her. Facts about their marriage. But he was focused on the bigger picture, a long-term answer for them. Their future as a family. She would see that, if she suddenly remembered everything. She had to.

"You don't have to thank me, Alaina. You deserve it. And the program has been a success. The kids really benefit from it."

She looked at him them. Really and truly looked at him. He held her gaze, reading the warmth in her sky-blue eyes. The eyes of his wife and the eyes of a stranger at the same time.

Thomas began to stir, making little clucking noises. Poor guy. They were disturbing his much-needed sleep.

"I think we might be too loud."

"I guess that's our cue. We've got to let sleeping babies sleep." He took the monitor so he could give it to the matronly night nurse. "Besides, there is one more surprise for you. But it's back downstairs."

* * *

Alaina followed him back down the stairs and into the family room. They didn't bother with the actual light, but chose to sit beneath the glow of the Christmas tree.

"Close your eyes." His whisper tickled her ear. She let her eyes flit shut. A box was placed gently in her lap.

"All right. You can open them. And the present." Porter sat across from her, on the ground. Eyeing the box, she tore into the perfectly wrapped package. She lifted the flap.

And gasped in delight and breathed in the scent. Her soul sang.

Canvas paper. Acrylic paint. Oil paint. Chalk. Paintbrushes and sketching pencils. Everything she needed for a quick art set.

"Oh, Porter. You didn't have to… I mean…you could have waited for Christmas…" Her voice hitched in her throat. Emotions pulsed. Her breathing sped up in anticipation. She couldn't wait to pour out her emotions on the page.

He cupped her shoulders. "I'm a pretty simple guy. I want my family to have what they want. What they need. And I thought it would be a good outlet for you. I think this is the longest you've ever gone without some creative project."

In the deepest part of her being, she was truly touched. He had been trying so hard to connect with her. To do things to make her feel more comfortable. Even if their life before the accident hadn't been perfect, the man before her now was putting in a real effort.

"Porter, it's perfect. Thank you." She grabbed his

hand, beginning to feel as if she knew the texture and feel of him. He tucked her hair behind her ear.

"Of course."

"Can I ask another question?"

"Always."

"How did we decide on the name Thomas?" It had been her father's name. She hoped that had been the reason, but she didn't trust much about her instincts these days. A pang of sorrow shot through her. Her father would never know her son. She took a shaky breath. His loss felt so recent.

Porter inched toward her. They were side by side. His shoulder brushed hers and she leaned into him. Breathed in the dark clove scent of his cologne.

"We chose the name for your father. It wasn't much of a discussion. I never had a father and your father sounded wonderful even if I never had the honor of meeting the guy. It seemed right. Fitting." He wrapped his arm around her, and she buried her face in his chest. The tightness of his arm on hers ramped up her heartbeat. He was beginning to feel like someone she could talk to. Trust was still an iffy idea, but she was moved by his actions today.

She couldn't deny it. She was ready to take this to the next step. She craved intimacy with him. Her body ached for him, recognizing him on an instinctive level that went beyond memories.

"I know there must have been difficulties between us. Probably a strain because of the infertility," she began to say. She had to finish before she lost her nerve. "And probably a bunch of other things that I don't need to know right now...but I'm glad that we are trying to become a family now. And I was wondering if you could stay the night with me. Just sleeping. Nothing else. What do you think?"

His eyebrows shot upward. "I think I would be an idiot to say no."

Seven

Alaina couldn't believe she'd asked to share a bed with her husband. Not sex. Just sleeping.

She stood in her bathroom, changing into the pajamas she'd chosen. Choosing them had been tough. What to wear to sleep with a man she was attracted to, but wasn't ready to have sex with? If she wore a nightgown or a T-shirt, that would invite his hand to tunnel upward.

If she wore something silky, then that would feel like skin, sexy. But she didn't want to be frumpy. She couldn't help but feel vain in wanting to look attractive for her husband. So she'd opted for colors that flattered her. A pale pink tank top, cotton but thin. And a striped pair of shorts, so yes, their legs could brush.

Because she wanted this. Needed this, to be close to another human being. To her husband. Some part of her body knew they'd been together. Often. For a long time. There was a synchronicity in the way they moved through life that spoke of having done things together as a team, everyday things, sexual things.

When she'd first woken up from her coma, she'd felt as if the past five years hadn't existed. That it had only been a few months since she'd broken off her relationship with Douglas and taken out a restraining order.

But during the week in the hospital and then the week at the beach house, she had gained a sense of distance from the past. These weeks had helped ease the initial tension that had made her feel stuck in another time.

Had she moved beyond all those awful feelings left over from Douglas? She must have, since she'd got married. Even with her memories of the past five years gone, her sense of Douglas felt further away than when she'd first woken up in the hospital. It was as if her body was moving forward to absorb the lost time even if her brain didn't fill in the missing pieces.

Her past with Porter hadn't returned, but her feelings for him were definitely growing. Strong. Real.

Powerful.

She looked down at her engagement ring and the wedding band. For the first time, she felt as if maybe, just maybe, they fit.

When Porter had given her those art supplies, she'd felt connected to him. She'd been given a link to her past with those supplies in hand. It made her want to find more links to the past, make more connections. It made her want this night with her husband.

She tugged on her pj's, the soft cotton brushing against her breasts and sending a shiver of awareness through her.

This wasn't going to be as easy as she'd thought.

Deep breath in. One foot in front of the other. She could do this.

The bedroom was washed in warm yellow light from the oversize candle emblazoned with an anchor on the mahogany dresser. It cast flickers on the ship steering wheel that leaned from dresser to wall.

Matchy-matchy. Maybe she would try her hand at re-decorating this place. Make it feel less like a page out of a catalog and more like a home for a family always on the go. But she'd only make those decisions with Por-ter. Joint decisions. Like the decisions they had made earlier today with Thomas's gifts.

Porter slouched against the door frame, half looking at her. His black sweatpants hung low on his hips. A white T-shirt for a local Tallahassee baseball team en-hanced his athletic frame. Damn, he was sexy.

And he was hers.

Alaina toyed with the band on her shorts. "This is a little awkward."

"I'm sorry you feel that way."

"Me, too, but I said it, and then I couldn't take it back."

"You don't have to."

She took a deep breath. "I think I do." She yanked back the covers, then paused, inhaling hard. "I don't even know what side of the bed I sleep on."

"You're fine," he said.

"Are you saying that to be accommodating? Or is that the truth?"

"The truth. Your instincts are right. That's your side of the bed."

Something eased inside her. Maybe she needed to follow her instincts more with him.

Alaina climbed into bed and patted the space beside her. "Okay. Join me."

He lay on top of the spread. "Done, as requested."

"And I didn't die."

"Wow, now that's a turn-on."

Laughing, she shoved him gently with both hands and felt the resistance in his muscles as her skin met his. He let out a low chuckle, clearly amused.

She sagged back into the fluffy feather pillow. He reclined on his side, propping his head on his hand.

Alaina picked at the down comforter. "What's next? Our situation is so unconventional I don't know what the rules are."

"No rules as far as I'm concerned. We're making this up as we go."

Still, she wanted details, a sense of who'd they'd been. "How did we used to sleep? Did I sleep on your chest? Did we spoon? Me against you? You against me? Opposite sides of bed?"

"Why don't we just see where we end up?" He held out an arm.

After only an instant's hesitation, she rested her head on his shoulder and his arm wrapped around her. A sigh filled her. This. This was right. The feel of her body fitting against her husband's.

Sleep pulled at her eyelids. It had been an exhausting day. Being here with Porter felt so damn right. Familiar. As if by muscle memory, her body curled around him, and she took comfort in the steady rise and fall of his broad chest.

Her eyelids fluttered shut. How was it possible to be entirely at ease and so on edge all at once?

Sleep was the furthest thing from Porter's mind.

Then again, that was nothing new. Not since the accident. Since the endless blur of days and nights at the hospital. He'd taken to doing work in the odd hours of the evening. Using work as a way to keep his mind off the dire situation of his family.

But tonight, he was working for different reasons. He needed to keep himself occupied, to keep his hands off his wife. Tonight, concentration was difficult. Near impossible, with Alaina pressed against him.

It had been so damn long since he'd held her like this. Since the warmth of her body melted with his. He absently ran a hand through her hair. She drew in closer.

How had it been so long since they'd done this? Been in bed together, nestled against each other.

Too long.

Yes, he wanted to touch her, to make love to her, but he had to keep his goals in mind. For the first time in months, he felt as if they were working together. That they were in this for real. Not just him, but her, too. They were becoming a family. At least, he thought they were. His own experiences with family were shaky at best. And her family was gone. But *this* family—this family had a shot.

He returned his attention back to his tablet. Looked over some reports. Started to feel the pull of sleep.

But something was wrong. Alaina started to shake. She twisted away from him.

"Stop it." Her voice was a murmur. But there was desperation in it.

"Let go. Just…just. No. Stop." Her lovely face contorted with fear. She continued to thrash against an invisible assailant.

She was having a nightmare.

Gently, he shook her shoulder. "Alaina. You're okay. You're okay."

She gasped in air. Her blue eyes suddenly alert. Scanning the room. Focusing on him. Breathing rapidly, her body twitchy. "I'm sorry. I didn't mean to wake you. Oh, God, this plan isn't working out like I meant it… I should just go."

He clasped her arm. "Stay. Do you remember what you dreamed? Did you recall something from the past?"

"No, not really." She sagged back against him. "I was just having a nightmare about Douglas, about that time with him. Things get muddled in dreams, feeling out of control and scared. Did I tell you about Douglas?"

"Your ex-boyfriend before you met me? Yes, you did."

"What did I tell you?"

"Are you trying to pull information out of me? Have you forgotten parts of that time in your life, too?"

"I remember. He was verbally abusive. I didn't see that for a long time. Then he hit me…" She shook her head. "And then I was done. I walked out."

"That's what you told me." Once he'd learned about the jerk, Porter had made a point to keep tabs on the guy, make sure he honored that restraining order. "I'm sorry tonight is bringing back bad memories for you. This was supposed to be a positive experience."

"It would have been worse if I'd been alone. Let's try again."

"I'd like that, too." She maneuvered into the crook of

his arm. Laid a hand on his chest. He pulled her tightly against him, his mind churning with ways to help her feel at ease, to know he wouldn't let anything happen to her. Her breathing slowed, falling into the rhythmic pattern of a deep sleep.

And even with the determination to keep her safe from threats like Douglas, and to keep his hands to himself until she was ready for more, Porter couldn't deny he had no way to keep her safe from thoughts of the past.

The yellow-orange rays of dawn's first light filtered in between the tulle-like curtains, nudging Alaina awake. She glanced over at her husband, whose eyes were still closed, heavy with sleep.

Quietly, she slid from bed and crept down the hall to check on the baby.

Thomas greeted her with a chubby-cheeked smile.

"Are you hungry, my love?" she cooed, picking him up out of bed. She sat with him in the rocker while he drank from the bottle. This was her favorite time of the day, just the two of them alone. She fed him and rocked him even though he was awake. She talked to him and sang to him. Time passed in a vacuum, a couple of hours sliding by in a beautiful haze.

This was everything she'd always hoped motherhood would be. A calmness descended on her as she sat with Thomas. And a desire to crawl back into bed with Porter. To memorize all of his features. To hold these moments close so they couldn't slip away like the others.

Maybe it was time to start drawing again. A family portrait. She'd start with Porter. Capture the angles of his face, the strength in his chest. And the smile lines in his face. And somehow, maybe their years together would come rushing back as she revisited him.

After finishing with Thomas, she set him down for a nap. Kissed his forehead. Filled with love for the making of her little family. She'd sketch him next.

On tiptoe, she made her way downstairs, grabbed her new sketchbook and pencils and crawled back into bed. Sunlight streamed over Porter's face.

She began to outline him. Rough strokes on paper. She worked first on his face. She started to lose herself in the drawing, the world ebbing away from her.

Until a knock sounded from behind her. Alaina practically leaped out of her skin.

"Sleeping Beauty's still asleep, I see." Her mother-in-law called from the door, a diamond-and-silver snowflake broach pinned to the collar of her shirt. Porter let out a loud snore and turned on his side.

"Have breakfast with me? I could use some toast. And girl time." She motioned for Alaina to follow her down the hall.

"Sounds great. I am a bit hungry myself." Alaina stacked her sketchbook and pencils on the bedside table. If she stayed here much longer, she might not be able to resist temptation. She needed some space to gather her thoughts—and her mother-in-law might well have insights that could help her decide how to move forward in the marriage.

She hurried after Courtney into the hallway toward the back stairway leading to the kitchen.

When she'd caught up to her mother-in-law, Courtney glanced over her shoulder on her way down the steps. "I've never seen you draw before. You know, you get the same look on your face as Porter does when he is working on a building design."

"I do?"

She nodded, clasping the polished steel railing. "Porter's always been a hands-on guy. Started back in middle school. He was always building things. Once, he built a table for me for Christmas. He was sixteen then. Said he'd loved the sweat equity of the project. The ability to create something from nothing. I guess that's a bit like art, isn't it?"

"I suppose it's actually a similar process. Built not bought. I think that's why this house feels foreign to me. It's cookie cutter decor in a lot of ways other than some of the artwork. I'll take some imperfections in my decorations if it's coming from scratch."

"You sound like him. When he built that table, I think that's when he decided he didn't need me anymore." Courtney gave a slight laugh. But the sound was tinged with sadness.

They turned the corner into the kitchen and sat on the bar stools facing a view of the water, where a holiday boat parade was organizing. Festively decorated boats of all sizes congregated. A blow-up Santa in a bathing suit sat on the deck of one, but most of the vessels were outfitted more simply with green garland boughs.

"I'm sure he still needed you then. You helped shape him into the person he is today." A person she was still trying to understand. To relearn.

Her mother-in-law's eyebrows arched as she popped two slices of bread in the toaster. "Sometimes I wonder. He's built every house he's lived in as an adult. Sometimes I'm surprised he didn't build the yacht, too."

Alaina said, "Whoa, wait. We own one of those yachts?"

"You do. Usually my son has me stay out there rather than in the house, which, quite frankly, is an amazing spin on a mother-in-law suite. But still. We've always had troubles, my son and I."

Her mother-in-law straightened the rings on her fingers before she continued. "You know, I was madly in love with Porter's father. I was young—and the whole world seemed open to me when we were together. But he had other dreams. Other desires. He left shortly after Porter was born."

"I'm sure that was difficult. Raising Porter alone and working so much."

"Would you like the truth, Alaina? I was—and still am—brilliant in the courtroom. I can dissect a case like nobody's business. But motherhood? That never came to me. Not like it does to you."

Alaina nodded sympathetically, but didn't say anything. She knew Courtney had her quirks, but she never doubted that the woman loved her son. Family was just complicated. Alaina felt as if she knew that better than anyone. Funny what a few weeks in a coma had done for her perspective.

Porter was a man whom she was only just beginning to understand. But the tension between her husband and mother-in-law was starting to make sense to her. Courtney was all about buying premade items. It's why she'd insisted on the night nurse tending to Thomas.

But Porter—Porter was a man intent on creation. On actively building. He'd built a construction empire the same way he'd built that table. To prove he could take scraps and turn them into something usable. He'd built his life from the ground up, even though he could have easily used his mother's fortune. He hadn't backed down from the work it required.

And what about her? Alaina had spent the past two weeks in the haze of amnesia. Afraid of what she'd find if she pressed too hard. But Porter was aware of their history. Aware of their struggles. And he was still dedicated to their family. Maybe she needed to become aware, too.

And that meant digging around in the dirt a bit. And possibly talking to Sage.

As Alaina poured two cups of coffee in holiday mugs painted with angels, she made up her mind. Today was a day for exploring. And she would start with all the pieces of her past—even the uncomfortable ones. The time had come to reconstruct her life.

Starting with finding out more about how and why they'd purchased that yacht when she could have sworn such flashy purchases weren't her style.

Eight

Porter was still stunned over Alaina suggesting they go out to the yacht. He couldn't recall her ever suggesting that. In fact, the eighty-foot *Sunseeker* had been a contentious issue between them since he'd bought it two years ago. But he wasn't turning his back on the chance to get closer to her.

In the past, she'd always hated the vessel. Said it was too showy. Too flashy. It screamed their wealth, and that bothered her down to the core.

But Porter had never felt that way about the purchase. To him, it represented freedom. A chance to leave the world behind. To be completely untethered from the responsibilities of work and reliant on himself. And yes, he'd hoped it would offer them more time to relax together, bring them closer as their marriage began to fray.

The Florida winter sun warmed him. The captain had

dropped anchor and gone into town about a half hour ago. The luxury craft happily rocked with the waves and the current, other boats far enough away to give him and Alaina a sense of privacy he welcomed. Water lapped against the sides and a healthy breeze coated the deck. They'd intended to take Thomas with them, but his mother had offered to watch him. She had even insisted. Though they did hire a backup sitter for all the tasks Courtney was not enthusiastic about performing.

He'd come out of the cabin with two bottles of water. One for him and one for Alaina.

Every day he was feeling closer to her, closer than he could remember feeling before. They were building something, a new connection. And since last night he felt a change between them. Something that had been missing for a long time before the accident.

He took a moment to appreciate her. Just the way she was in this moment. She'd dressed in layered tank tops and leggings, flip-flops half on, half off. She was sprawled on the white cushioned deck chair. Hunched over a pad, sketching furiously. The wind teased her blond hair. She was beautiful.

"May I see your drawings?"

She sketched with charcoal, not looking up. "Are you sure you want to look? There are ones of you in here."

"Did you draw me as a gargoyle? Or a cyclops?" he asked, lounging back in a deck chair and propping his foot on the bolted down table between the seating.

She glanced up. "Why would I do that?"

"Since we talked about our past arguments."

Fish plopped in the brief silence before she answered, "You've been nothing but understanding and patient with me, with this whole situation. No matter what else happens, I won't forget that."

"Whatever else happens?" Trepidation kinked the muscles in his neck.

"If you get tired of having an amnesiac wife."

"I could never get tired of you."

Her cheeks flushed pink as she glanced at him through her eyelashes. His mind swirled, thinking of last night. Of her body pressed against his and the scent of her coconut shampoo. And how he'd wanted so much more than to just sleep next to her.

How he still wanted that.

She seemed to read his thoughts, her blush fading. Awareness flitted across her face. An expression that almost looked like longing.

The sound of another fish jumping out of the water brought them back to reality. He shook his head.

She passed over the pad of drawings. "Here. Feel free to look."

She tucked her hair behind her ear and chewed her nail as he flipped through the book.

There were pages upon pages of sketches. Some scenes of the beach house. Some of boats in the harbor. Thomas in a Santa hat.

All so damn good, the details grabbing his heart. "You've been busy."

"I feel like there are thoughts needing to pour out. I don't have to think or talk, just... Oh, I don't know how to describe it other than to say it's like meditation."

He flipped to the next page. Half-finished drawings of him sleeping. She seemed to fixate on his face. Mostly his eyes. As if she was trying to figure out something about him. Her sketches were beautiful. Hyperrealistic. He'd forgotten how talented she was with charcoal and pencils.

The last sketch in the book sucked the air from his chest. It was a montage of images. Items of their joint past. Did she remember?

It was a scene of a room. On the desk, there was a globe with a cracked stand. A Moroccan rug on the ground. All souvenirs—all representing moments in their life together. If she didn't know what these were, what did the drawings mean? Why had she stumbled onto these particular items? He couldn't decide whether to tell her or not. What would be helpful?

Truth. As much as he could give her.

"There are items here that you received over those missing years, gifts I gave you."

She gasped. "Like what?"

"The rug right here." He pointed to the sketch, careful not to smudge the material, "It was the first gift I ever gave you. When you were living in that tiny apartment with the tile in your bedroom. You said you hated how cold your feet were in the mornings. Even then, I knew you liked those rich colors. Items with a bit of history. I picked it up on a business trip."

She considered his words, staring hard at the sketch. "I woke up with this scene in my head. I thought it was from a dream…but maybe my memories are trying to come back after all."

"It's quite possible."

"What else is from our past?"

"The globe with the cracked stand."

"That's a strange gift. Where's it from?" She crinkled her nose and adjusted her sunglasses again.

"Well it didn't start out cracked. It cracked in our

move. But I got it for our one-year anniversary. It was a blank globe. Ceramic. You painted it. It's got quotes over where the countries ought to be. Quotes about art and life. I've always thought you should replicate it and sell them."

She smiled at him. "Do you think the art supplies gift made me think of that?"

"Could be."

"What about being on the yacht? What will that help me remember?"

"Honestly? Arguing. You were angry with me for buying this. You thought the money could have been better spent. But then we fought about pretty much everything then."

"I appreciate you being honest."

"I want you to trust me. You believe that, right?"

"I do. I'm just not sure you want me to remember everything. You seem very into this fresh start. All the control is on your side since you have the pieces of the past and I only get what other people tell me."

He couldn't deny the truth in that. He owed her more, better. Hell, he owed her the unvarnished truth, but couldn't bring himself to go quite that far when they were so close to having everything they'd wanted. Time on the yacht offered them a window of time away from the world and he needed to embrace that fully.

"Alaina, I have an idea. Let's use this time to pretend we're two different people. Strangers who've met and are stuck on this ostentatious yacht together. Strangers attracted to each other and ready to get to know each other." He loosened the cap on the water bottle and handed it to her.

His gaze met hers, and he could swear the air crackled with the static of a lightning strike even though there wasn't a cloud in the sky.

She grabbed it and flashed him a grin. "I'm game."

Vibrant pinks of the sunset blurred into deeper purples. The heat of the day was behind them, the cool ocean breeze nudging Alaina's skin toward goose bumps. She ran a hand over her exposed leg, hoping to generate some warmth.

Embers of sunlight caused the yacht to glow. While she was conscious of how expensive this outing was, she had to admit there was some charm to it all. The lulling rock of the yacht in the water. The heavy smell of salt in the air. Relaxing. Intimate. It was easy to feel as if they were the only two people in the whole world with the captain and crew dismissed for a few hours and other boats so far away.

And in some ways, that'd been a good thing.

But she still couldn't help feeling slightly uneasy. He hadn't denied wanting this fresh start, or taking the power it gave him. Even when she agreed to get to know him anew, she wondered what he really thought of her. Of all of this.

"You look chilled." Porter pushed his deck chair closer to hers. He had a thick blanket in his hand. It was covered in a sprawling cursive print. She squinted in the dying light to see what it said. Looked like lines from a novel. Was that a purchase she'd made?

"I've definitely been warmer. That's for sure." Although there was heat building inside her just from looking at him, having him near. Their night sleeping together had brought a new level of intimacy to their relationship. One that made her yearn to take that to the next level.

"Luckily for you, I come prepared." He draped the blanket across her shoulders, his hands brushing her shoulders and sending another shiver through her.

Definitely the electric sort of shiver born of heat not cold.

She pulled the blanket-tight, closing it around her body against the ache for contact with him. Did he want this as much as she did? What would happen afterward?

"So generous," she teased him, but she was grateful for his attentiveness. Even her nose was cold.

"I don't know about that. There is a catch, you see." The sunset glinted in his eyes. His beard-stubbled face was serious.

"Oh?"

"It's going to cost you a date, lady. And you're going to have to share that blanket." A mischievous twinkle danced in his dark eyes, reaching his lips.

Butterflies filled her stomach, and her breasts tingled with increasing need. His relaxed smile sparked a fierce need for him; the new ease of being with him stirred her. Deeply.

He was asking for more than a shared night in a bed and she could sense they both knew that.

Clenching the blanket tighter in her fists, she returned his gaze steadily. "I don't know about that. That's a pretty tall demand."

Feeling bold and ready to take a risk that she prayed would pay off, she held out a side of the blanket for him to sit next to her. He filled the gaping space in an instant with his big, warm presence.

"How 'bout a game?" he asked, gathering her closer, his hard thigh against her legs.

"I like games." She liked *him*. A lot.

"Thought you might. I'll ask a question. And you have to answer it. And then you can do the same to me." He pivoted his body to face her.

She nodded, her hair snagging on his five o'clock shadow. "I like it. But I'm going first. Worst drink you've ever had?"

"Worst drink? Hmm. In college, a friend dared me to drink a bar mat—which is basically a mix of all the alcohol that spills during the night as a shot. I never made that mistake again." He shuddered at the memory.

"That is absolutely disgusting." She laughed, unable to imagine him losing control in any way. "What in the world made you go along with that?"

"Now, now, Alaina." He nudged her shoulder gently. "You only get one question at a time. It's my turn. If you had to be stuck in one television show for the rest of your life, which one would it be?"

Now that was a hard one. "Well. And you keep in mind I'm working with outdated information. But I'd have to say I'd like to be stuck in *Scooby-Doo*. The original series. I could totally drive around in the Mystery Machine. I half wanted to be a detective when I was younger because of that show. Definitely my favorite growing up."

"*Scooby-Doo?* I would never have guessed that one. You'd have the brains of Velma and the beauty of Daphne. You would've been the powerhouse." He put his arm around her back, drawing her closer to him as he leaned them down to look at the first evening stars.

She turned to half lie on his chest, her ear pressed

against the steady thud of his heart. "Ha-ha. Absolute favorite meal? Like the kind you could eat again and again and never get sick of?"

He exhaled deeply. "You do know how to ask the tough questions. I would eat Dunkaroos for every meal. I love the frosting."

"Porter…really? Out of all the food in the world… Dunkaroos?" She lifted her head off his chest to stare at his face. Smile lines pushed at his cheeks as he attempted to look completely serious.

"Oh, yeah. Completely." She arched her brow at him. But the smile stuck to her face, anyway.

"My turn again. Let's see—who was your first kiss?"

"Oh, lord. I haven't thought about Bobby Dagana in ages. I was fourteen. He walked me home and kissed me on my doorstep. But my mom saw the whole thing happen and teased me for the rest of the day."

"If I had known you when we were younger, I would have kissed you before Bobby Dagana had ever thought about it." He massaged the back of her head. Fingers tracing circles in her scalp.

"Mmm. That feels nice. Could you keep doing that while I think of another question?" She held on to his side, hooked her fingers in his belt loop. She could have sworn the vessel rocked under her feet even as she knew that would be virtually undetectable on the large luxury yacht.

"Nope. Sorry. That's your question… I'm kidding." He captured a lock of her hair and wrapped it around his finger.

"What are you thinking about right now?" Her heart was in her throat as she waited for the answer. The seconds felt like mini eternities.

"Honestly? You. How beautiful you are. How lucky I am." He said it without a trace of sarcasm or humor. He squeezed her arm. Silence fell between them.

She swallowed hard. "Really lucky to have your life turned upside down because I can't remember even meeting you?"

Her eyes stung with tears.

"Ah, Alaina," he sighed, stroking her face. "I don't deserve you."

"Why do you say that?"

"Because you came out here with me today, even though you seemed to have sensed the yacht wasn't neutral territory for us. Why *did* you come out on the yacht with me?"

Where the hell had that come from?

Porter wanted to kick himself. He'd been five seconds away from romancing his wife back into his bed again. Then he'd sabotaged it by asking a question to stop their progress in its tracks.

"The yacht seems to have been a bone of contention between us and I wanted to try to heal that."

"Did you remember something about it?" He felt as if his marriage was one big ticking time bomb, set to explode the second she regained her full memory. He had to make the most of their time together before that happened.

"It's more like a sensation, feelings." She tapped her temple, her forehead furrowed. "Intuition, I guess. But no, I don't remember."

A reprieve. For now.

He searched for the right words to strike a balance between honesty and gaining her trust without spilling all. "We did argue, pretty heatedly. You thought it was a waste of money, that we didn't need it, wouldn't be using it often enough to warrant the expense."

"It is a nice boat." She drew a lazy circle on his chest with her finger.

He struggled to focus.

"Boat? That's something you ski behind or paddle."

"Ah, so the big boat is important to you." She patted his chest. "That's rather Freudian."

He didn't take the bait and argue with her as he would have in the past. Instead, he worked to explain his feelings rather than offer up a knee-jerk reaction. Over the past few weeks, he'd pushed aside her feelings for his own, and he knew if he wanted his family to stay intact, he needed to try a different strategy.

"The escape is important to me. There's no office here. It's the anticonstruction site, no land."

"Oh." She blinked fast, her hands falling to her lap. "Did you tell me that before?"

"I didn't," he admitted. "I should have."

She stayed silent so long he wondered if she would change the subject altogether.

Then she looked up at him, her blue eyes searching his face. "Would I have heard you?"

He hadn't expected that from her. Maybe they were both changing, making something good happen from the hell of the car accident that had stolen her memory.

"Maybe. Maybe not. I honestly can't answer that, Alaina. And you've mentioned before that it's not fair I'm the filter for all your memories and questions." He reached forward and slid a disc holder off the table. "We're tied to this house for now. But I compiled all the videos and photos of our Tallahassee home. When we get back, if you're ready and want to, I will try my best to help you connect with people who knew both of us."

"Thank you. Truly. This means more to me than... well, more than any expensive gift." She took the disc from him and held it to her chest. "This is what I'm talking about. You're really trying to hear what I need, to help us trust each other. I can feel that."

Trust. Now that was a sticky word. But the doctor had warned against pushing her too fast. Maybe that was a convenient excuse now for not being more open, but damn, she felt good in his arms. He didn't want to say anything to make her pull away.

She set the disc aside and rested her palms on his chest, the invitation clear in her gaze. "And I want to be closer to you, even if it's just on a physical level."

They'd been married a long time. He recognized the authenticity of the desire in her eyes, the passion in her husky voice. Some things between them didn't need words or memories. Their bodies recognized each other.

Still, he had to ask, to keep what fragile trust they'd built.

"Alaina," he said, taking her face in his hands, "are you sure this is what you want?"

"Absolutely certain," she whispered against his mouth an instant before she kissed him.

In a flash of insight, as he wrapped his arms around her, he realized why he'd asked about the boat. To deflect her from pressing for more on why he felt he wasn't a good husband. He was changing, learning from his mistakes, but he still wasn't ready to admit he hadn't been up-front about how close they'd been to divorce before the accident. He wanted to make his family whole before they dealt with that truth.

He was a jerk.

And the worst part? He still couldn't bring himself to back away from this chance to have Alaina again.

Every step of the way to their cabin below, she kissed him. Deeply. Urgently.

Hungrily.

Alaina savored the taste of Porter on her tongue. The sensations pulsing through her were new and familiar all at once. Surreal. Sensual.

The touch of his hand, the rasp of his beard-stubbled face, the scent of him—all of it turned her inside out. Nothing in her life made sense. Her past was a jumble. Her present a strange haze.

But she was certain of this. Of needing Porter. Of their undeniable chemistry. Of the evening that had sparked her back to life in a way she was somehow certain she'd never felt before.

Her feet tangled with his as they moved through the corridor, sconces lighting the way toward the main cabin. He met her kiss for kiss, snaking his hands into the mess of her wavy hair. His steps slowing, he pressed her against the wall to deepen the contact. Pressed her closer to him. Her back against the polished cypress wainscoting.

And then he broke the kiss to stare at her. His coal-dark eyes searched her face, looking for an answer to his unasked question. And she knew. He was wrestling with this step and the fact that she didn't recall their marriage.

But she recalled their now. She felt the connection. She didn't believe in love at first sight, but there was a sense of their history still binding them, curling through some part of her mind.

So she leaned in for another kiss and reassured him.

"I want this." She breathed against his mouth. Then nipped his lower lip. She let her hand travel to the tender flesh between his shirt and pant line.

His head fell back with a growl of desire. Need fueled the air between them. He lifted her legs to wrap around his waist. She hooked her heels behind him, her core pressed to his, her arms looped around his neck. Her body was on fire for him.

Porter.

Her husband.

He carried her the rest of the way down the hall, past framed photos of Florida island scenery and fishing expeditions. And she had to admit, this yacht had a romantic appeal. She appreciated the sense of escape, being away from the world, just the two of them floating alone in the world.

Porter shouldered open the door to their master bedroom, and then shouldered the door closed after him. The lighting was dimmer here, but she didn't care much about the surroundings anymore. Only the man touching her.

And that big bed waiting for them.

Gently, he eased her back onto the soft comforter carefully, stretching out on top of her. He propped himself on his forearms, but there was no missing the rigid length of him pressing against her belly.

A smile spread across her lips as she met his gaze. In his face, she saw his desire matched hers. Frenzy. Fire. Longing.

"Alaina. I've missed you. So damned much." He

punctuated each word with a kiss before angling back up onto an elbow, putting enough space between them to pluck at their clothes.

One, then the other, he peeled off her layered shirts and bared her lacy bra to the moonlight and low flickering sconces. Reverently, he ran gentle fingers across the peaks of her breasts. Her nipples tightened in response. Anticipation lit beneath her skin and she reached for him, needed to feel his bare flesh against hers. She skimmed off his shirt and unzipped his jeans with impatience, her hands brushing his as he peeled away her leggings.

Finally, finally, they were both naked. The heat of his skin seared her and she wondered how she could have ever forgotten this man.

Porter lowered himself on top of her. Skimmed her collarbone with kisses. Traveled with soft lips back to her mouth. He held one of her hands above her head as he skimmed off her underwear.

She arched her body toward him. Slick with need for him. His fingers teasing her, taking her desire to another level.

His breath was against her skin again. Kissing her hip, hands sketching along her breasts, then his mouth there as well, licking and drawing her in until she bit back a cry of ecstasy.

She pushed herself up, meeting Porter's eyes as she reached for the hard length of him. His jaw flexed, eyes fluttering as she stroked him. His lips found hers again. Needing the contact.

Hooking her legs around his waist again, she pulled him closer. Pulled him into her, the thick press of him filling her. They were anchored together. Joined by something more than the physical.

There was a deliberate rhythm to their coupling. The frenzy shifting into something even more intimate. Something that didn't rely on the past, that only existed between the people they were now. A throaty moan rolled through her. Made her dizzy as he stroked her. She writhed, hands twisting in the blanket.

Each deep thrust sent her closer to a wave of ecstasy about to crest. They pushed farther up the deck chair until she was pressed up against the edge. Their bodies moved as one in a familiar rhythm.

He kissed her deeply on her mouth. Her neck. She practically melted into him as he brought her to the cusp of release, slowed, held back, then thrust deeper to drive her the rest of the way into completion.

She wrapped her legs tighter around him, her heels digging into his ass. She kissed him, fiercely, deeply, taking his hoarse shout of completion into her mouth, aftershocks rippling through her again and again.

Their first time together.

Or rather her first time with him.

That thought threatened to steal the bliss still shimmering through her.

As she held him, their bodies slick with sweat, she knew. They'd done this before. She knew him, not in a concrete memory, but in an elusive feeling she wanted to grasp and hold on to but couldn't quite reach.

However she knew, this man was her husband.

Nine

Peace settled inside him like a whisper, like the breeze coming in off the ocean. Alaina had pulled on his polo shirt to keep out the night chill. It looked right on her. She pressed herself against him, head resting on his shoulder. Her soft arms draped over his bare chest. The downy blanket closed them in together, cocooning them in that peace.

Except with that peace came the reminder that he still hadn't told her everything about the state of their marriage before the accident. They'd moved to another level here and he couldn't keep hiding the facts from her for much longer under the excuse of protecting her or rebuilding their family.

She had always been a strong, independent woman. That hadn't changed. He could feel the restlessness in her to regain her life. He owed it to her to do everything he could to help. And he would. He resolved to give her—them—the foundation, the memory, of a beautiful Christmas together, and then just before New Year's he could tell her everything he could about their past. Hopefully she, too, would see that the New Year offered a new beginning, symbolically and literally.

At first, keeping Alaina had been about re-establishing their family at all costs, but as he learned new things about her and realized the mistakes he'd made that had contributed to their discord, he knew he didn't just want the family. He wanted her. He wanted them. Together. In love.

He'd do anything to keep her with him like this. He hadn't realized how broken they'd been before. But tonight—tonight they'd connected as they had when they were just falling in love.

A new conviction overtook him. Porter wanted to help ease her memories back. He was not afraid of her leaving. Of her wanting a life without him. They fit. They were a team.

A family.

"What was our first time together like?" Alaina's voice carried on the wind.

Porter took a deep breath. "Are you sure you wouldn't rather remember that on your own and not have my words tangled up in those memories?"

She looked up her chest at him, her blue eyes still hazy with passion. "I want to hear how you remember us."

"Okay, then." His hand settled on the soft curve of her hip. "I'll do my best to set the stage for you. I came to your apartment for dinner. You swore you could make the best steak and stuffed mushrooms. I brought a bottle of wine. You were in a bright green dress. Red lipstick. Your hair was curled. We ate. And you were right." Paused to kiss her. He never wanted to stop kissing her.

He whispered in her ear, "Best steak and stuffed mushrooms ever. And then." He nipped down her neck again, tasting the mix of sea salt and sweat. "The rest is history."

A breathy sigh escaped her lips a second before she angled to press her mouth to his. "Let's make history again."

He growled his approval.

Her hands slid around his waist and shifted on his lap. He spanned her waist and brought her closer. She wriggled against his erection, sending a fresh jolt of desire through him. The scent of her shampoo, the salty air and their lovemaking combined into a heady aphrodisiac.

The blanket, in addition to the dark, gave them an air of privacy. And even though all the boats were too far away for anyone to see them, there was also a sexiness to being out in the open this way with her, under the stars. Sex between them had always been good, even with the stress of the fertility treatments, but there was a freedom between them now.

A new connection tonight.

Her hands skimmed across his bare chest, her head falling back to expose the curve of her neck, encouraging him wordlessly. He didn't need more of an invitation to make the most of this chance to be with her again.

He slipped his hands under the shirt—his shirt on her, the cotton warm from her body. Her silky smooth skin called to him, enticed him to explore further. He skimmed up to cup her breasts, circling his thumbs over her nipples as he kissed the curve of her neck. Her low moan of excitement encouraged him to continue. He stroked down her side, tucking his fingers into her panties, the string along her hip a fragile barrier that gave way with a twist and snap.

Humming her approval, she made fast work of unzipping his jeans. He swept away her underwear, the scrap of satin almost as soft as her skin. The moist heat of her pressed against him. He'd never wanted her—or anyone—more than at this moment. She was everything, his every fantasy come to life. She was… Alaina.

Resting her hands on his shoulders, she raised up, then lowered herself onto him, taking him inside her. Exactly where he wanted to be for as long as possible. A challenge with her hips rolling against him in an arousing wriggle.

He cupped her bottom and brought her closer still, thrusting up as she threaded her fingers through his hair, tugging slightly. Her husky sighs drove him crazy with wanting her, drove all thoughts of their past away until only the present mattered.

And hell yeah, he knew he was making excuses to be with her even with secrets between them. But right then, he didn't care.

The wind blew her hair forward and around his face, as if binding them more closely. The silky strands teased his senses. Everything about her was sensual. Her hair, yes, even her hair turned him on, drove him closer to the edge until he bit back the urge to come, waiting for her. Touching her and stroking her until her breath hitched in that way he knew meant she was close, so close. And then her orgasm massaged him over the edge to his own release. Their groans tangled up, tossed around in the wind like her hair.

Each ripple of his release rolled through him like waves along the water, one after the other. Elemental. So damn perfect, all the more so because she sighed her bliss against his neck.

Cradling her to him, he reclined back onto the deck, holding her, the blanket still secured around them. He drew in ragged breaths of ocean air, his heart hammering in his chest.

Alaina sagged back until they lay side by side with a deep exhale. "Porter, it's not fair that you know exactly what I want and I know so little about what turns you on."

"So little?" He laughed. "Trust me—your instincts are spot-on."

"Hmmm... Maybe I'm remembering things on a subconscious level."

Her words chilled him into silence for an instant before he said, "Like what?"

"Nothing specific really." She linked hands with him. "Just impressions. A sense of knowing you."

He squeezed her hand. "I like the sound of that. We're still married underneath everything that's happened."

She just made that *hmmm* noise again and let the silence settle.

He rolled onto his side, propping his head on his hand. "Should we turn in?"

She traced his bottom lip. "I want to sleep here with you on the boat, but I can't leave Thomas overnight. Even knowing he's just there on shore—"

Porter kissed her fingertips. Drew her close. "I understand and I agree. Let's go see our son."

He wanted their focus to be on their family, their future, and Thomas was an important part of what would bind them together even after she regained her memories. If Porter could give Alaina the perfect family Christmas, she would understand why he wanted their family to remain intact, why he'd waited to tell her the truth about their tumultuous past. She'd understand, and she'd forgive him so they could create a happy, stable family environment for their son.

Or at least he thought she would forgive him. The trouble with Alaina's amnesia, however, was that she wasn't the same woman he'd once known.

The moon glow washed the beach in a pale silver light, softening the edges of their mansion like a watercolor image. Alaina took it in, seeing a beauty in the place she'd missed before. This might not be her personal pick of a home, but there was a blessing in having access to this kind of magnificent landscape and a peaceful escape where she could recover.

She curled in a tight ball, hugging her knees, wrapped in a blanket on the hammock. The light breeze rocked her back and forth, keeping time with the crash of the waves.

She'd come out here after they'd checked on Thomas while Porter went to scavenge for food. She'd brought a laptop with her to watch the disc he'd made, filled with images of their home. Such a thoughtful gesture.

And the more she glanced at the photographs of her life, the more she was excited for the return trip to Tallahassee. For life with Porter and Thomas. For her shot at having a family.

She looked up from the laptop, glancing at the house next door, Sage's home. Could the woman's comment about another man visiting be trusted? Was there a hidden agenda in her statement?

Or could there have been another man? Alaina didn't feel as if she ever could have been the sort to cheat on her husband but what did she really know about their marriage?

A burn started along her skin as she thought of her stalker ex-boyfriend from long ago. Could he have been lurking around again after so many years? Porter hadn't mentioned him, but perhaps she should bring up the subject of Douglas and simply ask that they look into his whereabouts.

An outline of an approaching figure took shape out of the misty night. Her eyes adjusted from the glare of the laptop to the darkness of the moonlit beach and she recognized her husband. Sagging with relief, she closed her laptop and set it aside to focus on this renewed connection with Porter. He strode down the bluff, sure-footed, a pizza in one hand, baby monitor in the other.

His smile widened as he placed the box on the Adirondack chair and sat next to her on the hammock.

"You're the only woman I ever met who would rather be romanced with deep-dish pizza than the offer of lobster." Porter passed her a slice.

Steam oozed off the cheese—the scent of tomatoes, garlic and oregano dancing around her. She blew cool air on her slice, eager to dive in. "The videos you put together of the Tallahassee house were very thoughtful.

I haven't gotten to watch them all, but I took a quick peek and I like the house."

"I'm glad. We'll be celebrating New Year's there with our son."

"And your mom?"

"She won't be with us. I'm still not sure why she's here." Even in the muted light, she could see his eyes darken at the mention of his mother. His mouth went tight.

In the deepest part of her core, Alaina wanted to set her family right. Her whole family, which included Courtney, too.

"She loves you. She wants to see your child." She set the plate of pizza down and ran a comforting hand down his back.

"Our child. You're a good mother, Alaina." He kissed her forehead.

"Thank you. These definitely aren't the easiest of circumstances to become a first-time parent." She looked down at her slice of pizza. "Your mother said I used to volunteer in the NICU, back when we were trying to conceive."

"You did. You were so generous and brave to do that. Like I said, you're a born mother."

She'd tried to envision herself in the hospital holding babies. Had volunteering helped ease the ache inside her over not being able to become pregnant? Or had it deepened her sense of loss?

"Your mother and I may be different, but that doesn't mean she loves you any less than I love Thomas."

"Like I said, you're generous. She wasn't very nice to you when we got married."

"Why was that?" She'd gathered that much. Pieced

it together from her conversations with her mother-in-law. But Alaina wondered if that even mattered now. The introduction of their child reminded Alaina that there was more at stake in this family than petty fights.

"I was never really sure and you didn't bad-mouth her so I never found out."

Alaina nodded, wondering if the animosity had just been a misunderstanding. And realizing that her mother-in-law had never intentionally sabotaged them. She'd kept her reservations about Alaina to herself. And there was something to be said for that. "She must not have bad-mouthed me, either, or you would know what the problem was."

"I hadn't thought about that."

"I just think it is something to consider. And besides, your mom and I are fine now. We have a fresh start. And she wants to be a part of the family—a part of our lives. Part of Thomas's life. I can feel it." A gust of wind pushed the ends of her hair into her eyes. She removed a ponytail holder from her wrist and piled her hair on top of her head in a messy bun.

"Oh, yeah. She wants to be part of the family. But only when it suits her." Bitterness dripped from his words. He ran a hand through his hair, exhaling deeply.

She picked up his hand in hers and twined their fingers together. "So…what should we get your mom for Christmas? And should we think of a neutral gift for her tax-attorney boyfriend? You know, just in case he is here. I'd hate for him to have nothing to open up if he spends Christmas with us."

Porter's jaw tightened and he dropped her hand. "I'm cold, aren't you?"

"Not terribly. Not with you and this blanket." She

tried to catch his eye. To get him to stay and talk to her. To calm down and let her in. They could work through this together if he would only open up.

Was this something that used to happen in the past? Were these the kinds of arguments they'd had before?

"I think it's time to go inside. We have a big day tomorrow. Lots of wrapping to do. We don't want to get sick." He started to gather the remains of the pizza and dishes. He kissed her forehead again, then he started for the beach house, retreating into the dark space between the beach and the mansion.

Leaving her with a cold feeling in her stomach no blanket could insulate.

Of all the times for his temper to explode, this was probably the worst one imaginable.

Porter had sought sanctuary in his office. Tried to lose himself in work. To cool down. To figure out why he had got so angry with Alaina.

He knew he'd been unreasonable. And he was afraid he'd blown his second chance with her. Maybe she'd see he wasn't worthy of her love and time. Maybe this would be the trigger that brought all of her memories rushing back. But not the good memories. The dark ones. All of their fights.

Without even realizing it, he'd bumped over from his spreadsheet and projections charts to the internet. He'd begun to scour his normal stockpile of online shopping websites. Looking for a gift for his mother. Alaina was right. He needed to figure something out.

And not just a gift for his mom. Also how to fix the space he'd placed between him and his wife. Again. Had he been too selfish keeping their past a secret? Put

Alaina at too much of a disadvantage by not sharing the darker parts of their marriage?

A knock pulled his attention to the door, and damn, how ironic, there his mother stood.

"Good evening, Porter. I was just thinking about what I should get Thomas for Christmas. Now, I know you and Alaina just finished your big shopping trip, but I thought we'd compare lists."

Now his mother was ready to play Santa? After all these years of virtually ignoring the holidays? Not that he begrudged his son the presents by any means, but he also didn't want Thomas to expect something from Courtney only to have her go back to her old ways later. Porter pursed his lips. Felt them turn white with tension.

"Clothes would be fine." It came out like a bark. "Or set away money for his college education. Whatever you want."

Courtney nodded, straightening her green silk scarf as she stepped deeper into the room. "This place reminds me so much of that Christmas we spent in the Keys when you were younger. Do you remember?"

"I do. But I think the beach house is closer to the house you rented the Christmas we went to Virginia Beach."

"Sometimes the places run together for me. I never liked to repeat holiday locations. Too depressing." A sad sort of smile set on her mouth.

Old habits died hard. When was the last time he and Alaina had spent a holiday in Tallahassee? He could have brought them home. To start their lives together in the space they'd cocreated. But instead, he'd fled and brought them here. Maybe there were some similarities between him and his mother after all.

"So are you serious about this guy?" Porter asked, shutting down his computer for the night.

Courtney shook her head. "No. I'm done with the search for my forever love. After your father left me... well, I'm not sure I've ever been the same. I loved him. I really did. But then he left and I was pregnant..." Her voice trailed off. She stared at her son with shining eyes.

"Mom...I'm sorry." A pang ricocheted through his heart. He'd had no idea she'd ever felt that way about anyone.

"Oh, honey. Don't look at me like that. I know things haven't been perfect for us. But I'm so glad that this was the path of my life. It gave you to me, and I've never once regretted it," she said, wrapping him in a hug.

It wasn't a particularly tight hug, but it wasn't one of those air hugs that she normally gave. From his mom, this was a lot.

He'd been so focused on his experience of childhood, on what she'd lacked as a mother, that he'd failed to see she was every bit as damaged as he was by the guy who'd bailed on them.

Never before had he considered what his father had done to his mother. Never had he thought about how betrayed and lonely his mother must have felt.

He was a selfish bastard for missing that.

"Thanks, Mom. I'm glad you're in Thomas's life." He hugged her back before stepping away.

Just as Alaina's scream echoed from above.

Ten

Alaina shot upright on the bed where she'd fallen asleep on top of the covers. The nightmare filled her brain like toxic fumes. Except it wasn't a dream. It was a memory, but from five years ago. One she hadn't forgotten but had instead pushed back because it was too painful to remember on a daily basis.

Why was she dreaming of an ex-boyfriend now? Of that hellish last time she'd seen Douglas? Of what he'd done to her?

Porter charged through the door, looked around the room as if searching for an intruder, then rushed to their bedroom, his face filled with concern—and fear. "Alaina, what's wrong? Are you okay?"

Thomas started shrieking in the next room, his plaintive cries cutting through the fog in her mind. She slid her feet off the bed. "I need to go to him—"

Courtney called from the open doorway, apparently having followed her son upstairs, "I'll take care of the baby. You two...talk. I promise not to drop him," she said in a halfhearted joke that fell a little flat. Then she left, heels clicking double time down the hall.

Heart still racing, Alaina waited until her son's cries quieted at Courtney's cooing and only then did she sag back against the headboard. Porter crossed to close the door, then returned to her, sitting on the edge of the bed while she tried to catch her breath. Returning to the present was tough. The night terror's claws were still buried deep in her.

Porter stroked her tangled hair back from her face. "What's going on?"

"I had another nightmare about Douglas." It seemed a pale word for what she'd experienced. Especially since the event had really happened to her five years ago.

She shivered at the thought. Intellectually, she knew it was long ago, but it felt so much closer to the present because of the amnesia. The chill settled deep in her gut and she tugged the down comforter tighter around her even though it made no sense that she would be so cold.

"How was this dream different from the other one about him?"

"This time, he didn't just stalk me, or slap me. Douglas hurt me...more. So much more."

He went still. Very still. "More?"

"You know what I mean." She made a vague gesture with her hands, as if they could speak what she hated to verbalize.

"I'm not sure I do."

"You must know." She looked up at him sharply. "We were married for almost four years. You have to know what he did to me." A desperate, fearful note entered her voice as she searched his face. Hoping the answers were there.

It was bad enough she had to relive it in her dreams. She didn't want to. So many times she'd resented that Porter needed to fill in the blanks in her memory. But she didn't want to recall one second more of this than she already did.

His eyes narrowed. "You told me how he verbally abused you. Your fights escalated and he hit you. You left him because of that, then he stalked you. Completely unacceptable, and you told him it had to stop." He grabbed for her hand gently.

A simple touch, but it gave her the courage she'd been lacking.

A courage that was all the more necessary as she realized she might have omitted a very big facet of her past from him. Why would she have done that?

"I honestly never explained to you what happened after I left him?" she pressed. "Why I got the restraining order?"

"I assumed you spoke with the police right away." He frowned. For an odd moment their roles were reversed as she had answers that he didn't know about.

She couldn't say she liked the feeling on this side of the fence, either. "I did speak to the police, then and later. And you really don't know this? You never did a background check on me?"

"I'm insulted you would think that of me."

"You seem like the kind of guy who would learn as much as you could about an important person in your life."

"I seem like a control freak, you mean?" A laugh escaped his lips, an effort to put her at ease she realized.

"No, um, you just seem assertive." She searched for the right words but her nerves were so damn frayed. "Detail oriented."

"Well, that's diplomatic."

She dropped her gaze, cheeks burning at the memory. The reality catching in her throat. "You're not like Douglas at all." She understood that absolutely. "But I think maybe since I woke up from the coma I've been fearing that you're like him. That the amnesia upsets the balance of control between us, and on some level that's been frightening to me."

"I'm not sure I'm following what you're trying to tell me." He pinched the bridge of his nose. "What happened that gave you nightmares? Did you remember the time he showed up here?"

She looked up sharply. "He came *here*?"

"Once, yes, he did. You freaked out. I arrived home just in time, and…" He clenched his hands in fists. "I hit him and the police were called. He did a little time in jail for violating the restraining order and that was that. We never saw him again. Last I heard he got arrested for assault and is back in prison."

That must have been what Sage saw. There wasn't some other man she'd been seeing during her marital troubles. There hadn't been cheating in the marriage because no way in hell would she have ever, ever slept with Douglas again. And thank God, he was out of her life, unable to reach her.

Relief melted through her, dulling the edges of her fear enough that she could say the words out loud to Porter.

Her husband, a man who'd been there for her, who supported her as an equal. She might not have shared the full truth before, but she needed to share it now.

"Douglas did more than hit me once before we split up. When he started stalking me, I thought he would lose interest in time but it got worse." Even thinking about it, just remembering those months brought back the old terror, and then the pain.

Porter rubbed a hand along her back in soothing circles, staying silent but present, waiting.

"One night, after work, he was lurking around my apartment. I don't know how many times he'd done it before. He said he'd been watching me, studying my habits. And the time had come for us to be together again."

A breath hissed between Porter's teeth.

"Usually I had someone walk me to my car, but not that night. So yes, he'd probably been waiting every night and stayed away those other times because he was such a coward. He would have never dared come after me if I had a protector."

"Please don't say you're blaming yourself for whatever happened. You have to know you didn't deserve the hell and the betrayal that bastard brought into your life."

"No, I don't blame myself. I understand he would have found me alone sometime. It's impossible to stay on guard 24/7. He preyed on me because my family was dead and I had very few connections to check up on me." She said the words by rote, knowing them to be true, but still wondering what else she could have done. Maybe she should have moved across the country. "It's not unreasonable to expect to live my life."

His throat moved in a hard swallow. "Do you want to tell me what happened?"

She covered his hand quickly, realizing she should have told him right away. "He didn't rape me, if that's what you're thinking."

"I'm not thinking anything. I'm waiting for you to tell me."

She exhaled hard. "He beat the hell out of me in the parking lot. Completely. He hit me and kicked me, damn near killed me before he walked away as if we'd just had a disagreement over what cereal to have for breakfast. I crawled into the car and tried to drive myself to the hospital."

"Why wasn't he locked away for good, then?"

Alaina picked at an imaginary piece of lint. The memory swelled before her again, rising up in the depths of her stomach. She took a steadying breath. She needed more air in her lungs. "Family connections and a good lawyer were able to convince a jury my injuries resulted from driving into a ditch as I tried to take myself to the hospital."

"The auto accident that made it difficult for you to conceive." A flicker of understanding passed over his face.

"Yes. Except it wasn't an accident. And the jury didn't believe it, in spite of the restraining order. His lawyers said I was unbalanced and trying to set him up. They convinced the jury."

"That's such bull," he blurted out.

"I agree."

She'd felt so helpless and alone without even someone to sit by her side in court. She'd isolated herself from everyone but her work friends by then, not wanting Douglas to lash out at someone close to her. It was the double cruelty of domestic abuse—an abuser isolated a woman and then, scared and mortified, a woman isolated herself more.

"What happened?" he asked.

"In the end they settled on a restraining order against both of us." She stared at her hands. "And you truly didn't know this? I never told you?"

"You didn't." He shook his head, and then, looking at her, his shoulders tensed. "I hope you believe me."

"I do believe you, actually. But that makes me wonder why I didn't share this before now, though." Had she clung to some kind of old sense of shame? Or simply hoped for a new start? "It's strange, especially since that played a part in our inability to have kids—you said it was both of us, though."

"It was. The scar tissue around your fallopian tubes and my low sperm count worked against each other." He took her hands in his. "But that's all a moot point. I am so sorry for what you went through."

"You're not angry with me for not telling you?"

"I'm…frustrated. I wish I'd known. I wish you'd trusted me enough to tell me."

She wanted to ask him what was wrong between them that she wouldn't share something so important, but maybe he was puzzling through that even now. What was wrong with her? Why hadn't she trusted him? That question scared her most of all because in spite of her concerns since coming home from the hospital, she'd grown closer to him over the past couple of weeks. She could see them building a life together with their child.

But that nightmare was a threat to her future. She could feel it. A simmering unease filled her, rooted in the fact that she hadn't trusted him with such fundamental knowledge about her as a person. She hadn't confided her deepest fears to him and she didn't like what that revealed about their relationship. Or at least, their old relationship.

Was it foolish of her to hope they had started to build something stronger than what they'd had? Something that could really last? More than anything, she wanted to keep the connection they'd found. Especially when she felt so completely adrift in the world.

She needed Porter. Needed to reclaim that connection to him on an elemental level.

The last thing Porter expected right now was for Alaina to push him back onto the bed and straddle his lap. No doubting her intent, though. She planned for them to have sex. Now.

She unbuttoned his shirt with impatient fingers, crawling up his chest as she leaned down to kiss him. Thoroughly. With open mouth and open passion.

Sweeping his shirt away, she kissed her way down his chest, pausing to circle his flat nipples with her tongue. His body reacted even as his mind shouted to know what the hell was going on with her.

She kissed lower and lower still, unzipping his fly and freeing him. Stroking. Inching closer until her mouth closed over him and his head dug back into the pillow. Her tongue circled him, her hand working up and down the length of his shaft. His fingers twisted in the sheets as he held back the urge to pulsate to completion.

His heartbeat throbbed in his ears. Sweat beaded on his brow from the restraint of holding back.

She looked up at him through her lashes with a sultry expression. He wanted her to have whatever she needed, whatever would bring them closer, even on an elemental level.

His hands roamed along her shoulders and he lifted her upward before he lost control altogether. Even though it damn near killed him to stop.

He owed her the honesty he'd planned for the New Year. Except he couldn't seem to dismiss the knowledge that she hadn't been honest with him for their entire marriage, and about such an important part of her past.

A huge, daunting piece of her. Obviously, the fact that she'd battled through that nightmare of a relationship didn't change how he felt about her. But he worried what it suggested she felt about him that she'd withheld the truth.

"Alaina—"

She tapped his lips before sweeping off her nightgown. "Don't even try to talk me out of this. I know what I want. I know what I need. You. Now."

The sight of her naked other than her panties stunned him silent and made him burn to have her. Only her words stopped him short.

Did she sense that they were headed for trouble once she remembered? Did she know on some subconscious level that memories of their marriage were not all good? Is that why she wanted this moment before their future was taken away?

And then he realized he couldn't do this. Not this way, with so many secrets between them. He couldn't make love to her again until they had more level ground between them. She deserved better from him.

She'd been hurt enough. He couldn't undo his past

deceptions. But he could start fresh now and be the man she deserved.

He scooped up her nightgown, the silky fabric still warm from her body. He resisted the urge to press the nightie to his face and take in the scent of her.

Porter cleared his throat and tossed the gown onto the bed. "Alaina, this may be the right time for you, but it's not the right time for me."

She angled up and stared down at him, horror on her face. "Did what I told you about Douglas turn you off?"

Guilt kicked him. How could she think that? He hated that she'd entertained that thought for even an instant.

Sexy as hell, she was all defiance and challenge, inventing obstacles when they needed to talk. Really talk.

"No, I don't think that. Not at all." He sat up and wrapped a sheet around her. "I want you so much my teeth hurt. But, now that you're having these nightmares and flashes of memories, I wonder if we should be careful." His mind was racing with—hell, he didn't know what exactly. He just felt unsettled. "What if all of this is too much for you, stirring up too many emotions too fast, upsetting you. Maybe we should talk to the doctor again about working on helping you recover your memory."

She bowed her head, eyes averted. "Do you see me as flawed?"

The defiance slid away, leaving behind a vulnerability that rocked him.

He touched her chin, tipping her face so she could see the truth in his eyes. "Don't put words in my mouth. I care about you. I want what's best for you."

"Care? You *care* about me," she hissed, stepping

backward. "Be honest with me, Porter. Did we love each other?"

They did. So much. And yet still, he'd lost her. They'd decided to divorce, only reconciling temporarily for the baby.

"Then what's stopping you now? I don't understand."

Of course she didn't because he was holding back so damn much from her. He kept their past a secret out of fear of destroying this new peace between them, this chance to rediscover what they'd had.

The thought of losing her again shredded what was left of his restraint. "Nothing's stopping me." Not tonight. "Absolutely nothing."

He angled forward to kiss her and her purr of approval vibrated up her throat. Things were so right here between them. If only the outside world and concerns— and memories—didn't lurk just outside that door.

For now, he would have her, take and give all he could, hope that she would feel and understand how much she meant to him. He rolled her to her back on the bed, the mattress giving beneath them. With sure but swift hands, he swept off the rest of his clothes and her panties, his urgency sending them fluttering to the floor.

Her milky white skin glowed in the moonlight beaming through the window. She took his breath away.

"Alaina, I could never see you as anything but beautiful, magnificent. Mesmerizing. You take my breath away now every bit as much as you did then. I want you, Alaina, every single day, every minute since I met you, I have wanted you."

When they'd first been married, he'd taken his time learning every curve of her, every freckle and dimple.

They'd both talked of being made for each other. How had he lost sight of that?

Almost lost her?

He stretched out over his wife. Flesh to flesh. Truly becoming one as he slid inside her. Moved within her. The warm clamp of her body around him made his heart hammer harder in his chest,

Framing her face in his hands, he kissed her, open-mouthed, tongues mating, as well. He couldn't be close enough to her. Wanted more. He wanted forever. The reality of that exploded inside him, filling every corner. It wasn't just about making a family or being parents together. This was about being her husband, her lover, her love.

His feelings for her were more intense than before, steeled by the challenges they faced. He wouldn't take her or what they had for granted.

He loved her.

Three simple words that unleashed everything inside him, sending him over the edge into throbbing release as her cries of completion breathed over his ear. Her fingernails dug into his back as if she ached to stay anchored in this moment every bit as much as he did.

Forever.

His forehead fell to rest on her shoulder and he inhaled the sweet sultry scent of her mixed with an air of their perspiration mingling. The perfume of them together.

Wrapping his arms around her, he tucked her to him and slid onto his side. Her cheek pressed against his chest and she trailed her fingers along his stomach. The ceiling fan spun lazy circles overhead, cooling the air around them.

Reminding him the outside world and concerns couldn't be kept at bay forever. At any moment, she could remember. His time was running out. And even if it wasn't, he owed her the best he had to offer in all aspects of their life together.

"Porter, you never answered my question."

He searched his passion-fogged brain for exactly what she meant. "Which question?"

She raised up on one elbow to look into his eyes. "Did we love each other before I lost my memory?"

He weighed his answer carefully, because yes, he had loved her, so very much. But their past hadn't been as simple as that, and he owed her a more honest future. And he would give it to her.

Still, he needed to be careful not to put too much stress on her, especially so early in her recovery. The nightmares made it clear how her feelings were in turmoil. She was a strong woman, but she'd been through so much. So he would tread warily, step back, figure out and plan the best way and time to tell her.

For now, he had a question to answer. Did they love each other before she'd lost her memory?

He couldn't be sure how she felt at the end, but he'd loved her. Did he still?

God help him, could he love a woman who didn't even remember the first time they met? A woman who didn't know him well enough to love him and might never love him again?

Alaina's frustration level was through the roof. Porter had become distant, and was spending more and more time in his study.

Where was the tender lover? The attentive father?

Between the nightmares and being rejected by Porter, her brain was spinning.

Her life had been frustrating every day since she'd woken from the coma with five years of her life missing, but Porter had counseled her to be patient, all the while romancing her to restore their marriage.

And when she needed romance he shut her out.

Now it was only two days away from Christmas and she couldn't recall ever feeling less in the holiday spirit. How unfair to Thomas. This was his first Christmas. He deserved a house full of love and happiness.

Knotting the belt on her bathrobe, she walked down the quiet hall toward the nursery, the scent of pine from the tree filling the whole giant house. She needed to be near her son and soak up his sweet innocence. To find the peace of rocking him in her arms. And maybe she needed to cry.

Silently nudging the door open, she tiptoed into the room. Her son still slept, his chest rising and falling evenly as he sucked on his tiny fist. Needing the comfort of being close to him, she turned to settle into the rocker.

And stopped short.

Courtney slept on the daybed, a baby bottle of water and powdered formula on the end table. Her arm draped over the side. Why hadn't she noticed before now how much Porter looked like his mother?

Perhaps Alaina made a noise because her mother-in-law startled awake, yawning. "Oh, wow, I must have fallen asleep. I vow that night nanny has the best job ever."

Alaina laughed softly, chocking back the tears in her throat. "We all love Thomas, and I have to confess I appreciate the help." She mixed the bottle and shook the contents. Thomas would be awake at any moment and he would be hungry. "This has been an, um, unusual foray into motherhood."

"You would have done fine on your own. But I'm glad to be here. I thought, well, I wasn't sure how things would be between you and Porter. So I'm here." She stretched, her silk shirt untucked from her skirt. She reached down to retrieve her Jimmy Choo heels. "And I'm seriously in need of a bathroom and a cup of coffee. Do you need anything from the kitchen?"

"Coffee and a biscotti would be nice. No need to hurry, though," she answered, mulling over what Courtney had just said about being unsure of their marriage.

Or, wait, had she put it a different way... Alaina tried to recall the shifting words in her mind. She was having trouble sorting what was real or remembered, or just an impression.

Kind of like those drawings in her sketchbook—she didn't know which images came from real life and which ones were simple dreams until Porter told her.

Her brain was so rattled. She was such a freaking mess. She just wanted to feel certain about something. Anything. When Thomas made a soft cry, Alaina was only too glad for the reprieve from her thoughts.

She turned off the monitor and lifted him from the crib; his casted leg hung heavily. Her little boy needed her so much.

A quick diaper change later, she settled into the rocking chair and popped the bottle in his mouth, savoring the simple joy of snuggling him close and feeling his warm weight in her arms. She bent to brush a kiss through his baby-fine hair while his little fingers flexed and curled haphazardly around the bottle.

So precious.

More than anything she wanted to remember the day she and Porter had first met Thomas, the day they'd picked him up from the hospital. She ached to recall that moment when they'd first become parents to this beautiful boy. She wanted to be grateful for all she had, but she still couldn't shake the feelings of frustration for all that she'd been denied.

What would happen if she never remembered anything more? Just that thought sent a bolt of panic through her.

Three deep breaths later, she saw her mother-in-law in the doorway with two cups of coffee. Courtney set one mug down beside Alaina with a small plate of biscotti before sitting elegantly on the edge of the day-bed.

"Hmmm." Courtney sighed, holding her mug under her nose and inhaling. "Manna for an exhausted mama."

The java scent wafted from the cup, teasing the air. Alaina's mouth watered but she didn't want to hold the hot drink near her son. "Thank you again for your help caring for him since we brought him home from the hospital."

"Of course I want to help. I'm not the most maternal figure in the world, but we *are* all family." Courtney blew into her mug, then sipped. "I'm just so glad you and Porter have worked things out between you."

Worked things out?

Alaina schooled her face not to show her surprise. Her mother-in-law had let something very telling slip. This was Alaina's chance, the one she'd been waiting for, to unwittingly pry a piece of important information about the past from someone. But getting those words from Courtney wouldn't be easy. The woman was a savvy lawyer.

Alaina opted to encourage Courtney to finish her thought. "Porter and I have come to an understanding thanks to Thomas."

"Good. I'm so glad the two of you are staying together." She shook her head sadly. "Divorce is tough on children. Although, of course, Porter's father and I were never married, but I think you get my point. It was difficult on my son not having his dad in his life."

Divorce.

There it was. The word she'd feared. The secret Porter had been keeping from her.

They'd been on the brink of splitting up.

Eleven

The family room was still littered with wrapping paper and baby toys. Porter's eyes roved over the chaos, and he couldn't help but smile. It was exactly the way a child's Christmas should be. Presents spread all over the place and a room filled with family. His family.

So far, Thomas's first Christmas had been a success. Porter and Alaina had unwrapped all of Thomas's gifts and taken so many pictures. Even Barry had brought Thomas a gift—a giant puppy stuffed animal that took up a whole couch cushion on its own.

Everything was as it should be. Except for Alaina's demeanor. That had shifted over the past few days. He could sense her growing frustration. She was angry with him for the time he spent locked away in his office, but it had been all he could do to keep his hands off her while he figured out the best way to tell her he had been holding back important parts of their past. Yes, he'd done so in hopes of rebuilding their family and along the way rediscovered his love for her.

A love that was now in danger again.

If only the doctors could give him concrete answers on her recovery and the odds that painful news could set her back? He knew she was strong. He wanted to trust in what they had.

Except how did a man tell his wife during the holidays that oh, by the way, they'd been talking to lawyers about a divorce shortly before that car accident?

That stark truth didn't fit well into a Christmas bag.

But he wasn't so good at pretending all was well anymore. So when he stepped out of his office, conversation between them had been stiff. Formal.

His mother and her boyfriend had already retired for the evening, leaving Alaina and Porter alone. They'd put Thomas down for the night.

Alaina had begun to stuff a trash bag with the discarded and ripped wrapping paper. She moved with an efficiency and fluidity that radiated anger.

He moved the framed drawing of Thomas she'd given him for Christmas onto the shelf behind the couch. This would be the start of the redecorating process. The process of making this house a home, one that reflected their joint, eclectic tastes.

Assuming he could figure out how best to ease into telling her about their past without destroying their future—while still making sure he didn't somehow harm her recovery.

The radio played through a medley of Christmas songs, filling the space between them. This was his chance. He picked up a neatly wrapped box. He'd given her a ring earlier with Thomas's birthstone, circled with diamonds. But he still had another present for her, something more personal rather than just focused on them as parents, and he'd hoped that in this stolen moment, he would be able to show her how much he cared.

Cared?

He needed to stop using that lukewarm word. He knew he loved her. Deeply. There was no denying that.

The only question? Did his wife still love him?

He tightened the bow on the box and hoped like hell he could get this right with her.

He loved her, more than he could have thought possible.

Her voice halted him. "Were we on the edge of divorce when we adopted Thomas?"

Porter stared at her, unblinking. Heart hammering. "Why would you say that? Do you remember something?"

"Just answer my question." She set aside the bag of discarded wrappings, her posture tense. "Was our marriage over? Were we on the brink of splitting up when I had my accident? Answer me, damn it."

He could feel her anger and her worries even though her voice remained low, her body rigid.

"Our marriage was in jeopardy. Yes. How did you find out?" Were her memories warning her about how close they'd been to throwing it all away? He set aside the package he'd been about to give her.

"Your mother told me." Her tone was flat. Sharp. Accusatory.

He bit back a curse. Why would she do that? Clearly he hadn't told his wife yet and it was his place to share. The betrayal cut deeply. He was disappointed in his mother—and in himself for not handling this better. "I had hoped to wait until after Christmas to tell you, but I see that's only made things worse."

"You're right about that. This can't wait. Not any longer."

"I'm sorry, Alaina, so damn sorry for bungling this. This amnesia... Well, no more excuses. I'm sorry." He thrust a hand through his hair. "The truth is, yes, we planned to get a divorce."

"A divorce," she echoed hollowly. "We were truly on our way to divorce."

"We discussed it with an attorney. But even though we talked about it, we hadn't started official proceedings."

"Why not?" Her eyes flashed with a hint of hope, as if she wanted him to say they'd reconciled.

But he wouldn't lie to her. Not again.

"We'd decided to stay together temporarily, because of Thomas."

"I meant why didn't you tell me sooner, before Christmas week?"

"What good would that have done when you didn't remember? I wasn't supposed to push you—"

"Stop. Just stop the excuses. You misled me. Deliberately." Alaina's eyes narrowed.

"Excuse me for wanting to hold my family together. Yes, I saw it as a chance to repair things so you, Thomas and I could have a future together. Then along the way it became about more. I wanted to romance you. I wanted to win my wife back."

"Win? *Win?*" Her voice rose along with her obvious anger—and hurt. "Win me like I'm some kind of prize?"

Damn, that sounded cold. The truth really did sound better. "Win back your love."

"Marginally better," she conceded, "but still done in a way where you kept me in the dark. You could have said something, done something, to let me know things were more strained than just arguments." Her voice cracked and she paused to take a deep breath. "You know how hard this has been for me, to struggle with not having any memories of you."

Her accusation stung.

"You kept secrets of your own. You never told me what Douglas did to you. We were married, for God's sake. And you never told me." That truth had hurt. But he'd swallowed down the pain in an effort to solidify their future.

"Sounds to me like our marriage was a sham." She clenched her hands into fists. "I love that child in there, but I don't understand why we chose to adopt if we were about to divorce."

"We weren't about to divorce, damn it."

"Don't quibble. That's the same as lying to me. That stops now." The pain in her voice was audible. "Tell me exactly what happened before I lost my memory. What was the state of our relationship?"

The frustration and agony of those days were indelibly etched in his mind. He paced restlessly, but there was no escaping the past—or the present. "We'd been waiting for a child for a long while. Then right when we'd given up hope on each other, we got the call about Thomas. It was the wrong time, but he needed us. The surgery. We were afraid he would go into the foster system. So we agreed to stay together until the adoption became final."

"And you didn't think this was important for me to know?" Her arms crossed over her chest. Closing him out. Shutting him out.

"You were in no shape—"

"So you decided to climb into my bed again?"

"I wanted to put my family back together. I wanted to win you back and I saw the chance." He stopped his restless pacing and rested his hands on her shoulders. How could he make her see how far he'd come? How much he'd changed? That he wanted this second chance to work between them, not just for their family, but because he loved her.

"The chance to get your way." She shrugged off his hands. "Forget it. Forget everything. This hurts, Porter. This betrayal hurts too much for me to forgive."

Alaina rocked her baby. The nursery provided her with a calming reassurance. She belonged here with him and her heart swelled in pain at the idea of not having this part of her life. Despite the mess of the past few weeks, she knew that a family was all she'd really ever wanted. The time in the nursery with her son was healing to her soul.

Such a precious child. Hers.

And Porter's.

Thomas yawned in her arms, blinking up at her, eyes heavy with sleep.

"Thomas, you know I'll always love you. Always." Her murmur mixed into the gentle lullaby music playing from the mobile over the crib.

She shook her head, still trying to piece together the latest revelation.

Surveying the mural on the wall—the one she'd

painted—fuzzy images wafted in and out of her mind. Visits to doctor's offices and specialists. Vacations and hotel rooms. Snippets of a past half remembered, feeling a bit like a dream upon waking.

For a moment, she held her breath, almost afraid breathing would chase the memories away. But instead, the thoughts became clearer, more vivid. Pieces of her past five years began to materialize and to make sense.

And then something else entered her mind that left her stomach in knots.

With a clarity that frightened her, she remembered the car ride home after picking up Thomas. Things had been so strained in the last few months leading up to the adoption. And their inability to conceive had dredged up old memories. Memories of Douglas and the attack and what might have been if he'd never beat her senseless. All of that had come crashing back at her when they'd picked up Thomas and she'd had an all-consuming headache. The pain had only grown worse when she'd realized their son had reminded her of her past. The past she'd been running and hiding from.

A past she'd hidden from Porter. A man she had married and had loved.

A man she loved still.

Porter was on the hunt, storming through the house looking for his mother. He needed to talk to her. To figure out why she'd jeopardized his second chance with Alaina.

He found her in the kitchen, scooping out heaps of mint-chocolate-chip ice cream into a silver bowl embellished with mistletoe.

"Mother, what the hell were you doing?"

"What are you talking about?" She piled more ice cream into the bowl, staring coolly at him.

"You told Alaina that we were getting a divorce."

Courtney's face was impassive. She shrugged nonchalantly. "I told her the truth. Somebody needed to."

"That was my place." Leaning against the counter, he crossed his arms over his chest. He felt betrayed. It wasn't his mother's place to tell Alaina anything about their marriage. Porter inhaled deeply.

"So one would think. Too bad you didn't bother to give her that courtesy before you climbed back into bed with her." She fixed him with an unflinching gaze. The one she was famous for in the courtroom.

"That's really none of your business. I'm acting on the advice of her doctors, trying to ease her memory back."

As she shook her head dismissively, a tight grin spread across her face, not reaching her eyes. "You're using that as a cop-out so you can pursue her."

"I want my wife back. What's the problem with that?"

"The problem is the way you're going about it. I love you, son, but I also love Alaina. And no woman deserves to be tricked by a man who is supposed to love her."

She turned and walked away.

Tricked?

He wanted to call her back. To demand that she listen. He wasn't trying to fool anyone; he'd simply been trying to buy some time to get his family in order. He was simply trying to make Alaina fall in love with him again so she would love him as much as he loved her.

Love?

Yes, he loved her. Just because he hadn't said the words didn't make them any less true.

So why hadn't he thought to tell her?

Now that her initial shock had eased, Alaina wanted to do something to fix the rift between her and Porter. She didn't know exactly how much could be repaired, but she couldn't leave things this way. The only question was where to start. She took a deep breath of the salt air, watching the lights on the yachts twinkle in the twilight, remembering her time on *their* yacht.

She tugged her gaze back to her drawing pad, needing the comfort of her art now more than ever. Sketching a whimsical family portrait—a dream really—she whipped the charcoal across the pad. Pushing with her left foot, she rocked the hammock back and forth. An idea would come to her if she sat here long enough, she was sure of it.

Her brow furrowed as she ran through potential ways to start her conversation with Porter. To make him understand what she'd learned about herself since the accident. About her feelings for him.

If only she could voice her feelings with words as easily as they flowed from her fingertips onto paper— the three of them on their yacht in a tropical locale with a baby palm tree for a Christmas tree and toddler Thomas playing with a new toy boat. She had faith in them as a family. Faith that they could build a future with or without all her memories.

She had her faith in what she wanted from the future.

The sound of shoes shuffling on the ground drew her attention back to the present. Eyes focusing, she saw

Porter approaching, a box with glittering gold wrapping paper in hand.

Cocking her head to the side, she peered sideways at him. "What do you have there? You already gave me a gift." She held up her hand with the ring featuring Thomas's birthstone circled by diamonds." The setting was a delicate band of filigree that looked handcrafted.

"I have something else for you. Do you mind if I sit with you?"

She swung her feet off the side of the hammock. "Please."

He lowered himself to sit beside her, his strong shoulder brushing hers and reminding her of the physical chemistry they'd always shared, the heightened awareness she'd always felt around him.

She knew that because she remembered it now.

Wordlessly, he passed her the large gold box. She opened it to find—a binder full of house designs.

"I thought you would want to choose a new house yourself rather than having me assume I know what you want. I would like for us to live in that house together, but that's up to you."

Words failed her. His gift touched her, deep in her soul. She tore her eyes away from the drawings and sketches to meet his gaze, still stunned silent.

"Alaina, I apologize for not being up-front with you from the start."

"I'm the one who owes you an apology." She sighed deeply.

"I'm not sure what you mean."

Bracing for the talk they needed to have, she told herself that honesty and communication were their only hope at this point. That was how they'd patch things together. And it started now.

"I think I lost my memory before the accident," she admitted, although she wanted to see a specialist to discuss it. "I think it had something to do with being afraid to be a parent, being afraid of what happened to me with Douglas."

"I'll never let him near you again." Porter made it sound so simple, but her fears were far more jumbled than that. She didn't fear Douglas coming after her. She feared the wreck of a woman the attack had left behind.

"I realize he's back in jail. I should have told you years ago about what happened and I didn't. I'm in no position to judge you for holding things back. I think I spent so long telling myself that I would be okay, I forgot to show you the weakness behind the mask." Maybe she had hoped that if she forgot about it, that if she never brought it into their relationship, that would be almost the same as if it had never happened.

After her struggle with amnesia, she knew the brain had its own complicated coping mechanisms.

"Seems to me we both have issues with trust." He brushed a hand along her hair, a light caress she wanted to lean into. "What about now that you remember?" Even in the dying light, she could read the worry and fear sparking in his eyes. She was starting to realize just how afraid he was of losing her, of them drifting away from each other.

"I don't remember, not everything. Just snippets about the day of the accident."

"I assumed you remembered…" He rested his head against hers. "My mother said you deserve better from me, better than me. And God, Alaina, she's right. I should have handled everything differently from the moment you woke up in the hospital, from before then, actually."

The bits of Porter she remembered from before the accident would have never said something so tender or allowed himself to be so vulnerable. She recalled how locked in he'd been on the goal of building the family and life he'd thought they should have. She glanced at his gifts—the choices for house plans, the understated but heartfelt ring. These were the gifts of the man she had sensed he might become.

A man she could build her life with.

"I trust you. If you say you love me, then you do."

"But I haven't said it."

"Yet. You will." A smile spread across her lips as she reached for him, fingers twining with his.

"Confident, are you?"

"I'm learning to trust my feelings rather than rely on some black-and-white memory of the past. Feelings, emotions…love…well, that comes in layers and textures that defy simple images."

"Love, you say?" He moved closer. "You love me?"

"I'm still waiting for you to say the words first."

He squeezed her hand tight. Brought his lips to her fingertips and kissed her gently. Butterflies stirred in her stomach.

His mouth brushed hers again. "Then by all means, I'm more than ready. Alaina Rutger, you are the one and only woman for me, the love of my life, the mother of my child. My partner. My lover. My life."

She took his face in her hands. "Porter, my love, my partner, father of my child. You are my soul mate for all time even if our minds and memories fade." And she meant it. Every syllable.

Porter dropped to one knee. "Will you marry me?"

"But we're already married." Her eyes widened in a mixture of disbelief and excitement.

"You'll get your memory back someday. I'm confident of that. But even if you don't, I would like for us both to remember the day, the vows." The starlight and Christmas lights caught in his eyes, making them dance with the promise of family and love.

"I adore that plan. I adore you. Yes. Let's get married all over again."

"Renew our vows on New Year's at our Tallahassee house?"

"Perfection." She kissed him deeply. So sure of him. Of them. Of what they could accomplish together as a team.

He pulled away to whisper in her ear. "Yes, you are perfect, Alaina. Absolutely perfect."

Epilogue

One Year Later

"Merry Christmas, my love," Porter said, kissing his wife, the sun warm on his shoulders as they lounged on the upper deck of their yacht.

"Merry Christmas to you, too." She slid from her lounge chair to his, curling up beside him with a happy sigh. "This has been the most amazing family Christmas ever."

Their son napped in his cabin with his grandmother and her new husband keeping watch. Who would have thought Barry would be a keeper? But his mom was happy.

And so was Porter.

He stroked down his wife's arm, linking fingers with her. "I'm glad you found a way to enjoy the yacht."

"Trips together have been a fun escape—" she squeezed his hand back "—and a chance to grow closer as a family."

Waves slapped the side of the craft, chimes singing on their Christmas palm tree. He never would have believed this possible before her accident. But then, he hadn't bought the yacht with the intent of traveling. He'd missed the whole point of a vacation home and the boat, a symbol for his bigger problem.

Life was meant to be enjoyed.

And this past year he'd enjoyed his life more than he could ever remember doing, thanks to his fresh start with Alaina and Thomas.

He stroked a loose strand of blond hair behind her ear. "So you never told me. Why did you choose the Florida Keys for Christmas?"

She tapped her temple. "A week with minimal contact from the outside world?" She grinned. "What's not to love? I have my husband and son, my family, for the holidays."

Thomas was out of a cast for now, due for another surgery later, but free to crawl around in the sand. He would be a late walker because of his clubfoot, but the doctors expected a full recovery. He was a gloriously healthy child.

They had everything in their life that mattered.

It hadn't always been easy. But they worked at it, finding new paths to make their marriage thrive.

They played this game of surprise often. Her memory had never returned fully, so Porter had suggested she make choices and surprise him. Some small things like dinner dates or larger plans like vacations.

He soaked up the feeling of her skin against his, her

bikini leaving a delicious amount of flesh for him to explore with his eyes and hands. "I enjoy your choices for vacations."

"And I appreciate the way you've worked to help me feel more in control of my world. I wish I could have regained all of those missing years, but I'm beginning to accept that may never happen."

He searched her eyes for signs of the pain she'd experienced last year as she began to accept that her memory might not ever come back. She'd remembered good moments and some arguments they'd had, as well. He'd asked to hear every one of them, and as he'd listened, it had helped him hear her side of things. Helped them cement the bond they'd found after the accident.

They had made peace with that past and grown individually, as a couple, too.

He kissed her on her pink nose. "You still haven't fully answered my question. Why the Keys? There are plenty of places for isolation."

She sat up and pulled a box from under her lounge chair. "Why don't you pull the wrapping from your gift and see. That's why I asked you to come up here."

She passed him a two-foot square box with a huge red bow.

They'd already exchanged presents earlier and one of his had a note inside promising his "special" gift would be given later on the top deck. He'd assumed she meant sex.

This was another surprise.

He tore the large red ribbon from the gift box, lifted the lid. A framed sketch rested inside a satin lining. The charcoal image showed a family of three on their yacht in a tropical locale with a baby palm tree for a

Christmas tree and toddler Thomas playing with a new toy boat.

She rested her hand on his elbow. "I was drawing that a year ago when you found me in the hammock and told me you love me. This," she said, tapping the edge of the gift, "was my dream for our family. My hope. And now it's our reality."

"It is, isn't it?"

"The very best Christmas gift ever and I get to enjoy it year-round." Her smile was brighter than the noon-day sun. "Thank you."

He traced her mouth and winked. "I guess that means I should cancel our flight out of Miami to Paris."

Laughing, she kissed him, her palms flat against his chest. "Don't you dare. I can't wait to go to the Louvre."

She'd seen the photos of their first trip, one she'd forgotten. Seeing the frustration on her face over that lost moment, he'd known right away what to get her for Christmas.

He set aside the incredible sketch, a treasure for his office, and gathered his wife into his arms to make love. They would experience Paris all over again for New Year's. Some couples didn't get second chances at forever.

He was grateful for every minute of this second chance with Alaina. Each day a beautiful surprise with the love of his life.

* * * * *

TRIPLETS UNDER
THE TREE

KAT CANTRELL

To Diane Spigonardo. Thanks for the inspiration.

Prologue

Near Punggur Besar, Batam Island, Indonesia

Automatically, Falco swung his arm in an arc to block the punch. He hadn't seen it coming. But a sense he couldn't explain told him to expect his opponent's attack.

Counterpunch. His opponent's head snapped backward. *No mercy.* Flesh smacked flesh again and again, rhythmically.

The moves came to him fluidly, without thought. He'd been learning from Wilipo for only a few months, but Falco's muscles already sang with expertise, adopting the techniques easily.

His opponent, Ravi, attacked yet again. Falco ducked and spun to avoid the hit. His right leg ached with the effort, but he ignored it. It always ached where the bone had broken.

From his spot on the sidelines of the dirt-floored ring,

Wilipo grunted. The sound meant more footwork, less jabbing.

Wilipo spoke no English and Falco had learned but a handful of words in Bahasa since becoming a student of the sole martial arts master in southern Batam Island. Their communication during training sessions consisted of nods and gestures. A blessing, considering Falco had little to say.

The stench of old fish rent the air, more pungent today with the heat. Gazes locked, Falco and Ravi circled each other. The younger man from a neighboring village had become Falco's sparring partner a week ago after he'd run out of opponents in his own village. The locals whispered about him and he didn't need to speak Bahasa to understand they feared him.

He wanted to tell them not to be afraid. But he knew he was more than a strange Westerner in an Asian village full of simple people. More than a man with dangerous fists.

Nearly four seasons ago, a fisherman had found Falco floating in the water, unconscious, with horrific injuries. At least that was what he'd pieced together from the doctor's halting, limited English.

He should have died before he'd washed ashore in Indonesia and he certainly should have died at some point during the six-month coma his body had required to heal.

But he'd lived.

And when he finally awoke, it was to a nightmare of physical rehabilitation and confusion. His memories were fleeting. Insubstantial. Incomplete. He was the man with no past, no home, no idea who he was other than angry and lost.

The only clue to his identity lay inked across his left pectoral muscle—a fierce, bold falcon tattoo with a scarlet banner clutched in its talons, emblazoned with the word *Falco*.

That was what his saviors called him since he didn't remember his name, though it chafed to be addressed as such.

Why? It must be a part of his identity. But when he pushed his memory, it only resulted in his fists primed to punch something and a blinding headache. Every waking moment—and even some of those dedicated to sleep—he heard an urgent soul-deep cry to discover why he'd been snatched from the teeth of a cruel death. Surely he'd lived for a reason. Surely he'd remember something critical to set him on the path toward who he was. Every day thus far had ended in disappointment.

Only fighting allowed him moments of peace and clarity as he disciplined his mind to focus on something other than the struggle to remember.

Ravi and Wilipo spoke in rapid Bahasa, leaving the Westerner out of it, as always.

Wilipo grunted again.

That meant it was time to stop sparring. Nodding, Falco halted, breathing heavily. Ravi's reflexes were not as instantaneous and his fist clipped Falco.

Pain exploded in his head. *"Che diavolo!"*

The curse had spit from his mouth the moment Ravi struck, though Falco had no conscious knowledge of Italian. Or how he knew it was Italian. The intrigue saved Ravi from being pulverized.

Ravi bowed apologetically, dropping his hands to his sides. Rubbing his temples, Falco scowled over the late shot as a flash of memory spilled into his head.

White stucco. Glass. A house perched on a cliff, overlooking the ocean. *Malibu*. A warm breeze. A woman with red hair.

His house. He had a home, full of his things, his memories, his life.

The address scrolled through his mind as if it had always been there, along with images of street signs and impressions of direction, and he knew he could find it.

Home. He had to get there. Somehow.

One

At precisely 4:47 a.m., Caitlyn bolted awake, as she did every morning. The babies had started sleeping through the night, thank the good Lord, but despite that, their feeding time had ingrained itself into her body in some kind of whacked-out mommy alarm clock.

No one had warned her of that. Just as no one had warned her that triplets weren't three times the effort and nail-biting worry of one baby, but more like a zillion times.

But they also came with a zillion times the awe and adoration.

Caitlyn picked up the video monitor from her nightstand and watched her darlings sleep in their individual cribs. Antonio Junior sighed and flopped a fist back and forth as if he knew his mother was watching, but Leon and Annabelle slept like rocks. It was a genetic trait they shared with Vanessa, their biological mother, along with her red hair. Antonio had hair the color of a starless night, like his father.

And if he grew up to be half as hypnotically gorgeous as his father, she'd be beating the women off her son with a Louisville Slugger.

No matter how hard she tried, Caitlyn couldn't go back to sleep. Exhaustion was a condition she'd learned to live with and, maddeningly, it had nothing to do with how much sleep she got. Having fatherless eight-month-old triplets wreaked havoc on her sanity, and in the hours before dawn, all the questions and doubts and fears crowded into her mind.

Should she be doing more to meet an eligible man? Like what? Hang out in bars wearing a vomit-stained shirt, where she could chat up a few victims. "Hey, baby, have you ever fantasized about going all night long with triplets? Because I've got a proposition for you!"

No, the eligible men of Los Angeles were pretty safe from Caitlyn Hopewell, that was for sure. Even without the ready-made family, her relationship rules scared away most men: you didn't sleep with a man unless you were in love and there was a ring on your finger. Period. It was an absolute that had carried her through college and into adulthood, especially as she'd witnessed what passed for her sister Vanessa's criteria for getting naked with someone—he'd bought her jewelry or could get her further in her career. Caitlyn didn't want that for herself. And that pretty much guaranteed she'd stay single.

But how could she ever be enough for three children when, no matter how much she loved them, she wasn't supposed to be their mother? When she'd agreed to be Vanessa's surrogate, Caitlyn had planned on a nine-month commitment, not a lifetime. But fate had had different plans.

Caitlyn rolled from the king-size bed she still hadn't

grown used to despite sleeping in it for over a year. Might as well get started on the day at—she squinted at her phone—6:05 a.m. Threading her dark mess of curls through a ponytail holder, she threw on some yoga pants and a top, determined to get in at least twenty minutes of Pilates before Leon awoke.

She spread out her mat on the hardwood floor close to the glass wall overlooking the Malibu coastline, her favorite spot for tranquility. There was a full gym on the first floor of Antonio and Vanessa's mansion, but she couldn't bear to use it. Not yet. It had too much of Antonio stamped all over it, what with the mixed martial arts memorabilia hanging from the walls and the regulation ring in the center.

One day she'd clean it out, but as much as she hated the reminders of Antonio, she couldn't lose the priceless link to him. She hadn't removed any of Vanessa's things from the house, either, but had put a good bit away, where she couldn't see it every day.

Fifteen minutes later, her firstborn yowled through the monitor and Caitlyn dashed to the nursery across the hall from her bedroom before he woke up his brother and sister.

"There's my precious," she crooned and scooped up the gorgeous little bundle from his crib.

Like clockwork, he was always the first of the three to demand breakfast, and Caitlyn tried to spend alone time with each of her kids while feeding them. Brigitte, the babies' au pair, thought she was certifiable for breast-feeding triplets, but Caitlyn didn't mind. She loved bonding with the babies, and nobody ever saw her naked anyway; it was worth the potential hit to her figure to give the babies a leg up in the nutrition department.

The morning passed in a blur of babies and baths, and just as Caitlyn was about to return a phone call to her lawyer that she'd missed somewhere along the way, someone pounded on the front door.

Delivery guy, she hoped. She'd had to order a new car seat and it could not get here fast enough. Annabelle had christened hers in such a way that no bleach in existence could make it usable again and, honestly, Caitlyn had given up trying. There had to be some benefits to having custodial control of her children's billion-dollar inheritance.

"Brigitte? Can you get that?" Caitlyn called, but the girl didn't respond. Probably dealing with one of the kids, which was what she got paid well to do.

With a shrug, Caitlyn pocketed her phone and padded to the door, swinging it wide in full anticipation of a brown uniform–clad man.

It wasn't UPS. The unshaven man on her doorstep loomed over her, his dark gaze searching and familiar. There was something about the way he tilted his head—

"Antonio!" The strangled word barely made it past her throat as it seized up.

No! It couldn't be. Antonio had died in the same plane crash as Vanessa, over a year ago. Her brain fuzzed with disappointment, even as her heart latched on to the idea of her children's father standing before her in the flesh. Lack of sleep was catching up with her.

"Antonio," the man repeated and his eyes widened. "Do I know you?"

His raspy voice washed over her, turning inside her chest warmly, and tears pricked her eyelids. He even sounded like Antonio. She'd always loved his voice. "No, I don't think so. For a moment, I thought you were—"

A ghost. She choked it back.

His blank stare shouldn't have tripped her senses, but all at once, even with a full beard and weighing twenty pounds less, he looked so much like Antonio she couldn't stop greedily drinking him in.

"This is my house," he insisted firmly with a hint of wonderment as he glanced around the foyer beyond the open door. "I recognize it. But the Christmas tree is in the wrong place."

Automatically, she glanced behind her to note the location of the twelve-foot-high blue spruce she'd painstakingly arranged in the living room near the floor-to-ceiling glass wall facing the ocean.

"No, it's not," Caitlyn retorted.

Vanessa had always put the tree in the foyer so people could see it when they came in, but Caitlyn liked it by the sea. Then, every time you looked at the tree, you saw the water, too. Seemed logical to her, and this was her house now.

"I don't remember you." He cocked his head as if puzzled. "Did I sell you this house?"

She shook her head. "I…uh, live here with the owners."

The Malibu mansion was actually part of the babies' estate. She hadn't wanted to move them from their parents' house and, according to the terms of Vanessa's and Antonio's wills, Caitlyn got to make all the decisions for the children.

"I remember a red-haired woman. Beautiful." His expression turned hard and slightly desperate. "Who is she?"

"Vanessa," Caitlyn responded without thinking. She shouldn't be so free with information. "Who are *you*?" she demanded.

"I don't know," he said between clenched teeth. "I remember flashes, incomplete pictures, and none of it makes sense. Tell me who I am."

Oh, my God. "You don't know who you are?" People didn't really get amnesia the way they did in movies. Did they?

Hand to her mouth, she evaluated this dirty, disheveled

man wearing simple cotton pants rolled at the ankles and a torn cotton shirt. It couldn't be true. Antonio was dead.

If Antonio *wasn't* dead, where had he been since the plane crash? If he'd really lost his memory, it could explain why he'd been missing all this time.

But not why he'd suddenly shown up over a year later. Maybe he was one of those con men who preyed on grieving family members, and loss of memory was a convenient out to avoid incriminatory questions that would prove his identity, yet he couldn't answer.

But he'd known the Christmas tree was in the wrong place. What if he was telling the truth?

Her heart latched on to the idea and wouldn't let go.

Because— Oh, goodness. She'd always been half in love with her sister's husband and it all came rushing back. The guilt. The despondency at being passed over for the lush, gorgeous older Hopewell sister, the one who always got everything her heart desired. The covert sidelong glances at Antonio's profile during family dinners. Fantasies about what it would be like if he'd married her instead of Vanessa. The secret thrill at carrying Antonio's babies because Vanessa couldn't, and harboring secret dreams of Antonio falling at her feet, begging Caitlyn to be the mother of his children instead.

Okay, and she'd had a few secret dreams that involved some…carnal scenarios, like how Antonio's skin would feel against hers. What it would be like to kiss him. And love him in every sense of the word.

For the past six years, Caitlyn had lived with an almost biblical sense of shame, in a "thou shalt not covet thy sister's husband" kind of way. But she couldn't help it—Antonio had a wickedly sexy warrior's body and an enigmatic, watchful gaze that sliced through her when he turned it in her direction. Oh, she had it bad, and she'd never fully reconciled because it was intertwined with guilt—maybe she'd wished her sister ill and that was why the plane had crashed.

The guilt crushed down on her anew.

Tersely, he shook his head and that was when she noticed the scar bisecting his temple, which forked up into his dark, shaggy hair. On second thought, this man looked nothing like Antonio. With hard lines around his mouth, he was sharper, more angular, with shadows in his dark eyes that spoke of nightmares better left unexplained.

"I can't remem—you called me Antonio." Something vulnerable welled up in his gaze and then he winced. "Antonio Cavallari. Tell me. Is that my name?"

She hadn't mentioned Antonio's last name.

He could have learned the name of her children's father from anywhere. Los Angeles County tax records. From the millions of internet stories about the death of the former UFC champion and subsequent founder of the billion-dollar enterprise called Falco Fight Club after his career ended. Vanessa had had her own share of fame as an actress, playing the home-wrecking vixen everyone loved to hate on a popular nighttime drama. Her red hair had been part of her trademark look, and when she'd died, the internet had exploded with the news. Her sister's picture popped up now and again even a year later, so knowing about the color of Vanessa's hair wasn't terribly conclusive, either.

He could have pumped the next-door neighbor for information, for that matter.

Caitlyn refused to put her children in danger under any circumstances.

Sweeping him with a glance, she took as much of his measure as she could. But there was no calculation. No suggestion of shrewdness. Just confusion and a hint of the man who'd married her sister six years ago.

"Yes. Antonio Cavallari." Her eyelids fluttered closed for a beat. What if she was wrong? What if she just wanted him to be Antonio for all the wrong reasons and became the victim of an elaborate fraud? Or worse—the victim of assault?

All at once, he sagged against the door frame, babbling in a foreign language. Stricken, she stared at him. She'd never heard Antonio speak anything other than English.

Her stomach clenched. Blood tests. Dental records. Doctors' exams. There had to be a thousand ways to prove someone's identity. But what was she supposed to do? Tell him to come back with proof?

Then his face went white and he pitched to his knees with a feeble curse, landing heavily on the woven welcome mat.

It was a fitting condemnation. Welcoming, she was not.

Throat tight with concern, she blurted out, "Are you okay? What's wrong?"

"Tired. Hungry," he stated simply, eyes closed and head lolling to one side. "I walked from the docks."

"The docks?" Her eyes went wide. "The ones near *Long Beach*? That's, like, fifty miles!"

"No identification," he said hoarsely. "No money."

The man couldn't even stand and, good grief, Caitlyn had certainly spent enough time in the company of actors to spot one—his weakened state was real.

"Come inside," she told him before she thought better of it. "Rest. And drink some water. Then we can sort this out."

It wasn't as if she was alone. Brigitte and Rosa, the housekeeper, were both upstairs. He might be Antonio, but that didn't make him automatically harmless, and who knew what his mental state was? But if he couldn't stand, he couldn't threaten anyone, let alone three women armed with cell phones and easy access to Francesco's top-dollar chef's knives.

He didn't even seem to register that she'd spoken, let

alone acknowledge what he'd surely been after the whole time—an invitation inside. For a man who could be trying to scam her, he certainly wasn't chomping at the bit to gain entrance to her home.

Hesitating, she wondered if she should help him to his feet, but the thought of touching him had her hyperventilating. Either he was a strange man, or he was a most familiar one, and neither one gave her an ounce of comfort. Heat feathered across her cheeks as her chaste sensibilities warred with the practicality of helping someone in need.

He swayed and nearly toppled over, forcing her decision. No way around it. She knelt and grabbed his arm, then slung it across her shoulders. The weight was strange and, oddly, a little exhilarating. The touch of a man was alien, though, no doubt—she hadn't gone on a date in over two years. Her mind went blank as he slumped against her.

Looping her own arm around his waist, she pushed up with her legs, grateful for the core strength she'd developed through rigorous Pilates, both before and after the babies were born.

Gracious. He smelled like three-day-old fish and other pungencies she hesitated to identify—and she'd have sworn babies produced the worst stench in the world.

The man hobbled along with her across the threshold, thankfully revived enough to do so under his own power. When she paused in front of the pristine eggshell-colored suede sofa in the formal living area, he immediately dropped vertically onto the cushions without hesitation. Groaning, he covered his eyes with his arm.

"Water," he murmured and lay still as death.

And now for the second dilemma. Leave him unattended while she fetched a glassful from the wet bar across the foyer in Antonio's study? It wasn't that far, and she was being silly worrying about a near comatose man posing some sort of threat. She dashed across the marble at breakneck pace, filled the glass at the small stainless-steel sink and dashed back without spilling it, thankfully.

"Here it is," she said to alert him she'd returned.

The arm over his eyes moved up, sweeping the long, shaggy mane away from his forehead. Blearily he peered at her through bloodshot eyes, and without the hair obscuring his face, he looked totally different. Exactly like Antonio, the man she'd secretly studied, pined over, fantasized about for years. She gasped.

"I won't hurt you," he muttered as he sat up, pain etching deeper lines into his face. "Just want water."

She handed it to him, unable to tear her gaze from his face, even as chunks of matted hair fell back over his forehead. Regardless of her immense guilt over his presumed identity, she couldn't go on arguing with herself over it. There was one way to settle this matter right now.

"Do you think you're Antonio?" she asked as he drank deeply from the glass.

"I…" He glanced up at her, his gaze full of emotions she couldn't name, but those dark, mysterious eyes held her captive. "I don't remember. That's why I'm here. I want to know."

"There's one way." Before she lost her courage, she pointed to her chest over her heart as her pulse raced at the promise. "Antonio has a rather elaborate tattoo. Right here. Do you?"

It wouldn't be impossible to replicate. But difficult, as the tattoo had been commissioned by a famous artist who had a unique tribal style.

Without breaking eye contact, he set his water glass on the side table and unbuttoned his shirt to midchest. *Unbuttoned his shirt*, as if they were intimate and she had every right to see him unclothed.

"It says Falco. What does it mean?" he asked.

The truth washed through her even before he drew his

shirt aside to reveal the red-and-black falcon screaming across his pectoral muscle. Her gaze locked on to the ink, registering the chiseled flesh beneath it, and it kicked at her way down low with a long, hot pull, exactly the way she'd always reacted to Antonio.

She blinked and refocused on his face. The sight of his cut, athletic torso—sun browned and more enthralling than she'd ever have expected—wouldn't fade from her mind.

That tattoo had always been an electrifying aspect of his dangerous appeal. And, oh, my—it still was.

"It means that's proof enough for me to know you're Antonio." She shut her eyes, unable to process the relief flooding through his gaze. Unable to process the sharp thrill in her midsection that was wholly erotic…and felt an awful lot like trouble. Stunning, resplendent, *forbidden* Antonio Cavallari was alive. "And we have a lot of hurdles in front of us."

Everything in her world had just slid off a cliff.

The long, legal nightmare of the past year as she'd fought for her right to the babies had been for nothing. Nearly two years ago, she'd signed a surrogacy agreement, but then a year ago Vanessa and Antonio had crashed into the South China Sea. After months of court appearances, a judge had finally overturned the rights she'd signed away and given her full custody of her children.

Oh, dear Lord. This was Antonio's home. It was his money. *Her children were his.* And he had every right to take them away from her.

Two

Antonio—he rolled the name around on his tongue, and it didn't feel wrong like Falco had. Before Indonesia, he'd been called both Antonio and Falco by blurry-faced people, some with cameras, some with serious expressions as they spoke to him about important matters. A crowd had chanted *Falco* like a tribal drum, bouncing off the ceiling of a huge, cavernous arena.

The headache nearly flattened him again, as it always did when he tried too hard to force open his mind.

Instead, he contemplated the blushing, dark-haired and very attractive woman who seemed vaguely familiar but not enough to place her. She didn't belong in his house. She shouldn't be living here, but he had no clue where that sense came from. "What is your name?"

"Caitlyn. Hopewell," she added in what appeared to be an afterthought. "Vanessa is—was—my sister." She eyed him. "You remember Vanessa but not me?"

"The redhead?" At Caitlyn's nod, he frowned.

No, he didn't remember Vanessa, not the way he remembered his house. A woman with flame-colored hair haunted his dreams. Bits and pieces floated through his mind. The images were laced with flashes of her flesh as if he'd often seen her naked, but her face wouldn't quite clarify, as though he'd created an impressionist painting of this woman whose name he couldn't recall.

Frustration rose again. Because how was it fair that he knew exactly what an impressionist painting was but not who *he* was?

After Ravi had knocked loose the memories of his house, Antonio had left Indonesia the next morning, hopping fishing boats and stowing away amidst heavy cargo containers for days and days, all to reach Los Angeles in hopes of regaining more precious links with his past.

This delicate, ethereally beautiful woman—Caitlyn—held a few of these keys, and he needed her to provide them. "Who is Vanessa to me?"

"Your wife," she announced softly. "You didn't know that?"

He shook his head. Married. He was *married* to Vanessa? It was an entire piece of his life, his persona, he'd had no idea existed. Had he been in love with her? Had his wife looked for him at all, distraught over his fate, or just written him off when he went missing?

Would he even recognize Vanessa if she stood before him?

Glancing around the living room for which he'd instantly and distinctly recalled purchasing the furnishings—without the help of anyone, let alone the red-haired woman teasing the edges of his memory—he asked, "Where is she?"

"She died." Grief welled up across her classical features. The sisters must have been close, which was probably why

Caitlyn seemed familiar. "You were both involved in the same plane crash shortly after leaving Thailand."

"Plane crash?" The wispy images of the red-haired woman vanished as he zeroed in on Caitlyn. "Is that what happened?"

Thailand. He'd visited Thailand—but never made it home. Until now.

Eyes bright with unshed tears, she nodded, dark ponytail flipping over her shoulder. "Over a year ago."

All at once, he wanted to mourn for this wife he couldn't remember. Because it would mean he could still experience emotions that stayed maddeningly out of reach, emotions with clinical definitions—love, peace, happiness, fulfillment, the list went on and on—but which had no real context. He wanted to feel *something* other than discouraged and adrift.

His head ached, but he pressed on, determined to unearth more clues to how he'd started out on a plane from Thailand and ended up in a fishing village in Indonesia. Alone. "But I was on the plane. And I'm not dead. Maybe Vanessa is still alive, too."

Her name produced a small ping in his heart, but he couldn't be certain if the feeling lingered from before the crash or if he'd manufactured it out of his intense need to remember.

Hand to her mouth, Caitlyn bowed her head. "No. They recovered her...body," she murmured, her voice thick. "They found the majority of the fuselage in the water. Most of the forty-seven people on board were still in their seats."

Vivid, gory images spilled into his mind as he imagined the horrors his wife—and the rest of the passengers—must have gone through before succumbing to the death he'd escaped.

"Except me."

For the first time, his reality felt a bit like a miracle instead of a punishment. How had he escaped? Had he unbuckled himself in time to avoid drowning or had he been thrown free of the wreckage?

"Except you," she agreed, though apparently it had taken the revelation of his strange falcon tattoo to convince her. "And two other passengers, who were sitting across the aisle from you in first class. You were all in the first row, including Vanessa. They searched for survivors for a week, but there was no trace."

"They were looking in the wrong place," he growled. "I washed up on the beach in Indonesia. On the south side of Batam Island."

"I don't know my geography, but the plane crashed into the ocean near the coast of Malaysia. That's where they focused the search."

No wonder no one had found him. They'd been hundreds of miles off.

"After a month," she continued, "they declared all three of you dead."

But he wasn't dead.

The other two passengers might have survived, as well. *Look for them.* They might be suffering from memory loss or ghastly injuries. They might be frightened and alone, having clawed their way out of a watery crypt, only to face a fully awake nightmare. As he had.

He had to find them. But he had no money, no resources— not at this moment anyway. He must have money, or at least he must have had some once. The sum he'd paid for this house popped into his head out of nowhere: fifteen point eight million dollars. That had been eight years ago.

Groaning, he rubbed his temples as the headache grew uncontrollable.

"Are you okay?" Caitlyn asked.

Ensuring the comfort of others seemed to come naturally to this woman he'd found living in his house. His sister-in-law. Had she always been so nurturing?

"Fine," he said between clenched teeth. "Is this still my house?"

He could sell it and use the proceeds to live on while he combed the South China Sea.

Caitlyn chose that moment to sit next to him on the couch, overwhelming him with the light scent of coconut, which, strangely, made him want to bury his nose in her hair.

"Technically, no. When you were declared dead, it passed to your heirs."

"You mean Vanessa's?" Seemed as if his wife's sister had made out pretty well after the plane crash. "Are you the only heir? Because I'm not dead and I want my money back."

It was the only way he could launch a search for the other two missing passengers.

"Oh." She stared at him, her sea-glass-blue eyes wide with guilt and a myriad of other emotions he suddenly wished to understand.

Because looking into her eyes made him feel something. Something good and beautiful and he didn't want to stop drowning in her gaze.

"You don't remember, do you?" she asked. "Oh, my gosh. I've been rambling and you don't even know about the babies."

Blood rushed from his head so fast, his ears popped.

"Babies?" he croaked. Surely she didn't mean babies, plural, as in more than one? As in *his* babies?

"Triplets." She shot him a misty smile that heightened her ethereal beauty. Which he wished he could appreciate, but there was no way, not with the bomb she'd just dropped. "And by some miracle, they still have a father. You. Would you like to meet them?"

"I…" A father. He had children? Three of them, apparently. "They're really mine?" Stupid question, but this was beyond—he shook his head. "How old are they? Do they remember me?"

"Oh, no, they weren't born yet when you went to Thailand."

He frowned. "But you said Vanessa died in the plane crash. Is she not their mother?"

Had he cheated on his wife with another woman? Catholic-school lessons from his youth blasted through his mind instantly. Infidelity was wrong.

"She's not," Caitlyn refuted definitively. "I am."

Guilt and shame cramped his gut as he eyed Caitlyn. He'd cheated on his wife with his *sister-in-law*? The thought was reprehensible.

But it explained the instant visceral reaction he had to her.

Her delicate, refined beauty didn't match the obvious lushness of the redhead he'd married. Maybe that was the point. He really preferred a dark-haired, more classically attractive woman like Caitlyn if he'd fathered children with her.

"Were we having an affair?" he asked bluntly. And would he have a serious fight to regain control of his money now that his mistress had her hooks into it?

Pink spread across her cheeks in a gorgeous blush, and a foreign heaviness filled his chest, spreading to heat his lower half. Though he couldn't recall having made love to her before, he had no trouble recognizing the raw, carnal attraction to Caitlyn. Obviously, she was precisely the woman he preferred, judging by his body's unfiltered reaction.

"Of course not!" She wouldn't meet his gaze, and her blush deepened. "You were married to my sister and I would never—well, I mean, I did meet you first and, okay, maybe I thought about…but then I introduced you to Vanessa. That was that. You were hers. Not that I blame you—"

"Caitlyn."

Her name alone caused that strange fullness in his chest. He'd like to say it again. Whisper it to her as he learned what she tasted like.

She glanced up, finally silenced, and he would very much like to understand why her self-conscious babbling had caused the corners of his mouth to turn up. It was evident from the way she nervously twisted her fingers together that she had no concept of how to lie. They'd never been involved. He'd stake his life on it.

He cleared his raspy throat. "How did the children come to be, then?"

"Oh. I was your surrogate. Yours and Vanessa's. The children are a hundred percent your DNA, grown in my womb." She wrinkled her nose. "That sounds so scientific. Vanessa couldn't conceive, so I volunteered to carry the baby. Granted, I didn't know three eggs were going to take."

She laughed and he somehow found the energy to be charmed by her light spirit. "So Vanessa and I, we were happy?"

If only he could remember her. Remember if they'd laughed together as he vaguely sensed that lovers should. Had they dreamed together of the babies on the way, planning for their family? Had she cried out in her last moments, grief stricken that she'd never hold her children?

"Madly in love." Caitlyn sighed happily. "It was a grand story. Falco and the Vixen. The media adored you guys. I'll go ask Brigitte, the au pair, to bring down the babies."

Reality overwhelmed him.

"Wait." Panicked all of a sudden, he clamped down on her arm before she could rise. "I can't… They don't know me."

He was a father. But so far from a father, he couldn't

fathom the idea of three helpless infants under his care. What if he broke one? What if he scared them? How did you handle a baby? How did you handle *three*?

"Five minutes," she said calmly. "Say hello. See them and count their fingers and toes. Then I'll have Brigitte take them away. They'll get used to you, I promise."

But would he get used to them? "Five minutes. And then I'd like to clean up. Eat."

Breathe. Get his bearings. Figure out how to be Antonio Cavallari again before he had to figure out how to be Antonio Cavallari plus three.

"Of course. I'm sorry, I should have thought of that." Dismay curved her mouth downward.

"There is no protocol when the dead come back to life," he countered drily and smiled. Apparently he'd found a sense of humor along with his home.

His head spun as Caitlyn disappeared upstairs to retrieve the babies and Brigitte, whoever that was. A few minutes later, she returned, followed by a young blonde girl pushing a three-seated carriage. Everything faded away as he saw his children.

Three little heads rested against the cushions, with three sets of eyes and three mouths. Wonder and awe crushed his heart as he drank in the sight of these creatures he'd had a hand in creating.

"They're really mine?" he whispered.

"Really, really," Caitlyn confirmed at normal volume, her tone slightly amused.

She picked up the one from the first seat and held him in the crook of her arm, angling the baby to face him. The blue outfit meant this was his son, didn't it?

"This is Leon." Her mouth quirked. "He's named after my father. I guess it's too late to ask if that's okay, but I thought it was a nice tribute to Vanessa's role in his heritage."

"It's fine."

Antonio was still whispering, but his voice caught in his throat and he couldn't have uttered another sound as his son mewled like a hungry cat, his gaze sharp and bright as he cocked his head as if contemplating the secrets of the universe.

His son. Leon.

Such a simple concept, procreating. People did it every day in all corners of the world. Wilipo had fourteen children and as far as Antonio could tell, never thought it particularly miraculous.

But it *was*.

This little person with the short baby-fine red hair was his child.

"You can say hello," Caitlyn reminded him.

"Hello." His son didn't acknowledge that Antonio had spoken, preferring to bury his head in Caitlyn's shoulder. Had he said the wrong thing? Maybe his voice was too scratchy.

"He'll warm up, I promise." She slid Leon back into the baby seat and picked up the next one.

The pink outfit filled his vision and stung his eyes. He had a daughter. The heart he could have sworn was already full of his son grew so big, he was shocked it hadn't burst from his rib cage.

"This is Annabelle. I always wanted to have a daughter named Annabelle," Caitlyn informed him casually, as if they were discussing the weather instead of this little bundle of perfection.

"She has red hair, too," he murmured. "Like her brother."

Her beautiful face turned up at the sound of his voice and he got lost in her blue eyes.

He had a very bad feeling that the word *no* had just vanished from his vocabulary, and he looked forward to spoiling his daughter to the point of ridiculousness.

"Yes, she and Leon take after Vanessa. Which means Annabelle will be a knockout by the time she's fourteen. Be warned," she said wryly with a half laugh.

"I know martial arts," he muttered. "Any smarmy Romeo with illicit intentions will find himself minus a spleen if he touches my daughter."

Caitlyn smirked. "I don't think a male on the planet would come within fifty yards of Annabelle if they knew you were her father. I was warning you about *her*."

With that cryptic comment, she spirited away his daughter far too quickly and replaced her with the third baby, clad in blue.

"This is Antonio Junior," Caitlyn said quietly and moved closer to present his other son. "He looks just like you, don't you think?"

Dark hair capped a serious face with dark eyes. Antonio studied this third child and his gut lurched with an unnatural sense of recognition, as if the missing pieces of his soul had been snapped into place to form this tiny person.

"Yes," he whispered.

And suddenly, his new lease on life had a purpose.

When he'd set off from Indonesia to find his past, he'd never dreamed he'd instead find his future. A tragic plane crash had nearly robbed these three innocent lives of both their parents, but against all odds, Antonio had survived.

Now he knew why. So he could be a father.

As promised, Caitlyn rounded up the babies and sent them upstairs with Brigitte so Antonio could decompress. Brigitte, bless her, didn't ask any more questions about Antonio's presence, but Caitlyn could tell her hurried explanation that he'd been ill and unable to travel home hadn't satisfied the au pair. Neither would it be enough for the hordes of media and legal hounds who would be snapping at their heels soon enough.

The amazing return of Antonio Cavallari would make worldwide headlines, of that she was sure. But first, he needed to rest and then see a discreet doctor. The world didn't have to know right away. The household staff had signed nondisclosure agreements, and in Hollywood, that was taken so seriously, none of them would ever work again if they broke it. So Caitlyn felt fairly confident the few people who knew about the situation would keep quiet.

She showed him to the master suite, glad now that she'd never cleaned it out, though she'd have to get Rosa to pack up Vanessa's things. It was too morbid to expect him to use his former bedroom with his late wife's clothes still in the dresser.

"I'll send Rosa, the housekeeper, up with something to eat," she promised and left him to clean up.

She wandered to the sunroom and pretended to read a book about parenting multiples on her e-reader, but she couldn't clear the jagged emotion from her throat. Antonio's face when he'd met his children for the first time... It had been amazing to see that much love crowd into his expression instantly. She wished he could have been there in the delivery room, to hold her hand and smile at her like that. Tell her everything would be okay and he'd still think she was beautiful even with a C-section scar.

Except if he *had* been there, he'd have held Vanessa's hand, not hers, and the reality squelched Caitlyn's little daydream.

The babies were his. It wouldn't take long for a judge to overturn her custody rights, not when she'd signed a surrogacy agreement that stated she'd have no claim over the babies once they were born.

But the babies were hers, too. The hospital had listed her name on their birth certificates as their mother—who else would they have named? She'd been their sole parent for nearly eight months and before that, carried them in her womb for months, knowing they weren't going home with Vanessa and Antonio as planned, but with her.

It was a mess, and more than anything, she wanted to do what was best for the babies. Not for the first time, she wished her mother was still alive; Caitlyn could use some advice.

An hour later, Antonio reappeared.

He filled the doorway of the sunroom and the late-afternoon rays highlighted his form with an otherworldly glow that revealed the true nature of his return to this realm—as that of an angel.

She gasped, hand flying to her mouth.

Then he moved into the room and became flesh and blood once again. But no less beautiful.

He'd trimmed his full beard, revealing his deep cheekbones and allowing his arresting eyes to become the focal point of his face. He'd swept back his still long midnight-colored hair and dressed in his old clothes, which didn't fit nearly as well as they once had, but a man as devastatingly handsome as Antonio could make a bedsheet draped over his body work.

Heat swept along her cheeks as she imagined exactly that, and it did not resemble the toga she'd meant to envision. *Antonio, spread out on the bed, sheet barely covering his sinewy, drool-worthy fighter's physique, gaze dark and full of desire...for her...* She shook her head. That was the *last* thing she should be thinking about for a hundred reasons, but Antonio Junior, Leon and Annabelle were the top three and she needed to get a few things straight with their father. No naked masculine chests required for that conversation.

"You look...different," she squawked.

Nice. *Tip him off that you're thinking naughty thoughts.*

"You kept my clothes?" He pointed to the jeans slung low on his lean hips. "And my shaving equipment?"

All of which he apparently remembered just fine as he'd slipped back into his precrash look easily. Antonio had always been gorgeous as sin, built like a lost Michelangelo sculpture with a side of raw, masculine power. And she was still salivating over him. A year in Indonesia hadn't changed that, apparently.

She shrugged and tried to make herself stop staring at him, which didn't exactly work. "I kept meaning to go through that room, but I thought maybe there would be something the babies would want. So I left it."

"I'm glad you did. Thank you." His small smile tripped a long liquid pull inside and she tamped it down. Or she almost did. It was too delicious to fully let it go.

Serious. Talk. Now, she told herself sternly.

"I had a gym," he said before she could work up the courage to bring up item one on her long list of issues. "Did you leave it alone, too?"

"It's untouched."

"I need to see it. Will you come with me?"

Surprised, she nodded. "Of course."

Was it wrong to be thrilled he'd asked her to be with him as he delved into his past?

Well, if that was wrong, it was probably just as wrong to still have a thing for him all these years later. If only she hadn't given up so easily when she'd first met him— it was still one of her biggest regrets.

But then, her relationship rules didn't afford much hope unless a man was interested enough to hang around for the long haul. She'd thought maybe Antonio might have been, once upon a time. The way he'd flirted with her when they'd met, as though he thought she was beautiful, had floored her…and then Vanessa had entered stage left, which had dried up his interest in the chaste sister.

She followed him as he strolled directly to the gym, mystified how he remembered the way, and halted next to him as he quietly took in the posters advertising his many fights, his championship belts and publicity shots of himself clad in shorts and striking a fierce pose.

There was something wicked about staring at a photo of Antonio half clothed while standing next to the fully dressed version, knowing that falcon tattoo sat under his shirt, waiting to be discovered by a woman's fingers. *Her* fingers. What would it feel like?

Sometimes she dreamed about that.

"Do you remember any of this?" she asked as the silence stretched. She couldn't keep thinking about Antonio's naked chest. Which became more difficult the longer they stood there, his heat nearly palpable. He even smelled like sin.

"Bits and pieces," he finally said. "I didn't know I had martial arts training. I thought I was remembering a movie, because I wasn't always in the ring. Sometimes I was outside the ring, watching."

"Oh, like watching other fighters? Maybe you're remembering Falco," she offered. "The fight club."

He shook his head as if to clear it. "I feel as if I should know what that is."

He didn't remember Falco, either? Antonio had lived and breathed that place, much to Vanessa's dismay on many occasions. Her sister had hoped to see her husband more often once his time in the ring was up, but the opposite had proved true.

Caitlyn led him to a picture on the wall, the one of him standing with two fighters about to enter the ring. "Falco is your MMA promotional venue. You founded it once your career ended. That's where you made all your money."

"When did I stop fighting?"

"It wasn't long after you and Vanessa got married. You don't remember that, either?" When he shook his head, she told him what little she knew about his last fight. "Brian

Kerr nearly killed you. Illegal punch to the back of your head and you hit the floor at a bad angle. Knocked you out. You were in the hospital unconscious for two days. That's probably why your amnesia is so pronounced. Your brain has sustained quite a bit of trauma."

Really, he should have already been checked out by a competent doctor, but he'd refused when she'd mentioned it earlier. It wasn't as if she could make him. Caitlyn had no experience with amnesia *or* a powerful man who wouldn't admit to weakness.

Deep down, she had an undeniable desire to gain some experience, especially since it came wrapped in an Antonio package.

He stared at the picture for a moment. "Falco is the name of my company," he announced cautiously as if testing it out. "It's not *my* name."

Her heart ached over his obvious confusion. She wanted to help him, to erase that small bit of helplessness she would never have associated with confident, solid Antonio Cavallari if she hadn't seen it firsthand.

"Falco was your nickname when you were fighting. You transferred it to your promotional company because I guess it had some sentimental value." Not that he'd ever discussed it with her. It was an assumption everyone had made, regardless.

"What happened to my company while I was missing?"

Missing—was that how he'd thought of himself? She tried to put herself in his place, waking up with few memories, in a strange place, with strange people who spoke a different language, all while recuperating from a plane crash and near drowning. The picture was not pretty, which tugged at her heart anew.

"I, um, have control over it." And it had languished like the bedroom and his gym.

What did she know about running an MMA promotional company? But she couldn't have sold it or tried to step into his shoes. In many ways, his place in the world had been on accidental hold, as if a higher power had stilled her hand from dismantling Antonio's life. It had been here, waiting for him to slip back into it.

His expression hardened and the glimpse of vulnerability vanished. "I want control of my estate. And my company. Do whatever you have to do to make that happen."

The rasp in his voice, which hadn't been there before he got on that plane, laced his statement with a menacing undertone. He seemed more like a stranger in that moment than he had when he'd first appeared on her doorstep, unkempt and unrecognizable.

It was a brutal reminder that he wasn't the same man. He wasn't a safe fantasy come to life. And she wasn't her sister, a woman who could easily handle a man like Antonio—worse, she wasn't the woman he'd picked.

"It's a lot to process, I realize," she said slowly as her pulse skittered out of control. This harder, hooded Antonio was impossible to read, and she had no idea how to handle this unprecedented situation. "But you just got back to the States. You don't even remember Falco, let alone how to run it. Why don't you take a few days, get your bearings? I'll help you."

The offer was genuine. But it also kept her in his proximity so she could figure out his plans. If she got a hint that he was thinking about fighting her for custody of the triplets, she'd be ready. She was their mother, and this man—who was still very much a ghost of his former self—was not taking away her children.

Three

Antonio shifted his iron-hard gaze from the pictures on the wall to evaluate Caitlyn coolly, which did not help her pulse. Nothing in her limited experience had prepared her to face down a man like Antonio, but she had to make him agree to a few ground rules.

"You cannot fathom what I've been through over the past year," he stated firmly. "I want nothing more than to pick up the pieces of my life and begin the next chapter with these new cards I've been dealt. I need my identity back."

Which was a perfectly reasonable request, but executing it more closely resembled unsnarling a knotted skein of yarn than simply handing over a few account numbers. This was one time when she couldn't afford to back down.

Caitlyn nodded and took a deep breath. "I understand, and I'm not suggesting otherwise. The problem is that a lot of legalities are involved and I have to look out for the interests of the children."

His gaze softened, warming her, and she didn't know what to do with that, either.

"I'm thinking of the children, as well."

"Good. Then, it would be best to take things slowly. You've been gone for a long time and the babies have a routine. It would be catastrophic to disrupt them."

He pursed his lips. "If you're concerned that I might dismiss the nanny, I can assure you I have no intention of doing so. I couldn't care for one child by myself, let alone three."

Her stomach jolted and she swallowed, gearing up to lay it on the line. "You won't be by yourself. I'll still be here."

If only her voice hadn't squeaked, that might have come across more definitively. Besides, she was still breast-feeding and didn't plan to stop until the triplets were a year old. She was irreplaceable, as far as she was concerned.

"You're free to get back to your life," he said with a puzzled frown. "There's no reason for you to continue in your role as caretaker now that I've returned."

"Whoa." She threw up a palm as the back of her neck heated in a sweaty combination of anger and fear. "Where did you get the idea that I'm just a caretaker? The babies are *mine*. I'm their mother."

Nothing she'd said thus far had sunk in, obviously.

Antonio crossed his arms and contemplated her. "You said you were the surrogate. A huge sacrifice, to be sure, but the children would have been mine and Vanessa's. You've been forced to care for them much longer than anyone has a right to ask. I'm relieving you of the responsibility."

Her worst nightmare roared to life, pulsing and seething as it went for her jugular.

"No!" A tear rolled down her face before she could stop it as she tried to summon up a reasonable argument against the truth in his words. "That's not what happened. I care for them because I love them. They became mine in every sense when I thought you and Vanessa were both gone. I *need* them. And they need me. Don't take away my babies."

A sob choked off whatever else she'd been about to say. The one and only time she'd ever tried to fight for something, and instead of using logic and reason, she'd turned into an emotional mess.

Concern weighted Antonio's expression as he reached out to grasp her hand in a totally surprising move. His fingers found hers and squeezed tightly, shooting an unexpected thrill through her that she couldn't contain. Coupled with the emotional distress, it was almost overwhelming.

"Don't cry." The lines around his eyes deepened as he heaved a ragged sigh. "I don't know how to do this."

"But you don't have to know," she countered, clinging to his hand like a lifeline. "That's what I'm trying to tell you. Don't change anything. It's Christmastime and we're family, if nothing else. I'll stay here and continue to care for the babies, then we can spend this time figuring it out together. After the first of the year, maybe the path will seem clearer."

Please, God.

Relief coursed through her as he slowly nodded. "I want to be as fair as possible to everyone. If you don't have a life to get back to, then it makes sense for you to stay here. At least until January."

"This *is* my life."

Or at least it was now, since she'd given up her job as an accountant. She had no desire to be anything other than the mother she'd become over the past year. And now she had until the first of January to find a way to stay in that role. If Antonio decided his children would be better off in another arrangement, she had little to say about it.

What would she do without the family she'd formed?

"Caitlyn, I appreciate what you've done." His dark eyes

sought hers and held, his gratitude genuine. "You stepped into my place to care for my children. Thank you."

That he recognized her efforts meant the world to her. He was a good man, deep inside where brain trauma couldn't touch. As she'd always known.

She nodded, still too emotional to respond, but the sentiment gave her hope. He wasn't heartless, just trying to do the right thing.

Somehow, Antonio had to recognize that *she* was the right thing for the children and then the two of them could figure out how to be co-parents. After learning how to handle triplets, that should be a walk in the park.

The next two days passed in a blur. When Caitlyn had mentioned legalities, Antonio had half thought it was an excuse to avoid giving up control of his money. But she'd vastly understated the actuality. An avalanche of paperwork awaited him once the man who'd been his lawyer for a decade became convinced Antonio had really returned from the dead.

Funny how he'd instantly recognized Kyle Lowery the moment his lawyer's admin had ushered Antonio and Caitlyn into the man's office. His memory problems were inconsistent and frustrating, to say the least.

Antonio's headache persisted and grew worse the more documents Kyle's paralegal placed in front of him. The harsh lights glinting from the gold balls on the Christmas tree in the corner didn't help. Antonio wished he could enjoy the spirit of the season.

But Christmas and family and all of the joy others seemed to associate with this time of year meant little to him. Caitlyn had told him that his parents had died some time back, which probably explained why he remembered them with a sense of distance, as if the scenes had happened long ago.

After many more stops and an interminable number of hours, he had: a temporary driver's license, a temporary bank card, a promise of credit cards to come, a bank teller who'd fallen all over herself to give him access to his safe-deposit box…and a dark-haired enigma of a woman who'd stuck to his side like glue, determined to help him navigate the exhausting quagmire reentering his life had become.

Why was she still here?

Why did her presence make him so happy? She somehow made everything better just by being near him. And sometimes, she looked at him a certain way that burrowed under his skin with tingly warmth. Both had become necessary. Unexpectedly so.

He studied her covertly at lunch on the third day after he'd pounded on the door of his Malibu house, delirious and determined to find answers to the question marks in his mind.

What he'd found still hadn't fully registered. Caitlyn was an amazing woman and his kids were surprising, funny little people. Together, they were a potent package. But how did that make sense? She wasn't their biological mother.

While Antonio absently chewed on a thick sandwich designed to put back some of his lost weight, Caitlyn laughed at Leon as he shoved his food off his tray to the floor below.

She'd insisted on the triplets sitting at the table when the adults had meals, even though the babies ate little more than puree of something and bits of Cheerios. Antonio wouldn't have thought of having infants join them, but with the additions, eating became something more than a routine. It was a chance to spend time with his children without expectation since Brigitte and Caitlyn handled everything.

Secretly, he was grateful Caitlyn hadn't skipped through

the door the moment he'd given her the out. In the hazy reaches of his mind, he had the distinct impression most women would have run very fast in the other direction from triplets. He couldn't understand Caitlyn's motivation for staying unless she thought she'd get a chunk of his estate as a thank-you. Which he'd probably give her. She deserved something for her sacrifices.

"Your turn."

Antonio did a double take at the spoon in Caitlyn's outstretched hand and blinked. "My turn to what?"

"Feed your daughter. She won't bite you." Caitlyn raised her brows and nodded at the spoon. "Of the three, Annabelle is the most laid-back about eating, so start with her."

Since he couldn't see a graceful way to refuse, he accepted the spoon and scooted closer to the baby's high chair, eyeing the bowl of…whatever it was. Orange applesauce?

Scowling, he scooped some up and then squinted at the baby watching him with bright eyes. How was he supposed to feed her with her fingers stuck in her mouth?

"Come on, open," he commanded.

Annabelle fluttered her lashes and made an uncomplimentary noise, fingers firmly wedged where the spoon was supposed to go.

He tried again. "Please?"

Caitlyn giggled and he glanced at her askance, which only made her laugh harder. He rolled his shoulders, determined to pass this one small test, but getting his daughter to eat might top the list of the most difficult things he had to do today.

Antonio had learned to walk again on the poorly healed broken leg that the Indonesian doctor had promised would have to be amputated. He'd defied the odds and scarcely even had a limp now. If he could do that, one very small person could not break him.

He tapped the back of Annabelle's hand with the edge of the spoon, hoping that would act as an open sesame, but she picked that moment to yank her fingers free. She backhanded the spoon, flinging it free of Antonio's grip. It hit the wall with a *thunk*, leaving a splash of orange in a trail to the floor.

Frustration welled. He balled his fists automatically and then immediately shoved them into his lap as horror filtered through him. His first instinct was to fight, but he had to control that impulse, or else what kind of father was he going to be?

Breathing rhythmically, he willed back the frustration until his fists loosened. Better.

His first foray into caring for his kid and she elected to show him her best defensive moves. Annabelle blinked innocently as Antonio's scowl deepened. "Yeah, you work on that technique, and when you've got your spinning backhand down, we'll talk."

Spinning backhand. The phrase had leaped into his mind with no forethought. Instantly other techniques scrolled through his head. *Muay Thai.* That had been his specialty. His "training" with Wilipo had come so easily because Antonio should have been teaching the class as the master, not attending as the student.

Faster now, ingrained drills, disciplines and defense strategies exploded in his mind. Why now instead of in his gym, surrounded by the relics of his former status as a mixed martial arts champion?

The headache slammed him harder than ever before and the groan escaped before he could catch it.

"It's okay," Caitlyn said and jumped up to retrieve the spoon. "You don't have to feed her. I just thought you might like it."

"No problem," he said around the splitting pain in his temples. "Excuse me."

He mounted the stairs to his bedroom and shut himself away in the darkened room, but refused to lie on the bed like an invalid.

Instead, he sank into a chair and put his head in his hands. This couldn't go on, the rush of memories and the headaches and the inability to do simple tasks like stick a spoon in a baby's mouth without becoming irrational.

But how did he change it?

Coming to LA was supposed to solve everything, give him back his memories and his life. It had only highlighted how very far he had yet to go in his journey back to the land of the living.

An hour later, the pain was manageable enough to try being civilized again. Antonio tracked down Caitlyn in the sunroom, which seemed to be her favored spot when she wasn't hanging out with the babies. Her dark curls partially obscured the e-reader in her hands and she seemed absorbed in the words on the screen.

"I'll visit a doctor," he told her shortly and spun to leave before she asked any questions. She'd been after him to see one, but he'd thus far refused, having had enough of the medical profession during his months and months of rehabilitation in Indonesia.

No doctor could restore his memories, nor could one erase the scars he bore from the plane crash.

But if a Western doctor had a way to make his headaches go away, that would be stellar. He had to become a father, one way or another, and living in a crippling state of pain wasn't going to cut it.

"I'll drive you." She followed him into the hall. "Just because you have a driver's license doesn't mean you're ready to get behind the wheel. We'll take my—"

"Caitlyn." He whirled to face her, but she kept going, smacking into his chest.

His arms came up as they both nearly lost their balance

and somehow she ended up pinned to the wall, their bodies tangled and flush. His lower half sprang to attention and heat shot through his gut.

Caitlyn's wide-eyed gaze captured his and he couldn't have broken the connection if his life depended on it. Her chest heaved against his as if she was unable to catch her breath, and that excited him, too.

"Caitlyn," he murmured again, but that seemed to be the extent of his ability to speak as her lips parted, drawing his attention to her mouth. She caught her plump bottom lip between her teeth and—

"Um, you can let go now," she said and cleared her throat. "I'm okay."

He released her, stepping back to allow her the space she'd asked for, though it was far from what he wanted to do. "I'm curious about something."

Nervously, she rearranged her glossy hair, refusing to meet his eyes. "Sure."

"You said that you introduced me to Vanessa. How did you and I meet?" Because if he'd ever held Caitlyn in his arms before, he was an idiot if he'd willingly let her go.

"I was Rick's accountant." At his raised brows, she smiled. "Your former manager. He'd gone through several CPAs until he found me, and when I came by his house to do his quarterly taxes, you were there. You were wearing a pink shirt for a breast cancer fund-raiser you'd attended. We got to talking and somehow thirty minutes passed in a blur."

Nothing wrong with her memory, clearly, and it was more than a little flattering that she recalled his clothing from that day.

"And there was something about me that you didn't like?" Obviously, or she wouldn't have matched him up with her sister. Maybe she'd only thought of him as a friend.

"Oh, no! You were great. Gorgeous and gentlemanly." The blush that never seemed far from the surface of her skin bloomed again, heightening the blue in her eyes. "I mean, I might have been a little starstruck, which is silly, considering how many celebrities I've done taxes for."

That pleased him even more than her pink-shirt comment, and he wanted to learn more about this selfless woman who'd apparently been a part of his life for a long time. "You're an accountant, then?"

"Not anymore. I gave up all my clients when…Vanessa died." She laughed self-consciously. "It's hard to retrain my brain to no longer say 'when Antonio and Vanessa died'."

The mention of his wife sent an unexpected spike of sadness through his gut. "I don't remember being married to her. Did you think we'd be a good couple? Is that why you introduced us?"

All at once, a troubling sense of disloyalty effectively killed the discovery mode he'd fallen into with Caitlyn. He had no context for his relationship with Vanessa, but she'd been his wife and this woman was his sister-in-law. He shouldn't be thinking about Caitlyn as anything other than a temporary mother to his children. She'd probably be horrified at the direction of his thoughts.

"Oh. No, I mentioned that she was my sister and you asked to meet her. I don't think you even noticed me after that. Vanessa is—was—much more memorable than me."

"I beg to differ," he countered wryly, which pulled a smile out of her. "When I close my eyes, yours is the only face I can picture."

Apparently he couldn't help himself. Did he automatically flirt with beautiful women or just this one?

More blushing. But he wasn't going to apologize for the messed-up state of his mind or the distinct pleasure he'd discovered at baiting this delicate-skinned woman.

He'd needed something that made him feel good. Was that so wrong?

"Well, she was beautiful and famous. I didn't blame you for wanting an introduction. Most people did."

"Famous?" Somehow that didn't seem like valid criteria for wishing to meet a woman.

Caitlyn explained that Vanessa starred on *Beacon Street*, a TV show beloved by millions of fans, and then with a misty sigh, Caitlyn waxed poetic about their fairy-tale wedding. "Vanessa wanted a baby more than anything. She said it was the only thing missing from your perfect marriage."

He'd heard everything she'd said, but in a removed way, as if it had happened to someone else. And perhaps in many respects, it had. He didn't remember being in love with Vanessa, but he'd obviously put great stock in her as a partner, lover and future mother of his children.

Part of his journey apparently lay in reconciling his relationship with the woman he'd married—so he could know if it was something he might want to do again, with another woman, at some point in the future. He needed to grieve his lost love as best he could and move on.

Perhaps Caitlyn had a role in this part of his recovery, as well. "I'd like to know more about Vanessa. Will you tell me? Or is it too hard?"

She nodded with a small smile. "It's hard. But it's good for me, too, to remember her. I miss her every day."

Launching into an impassioned tribute to her sister, Caitlyn talked with her hands, her animated face clearly displaying her love for Vanessa. But Antonio couldn't stop thinking about that moment against the wall, when he'd almost reached out to see what Caitlyn's glossy hair felt like. What might have happened between them all those years ago if he hadn't asked Caitlyn to introduce him to Vanessa?

It was madness to wonder. He would do well to focus

on the present, where, thanks to Caitlyn, he'd forgotten about his headache. She'd begged him to allow her to stay under his roof and, frankly, it was easy to say yes because he needed her help. Incredible fortune had smiled on him since the plane crash, and he couldn't help feeling that Caitlyn was a large part of it.

Four

Instead of taking Antonio to the doctor, Caitlyn arranged for the doctor to come to the house the following afternoon. Antonio needed his space for as long as possible, at least until he got comfortable being in civilization again—or at least that was Caitlyn's opinion, and no one had to know that it fit her selfish desire to have him all to herself.

As a plus, Caitlyn wouldn't have to worry about wrestling Antonio into the car in case he changed his mind about seeing a doctor after all. Not that she could have. Nor did she do herself any favors imagining the tussle, which would likely end with Antonio's hard body pinning her against another wall.

Recalling yesterday's charged encounter had kept her quite warm last night and quite unable to sleep due to a restless ache she had no idea how to ease. Well, okay, she had *some* idea, but her sensibilities didn't extend to middle-of-the-night visits to the sexy man down the hall. One did not simply walk into Antonio's bedroom with the intent of hopping into bed with him, or at least *she* didn't. Risqué nighttime shenanigans were Vanessa's style, and her sister had had her heart broken time and time again as a result. Sex and love were so closely entwined that Caitlyn was willing to wait for the commitment she'd always wanted.

Nor did she imagine that Antonio was lying awake fantasizing about visiting Caitlyn anytime soon, either. They were two people thrown together by extraordinary circumstances and they both had enormous, daunting realities to deal with that didn't easily translate into any kind of relationship other than…what? Friends? Co-parents? Trying to figure it out was exhausting enough; adding romance to the mix was out of the question.

Especially since Antonio could—and likely would—have his pick of women soon enough. A virgin mother of triplets, former accountant sister-in-law didn't have the same appeal as a lush, redheaded actress-wife combo, that was for sure.

The doctor buzzed the gate entrance at precisely three o'clock. Antonio ushered the stately salt-and-pepper-haired physician into the foyer and thanked him for coming as the two men shook hands.

All morning, Antonio had been short-tempered and scowling, even after Caitlyn told him the doctor was coming to him. Caitlyn hovered just beyond the foyer, unsure if she was supposed to make herself scarce or insist on being present for the conversation in case the doctor had follow-up instructions for Antonio's care.

Vanessa would have been stuck to Antonio's side. As a wife should. Caitlyn was only the person who had made the appointment. And she'd done that just to make sure it happened.

"Caitlyn," Antonio called, his tone slightly amused, which was a plus, considering his black mood. "Come meet Dr. Barnett."

That she could do. She stood by Antonio, but not too close, and exchanged pleasantries with the doctor.

"I saw you fight Alondro in Vegas," the doctor remarked with an appreciative nod at Antonio. "Ringside. Good match."

Antonio accepted the praise with an inclined head, but his hands immediately clenched and his mouth tightened; clearly, the doctor's comments made him uncomfortable. Because he didn't remember? Or had he lost all context of what it meant to be famous? Either way, she didn't like anyone making Antonio uncomfortable, let alone someone who was supposed to be here to help.

"Can I show you to a private room where you can get started?" Caitlyn asked in a no-nonsense way.

"Of course." Dr. Barnett's face smoothed out and he followed Caitlyn and Antonio to the master bedroom, where Antonio had indicated he felt the most at home in the house.

Score one for Caitlyn. Or was it two since a medical professional was on the premises?

She started to duck out, but Antonio stopped her with a warm hand on her arm. "I'd like you to stay," he murmured. "So it will feel less formal."

"Oh." A bit flummoxed, she stared up into his dark eyes. "It won't be weird if the doctor wants you to…um… get undressed?"

On cue, her cheeks heated. She'd blushed more around this man in the past few days than she had in her whole life.

His lips quirked and she congratulated herself on removing that dark scowl he'd worn all day. Too bad his new expression had come about because he likely found her naïveté amusing.

"It will only be weird if you make it weird." His head tilted as he contemplated her. "What kind of doctor's appointment do you think this is?"

She scowled in return. "I'll stay. But only if you stop making fun of me."

He winked. *Winked*. "I solemnly swear. Provided you stop saying things that are funny."

"And," she continued as if he hadn't tried to be charming and slick, when, in truth, it fluttered her heart to be so firmly in the sights of Antonio's weapons of choice. "I'll stay if you'll be perfectly honest with the doctor. If you aren't, I will be."

At that, he smiled. "Then, you'll definitely have to see me undressed."

"For what reason?" she hissed with a glance at the doctor, who was pretending not to listen to their far-too-loud discussion. Did Antonio have zero sense of propriety?

"Otherwise, how will you know what to say about my badly healed broken leg?" Antonio responded innocently and laughed as Caitlyn smacked his arm. Over his shoulder, he called, "Dr. Barnett, can we start out dressed or shall I strip immediately?"

Dr. Barnett cleared his throat. "We'll talk first and then I'll take some vital signs. A more...ah...thorough examination will only become necessary pending the outcome of our discussion. Ms. Hopewell is free to excuse herself at that point."

Even the doctor sounded as if Caitlyn's lack of experience around naked men was cause for hilarity. She firmed her mouth and sank into the chair Antonio indicated in the sitting area, which was thankfully far from the bed, then crossed her arms. *Men*.

And speaking of pigheaded males—why was she just *now* finding out Antonio had suffered a broken leg? It probably needed to be reset and it must pain him something awful and...it wasn't her business. She'd gotten him in front of a doctor; now someone with a medical degree could talk sense into the man, who apparently thought he'd turned immortal.

Dr. Barnett settled into a wing-back chair with a clipboard he'd pulled from his bag of tricks. After a quick back-and-forth with the patient to determine Antonio's age, approximate height and weight, the doctor took his heart rate and peered into his throat.

"Now, then." The doctor contemplated Antonio. "Ms. Hopewell indicated that you have trouble remembering your past. Can you tell me more about that?"

"No," Antonio said smoothly, but Caitlyn heard the obstinacy in his voice. "You're here because I have headaches. Make them go away."

Caitlyn frowned. *That* was the thing he was most worried about?

The doctor asked a few pointed questions about the nature of Antonio's pain, which he refused to answer. Dr. Barnett pursed his lips. "I can write you a prescription for some heavy-duty painkillers, but I'd like to do a CT scan first. I'm concerned about your purported memory loss coupled with headaches. I'd prefer to know what we're dealing with before treating the symptoms."

"No tests. Write the prescription," Antonio ordered and stood, clearly indicating the appointment was over whether the doctor wished it to be or not. "Ms. Hopewell misrepresented the nature of the medical care I need."

Caitlyn didn't move from her chair. "How long will the CT scan take? Will you get results immediately or will it only lead to more tests? Will you also look at his leg?"

Someone had to be the voice of reason here.

"It doesn't matter, because that's not the problem," Antonio cut in with a scowl. "I'm not sick. I'm not an invalid, and my leg is fine. I just need something to make my headaches manageable."

Dr. Barnett nodded. "Fine. I'll write you a prescription for a painkiller, but only for enough pills to get you through the next few days. If you go to the radiology lab and get the CT scan, I'll give you more."

"Blackmail?" Antonio's lips quirked, but no one would mistake it for amusement. "I'll just find another doctor."

"Perhaps." Dr. Barnett shrugged. "Hollywood is certainly full of dishonest medical practitioners who will write prescriptions for just about anything if someone is willing to pay enough. Just keep in mind that many of those someones wind up in the morgue. I will never be a party to putting one of my patients there."

That was enough to convince Caitlyn she'd selected the right doctor, and she wasn't going to stand by and let Antonio destroy an opportunity to get the help he needed, not when he had three very good reasons to get better the medically approved way. "Dr. Barnett, please write the prescription for the amount of pills you think is appropriate and leave me the information about the radiology lab. We'll discuss it and get back to you."

Antonio crossed his arms, his expression the blackest it had been all day, but thankfully he kept his mouth closed instead of blasting her for interfering.

The doctor hastily scrawled on his pad and tore off the top page, handing it to Caitlyn with a business card for the radiology lab. She saw him out and shut the front door, assuming Antonio had stayed holed up in his room to work off his mood.

But when she turned, he was leaning against the wall at the other end of the foyer, watching her with crossed arms and a hooded, hard look. His expression wasn't as black as it had been, but somehow it was far more dangerous.

Startled, she backed up against the door, accidentally trapping her hands behind her. Feeling oddly exposed, she yanked them free and laced her fingers together over her abdomen, right where a strange sort of hum had started.

"I'm not getting a CT scan," he said succinctly. "I didn't ask you to call the doctor so you could railroad me into a bunch of useless tests. I had enough of doctors in Indonesia who couldn't fix me."

She shook her head, not about to back down. This was too important. "But what if the tests help? Don't you want to get your memory back?"

"Of course." A hint of vulnerability flitted through his gaze and the hum inside her abdomen sped up. "There's only one thing that's helped with that so far and it wasn't a doctor."

The atmosphere in the foyer pressed down on her, almost agonizing in its power. She couldn't think when he was like this, so focused and intense, funneling all of his energy toward her. It woke up her nerve endings and they ruffled under the surface of her skin, begging her to move with a restless insistence. But move where?

"What helps?" she asked softly, afraid of spooking him. She couldn't predict if he'd leave or advance on her and, at this point, she couldn't say which she'd prefer.

"Fighting." The word reverberated against the marble, ringing in her ears.

She gasped, hand flying to her mouth. Surely he didn't mean actual fighting. As if he intended to return to his former sport.

"I need to get in the ring again," he confirmed, his dark gaze on hers, searching for something she couldn't give him. Pleading with her to understand. "I have—"

"No," she interrupted as her stomach dropped. "You can't. You have no idea what's going on inside your skull and you want to introduce more trauma? Not a good idea."

He'd only returned to civilization a few days ago, broken on the inside. He needed...something, yes, but it wasn't picking up his former MMA persona as if no time had passed. As if he was still whole and healthy. As if he had nothing important to lose.

"This is not your call, Caitlyn," he said gently. Too gently. He'd already made up his mind. "This is my life, my head. I'm a fighter. It's what I do."

She stared up at him, and the raw emotion swimming through his eyes took her breath. "You haven't been a fighter for a long time, Antonio. You're a businessman now."

That was the man she knew well, the safe, contained version of Antonio. When he'd quit his MMA career to manage what went on in the ring for other fighters, it was the best of both worlds. Antonio still had all the outer trappings of his lean fighting physique, which—*let's be honest*—was wickedly delicious enough to get a nun going, but he'd shed the harsh brutality of Falco.

She liked him as a businessman. Businessmen were constant, committed. The way she'd always thought of Antonio. If he wasn't that man, who was he?

"I might have been before the crash, but I don't remember that part of me." Bleakly, he stared off into the distance and her heart plummeted. "That Antonio might as well be dead. The only Antonio *I* know is the one who lives inside my heart, beating against the walls of my chest, alive but not *whole*. That Antonio screams inside my head, begging to be free of this web of uncertainty."

God, how poetically awful and terrible. Her soul ached to imagine the confusion and pain he must experience every minute of every day, but at the same time, she thrilled in the knowledge that he'd shared even that small piece of himself.

His gaze snapped back to hers and she'd swear on a stack of Bibles he hadn't moved, but his heat wrapped around her, engulfing her, and she was powerless to stop it from affecting her. She wanted to step back, quickly. As fast as her legs could carry her. But he'd backed her against the wall…or she'd backed herself against the wall by starting this madness. By assuming she could convince a man who'd survived a plane crash to see a doctor.

Madness.

Because her body ached for Antonio to step into that scant space between them, which felt uncomfortably slight and yet as massive as the ocean that had separated him from his old life.

She wanted to support him. To care for him. To help him reenter his life in whatever way made sense to him. Who was she to say he shouldn't be in the ring again? Vanessa hadn't liked him fighting, either, but her sister had held many weapons in her arsenal that might have prevented the man she'd married from doing something dangerous.

Caitlyn had nothing.

"Please understand." He held her captive without words, without touching her at all, as his simple plea burned her throat. "I have to unleash my frustration on an opponent who can take it. Who's trained for it. Before I take it out on someone else."

Her teeth caught her lip and bit down as his meaning sank in. He sought a healthy outlet for his confusion, one that was familiar to him. Why was that so bad?

She'd been trying to keep him away from the media, away from his former employees and business partners, who might ask uncomfortable questions he couldn't answer. Perhaps she'd worried unnecessarily. Most likely, he'd be firmly in the public eye for the rest of his life, whether she liked it or not, and she couldn't keep him to herself forever. It was ridiculous to even pretend they could hide away in this house, even for a few days.

And then he reached out, encompassing her forearm with his palm. "I need you—" He swallowed and faltered.

"I need you in my corner, Caitlyn. I don't have anyone else."

Wide-eyed, she covered his strong fingers with hers. Reassuringly, she squeezed, reveling in the contact as warmth flooded the places where their skin touched. *She* was comforting *him* in what was clearly a difficult conversation for them both.

He needed her. More important, he needed her to validate his choices, no matter how crazy they seemed.

A little awed by the realization, she nodded because speaking wasn't an option as he rested his forehead on hers, whispering his gratitude. She closed her eyes against the intimacy of the thank-you, feeling as if she'd just fought an exhausting battle, only to look up and see the opposing general's second flank swarming the battlefield.

"I'll take you to Falco," she promised, her voice croaking, and wished she only meant she would take him to the building housing the empire he'd founded called Falco Fight Club. But she suspected she would really be taking him back to his former self, when he *was* Falco, a champion fighter who regularly took blows to the head.

God help her for enabling this lunacy.

Caitlyn insisted on driving to Falco, and Antonio humored her only because his pounding head had blurred his vision. Slightly. Not enough to give the doctor's ridiculous CT-scan idea any credence. He'd had plenty of brain scans in the past and the final one had ended his career.

He'd given up trying to understand why he could recall the last CT scan he'd endured, but couldn't remember the woman he'd been married to for—what? Four or five years? He didn't even know. He couldn't even fully picture her face, just bits of it in an insane collage.

They picked up Antonio's prescription on the way, but he waited to take a pill since the warning said the medication might make him drowsy. He definitely wanted to be alert for this first trip to his place of business.

The building came into view and Caitlyn pointed at it, saying Antonio had bought the lot and built Falco from the ground up, approving the architect's plans, surveying the drywall as it went up and hand selecting the equipment inside.

He waited for some sense of recognition. Pushed for it with widened eyes and a mostly empty mind. But the simple glass and brick looked like hundreds of other buildings in Los Angeles.

Falco Fight Club. The red-and-black letters marched across the brick, signifying this as the headquarters for the global MMA promotional company Antonio had founded. Under the name, a replica of the falcon tattoo on Antonio's pectoral had apparently been worked in as Falco's logo.

He briefly touched the ink under his shirt. This was part of his past, and likely his future as well, though he knew nothing about the business side of Falco. Nor did he have a driving desire to reclaim the helm...not yet.

He was here for what happened inside the ring.

Grimly, he climbed from the Range Rover Caitlyn drove more carefully than a ninety-year-old priest, and hesitated, suddenly fearful at crossing the threshold. What if he climbed into the ring and none of his memories came back? What if Caitlyn was right and additional trauma to his head actually caused more problems? He was a father now; he had other people to think about besides himself.

Caitlyn's presence wrapped around him before she slipped her smooth hand into his. It felt oddly...right to have her by his side as he faced down his past. She didn't say a word but stood with him as he surveyed the entrance, silently offering her unconditional support, even though she'd been adamantly against him fighting.

Somehow, that made his unsettling confusion acceptable. No matter what happened inside Falco Fight Club, he'd found his old life, and after a year of praying for it, he'd count his blessings.

The falcon emblem on his chest mirrored the one on the bricks in more ways than one—both decorated a shell housing the soul of Antonio Cavallari, and somewhere inside lay the answers he sought. He wouldn't give up until he had reclaimed *all* of his pieces.

"Is the company still in operation?" he asked, wishing he'd unbent from his bad mood enough to ask the question in the car. But his headache had grown worse as the day wore on, and he was weary of dealing with pain and questions and the blankness inside his head.

She nodded. "I get monthly reports from the interim CEO, Thomas Warren. He's been running it in your stead, but I have no idea if he's doing a good job or not. I was hoping you'd want to take over at some point, but I think everyone would understand if you didn't do so right away."

"Do they know?" He inclined his head toward the building, and even that renewed the pounding at his temples. Maybe he should take a painkiller anyway. It might dull the embarrassment and frustration of not knowing who "they" were.

She squeezed his hand and let it go, then shoved hers into her pocket. He missed the feel of her skin on his instantly and almost reached for her but recognized the wisdom in not appearing too intimate in public.

"Thomas called me yesterday after your lawyer gave him the heads-up that you were back," she said. "But I didn't tell him anything other than to confirm it was true, which was all he asked. I didn't know how much you'd planned to divulge."

"Thanks." He didn't know, either, but the truth would likely come out soon enough when Antonio stepped inside and had to be led around his own building like a blind person.

"Antonio." She hesitated for a moment. "I've been trying to shield you from the media, but you should know that coming to Falco is probably going to trip their radar. You should be prepared for a full onslaught at any time."

A crush of people, cameras, microphones, babbling. The chants of "Falco, Falco, Falco." The montage was the clearest yet of elements from his past. The memory washed over him, or rather it was a blend of several memories bleeding together, of him leaving the ring to follow his manager as Rick pushed through the crowd.

With the images came the expected renewed headache. The increased pounding and pressure wasn't so difficult to deal with if it came with new memories. But it was a brutal trade-off.

"I…" He'd been about to say he was used to reporters and cameras. But then he realized. The media wouldn't be interviewing him about his latest bout with Ramirez or Fuentes. He wasn't a fighter anymore.

Instead, the media would ask him painful questions, like, "Why don't you remember your wife?" and "What did you do for a whole year while you were gone?"

They might even ask him something even more difficult to answer, like, "How does it feel to find out you're a father after all this time?" Would the media want to crack open his life and take pictures of his children? He didn't want the babies exposed to anyone who didn't necessarily have their best interests at heart.

Caitlyn had been *shielding* him from the media. As if she wanted to protect him. It snagged a tender place inside, and he had no idea what to do with that.

"I shouldn't have come here," he muttered and turned to climb back into the Range Rover.

Fight or flight. The more he delved into his past, the

more appropriate the name Falco became. Seemed as if Antonio was constantly poised to use his talons or his wings, and he didn't like it. But he had no idea how to change it, how to achieve a happy medium where he dealt with life in a healthy way.

"Wait."

Caitlyn stopped him with a warm hand on his shoulder and the area under her palm tingled. Did all women affect him so greatly, or just this one?

Aggravated because he couldn't remember, Antonio moved out of her reach but paused before sliding into the passenger seat.

"I wasn't trying to talk you out of going inside," she said, concern lacing her tone. Enough so that he turned to face her. "This is important to you, and I think you need to do it. Five minutes. We'll walk around, say hello and then leave. The press won't have time to congregate in that length of time if you'd prefer not to be accosted."

"And then what?" he asked far more sharply than he'd intended, but she didn't flinch. "The hurdles will still be there tomorrow and the next day."

And he didn't just mean the press. All at once, the up-hill battle he faced to reclaim his memories, coupled with the constant physical pain, overwhelmed him.

"That will be true whether you take this step or not." She held out her hand for him to clasp, as if she'd known exactly what he needed.

Without hesitation, he slid his hand into hers and held it, wordlessly absorbing her energy and spirit, and it calmed him instantly. Miraculously.

"Walk with me." She pulled him away from the car and shut the door. "I'll do all the talking. If you want to spar with someone, the training facility is adjacent to the ad-ministrative offices. I'm sure one of the guys would indulge you in a round. There's always a ton of people either in the rings or strength training on the gym equipment."

"How do you know so much about my company?" he asked as he let her lead him toward the door, his pulse hammering in his temples. From nerves, trauma, the silky-sweet scent of Caitlyn? He couldn't tell. Maybe it was all three.

"I spent time here occasionally over the past year." A shadow passed through her expression. "I've brought the babies a couple of times, hoping to infuse your heritage into them. Silly, I know. They're too young to understand it."

She laughed and he felt an answering tug at his mouth. How did she do that? He'd been all set to command her to drive away as fast as she could, and when he got home, he'd probably have barred himself in his room to indulge in a fit of bad temper. Instead, Caitlyn had gotten him across the parking lot and pulled a smile from him, as well.

All in the name of physically, mentally and spiritually guiding him through a place she hadn't wanted him to go.

What an amazing, beautiful, selfless woman. The mother of his children. There was nothing temporary about her role; he saw that now. Her love for them shone through in every action, every small gesture.

Caitlyn Hopewell was his children's mother, and it was an odd addition to her attractiveness. But there it was.

That ever-present sense of disloyalty squelched the warmth in his chest that had bloomed at the sound of Caitlyn's laugh. Caitlyn was sensual and beautiful and likely that meant her sister'd had those qualities, as well. But why couldn't he remember being so outrageously attracted to Vanessa? Why couldn't he remember her touch the way he could recall with perfect clarity what Caitlyn's hand felt like on his shoulder? Surely he'd fallen for Vanessa for a myriad of reasons, especially if he'd married the redheaded sister instead of the dark-haired one. His late wife's attributes and personality must have eclipsed Caitlyn's.

But he couldn't fathom how, not when innocently thinking about Caitlyn caused a burn in his gut he couldn't explain away. It was pure, sensual attraction that he wished to explore.

How was he supposed to move past his relationship with Vanessa and potentially have a new one—especially if the woman was Caitlyn—when thinking about moving on caused a wretched sense of unfaithfulness?

Five

Antonio stepped through the glass doors to Falco with a silent sense of awe. The reception area held a hushed purpose, as if to say important matters happened between these walls, and it hit him oddly to imagine he owned all of this, had made it happen, had created this company himself through his own ingenuity and resolve.

White marble stretched under his feet, edged with red and black. Framed promotional pictures lined the walls on both sides, similar to the ones in his home gym, featuring fierce-faced fighters with raised gloves or crossed arms sporting bulging biceps. Many wore enormous title belts with distinctive, rounded shields in the center, proclaiming the fighter a world champion.

His own face stared back at him from three of the frames, one each for his three welterweight titles. The memory of posing for the shots crowded into his head, crystal clear.

But he couldn't remember picking out the marble under

his feet or the lot under the foundation or ever having walked into this building before today. It was becoming evident that his most severe memory loss encompassed the events that had happened after that final knockout Caitlyn had spoken of, the one that had ended his fighting career.

Perhaps the CT scan wasn't such a far-fetched next step. If there was something in his brain locking up his memories of that period, shouldn't he explore options to remove the block? Of course, he barely remembered Vanessa and he didn't remember Caitlyn at all, though he'd clearly known them both prior to his career-ending coma. So nothing was guaranteed.

After all, none of the Indonesian doctors had helped. Nothing had helped. And he hated hoping for a cure that would eventually amount to nothing.

In deference to the holidays, the reception area held a small decorated tree, and holly boughs covered nearly every surface. A classic Bing Crosby tune filtered through the sound system and he recognized it, of course, because his brain retaining Christmas songs made perfect sense. The receptionist looked up from her desk, blonde and perky, smiling with genuine happiness when she saw Antonio.

"Mr. Cavallari!" She shook her head, her wide-eyed gaze searching his face. "It's as if the past year never happened. I can't believe it. You look exactly the same."

Antonio nodded, because what else would he do when he couldn't remember this woman's name, though he'd probably hired her.

"Hi, Mandy," Caitlyn said smoothly, as if she'd read his mind. "Antonio would like to see what you've done with the place in his absence. I assured him that Thomas and his stellar team kept things in order, but there's nothing like an in-person tour, right?"

Rescued again. Antonio squelched the gratefulness

flooding his chest, because how long could Caitlyn's savior superpowers actually last? It was a fluke anyway. There
was no way she'd picked up on his distress. They barely
knew each other and besides, her ability to read his mind
had to be flawed; *he* didn't even know what was in his
head most of the time.

"Of course." The receptionist—Mandy—smiled at Caitlyn and picked up the phone on the desk to murmur into
it, then glanced up again. "Thomas will be here momen-
tarily to show you around. Glad you're…um…*here*, Mr.
Cavallari."

Here, meaning not dead. That was definitely a plus and
cheered him slightly. "Thanks, Mandy. I plan to be around
for a long time."

A man with a graying crew cut wearing an expensive,
tailored suit bustled into the reception area. *Thomas*.

A memory of the two of them standing in nearly this
same spot popped into Antonio's head, from Thomas's
first day on the job. Relief stung the back of Antonio's
throat. His memories were in there somewhere. It just took
the right combination of criteria for them to battle to the
forefront.

Thomas Warren was flanked by a couple of younger
men in sweatpants and hoodies. Fighters. They wore almost identical expressions with a slight menacing edge,
and they both leaned into the room, fists lightly curled as
if preparing to start swinging.

Antonio recognized the stance instantly—he'd entered
thousands of rooms that way. Still did, even now. Or perhaps he'd only picked it up again recently. Had he lost that
ready-to-fly edge in the past few years, only to regain it
after awakening to a blank world where simply entering a
room brought on a barrage of questions and few answers?

These were the pieces of Antonio Cavallari he hoped
to recover inside this building.

"Thomas." Antonio held out his hand to the older man, who shook Antonio's hand with a critical once-over.

"It's true." The interim CEO of Falco Fight Club narrowed his gaze, mouth slightly open as he fixated on Antonio's face. "I guess you can call me a doubting Thomas because I really didn't believe it until I saw you for myself. Come, let me show you the improvements we've made in your...ah, absence."

Seemed as if everyone was going to stumble over the proper verbiage to explain they'd assumed Antonio had died in the plane crash. He didn't blame them; he didn't have any clue what you were supposed to say, either.

"Let's put pretense aside," Antonio said before he'd fully determined what he planned to say. "You thought I was dead and spent the past year accordingly. I may disagree with some, or even all, of your decisions, but I fail to see how I could find fault with them. You did what you thought was right and I have no intention of walking in here to undo everything you've done."

Thomas's eyebrows rose. "Fair enough. It is an unprecedented situation and I appreciate that we might both need to maintain flexibility."

Thomas inclined his head and indicated Antonio should follow him into the interior of the building.

The two fighters fell in behind as well, and Antonio had the distinct sense the men were either intended as intimidation or accessory. It didn't matter which; either one was as laughable as it was baffling.

The short tour generated little in the way of jogging his memories, but the visit to Falco itself had already yielded a valuable harvest. Antonio had the unique opportunity to appreciate what he'd built using his own fortitude and business savvy as he surveyed it for what was, for all intents and purposes, the first time.

The vast influence of Falco unrolled before him as he

learned of his vision for bringing glory back to the sport of mixed martial arts with a promotional powerhouse that had no ties to a media conglomerate. Untainted by corporate politics or the need for a healthy bottom line, Antonio had pushed boundaries, opening MMA to unconventional fighting disciplines, training some of the most elite fighters in the world and gaining entry to off-the-beaten-path venues. Most important, he'd insisted all his fighters be allowed to compete for titles based on their records, not handshake promotional deals.

And he'd been wildly successful, beyond anything he'd envisioned when Caitlyn mentioned Falco was where he'd made all his money. When he'd asked Thomas to show him the books, his eye had shot straight to the profit line, as if he'd last glanced at a balance sheet yesterday. The number of decimal places couldn't be right, and Antonio had nearly chalked it up to a clerical error until he glanced at the rest of the line items.

Not a mistake. Billions of dollars flowed through his company. It was dizzying. He should have paid more attention to the balances of his accounts when Caitlyn had transferred control of his estate back to him at his lawyer's office the other day.

No wonder Caitlyn hadn't taken the first opportunity to get out of Dodge when he'd offered to relieve her of baby duty. He could easily give her eight or nine figures for her trouble and never think twice about it, which was probably what she was hoping for. She seemed to genuinely care about the children, but everyone wanted something, and that something tended to be money.

"I want to see the training facility," Antonio announced abruptly.

"Absolutely." Thomas led the way to the adjacent building.

Energy bolted through his body as he anticipated climbing between the ropes. That had been his sole purpose in coming here and it had thus far been eclipsed by a slow slide back into Businessman Antonio.

Which didn't seem as bad as it once might have.

Maybe part of his journey lay in coupling both halves of his soul—the fighter and the suit—under one banner. But it wouldn't be today. He needed to get his wits about him, what few remained, and the ring was the only place where he'd experienced any peace in the past year.

As he entered the training facility, Antonio's lungs hitched as his eye was drawn to the equipment closet, to the three rings, one with a regulation metal cage surrounding it, to the workout area. Exactly where he'd known they would all be placed. Because he truly remembered, or because he'd modeled the layout on another facility from before the career-ending knockout?

Eager to find out, he strode through the cavernous room, drawing the attention of the muscled men—and surprisingly, a few women—engaged in various activities. One by one, weights drifted to the ground and sparring partners halted, gloves down, as they stared at him.

"That's right," he called to the room at large. "I've arisen from my watery grave. Who's brave enough to go a round with a ghost?"

"Cavallari, you sly dog." A grinning Hispanic male, early twenties, jogged over from his spot at a weight bench and punched Antonio on the arm as if he'd done it often. "They told us you were dead. What have you been doing, hiding out to get back in professional shape without any pressure? Smart."

What a ridiculous notion. Ridiculously brilliant. Maybe he'd adopt it as his easy out if the media did start harassing him about his whereabouts over the past year.

"Hey, Rodrigo," Caitlyn called, and when Antonio

glanced at her, she winked, and then murmured under her breath, "Rodrigo was a good friend. Before."

When they got home, he'd treat her to the most expensive bottle of wine in his cellar. And then when she was good and looped, he'd carefully extract her real agenda.

No matter how much she seemed to love his kids, no one did nice things without a motive. He wanted to know what hers was.

"Are you my volunteer?" Antonio jerked his head at the nearest ring, eyes on his potential sparring partner.

"Sure, boss." Rodrigo shadowboxed a couple of jabs at Antonio's gut. "Like old times. Just go easy on me if your secret training put you out of my league."

Rodrigo's grin belied the seriousness of the statement—did he not believe Antonio had actually trained over the past year or did he assume that regardless, they'd still be matched in skill? Apparently, they'd sparred before and had been on pretty equal ground.

"Likewise," Antonio commented, mirroring Rodrigo's grin because it felt expected. Honestly, he had no idea how they'd match up. He couldn't wait to find out.

Something inside rotated into place, as if two gears had been grinding together haphazardly, and all at once, the teeth aligned, humming like a well-oiled machine.

His headache had almost receded and if God had been listening to his pleas at all, the next few minutes would knock loose a precious memory or two.

Before long, Antonio had slipped into the shorts Caitlyn had insisted he bring from home. She watched him face off against Rodrigo in the large ring, both men barechested and barefoot. It hadn't taken the office grapevine but about five minutes to circulate the news that Antonio Cavallari was both back and in the ring. Nearly everyone from FFC's administrative building had crowded into the training facility and around the cage with expectant faces, murmuring about Antonio's return.

You couldn't have pried most of the women's gazes from Antonio with a crowbar, Caitlyn's included, though she at least tried to hide it. But he was magnificent, sinewy and hard, with that fierce tattoo so prominent against his golden body. His still-longish hair was slicked back from his forehead, highlighting his striking eyes as they glittered like black diamonds.

Apparently she liked him as a fighter just as much as she liked the savvy businessman. Maybe more. Her raw reaction at the sight of Antonio in the ring was powerful and uncomfortably warm. Hot, even. And far lower than seemed appropriate in public.

It was shameful. Shameful to be so affected by her sister's husband, shameful that she'd carried a yet-to-be-extinguished torch for Antonio all of these years. Most shameful of all was that at least half of his appeal lay in his primal stance as he waited for an opening to do bodily harm to another human. She'd always thought of him as the perfect man—committed, beautiful, steady. And it frightened her to be so attracted to him for purely carnal reasons.

But she couldn't stop the flood of elemental longing any more than she could explain how over-the-top sexy the man had become once he slipped into his glory in the ring.

She'd never seen him fight live. Once he and Vanessa had hooked up, she'd spent a lot of time feeling sorry for herself and as little time as possible around the two of them. It was too hard to be reminded that he'd picked the glamorous Hopewell sister instead of the quiet, unassuming one. Not that she blamed him; most men had overlooked Caitlyn in favor of Vanessa, and Caitlyn had never been bitter about it. Until Antonio.

She'd spent the entirety of their marriage hiding her hurt and disappointment and jealousy, the entirety of their relationship wishing she could have her sister's marriage... and then the past year feeling guilty and sick about the uncharitable thoughts she'd had.

Now she just wanted to feel as if she didn't have to apologize for being alive when her sister wasn't. For being a woman affected by a prime specimen of man as he engaged in physical combat. Was that so wrong?

The men circled each other, trash-talking. Suddenly, Antonio lashed out in a blur of intricately executed moves, both beautiful and lethally graceful. Her breath caught as she drank in the visual panorama. Antonio's body moved fluidly, as if it had been made specifically for this purpose, and it was stunning to behold.

In enabling him to return to the ring, she'd unwittingly exposed herself to a piece of his soul that was the opposite of harsh, the opposite of brutal. It was breathtaking.

Caitlyn blinked as Rodrigo hit the mat without having lodged one defense.

Violence was unfolding before her very eyes and the only thing she'd noticed was how exquisitely Antonio had executed it. Something was very wrong with her.

The crowd murmured as Rodrigo shook his head and climbed to his feet, rubbing his jaw.

"Lucky shot, boss," he grumbled.

Not that she had any basis for judgment, but Caitlyn didn't think so. As the men went at it again, Antonio's superior skill and style couldn't be mistaken, even by an untrained eye such as hers. Rodrigo landed a couple of shots, but the younger man called a halt to the match after only a few more minutes, breathing heavily. Caitlyn grimaced at his split lip.

Rodrigo and Antonio shook hands and the crowd slowly dispersed, many of them stopping to welcome Antonio back or clap him on the shoulder with a few congratulatory words about his performance.

Caitlyn hung back, remaining as unobtrusive as possible while Antonio excused himself to shower and change. No one was paying attention to her anyway, which she considered a blessing as long as her insides were still so unsettled. This whole Falco Fight Club experience had shown her something about herself that she didn't understand and didn't know what to do with.

Antonio returned. His gaze cut through the crowd and locked on to hers, his eyes dark with something untamed and unnameable and she shivered. It was as if he knew exactly where she was in the crowd. And exactly what she'd been thinking about while watching him fight.

Her cheeks heated and she blessed his distance because, hopefully, that meant he couldn't tell. But the distance disappeared as he strode directly to her.

Though clothed, his potency hadn't diminished in the slightest. Because she knew what his hard body looked like under his crisp white shirt and slacks. Heat rolled between them and his gaze fell to her mouth for a moment as if he was thinking about dropping a kiss there.

Her lips tingled under his scrutiny. Madness. She'd fallen under some kind of spell that caused her imagination to run away with her, obviously.

"I'm ready to go home," he murmured and the moment broke apart. "I've had enough for one day."

"Sure," she managed to get out around the tight, hot lump in her throat.

Goody. Now they could cram themselves into a tiny Range Rover for the drive home, where his masculine scent would overpower her, and she'd spend the drive reminding herself that no matter how sexy he was, the complications between them were legion.

Which was exactly what happened. She gripped the wheel, white-knuckling it onto the main street and, thankfully, Antonio fell silent.

Too silent. He'd just reentered his old world in the most immersive way possible. She desperately wanted to ask him about it.

Had he remembered any of Falco? All of it? What had it felt like for him to get in the ring again? Antonio hadn't fought professionally in years and, as far as Caitlyn knew, Vanessa had forbid him from even messing around with the guys in the ring because she feared he'd get hurt again.

Part of Caitlyn wondered if she'd helped facilitate his return to Falco because it was something her sister never would have done. As if it was some kind of sick contest to see if Antonio would realize Caitlyn was the better woman for him.

But she had no idea how to navigate the heavy vibe in the Range Rover, so she kept her mouth shut and let the silence ride.

When they got home, she followed him into the house from the garage, unable to stand the silence any longer. "How's your head?"

That was a safe enough topic, wasn't it?

He paused in the kitchen to get a glass of water and gulped the entire thing down before answering. "It hurts."

She leaned a hip on the granite countertop as close to him as she dared and crossed her arms over her still-unsettled insides. "Why don't you take a painkiller and rest."

"Because I'm not ninety and waiting around to die," he said shortly, then frowned. "Sorry, I don't mean to snap."

The line between his eyebrows concerned her and she regretted not encouraging him to talk to her while they'd been in the car. Her own uncertainties weren't an excuse to be selfish. "It's okay. You've had a difficult day."

His gaze latched on to hers and he surveyed her with a focused, hooded expression that pulled at something deep in her core. In or out of the ring—didn't matter. He exuded a primal energy that she couldn't stop herself from reacting to, and it was as frightening as it was thrilling.

The way Antonio made her feel had nothing to do with the safe, nebulous fantasy she'd carried around in her heart for years. *That*, she understood. The raw, ferocious draw between them, she didn't.

"Difficult?" he repeated. "Really? What gives you that impression?"

"Uh…because you're snapping at me?" When the corners of his mouth lifted, she smiled involuntarily in return. "It couldn't have been easy to get into the ring today in front of all your colleagues. How long has it been since you last went a round?"

"A couple of weeks. I trained six hours a day in Indonesia over the past few months. It was part of my rehabilitation."

"Oh, you never mentioned that." And why would he? She wasn't his confidante. But she'd kind of hoped he saw her in that role, as someone he could turn to, who would be there for him in a confusing world.

"It wasn't worth mentioning." A smile still played with his lips and she couldn't tear her gaze from his mouth as he talked. "Indonesia was about survival. Only. I fight—then and now—because I have to."

The confessions of his deepest self were as affecting as watching him fight had been. She wanted more but was afraid of what it might mean to get it. "I remember you said you needed to get in the ring to blow off frustration. Did it work?"

"Partially," he allowed. "I need a more skilled partner."

"Yes, even I could see that Rodrigo was outmatched."

A blanket of intimacy settled around them as a full, genuine smile bloomed on his face, and she reveled in it.

Brigitte bustled into the kitchen at that moment, shattering the mood. "Oh, you're back. Grand. Do you want to spend time with the babies before dinner?"

Taking a guilty step backward, Caitlyn tore her gaze from Antonio to focus on the au pair. "Um, yes. Of course."

She always played with the babies before dinner while Brigitte helped the chef, Francesco, put the children's meal together. What was wrong with Caitlyn that she hadn't noticed the time? Well, duh—Antonio was what was wrong with her.

"They're in their cribs waiting for you," Brigitte said sunnily and went to the fridge to pull out covered bowls of premashed fruit and veggies.

"Come with me." Caitlyn put a hand on Antonio's arm before she thought better of it. Heat prickled her palm and she snatched it back. "It'll be fun. Low pressure."

Fun, plus an excuse to stay in his presence under the pretense of guiding his steps toward fatherhood—but with the added distance the babies would automatically create.

Then she remembered his headache. "You don't have to if you'd rather be alone. I don't want to push you into a role you're not ready for."

"I'd like to," he said, surprising her.

He followed her upstairs and into the nursery. Leon stood in the center of his crib, both chubby hands gripping the edge to support his wobbly legs as he yowled like a wet cat. Annabelle sat with her back to the room banging one of the crib slats with a rattle while sweet Antonio Junior lay on his back staring at the mobile above his crib.

"There you go," Caitlyn murmured to their father. "This is a perfect encapsulation of your children's personalities. Leon does not like being forced to do something and he isn't a bit hesitant to tell you how unhappy he is. He'll be the first to learn how to climb out of his crib, mark my words. God help us then."

"Why?" Antonio eyed first his son and then Caitlyn as

she boosted Leon from his crib and into her arms, which predictably, quieted down his protests.

"Because then he'll be a holy terror, climbing out in the middle of the night while we're asleep." She nodded to the baby. "Would you like to hold him?"

"Yes," he said decisively and then his brows drew together as Caitlyn handed over the baby. "Do I have to do anything?"

"Nothing special, just make sure he feels secure."

She laughed as Leon peered up at his father suspiciously, as if trying to figure out whether he was okay with this new person. They'd learn the verdict in about two seconds.

Thankfully, Leon waved his fist around, which was his way of saying things were cool. Antonio's gaze never left his son's face, and his clear adoration shot straight through Caitlyn's heart with a painful, wonderful arrow.

Caitlyn spun to busy herself with Antonio Junior before the tears pricking at her eyelids actually fell in a mortifying display of sentiment. It was just a dad with his kid. Why should it be so tender and meaningful?

There were so many reasons locked up in that question, she could hardly start answering it—but first and foremost, because it was her kid, too, one she'd created with this man in a most unconventional way, sure, but that didn't make it any less powerful to watch the two interact.

Then there was the compelling contrast between this tender version of Antonio and the fierce warrior he'd been in the ring. The dichotomy created an even more compelling man, and he was already so mesmerizing, she could hardly think.

Antonio Junior hadn't made a sound since they'd entered the room, so Caitlyn checked on him as she often did, just to be sure he was still breathing. He'd always been quiet, carrying the weight of the world on his shoulders, and it bothered her that he'd adopted such a grave demeanor.

He definitely took after his father in that respect, where Leon was a demanding prima donna like Vanessa.

"That's my serious little man," she crooned to Antonio Junior and slid her fingertips across his fine dark hair as he refocused his gaze from the mobile to Caitlyn.

The sheer beauty of her child nearly took her breath. She'd always thought he looked like Antonio, but it had been an academic observation based on memory and expectation—they both had dark hair and dark eyes; of course the comparisons would come.

"Is he serious?" Antonio asked with genuine curiosity.

"Very. He's also quiet. Annabelle would probably be content to sit in her crib until the cows came home as long as she could make noise," Caitlyn called over her shoulder and, dang it, her voice caught on the emotion still clogging her throat. She cleared it, hoping Antonio had been too caught up in Leon to notice. "That's her favorite thing. Noise. She likes it best when she can bang on something and then imitate the noise with her voice and, trust me, she practices a lot."

"I don't mind," Antonio said softly, and she sensed him come up behind her long before she heard his quiet intake of breath. He peered over her shoulder into Annabelle's crib. "Hi, there, sweetheart."

Annabelle tipped her head up to focus on her father, her upside-down face beaming. "Gah."

"Is that her imitation of banging the rattle?" Antonio asked with a laugh. "Because she should practice some more."

"No, that's how she says hello."

Caitlyn's throat tightened again, which was silly when she was only explaining her children's quirks. But their father didn't know any of these things—because he'd been lost and alone half a world away while she'd lived in his house, cared for his children and spent his money. She wanted to make that up to him as best she could.

"Come on, you big flirt." Caitlyn hoisted Annabelle out of the crib and set her on the soft pink blanket already spread out on the nursery floor. "I realize pink is clichéd for a girl, but I thought Annabelle needed girlie things with two brothers."

"You don't have to justify your choices." Antonio crouched down on the blanket and settled Leon next to his sister. "I'd be the last person to tell you you're doing it wrong, and even if I have a conflicting opinion, I'd prefer to talk through it, not issue countercommands. You've done the best you can, and it couldn't have been easy to do it alone."

"It wasn't." One tear spilled over before she could catch it. "I worried every day that I wasn't enough for them."

Antonio glanced up from his perch on the fluffy pink blanket, which should have looked ridiculous but didn't in the slightest. "You've been amazing. More than enough. Look at how perfect these babies are. Healthy, happy. What more could you have provided?"

"A father," she whispered. And somehow the fates had granted that wish in the most unexpected, flawless way possible. "They deserve two parents."

A shadow passed over his face. "And for now, that's what they have."

For now? Was that a cryptic comment about the future of her place in this family?

"No matter what happens, I will always be their mother," she stated firmly, and if only her voice hadn't cracked, it might have sounded as authoritative out loud as it had in her head.

They needed to talk about the future, but she was afraid to bring it up, afraid to overload him with one more thing he didn't want to deal with, afraid he was only letting her stay because it was Christmas and she'd begged him not to kick her out.

But she had to get over it and go to the mat for her children. If anyone could understand the bone-deep need to fight for what you wanted, it would surely be Antonio.

"Yes," he said quietly. "You *are* their mother."

And that took the wind out of her sails so fast, she couldn't breathe. "Okay, then."

She'd have to bring up the future another time, after she'd recovered from all of this.

Six

Antonio's headache persisted through dinner, but he couldn't stomach the idea of taking the pills now that he actually had them. He'd lost so much of his past; losing his present to drowsiness held little appeal. Instead, he bided his time until Caitlyn and Brigitte put the babies to bed and then he cornered Caitlyn in the sunroom.

He hoped she wouldn't mind the interruption. It was time to dig into what Caitlyn wanted from him in exchange for the role she'd played thus far in his life and the lives of his children. And did she see a continued role? If so, what role did she envision for herself?

The sun had set long ago and Caitlyn read by low lamplight. He started to say her name but the words dried up on his tongue. Something inside lurched sweetly, as confusing as it was intriguing. Silently, he watched her, loath to alert her to his presence until he was good and finished sating himself on her ethereal beauty.

But she glanced up almost instantly, as if she'd sensed

him. He knew the feeling. There was an undeniable draw between them, and he'd bet every last dollar that she felt it, too. Maybe it was time to dig into that as well, and find out what role *he* wanted her to play.

"Have a glass with me?" He held up the uncorked bottle of wine he'd judiciously selected from his extensive wine cellar.

"Um, sure." Her fair skin bloomed with that blush he liked far more than he should. But what had brought it out? He had a perverse need to find out.

Which seemed to be the theme of this nighttime rendezvous. He'd barely scratched the surface of what made Caitlyn Hopewell tick, and exposing her layers appealed to him immensely.

Antonio poured two glasses of the deep red cabernet and handed one to Caitlyn, then settled into the other chair, separated from hers by a small wooden end table. For a moment, he watched the moonlight dance on the silvery surf so beautifully framed by the wall of glass opposite the chairs.

"I bought this house specifically for the view from this room," he commented instead of diving right in. "It's my favorite spot."

"Mine, too," Caitlyn agreed quietly.

"I figured. This is where I find you most often." He sipped his wine, rolling it around on his tongue as the easy silence stretched. For once, Caitlyn didn't seem determined to fill the gap with nervous chatter.

It was nice to sit with no expectations and not worry about his missing memories. His headache eased the longer he watched the waves crash on the shore below.

"Did you have something on your mind?" she blurted out and then sighed. "I mean, other than the regular stuff, like becoming a father and having amnesia and learning to live in civilization again and—"

"Caitlyn." He touched the rim of his glass to hers in silent apology for the interruption, but he wasn't really sorry. He liked that she gave him so many opportunities to say her name. "I wanted to have a bottle of wine with you. As you pointed out, if nothing else, we're a family by default. Nothing wrong with acting like one."

She didn't relax. "Except we're not a family, not really. You were all set to send me on my way until I convinced you to let me stay through the holidays. Then what, Antonio? I need to know what you plan to do."

Nothing like laying it on the line. Apparently, the easy silence hadn't been so easy for her. If she wasn't keen on a social drink, they didn't have to play nice. Shame. He'd have preferred to have the wine flowing before getting to the reason he'd tracked her down.

But clearly, her ability to read him wasn't a fluke, as he'd assumed earlier today.

"I'm not sure," he said carefully. "It's not January yet and I have a lot to consider. Tell me what you'd like to see happen."

Her fingers gripped the stem of the wineglass until her nail beds turned white. "That's difficult to answer."

Because she didn't want to come right out and say that on the first of January, she'd take a wire transfer with nine zeros tacked onto the end? "Then, maybe you can answer this for me. Why did you rescue me at Falco so many times today? It was as if you could read the room and tell exactly when I was floundering."

"Oh, um…" Her eyebrows drew together as her gaze flew to his face, searching it, and unexpected rawness sprang into the depths of her eyes. "I don't know. It was painfully obvious when you didn't remember someone. I hated that you were uncertain."

That rawness—it nearly eviscerated him with its strength. What did it mean? He had no context for it, not with her, not with any woman. And he wanted to know if it signified the same intense desire to explore each other, the way it did in him.

The draw between them grew tighter as he contemplated her. "Obvious?"

"Well, probably not to everyone," she corrected quickly. "To me anyway. I was, uh…paying attention."

Her gaze traveled down his body, and she didn't try to hide it, probably because she had no idea how to play coy. Heat flared in his loins as he became extremely aware of how the lamp highlighted the curves under her clothes. "I never thanked you for paying such close *attention*. I'm curious, though. What do you hope to gain from helping me?"

"Gain?" She cocked her head, confusion evident. "I'm helping you navigate your life because you need me. You told me so. I want to help."

"Why?"

"Because I like the fact that you need me!" Her eyelids flew shut and she shook her head. Leaping to her feet, she backed away. "I didn't mean to say that."

"Caitlyn." He'd upset her, and he didn't like the way it snagged at his gut to be responsible for the distress around her mouth and eyes.

He'd much rather be responsible for the raw intensity he'd glimpsed a moment ago.

When he slid from his chair and approached her, she stood her ground despite the fact that her body was poised to flee.

"Wait," he murmured. "What did you mean to say?"

She wouldn't meet his gaze. "I meant to say that the children are my first priority."

No, there was more here, more she didn't want to say, more she didn't want him to discover—and that unidentified something called to him.

Instinct alone guided his hand to her chin and he tipped

her head up to evaluate her stricken expression. "Mine, too. That's why I ask these questions. I want to know whether you're helping me in hopes of a nice payout. Or some other, yet-to-be-determined motive."

"Really, Antonio?" Fire flared in her blue eyes, surprising him in its intensity. "Do you have any context for what being a mother means? What it means to me personally?"

Her lips curled into a harsh smile and he couldn't stop watching her, fascinated by the physical changes in her as she schooled him. Even more surprising, she didn't pull away but pushed her chin deeper into his grip.

"Leon, Annabelle and Antonio Junior are my *children*," she continued, her voice dipping lower with each impassioned word. "Just as much as they're yours. More so. I carried them in my womb and I've raised them. I could do it on an accountant's salary and would have if the judge hadn't granted me conservatorship of their inheritance. Keep your money. This is about love."

Love. A nebulous notion that he should understand but didn't.

With that one word, the atmosphere in the sunroom shifted, growing heavier with awareness. Her body leaned toward his, bristling with vibrancy. No longer poised to flee but to fight.

It reached out and punched him with a dark thrill. She wasn't backing down. She was prepared to meet him halfway, taking whatever he dished out. But what would she do with it?

"Hmm." The sound purred from his throat as he slanted her chin a touch higher. "Let's examine that. What do you know about love?"

More important, did she know the things he wanted to learn?

"I know enough," she retorted. "I know when I look at those babies, my heart feels as if it's about to explode with so many wonderful, terrible emotions. I know what it feels like to lose my sister to an early death and sob for days and days because I can't ever tell her I love her again."

Yes, that tightness in his chest when he'd gazed at his own flesh and blood encapsulated in a tiny person for the first time. It *was* wonderful and terrible. And inexplicably, that decided it. She was telling the truth about her motives, and all interest in grilling her over them evaporated.

Now his agenda included one thing and one thing only—Caitlyn and getting more of her soft skin under his fingers.

Love for a child he understood, but it wasn't the full extent of the kind of love possible. The kind of love he must have had for Vanessa. *That* was the concept that stayed maddeningly out of reach. "What about love for a man? Romantically."

"What, as if you're going to prove my motives are ugly because I've never been in love?" Fiercely, she eyed him. "I know how it feels to want a man to tell you he loves you. You want it so badly that you can't breathe. You want him to touch you and kiss you. It hurts deep down every second that you don't get it. And when you do get it, you want it to last forever."

Electricity arced between them and he ached to close the distance between them, to give her everything on her checklist, right here, right now.

"Is that what you wanted to hear?" she said, her chest rising and falling with quickened breath. "Love is equal parts need and commitment. What do *you* know about love?"

"Nothing," he growled, and instantly, the reality of it crushed through his chest.

The love that she'd painted with her impassioned speech—he wanted that. Wanted to know that he *could* feel like that. But love grew over time, over shared experiences, over shared memories.

He'd been robbed of that when he crashed in the ocean. But he had a chance to start over with someone else, to move on from the past he couldn't reclaim.

This nighttime interlude had started out as a way to get her to explain her motives, but instead, she'd uncovered his. Everything he wanted was right here, gripped in his hand. So he took it.

Hauling Caitlyn forward, he fused his mouth to hers. Hungrily, desperately, he kissed her, and his body ignited in a firestorm of sensation. Her mouth came alive under his, taking and giving with each stroke, matching him in the power of her appetite. He soared into the heavens in the most intense flight he'd ever experienced.

His eyes slammed shut as he savored the tight, heated pulls in his groin that could only be eased by burying himself in this woman, body and soul. *More.* He worked her mouth open and her tongue met his in the middle in a perfect, hot clash of flesh. Her eagerness coursed through him, spurring him on, begging him to take her deeper.

His mind drained of everything except her. He felt alive in the most elemental way, as if he'd been snatched from the jaws of hell for this moment, this woman.

Scrabbling for purchase, he slid his arms around her, aligning her with his body and dragging her into the most intimate of embraces. She clung to his shoulders and the contact sparked through his shirt. The contrast of her soft curves sliding against his brutally hardened torso and thighs drove him wild with sharp-edged need.

So frustrating. Too many clothes in the way. His fingertips explored her automatically, mindlessly, craving her. He wanted every millimeter of her beautiful skin exposed, wanted to taste it, feel it, rake it with his gaze and incite that gorgeous blush she could never seem to stop.

The kiss abruptly ended. Caitlyn tore out of his arms, hair in wild disarray from his questing fingers. Chest heaving, she stared at him, eyes limpid and heated.

And then she fled without a word.

Still mortified over her brazen behavior, Caitlyn curled in a ball on her bed, praying none of the babies would wake up tonight. Praying that Antonio didn't take her display of wantonness as an invitation to knock on her door. Because she didn't know if she'd open it. Or never come out.

She'd kissed her sister's husband. And the guilt was killing her—almost as much as the fact that she wouldn't stop herself from doing it again.

That kiss had rocked her to the core.

And shattered all her harmless fantasies about what it might be like to kiss Antonio.

The gap between imagination and reality was so wide, she couldn't see across it. Never would she have imagined her body capable of feeling such raw *need*. Or such a desire to let Antonio take her further into the descent of sensual pleasure, a place she'd never gone with any man.

The way he made her feel scared her, no doubt. But she scared herself even more. She was afraid of her own impaired judgment. If she gave in to that swirl of dark desire—which had seemed like a very real possibility when Antonio had taken her into his arms—what happened then? Was Antonio gearing up for a marriage proposal? She had no idea how any of this worked. Where his thoughts were on the matter. How you even brought up such important subjects as commitment and love when a man had done nothing more than kiss you.

She needed these questions answered before she let these confusing new feelings brainwash her. The confusion was made even worse by the fact that it was *Antonio* on the other end of the equation. A different, harder, sexier, more over-the-top Antonio, who wasn't necessarily the man he'd been. She had no idea how to handle any of this.

And while she'd long ago accepted that she was already half in love with him, he hadn't professed any such thing to her. Sex was a big deal and until she knew he got that, no more kissing. Otherwise, she might find herself on the wrong side of a broken heart—as she'd always feared.

Along with a guilty conscience she couldn't shake, it was too much.

So they'd just have to pretend that scorching, mind-altering kiss had never happened.

By morning, she'd figured out that was impossible. The long, need-soaked night had not been kind.

Today's goal: get Antonio into a public place so he couldn't entice her again.

When he entered the breakfast nook, fresh from the shower, her heart did a crazy, erratic dance. It was sinful how perfect he was, how well his shoulders filled out a simple T-shirt, how his sinewy arms made her want to run her fingertips across them. Those arms… They'd held her expertly last night as he'd treated her to the most passionate kiss of her life.

How did the sight of him muddle her insides so much?

"Good morning," he murmured, his gaze full of knowledge.

"Hi," she squeaked in return. What did that dark, enigmatic look mean? That he remembered the taste of their kiss and wanted more?

Or was that a classic case of projection since that was what *she* was thinking? Would he even bring up the kiss, or was he of the same mind that it was better to forget about it?

Quickly, she tore her gaze from his and concentrated on her…oatmeal. At least that was what she vaguely recalled she'd been eating before he'd waltzed in and stolen her ability to use her brain.

"Would you like to go Christmas shopping with me today?" she asked and winced at the desperation in the question. As if she was dying to spend the day in his company instead of the truth—public places were her new best friend.

He pursed his perfect lips, which made it really hard not to stare at them. *Oatmeal.* She put her head down and shoveled some in her mouth.

"I'd like that," he said easily. "Will we shop for the children? Or are they too young for gifts?"

"Oh, no. It's their first Christmas. I planned to shower them with presents and lots of brightly wrapped boxes. You know how kids only like to play with the boxes? I thought it would be fun to have empty boxes as well as toys. Of course, I came up with all of that before you returned, so if it's too extravagant—"

"Caitlyn."

She didn't look up. Didn't have to in order to know she was rambling again. Her name was like a code word. Anytime she heard it, it meant *shut up*.

With a soft rush of cloth, he crossed the breakfast nook, pausing by her chair. He tilted her chin to force her to meet his gaze. The way he'd done last night, but this morning, she didn't have the fuel of righteous indignation to keep her semisane. Caught in the grip of his powerful presence, she watched him, unable to look away or breathe. His fingers were like live electrical conduits, zapping her skin with energy, and she was pretty sure the heat had climbed into her cheeks.

"Let's just go shopping, okay?" he asked. "Money is not subject to discussion today."

"Oh. Um, really?" That certainly wasn't the tune he'd

been singing last night. "I told you, I don't want your money, nor am I okay with treating you like a blank check."

She *had* said that, hadn't she? The atmosphere last night had been so vibrant and intense, there was no telling what she'd actually communicated now that she thought back.

"I believe you. So let's be clear. I'm paying. You are shopping." His smile broadened as she opened her mouth. "And not arguing," he added quickly before she could interrupt.

"So you don't have my name in your head next to a little check box labeled 'gold digger' anymore?" she asked suspiciously.

He shook his head and dropped his hand, which she instantly wished he'd put back simply because she liked his touch.

"I'm sorry. I was less than tactful last night. We still have the future to sort out, but I'm less concerned about that today than I was yesterday. I'm willing to see what happens."

"You know I'm breast-feeding the babies, right?" she blurted out, and yeah, that heat was definitely in her cheeks.

His gaze narrowed, but to his credit, he didn't outwardly react to such an intimate topic. "All three of them?"

She scowled. "Yes, all three of them. Why in the world would I be selective?"

For some reason, that amused him. "I wasn't suggesting you should be. Forgive my surprise. It just seems like a huge undertaking. Though, admittedly, my understanding of the mechanics is limited."

Yeah, she'd bet he understood breasts better than most men. "It's a sacrifice, for sure, but one I'm more than willing to make. But the point is, I can't just stop. So there's not a lot of room for seeing how it goes. I'm their mother, not an employee."

He nodded. "I'm beginning to see that point more clearly."

At last. There was no telling if he'd actually softened his stance or whether she could explain her feelings any better now than she'd thus far been able to. But the time seemed right to try.

She shut her eyes for a beat and laid it on the line. "Well, thank you for that. You asked me last night what I envision and honestly, I see us co-parenting."

"You mean long-term?" Even that didn't ruffle his composure, which, hopefully, meant it wasn't too far out of a suggestion in his mind.

"Forever. They're my children," she said simply. "I want to shop for Annabelle's prom dress, see them graduate from college, be there when they get married. The works. There's not one single thing I'd agree to miss."

His silence wasn't very reassuring. Finally, he nodded once. "I don't know how to do that. But I'm willing to talk about it after the holidays, like we agreed. It will give us time to think about what that looks like."

Breath she hadn't realized she was holding whooshed out. It was something. Not the full-bore yes she'd have preferred but more than she'd had five minutes ago.

"That's great. Thank you. It means a lot to me."

"It means a lot to me that you're willing to be their mother." His dark, hooded expression sought hers and held again and she shivered under the intensity. "They need a mother. Who better than the one who carried them for nine months?"

"That's exactly what I've been trying to tell you," she said and wished she could have pulled that off with a smirk, but it probably just sounded grateful.

"Let me eat some breakfast and we'll go shopping." He smiled as Francesco hustled into the breakfast nook, carrying a bowl of oatmeal and some coffee with two teaspoons of sugar, milk and a shot of espresso, the way Antonio liked it.

Not that she'd memorized his likes and dislikes over the years, but she found it interesting that his coffee preference hadn't changed even through the nightmare of amnesia.

"I'll drive," she told him. "Unless your headache is better?"

"It's not as bad today." He glanced at her. "I took a painkiller last night. Figured it was the only way I'd get to sleep after you ran out on me."

Amusement danced through his gaze along with a hint of heat that she had no trouble understanding. And on cue, there came the stupid blush. "I'm sorry. That was juvenile."

"Why did you take off, then?" Casually, he spooned up some oatmeal as if the answer didn't matter, but she caught the tightness around his mouth.

"It was too much," she said carefully. And honestly. "We have a lot of challenges in front of us. I'd like to focus on them without…complications."

That part wasn't the whole truth, but it was certainly true enough.

"That's a good point." Antonio polished off his breakfast without fanfare and without arguing.

Caitlyn frowned. Was she that easy to resist?

It didn't matter. No more kissing. That was the rule and she was sticking to it.

She stood and moved toward the door of the breakfast nook, hoping it didn't appear too much as if she was running away again, but Antonio confused her and she wanted to find a place where she could breathe for a few minutes. "I'll be ready to go shopping in about thirty minutes, if that's okay."

"Caitlyn."

She paused but didn't turn around.

"You focus on your challenges your way, and I'll focus on my challenges my way."

"What's that supposed to mean?" she whispered, afraid she wasn't going to like the answer.

"It means I'm going to kiss you again. The complications aren't great enough to stop me. You'd best think of another argument if you don't want me to."

Seven

The Malibu Country Mart at Christmastime might not have been the smartest choice for keeping her distance from Antonio. For the fourth time, the crush of holiday shoppers forced them together, and for the fourth time, his thigh brushed Caitlyn's hand.

She snatched it back before considering how telling a gesture it was.

Of course, his parting comment at breakfast had obviously been designed to throw her off balance, so alerting him to the fact that he'd succeeded shouldn't be that big of a deal.

"There's Toy Crazy," she squawked and cleared her throat, pointing with her still-tingling finger. "Let's hit that first."

Antonio nodded without comment about her affected voice, bless him, and they walked in tandem to the store.

A Salvation Army bell ringer called out season's greetings as they passed, and the holiday decor added a cheerful mien to the shopping center that Caitlyn wished she could enjoy. She loved Christmas, loved the holiday spirit and had been looking forward to the babies' first experience with the festivities.

Now everything with Antonio was weird and uncertain and she hated that. For so long she'd dreamed of having a relationship with him, and nothing had happened like she would have thought. *He* was nothing like she would have thought, so different than the man he'd been before the crash. Darker, fiercer Antonio wasn't the tame businessman her sister had married, and Vanessa was far more suited to handle this version of the man than Caitlyn was.

Antonio had flat-out told her he was going to kiss her again. What did she do with that? How did she come up with a better argument than "It's complicated"? Especially when there wasn't a better argument.

"After you," Antonio murmured and allowed Caitlyn to enter the toy store ahead of him, then followed her closely as they wandered into the fray.

Dolls and rocking horses and toy trains dominated the floor space, jockeying for attention amidst the shoppers. Caitlyn grabbed a cart and jostled through the aisles in search of the perfect toys for their children. True to his words at breakfast, Antonio didn't allow her to look at prices, and insisted she put everything in the cart she wanted.

Somewhere along the way, the sensual tension faded and the task became fun. They were just two parents picking out presents for their kids: swapping suggestions, agreeing with each other's ideas, nixing the toys that one of them felt wasn't age appropriate—mostly Caitlyn took on that role, especially after Antonio joyfully picked out remote-control cars for Leon and Antonio Junior. Honestly. The boys couldn't even walk yet.

Before long, the cart overflowed and Caitlyn had shared

more smiles with Antonio than she'd expected, given yesterday's kiss.

"I don't think anything else will fit," she announced.

"Then, I suppose we're finished." Antonio nodded toward the front of the store. "Unless you want to get another cart and keep going."

She laughed. "No, I think this is enough to spoil three children rotten."

Antonio smiled and pushed the cart toward the register. He'd manhandled it away from Caitlyn about halfway through without asking, insisting it had grown too heavy for her to maneuver. How could she argue with chivalry?

After they paid and Caitlyn got over her sticker shock, she let Antonio carry the umpteen bags.

But she didn't make it two feet toward the door. Antonio nearly plowed into her when she stopped. 'Twas the season to spend money as if it was going out of style, but it was also the season to spread good cheer to those who wouldn't be waking up to their parents' overindulgence.

"I just remembered that I wanted to donate something to Toys for Tots." Caitlyn picked up a Barbie doll and a GI Joe action figure located near the register. "I'll pay for this out of my own money."

Antonio's brows drew together. "What's Toys for Tots?"

He didn't remember Toys for Tots? Amnesia was such a strange beast, constantly surprising her with the holes it had created in Antonio's mind. Her heart twisted anew as she imagined how difficult his daily life must still be.

"It's a charity sponsored by the US Marines that gives toys to underprivileged kids. Not everyone has a billionaire for a father," she joked. "I like to donate every year, but I selfishly got caught up in my own children this year and nearly forgot."

His expression flickered with a dozen inexplicable emotions.

"Wait here," he instructed. "I'll be right back."

Mystified, she watched him thread back through the crowd and say something to the girl behind the register. Wide-eyed, she nodded and called to another worker. They spoke furiously to each other and then the second worker came alongside the first to speak to Antonio. He handed her something and then returned to Caitlyn's side with a small smile.

"Sorry, but you can't use your own money to buy toys for the kids without fathers."

Kids without fathers. That wasn't what she'd said, but he'd interpreted the term *underprivileged* in a way that had affected him, obviously. And many of the Toys for Tots recipients probably *didn't* have fathers.

"Don't argue with me," she told him sternly. "I didn't say anything about you paying for the babies' gifts, but this is something for me to do on my own."

"I don't mean I don't want you to. I mean, you can't. I bought out the whole store," he explained, and didn't even have the grace to look chagrined.

"You...what?"

"I told the clerk that she should check out the people already in the store and I'd buy whatever was left." He looked downright gleeful. "So we're going to hang out until they clear the store and then she's going to run my credit card."

Her heart thumped strangely. "That's...extravagant. And generous. What brought that on?"

He shrugged. "I don't think I've ever done anything for others before. That charity event you mentioned, the one where I wore the pink shirt. On the day we met," he prompted, as if she'd ever forget. "I did that because it was part of my contract. Not because I believed in the cause. I'm a father now. It means something to me and I want to be a better person than I was."

Tears pricked her eyes and she fought to keep them from falling. "You already are, Antonio."

Somehow her hand ended up in his and he squeezed it tight. "You're the one who brought it up."

What, as if she had something to do with Antonio's beautiful gesture? "Not so you could unload an entire toy store on the marines!"

He laughed and it rumbled through her warmly. *This* was what she'd dreamed of all those lonely nights when she imagined what it would be like to have a relationship with Antonio. Here they were, holding hands, standing near each other, and it was comfortable. Nice.

Not desperate and sensual and dark the way that kiss had been. Which one was the real Antonio?

His thumb stroked her knuckle and heat curled through her midsection. Okay, so he had the capacity to be both, which wasn't an easy thing to reconcile.

"I'll call someone to pick up the toys after the customers are gone and arrange for everything to be taken to the drop-off location," he said.

Yeah, there was nothing wrong with that part of his memory—he had no trouble recalling how to be large and in charge. And she hated that she found that shockingly attractive, too. As much as his generosity and his warrior-like persona and the way he was with the babies.

Who was she kidding? *All* of him was attractive.

When they got home, she spent an hour with the babies feeding them, which was time with her children that she treasured. They wouldn't breast-feed forever and while it had its challenges, such as having to use a breast pump after she'd had wine with Antonio the other night, she would be sad when this special bonding period was over.

Brigitte took over when Caitlyn was finished and they chatted for a few minutes. Leon was teething and making his displeasure known. Brigitte made a few suggestions and they agreed to try a different approach.

Should they include Antonio in discussions about the children's care? Caitlyn hadn't even thought to ask him but she really should. That was what being co-parents was all about.

She went in search of him and found him in his gym. Shirtless. And putting his hard body through a punishing round of inverted push-ups. Muscles bunched as he lowered himself to the ground and back up. His torso rippled and his skin glistened with his effort.

Dear Lord. A more exquisitely built man did not exist anywhere in the world.

Her mouth dried up. She couldn't peel her eyes from his body. Watching him put a burn in her core that ached with unfulfilled need. Somehow, the fact that he didn't know she was there heightened the experience, heating her further.

What was she *doing*?

She backed away, horrified to be gawking like a teenager. Horrified that she'd allowed herself to have a carnal reaction to Antonio.

"Caitlyn."

She glanced up. He'd climbed to his feet and stood watching her with a slightly amused expression. His torso heaved with exertion, and the falcon on his pectoral seemed poised to fly off his chest with each breath.

"Did you want something?" he asked, eyebrows raised.

So many things… "Uh—"

Wide-eyed, she watched him approach and speaking wasn't much of an option. His masculinity wrapped around her in a sensual cloak that settled heavily along her skin, warming it.

"Maybe you wanted to work out with me?" he asked, his head cocked in contemplation.

He was too close. Her body woke up in thrumming anticipation.

"I...um...do Pilates." *What did that have to do with anything, dummy?* She could still lift weights or something in Antonio's company, couldn't she? She shook her head. What was she thinking? That wasn't even why she'd tracked him down.

He reached out and toyed with a lock of her hair, smoothing it from her cheek, letting his fingers trail across her throat as he tucked the strand behind her back.

"Maybe you're here to deliver that argument we talked about earlier?" he murmured.

"Argument?"

Her mind went blank as Antonio's hand slipped from her shoulder to her waist. His naked chest was right there, within her reach. Her fingertips strained to trace the ink that bled into his skin, branding him as Falco. A fierce bird of prey.

"Against me kissing you. If you've got one, now would be the time to say your piece."

She glanced up into his eyes and the typhoon of desire swirling in their dark depths slammed through her. That sensual flare—it was desire *for her*.

She was his prey. She should be frightened. She was... and yet perversely curious what *would* happen next if she let things roll.

"We're, uh... That is..." She yelped as his arm slid around her waist, tugging her closer.

Her breasts brushed his bare torso, and even through her clothes, the contact ignited her already tingling core, flooding her with damp warmth.

"Caitlyn," he murmured. "Don't deny this. Hush now, and let me kiss you."

And before she could blink, he cupped her chin and lifted her head, bringing her mouth to his in one expert shot. The touch of his lips sang through her and she fell into Antonio, into the dark need, into her own pleasure.

Hot and hungry, he kissed her, hefting her deeper in his arms so their bodies snugged tight. She couldn't stop herself from spreading a palm on his heated flesh, right across his heart. Where the falcon lived.

His tongue coupled with hers, sliding against hers with rough insistence, and the sparks it generated ripped a moan from her throat.

Her core liquefied. No man had ever made her feel like this, so desperate and incomplete, as if she'd never be whole without him. She wanted…more. Wanted things she had little concept of. Wanted him to teach her about the pleasure she sought but hadn't yet realized.

Antonio gripped her shirt at the waist and pulled it from her pants before she could protest. Suddenly, his fingertips slid up her spine, magic against her bare flesh. She reveled in it, losing herself in his touch. He palmed her rib cage and thumbed one breast through her bra. Her core throbbed in time with her thundering pulse. Her head lolled backward as he mouthed down her throat to suck at the hollow of her shoulder blade, his unshaven jaw scrubbing her sensitive skin, heightening the pleasure tenfold.

That questing thumb worked its way under her bra and the shock of his rough, insistent touch against her nipple rocketed through her with a spike of dangerous lust.

"Antonio," she croaked and somehow got a grip on his wrist to pull it free from her clothing. "That's too far. It's too much. I can't—"

She bit off the rest—she sounded exactly like the inexperienced virgin she was. She peeled her hands from his chest and tore out of his grip.

"Don't run away," he commanded quietly. "Not this time. I enjoy kissing you. I want to make love to you. But you keep stopping me. Why?"

Afflicted, she stared at him, totally at a loss. "You want to…"

She couldn't even say that out loud. *He wanted to sleep with her.* Of course he did; she'd led him on like a wicked temptress who was perfectly prepared to strip naked right there in his gym and go at it on the floor.

This was her fault. She had no clue how to handle a man like Antonio, who was built like a woman's fantasy come to life. Who probably thought of sex as the next logical step in this type of attraction. No wonder she was screwing this up.

"I'm not like that," she said firmly. "I don't run around sleeping with people indiscriminately."

Something dangerous whipped through his expression. "I'm not 'people' and I object to being classified as such. You're cheapening what's happening between us. Also, I don't think that's the reason. You're afraid to be intimate with me."

He was offended. And disappointed in her. It scratched at her insides painfully. He'd cut through her surface protests to find the truth of her uncertainty. The realization that he understood her so well, even better than she'd understood her reticence, coated her throat, turning it raw.

"Yes," she whispered. "I need space."

She left the gym and he didn't try to stop her. Good. She needed to sort out her confusion. Antonio wasn't some random guy who'd love her and leave her, and of course he'd seen right through that excuse. Good grief, he had *commitment* written all over him—it was a huge part of his appeal.

Still was, but the physicality of her attraction far eclipsed it. Somehow. He'd brought out a part of her she'd never known existed. Around Antonio, she became a sensual, carnal woman that she didn't recognize, who liked his fierce side, his raw masculinity. Who wanted to delve into the pleasures of his touch with no regard to the emotional connection she thought she'd valued above anything else. And it scared her.

Because she didn't want to be like Vanessa. And yet, Caitlyn craved the type of relationship her sister had had with Antonio. It was a paradox, one she didn't know how to resolve.

Antonio had offered himself up on a silver platter. And she never dreamed she'd be fighting herself over whether to accept.

Antonio gave Caitlyn her space.

It was the last thing he wanted to do, but he had enough wits about him to recognize that Caitlyn required delicacy. Not his forte. But he'd learn it to get what he wanted.

The long night stretched, lonely and uncomfortable. The enormous four-poster bed would fit five people, but there was only one person he wanted in it. He had the vague sense that he must have slept in this bed with Vanessa, but he didn't think of his late wife at all. Instead, his vivid fantasies involved a dark-haired beauty who'd tied him up in knots.

Twice.

The first kiss had floored him. The second kiss had thrown him into a whole other level of senselessness. What had started as a way to help him move on from his marriage had exploded into something far more intriguing than he'd dreamed. When he kissed Caitlyn, her essence crawled inside him, haunting him. Pleasing and thrilling at the same time.

He wanted more. So much more. He shifted, unable to find a comfortable position, and the too-soft mattress doubled as a torture device. His half-aroused state didn't help.

The next morning, he bought a town car and hired a full-time driver to shuttle him back and forth to Falco. He

still didn't feel comfortable driving, not with the headaches that sometimes cropped up out of the blue. Naviga-
tion sometimes tripped him up as well, especially while
trying to get to a place he didn't remember. His house—
no problem. Falco wasn't on the approved list of memories
his brain had apparently created.

Fighting was his only outlet for the constant frustra-
tions. And his opportunities for it were limited.

Once at Falco, he first arranged for a private detective
to start searching for the remaining two unaccounted-for
passengers from his flight to Thailand. He gave the highly
recommended man one instruction—spare no expense. If
those two people were out there, Antonio would help them
get back their lives.

Then he spent the afternoon with Thomas untangling
legalities. They worked through the brunt of it until Antonio thought his head would explode with details and pain.
This office job was where he belonged, where he'd built a
company out of the ashes of his first love.

He didn't want it.

In reality, Antonio longed to climb back in the ring.
The business side of this promotional venue he'd created
didn't call to him as it once must have. Some aspects felt
comfortable and familiar, though he didn't have conscious
memories of strategy and balance sheets. Surely sitting behind his desk and monitoring his empire had once made
him supremely happy.

As Thomas gathered up his paperwork, Antonio swiv-
eled the high-backed chair toward the window, which
overlooked a landscaped courtyard with a wishing-pool
fountain in the center. He must have enjoyed this view
often, as Caitlyn mentioned that he'd been a workaholic,
often clocking eighty-hour weeks.

"Thomas, what would it take to get me back in rotation?" Antonio asked without taking his gaze off the gur-

gling fountain. Not only was it a shocking request in and of itself, but worse, the man who owned an MMA promotional company should probably know the answer already.

"You want to fight again?" Thomas kept any surprise from his tone, which Antonio appreciated. "As a contender? Or just exhibition?"

His mouth quirked involuntarily. "It's not worth doing if you're not going for the title."

The ins and outs of being a professional fighter he had no problems remembering. The pain and the training and the brutal conditioning...all worth it for a shot at glory.

But Antonio had underlying reasons. Reasons why he was a fighter in the first place. It was a part of him, an indelible piece of his makeup that even a near lobotomy of his memory couldn't extricate.

Thomas cleared his throat. "Well, you certainly proved the other day that you're in good enough shape for it. But you stopped fighting for a reason. What's changed?"

"*I* have. Make it happen."

After Thomas left, restlessness drove Antonio to the training facility, where several people called out greetings, none of whom he recognized, and without his mind-reading guide to assist, there was no chance he'd come up with names. If only Caitlyn hadn't requested her space, he'd have gladly brought her with him.

Trainers worked with fighters of all shapes and sizes, some in the rings, some at the bags. Along with the grunts and slaps of flesh, a sense of purpose permeated the atmosphere. Falco had been born out of Antonio's love of mixed martial arts, but he felt far more comfortable in this half of it than in the CEO's office.

He watched a couple of heavyweights duke it out in the circular-cage ring. Round, so one fighter couldn't force the other into an inescapable corner as so often happened in traditional boxing. MMA strove to even the playing field, to create fairness. The two heavyweights sparred under the watchful eye of a middle-aged man who moved with the fighters gracefully and knowledgeably. A former fighter, clearly, and Antonio liked his coaching style instantly.

Both men in the ring were good and they likely practiced together often. But one was better, with a stellar command of his body and a force of will the second man couldn't match.

Even without clear memories of planning or creating this place, Antonio recognized that he'd spared no expense when purchasing and maintaining the equipment. He'd also managed to attract world-class athletes and trainers, who'd sustained his company while he'd been in Indonesia.

Everyone here had come to improve their technique, to become better fighters, to win. Including Antonio. What happened in the ring made sense, followed a set of rules, a flow. The discipline and repetition settled him and allowed his damaged mind to take a breather.

"Who wants a piece of me?" he called.

"I'm up for it, if you are, old man."

Slowly, Antonio turned to face one of Thomas's right-hand men. A dark gray hoodie partially obscured the younger man's face, but his slight smirk beamed brightly from the depths.

The fighter vibrated with animosity, and Antonio's radar blipped. The man didn't like him. Dirty fight. Excellent. Darkness rose inside him and he didn't squelch it.

He'd been itching for this since his last round with Ravi in Punggur Besar. Rodrigo hadn't matched even a tenth of Antonio's skill and the fight had left him unsatisfied. Plus, Antonio and Rodrigo must have been friendly at some point in the past and that alone had caused Antonio to hold back.

There would be no holding back required with this matchup.

Antonio let his gaze travel down the length of his opponent and snorted his derision. "Hope your moves back up your mouth."

"Only one way to find out."

"What do they call you?" His real name was irrelevant, but the nicknames fighters adopted often gave clues about their style, their mind-set.

"Cutter." The insolent lift of his chin revealed eyes so light blue, they were almost colorless. "Because you're gonna walk away with my cuts all over your face."

Or in some cases, when you were good at reading your competition, nicknames revealed their weaknesses. Cutter was arrogant. Overconfident. Eager to prove himself against the legendary Falco.

Of course, Antonio had known all of that the moment Cutter had labeled him "old man." And this punk was about to be schooled on what age meant for a man's technique and skill.

In minutes, Antonio and Cutter had suited up and squared off. Antonio sized him up quickly now that his opponent wasn't hiding under shapeless clothing. Muscular but not too bulky. Blond hair shaved close to his scalp. Viking-style tattoos across his torso and wrapped around his biceps. Feral sneer firmly in place. Nothing to differentiate him from the dozens of other fighters in his age and weight class—which was probably what pissed Cutter off the most.

The metal cage gleamed around them, providing a safe backdrop for the two men to tear each other up, no holds barred. No chance of being thrown from the ring...and no chance of escape.

There was nowhere to hide and nowhere to run. And blood would be spilled before long.

The younger man feinted and went low. Amateur. Antonio circled away and spun to catch him off guard with a sideways kick to his hip.

Cutter's retribution came in a series of attacks that kept Antonio busy deflecting. Duck. Spin. Feint. The rhythm became comfortable. Mindless.

In a split second, Antonio found a hole. *Attack.* His opponent was a lightweight, so Antonio had a few pounds on him, which he used ruthlessly to force Cutter against the fence. Going for the man's mouth was a no-brainer.

Antonio's fist connected and Cutter's flesh separated. The scent of blood rolled over him.

Cutter sprang forward with an amazing show of strength, fury lacing his expression and weighting his punches. A lucky cuff caught Antonio across the temple before he could block.

Pain exploded in his head, blurring his vision. Images of Vanessa's red hair ricocheted through his consciousness. Images of her in various scenarios. The two of them shouting at each other. Of her talking. Laughing. Of Antonio with her, skin bared, his hand on her flesh, mouth on hers.

Something about the memories pricked at him, sitting strangely. Something wasn't right. He couldn't—

He had no time to think.

Show no weakness. Blindly, he circled away, trying to give himself a moment to let his mind clear. The moment he regained his faculties, he went on the offensive. Uppercut, double kick. *No mercy.*

Often two fighters left the ring shaking hands. MMA was more gentlemanly than outsiders would assume. That wasn't the case in this ring.

In moments, it was finished. Antonio wiped the trickle of blood leaking into his right eye. Cutter lay crumpled on the mat, groaning.

Endorphins soared through his body like bullets. Memories of his wife crowded his mind. The metallic scent of blood stung his nose and he craved more.

"Anyone else want a go at me?" Antonio challenged.

No one volunteered.

Eight

Antonio sneaked into the house and closed himself off in his bedroom to clean up before anyone saw him. Anyone, meaning Caitlyn. The split skin near his eyebrow wasn't life threatening but it wasn't pretty, either. Nor was he good company, not with adrenaline still swirling through his body like a tornado.

A long, hot shower gave him decompression time, allowing him to force back the base urge to smack something again and again. Once he got going, it was hard to shut it off.

But he couldn't live in the ring. He had to find a balance between the need to fight and the rest of his life. Until he could, what kind of father would he be? How could he willingly expose his children to that?

Someone knocked on his bedroom door as he exited the bathroom, toweling off his damp hair. For modesty's sake, he draped the towel over his lower half and pulled open the door.

"Hi." Caitlyn's eyes strayed to his torso, lingered and cut back up again quickly. Pink bloomed in her cheeks.

He loved that blush, and with his body already caught in an adrenaline storm, it set off fireworks. His groin filled, primed for a whole different sort of one-on-one. Not a good combination when in the company of a woman who'd asked for space.

But then, she was also a woman who'd sought him out—in his bedroom. Maybe she'd gotten her space and was done with it.

Her eyebrows drew together as she focused on his face. "What happened? You're bleeding."

"I ran into something." He shrugged as her gaze narrowed. "Another guy's fist. I went to Falco this afternoon."

Her expression didn't change. "Do you need antiseptic? A Band-Aid?"

He bit back a smile. "No self-respecting fighter walks around with a Band-Aid on his face. Thanks for the concern, but it doesn't hurt."

It didn't hurt because his body was still flying on a postmatch trip that ignored the pain of a cut. Instead, he was solely focused on the ache caused by Caitlyn's nearness. She was exactly what his queued-up body craved.

"Come in," he murmured thickly and held the door open wider.

She shook her head, eyes wide. "I don't think that's a good idea."

Oh, it was a very good idea. Obviously she thought so, too, or she wouldn't have knocked on his door. "Then, why *are* you here, Caitlyn?"

The question seemed to confuse her. She bit her lip and it drew his gaze to her mouth, causing him to imagine replacing her teeth with his.

She glanced away and cleared her throat. "I, uh, meant

to talk to you about something, but I didn't realize you'd be…undressed."

"Didn't you?" He cocked his head. "That's what generally happens behind closed doors. Here, let me demonstrate."

But when he reached for the towel, intending to drop it and see where it led, she squeezed her eyelids shut. "No, no! That's okay. I get the point. I shouldn't have come to your bedroom, not after you'd just come back from Falco. I didn't realize you'd gone there, but you didn't come down for dinner, and I was worried and you're hurt and…this was a mistake."

Caitlyn whirled as if about to flee. Again.

Antonio shot out his hand to grip her arm before she took a step. "Caitlyn. Stop running away."

He needed her in a raw, elemental way. In other, more emotional ways he couldn't fully grasp. He didn't think it was one-sided, and the longer this back-and-forth went on, the clearer it became that they needed to deal with it head-on.

Smoothly, he turned her around to face him, searching her gaze for clues to her constant caginess. Confusion and something else skated through her expression.

"Come inside," he pleaded again.

If only he could get her on this side of the threshold, he'd feel less as if he was losing a grip on his sanity. If only he could get her to understand he was desperate to explore things he didn't fully grasp, things only she could teach him because she was the only woman he wanted.

"I can't." Her eyes were huge and troubled and her gaze flicked to the wound near his eyebrow. "I'm…scared."

The admission pinged through him, drawing blood with its claws of condemnation. He dropped his hand from her arm, flexing his raw fist, which smarted from connecting with bone in Cutter's face. Antonio lived and breathed to inflict bodily harm on other human beings, and she saw that about him.

She'd needed space because the falcon inside him frightened her. It *should* scare her.

He'd forced her to watch him fight the other day, forced her to remain in his presence now with evidence of his brutal nature plain as day on his face. Practically forced her into his room so he could have his carnal way with her because of his own selfish desires.

But she didn't leave when he let go. She had every right to. She deserved someone gentle and kind.

"I won't hurt you," he said brusquely, and cleared his throat. He'd done nothing to assure her otherwise. "I hate that you think I might."

Her rounded gaze flew to his and the glint of moisture nearly undid him.

"I'm not scared of *you*," she corrected, but her voice cracked halfway through. "Never of you. I…"

She swallowed and he watched the delicate muscles of her beautiful throat work. If she wasn't scared of him, what was it? And why was it so difficult for her to articulate?

"Then, tell me," he commanded softly, and reached out to grasp her hand in his so he could draw her forward. Almost over the threshold. She didn't resist, but neither did she rush. "What's going on in your mind when I do this?"

Slowly, he took her hand and placed it flat on his chest, over his thundering heart. Her touch nearly drove him to the carpet, but he locked his knees, sensing that if he could keep his wits about him, paradise might be within their reach.

Mute, she stared at her splayed hand under his. Her fingertips curled slightly as if she wanted to grip harder but couldn't.

"It's like granite," she whispered. "That's what I think

about. So hard. But underneath lies something so amazing."

"What?"

"You. Antonio." His name fluttered from her throat on a half groan and the sound almost broke him open.

"You say that as if my name is poetry." It was just a simple name. But one he'd sought in the reaches of his messed-up mind for so long. Hearing it on her lips… It was an elemental thrill.

He was Antonio. And yet not. Because he couldn't fully remember all of the parts that created the whole.

"*All* of you is poetic," she murmured, and drew in a ragged breath. "The way you walk, the way you hold your children. How you move in the ring. I couldn't stop watching you and it was, um…nice."

"You liked watching me fight?" The idea was ludicrous. But her dreamy smile spoke volumes.

"I didn't think I would, but it was amazing." She sighed, a breathy sound that hardened him instantly. "Watching you execute those perfect moves, your body so fluid and in such harmony. It's like a perfect song lyric that when you hear it for the first time, it climbs inside your heart and lives there."

His own breath came more quickly as he stared at her with dawning comprehension. "You have feelings for me."

That was what he'd seen in her expression, what he couldn't quite grasp. It was a wondrous, blessed revelation. As obvious all at once as the sun bursting over the horizon to announce daytime. But he had no context for how he felt. And he wanted to.

Blinking slowly, she bit her lip again and nodded. "I've tried not to. But I can't help it."

A hundred questions rocketed through his mind, but he stuck with the most important.

"Then, why?" he asked hoarsely. "Why do you run away? Why are you so scared of what's happening?"

"I..." She glanced off and the moment of honesty, of her raw confession, started slipping away.

Desperate not to lose it, he cupped her face in both hands and brought it to his, a breath away. "What, Caitlyn? Tell me. Please. I'm losing my mind here. And I don't have much left to lose."

His wry joke earned him a watery smile.

"I'm scared of *me*," she whispered. "I want...things. Things I barely understand. It's like in all the fairy tales where they tell the girl not to touch the spindle or not to eat the apple. I never understood why they couldn't help themselves. Because I never understood what it meant to truly *desire* something. Or someone. Until you. I don't know what to do."

She wanted him. And that made all the difference.

"There's only one right answer to that."

He leaned into the space between them and laid his lips on hers for a scant second, kissing her with only a thousandth of the passion he wished he could unleash. But didn't because she wasn't fully inside the room.

Once she stepped over the threshold, all bets were off.

Pulling back with an iron will that could only be developed by years of ruthless training, he evaluated her. "Do you like kissing me?"

"Yes," she murmured. "More than I should."

"Then, come inside. Let me kiss you. Let me give you that experience you described. Let me be the man who touches you and loves you."

He wanted that—badly. Wanted to feel her skin next to his, to feel alive alongside her. To feel as if the things she spoke of were more than just words but concepts his soul recognized.

Her eyes closed and her lips pursed as if in invitation,

as if she yearned for him to kiss her again. But then her eyes blinked open and she swallowed. Hard.

"I need to tell you something else." Her gaze sought his and held. "I've never had a lover before."

Antonio's expression didn't waver, bless him. "You're a virgin?"

Caitlyn nodded. Her tongue was stuck to the roof of her mouth, glued there by nerves and who knew what else—three or four of the seven deadly sins, most likely.

"That explains a lot. I'm sorry you didn't trust me with that fact sooner. That's why you asked for space." His chiseled lips turned down. "I didn't give it to you."

Her heart fluttered. Antonio had the patience of Job.

"You did," she corrected hurriedly. "You've been perfect. I'm the problem. That's what I've been trying to tell you. I don't have any experience at…you know. And I'm nervous. You're this beautiful, wonderful man with all these expectations about being with me, probably because I've led you on, and I'm… Well, I'm not Vanessa, that's for sure—"

"Caitlyn." The quirk of his eyebrow rendered her speechless, as he'd probably intended. "Are you trying to tell me that you think I'll compare you unfavorably to Vanessa?"

"Uh…" Clearly, yes wasn't the right answer. But it was the only one she had. "She was so gorgeous, with a body men salivated over. She knew how to please a man in bed, too, which she liked to brag about. It's hard to imagine following that."

His quick smile knocked her off-kilter. Was it *that* funny?

"Isn't it ironic, then," he mused, "that I can't remember Vanessa?"

"At all?" He couldn't remember his wife, the one he'd

ended his career for, whose babies he'd wanted to have so badly, he'd agreed to surrogacy?

Her gaze flicked to the year-old scar disappearing into his hairline. What kind of whack to the head had he endured that his memories were that insubstantial? It must have been vicious.

"Some." His tone grew somber. "I see flashes of her red hair and remember bits and pieces, like her laugh. It's all jumbled in my head. Sometimes it's her face and sometimes her body. But I don't remember being in love with her. I feel so disconnected from her, as if she wasn't real. I don't remember feeling like you said I should, as if I want to be with her so badly I can't breathe."

The despondency in his voice caught in her chest and made it hurt. "I'm sorry, Antonio. I didn't realize you hadn't regained your memories of her. That must be very difficult."

"What's difficult is that I want to move on." His lashes lowered and he speared her with that dark, enigmatic glance that set her blood on low simmer. "I want to be in the here and now, not stuck dwelling on the past I can't remember. I've found someone new, someone I *do* want so badly I can't breathe. I want to love her and fulfill her and let her do the same to me. But I can't seem to get her into my arms."

"Me?" she whispered.

Heat climbed into her cheeks, on cue. *Duh.* Of course he meant her. But her brain wasn't working quite right. Too busy filtering through the divine idea that Antonio wanted to love her.

"Yes, you." His thumb feathered across her hot cheek. "I not only can't compare you to Vanessa, I don't want to. I want what's possible now, for as long as we have together. I want to learn about the kind of love that you talked about. Teach me."

"How can I teach you anything? I'm not the one with experience."

His gorgeous lips turned upward into a killer smile. "I'm not the one with any experience I can remember. In a way, this will be the first time for both of us."

For some reason, that appealed to her. Immensely.

He didn't remember Vanessa and wanted to learn everything about love, sex, relationships over again. It was like the slate being wiped clean—Caitlyn could make this experience anything and everything she could imagine, be as wicked in his arms as she wished and wrap it up in a beautiful emotional connection that could last an eternity.

He'd come back from the dead a different person, and she'd often dwelt on the darker changes. It had never occurred to her that amnesia would be a positive in this one case.

Except he'd been born with a body designed for pleasure, and just as he'd not forgotten how to breathe, he likely hadn't lost any knowledge of how to make a woman quiver with desire. She couldn't do the same to him, no way.

"Are you sure this is what you want? With me? I mean, you might not precisely remember Vanessa, but you have to recall other women." *Shut up.* Nobody brought up former lovers on the brink of becoming the next one. She sighed. "See. I'm a big mess. That's so not attractive, I realize."

He glanced down at the two feet of space between them. "We've been standing in this doorway for ten minutes now, and for nine minutes and fifty-five seconds of it, I've been in danger of losing this towel due to the serious arousal you've caused me. Stop worrying so much about things that don't matter. Don't deny us any longer, Caitlyn."

He stepped aside, opening the doorway for her to enter if she chose.

This was it. Her opportunity to grab what she'd longed for. To put her guilt to rest and finally become a full-fledged, sexually realized woman at the hands of a master. A man who was probably the great love of her life, the only one she might ever love.

And his pretty speech about learning how to love at *her* hands surely meant he was open and willing to returning her feelings. He'd loved Vanessa, had married her and obviously yearned to have that sort of connection again. The sort of connection Caitlyn had dreamed of.

It was all within her reach.

Yet she hesitated, long enough for his eyebrows to rise.

What would happen if she stepped over the threshold, signaling to Antonio that she was ready to embark on a romantic relationship, and if it didn't work out? How would she co-parent their children with a broken heart? The past few years had been difficult enough when she'd revered him from afar. How much harder would it be to actually love and be loved by a man like Antonio, only to lose him because she wasn't the kind of woman who could handle him?

And what if he cut her out of her children's lives in retribution?

This was why she never got very far in a relationship with any man, including Antonio when she'd first met him. She was terrified of what came *after* she opened herself body and soul to someone.

As she let her gaze rest on his bare torso, on that glorious inked falcon, she wanted to let him melt her resistance.

Because it would be impossible to walk away.

She took a breath to calm her racing heart, which didn't work, and walked into Antonio's bedroom.

Nine

The door clicked shut behind her and Caitlyn froze.

She was inside a man's bedroom. She wouldn't leave it a virgin. She'd been saving herself for the right man, a man she was ready, willing and eager to love forever, and here he was…but this wasn't the safe fantasy she'd harbored for years. Was she *really* ready for this?

Oh, my. Antonio was going to see her naked, with her C-section scars and ridiculously shaped breasts that had served as a milk source for three hungry mouths for months.

Nearing full-blown panic, she tried to suck in a deep, calming breath. And choked on it as she thought back to getting dressed this morning. What underwear had she put on?

"Caitlyn."

She whirled. Antonio leaned against the door, arms crossed over his cut torso, towel dipping dangerously low. Her mouth went sticky and she averted her gaze. Then shifted her gaze back because, dang it, *surely* it was okay to look at him if they were about to make love. Maybe it was even expected. Part of foreplay.

"Do you want a glass of wine?" he asked casually.

"To drink?" When he laughed, she thought about punching him but would probably only hurt her hand. Mortified, she scowled. "I didn't know what you meant! Maybe it's some kind of sex thing, like you want me to pour it on you and lick it off."

His eyebrows rose and he treated her to a thoroughly wicked once-over. "Would you? Lick it off?"

The image of her tongue swirling over the ink on his chest popped into her mind and she couldn't shake it. As she imagined the taste of his golden skin melded with fruity red wine, her insides contracted. "Maybe. *Was* it a sex thing?"

He shrugged, a smile still playing about his expressive mouth. "As much as I want you right now, it could be. Seems a little messy, though. Let's save that for another time."

"How many times do you envision there being?"

"A thousand." His expression darkened carnally as if he was imagining each time individually and it was hot. "The things I want to do to you, to experience with you, might very well take a lifetime."

She couldn't blink, couldn't look away. Couldn't quite believe the sincerity ringing from his voice. She rubbed at the ache in her chest as she internalized that she'd heard precisely what he'd meant for her to hear. "A lifetime?"

Of course, it was what she'd yearned for. But it was another thing entirely to hear it from Antonio's mouth.

He tilted his head quizzically. "You aren't the kind of person who sleeps around indiscriminately. Neither am I. I want to be with you from now on. Awake, asleep. In bed, out of bed. Which part is confusing you?"

"All of it. Starting with 'hi' when I first knocked on the door," she muttered.

"So that wasn't a good subject, obviously. Here's what we're going to do instead," he said decisively, because of course he could read her like a book. "We're going to have a glass of wine. Then we're going to take this as slowly as you want to."

"Why?" Could she have sounded more suspicious? He was saying all the right things and she was botching this.

"The wine is to relax you," he explained, not seeming at all bothered by her lack of decorum. "Actually, both parts are to relax you. And both parts get me where I want to be. Inside you. Anticipation will make it sweeter, so I'm quite happy with the idea of taking my time. I've got a whole night and I'm not afraid to use it."

Dumbfounded, she let him lead her to his sitting area overlooking the coastline and sank onto the love seat he pointed to. Apparently, Antonio was botchproof. Good thing. She'd probably do ten more things to increase her mortification level before the night was through.

He selected a bottle of red wine from the rack on the wet bar and pulled the cork. Since his back was to her, she watched his bare torso unashamedly. Too quickly, he returned with two glasses full of deep red wine, handed her one and settled in next to her on the love seat. Clad in a towel.

It should be weird. He was completely naked underneath the terry cloth, which gaped at his thigh, revealing the muscular stretch of leg that led to his...good parts.

He glanced at her and then followed her line of vision. "Curious?"

Yes, wine was a fantastic idea. The alcohol needed to be swimming through her bloodstream, not sitting in a glass untouched. She gulped as much as she could get down, for fortification.

Because, oh, yes, she was curious. Burning with it.

"I've never seen a naked man before," she croaked.

Not enough wine, obviously, if she was still going to utter gems like that.

"Not even in pictures?"

She shook her head. "I'm a novice. I tried to tell you."

Antonio set down his glass on the side table with a hard click and then took her free hand in his. "Listen to me, because I don't want there to be any confusion about this."

Heart hammering in her throat, she stared at him as something tender sprang into his gaze.

"It means everything to me that no other man has ever touched you. That I get to be the first. It's an honor and I intend to treat it as such. You should never feel as if you have to apologize for this gift you're giving me."

"I…um." What did you say that *that*? "Okay."

That must have been the magic word. His thumb brushed over her knuckles and he let go of her hand to run his fingertips over the back of her wrist.

And kept going up her bare arm, watching her with that dark intensity as he touched her. Without a word, he took the glass from her suddenly nerveless fingers and set it next to his. A breath later, his mouth descended and took hers in a slow, deliberate kiss that melted her bones.

His sweet lips… They molded hers, explored. Slowly, as promised.

"Wait," he murmured, and his heat left her as he rose to click off the lights. Moonlight poured in from outside the glass, illuminating the love seat and throwing the rest of the room into shadow.

Antonio returned with the comforter from his bed and a couple of small squares that she eyed curiously until she realized what they were. Condoms. This had just turned real and her throat closed.

He spread the comforter in front of the floor-to-ceiling

window and stretched out on it, beckoning her to join him. "Just to set the mood."

But the sight of Antonio bathed in the glow from the moon froze her completely. He was beautiful, mystical. Too perfect to be real. She just wanted to soak him in, to gorge herself on his splendor.

He seemed to sense her thoughts and lay still, allowing her to gaze at him as much as she wanted. The scar marking the location of his once-broken leg forked up his calf, as seductively savage as the rest of him.

After an eternity, he reached for his towel and held it in both hands, poised to take it off. "Do you want to see all of me?"

Too numb to speak, she nodded, but before she could properly school her expression or her thoughts or her... anything, the towel fell away and... *Oh, my*. He was utterly divine in all his glory, hard everywhere, with a jutting erection she'd felt when he'd kissed her in the gym, but never in a million years would she have thought it would look like *that*.

She couldn't stop drinking him in. And he didn't seem to be in a hurry to stop her.

"By the way," he murmured, "you know you're going to do this for me in a minute, right?"

"Do what?" Then she clued in. "You mean lie in front of the window naked so you can stare at me?"

A wolfish smile bloomed on his face. "Let me know when you're ready."

"I don't think I'll ever be ready for that," she muttered.

He flipped onto his hands and knees and crawled to her, kneeling between her legs. "Then, I'll have to fix that. Because I want to see you in the moonlight. I want to watch your face as I make love to you. And you will most definitely need to be naked for that."

With exquisite care, he cupped her face with both hands and brought her lips to his.

This kiss was nothing like the one a minute ago, when there'd still been a towel and some modesty between them. There was nothing but Antonio between her legs, and when his mouth claimed hers in a scorching kiss, he palmed the small of her back and shoved her to the edge of the couch, almost flush with his body. Close, so close, and she arched involuntarily, seeking his heat.

His tongue plunged toward hers, possessing her with his taste, with his intoxicating desire. Moaning, she slid her arms around his strong torso, reveling in the feel of his sleek, heated skin under her palms. A small movement forward, just the slightest tilt of her hips, and his erection would brush her center.

And she ached for that contact. Desire emboldened her and she strained for it.

When it came, she gasped. He must have sensed her instant need for more because he pressed harder, rubbing in small circles. Heat exploded at her core and her head tipped back in shock.

He followed the line of her throat with his luscious lips, laving the tender skin expertly until he got a mouthful of her blouse. She nearly wept as his mouth lifted.

"I'm going to take this off," he murmured and fingered the first button for emphasis. "Okay?"

She nodded, appreciative that he respected her nerves enough to ask. Plus, she was very interested in getting his magic mouth back on her skin. "Seems fair. You're not wearing a shirt."

His warm chuckle had a hint of wicked that shuddered through her. Now, *that* was delightful.

"I'm not wearing anything. If you want to talk about fair…"

"You know what, you're right."

This imbalance *wasn't* fair. She stood quickly without thought of his proximity, and it was a testament to his superior balance that she didn't bowl him over.

He sat back on his muscular haunches, completely at ease in his own skin. She wanted to be that confident. To feel as if she belonged here, able to handle a man as virile and gorgeous as Antonio. There was only one way. She had to get over this virgin hump and take this night—her destiny, her *pleasure*—into her own hands. It wasn't Antonio's job to lead her through this.

He desired her. It was in his expression, in his words. In the hard flesh at his center. What purpose did it serve to protect her maidenly modesty? None.

She wanted him to take her in the basest sense. *Now.* And she wanted it to be hot. Sinful. Explosive. He could make that happen, she had no doubt. But he was holding back. She could feel it.

"I'm ready," she announced, and though her hands shook, she slipped the first button on her blouse from its mooring.

His eyelids lowered a touch as he watched her move on to the next button. "Ready?"

Third button. Fourth. "For you to see me. In the moonlight."

Heat flared in his expression and he hummed his approval. The sexy sound empowered her. Last button.

She slipped the blouse from her frame, gaze glued to his, and let it float from her fingers. That wasn't so bad. The clasp on her bra was a little harder to undo even though it was in front, and she couldn't even blame that on being a novice; she'd definitely taken her bra off a million times in her life, but never in front of a man, and this was it—the first time a man would see her bare breasts—and suddenly, the clasp came apart in her hands.

Well, that was the point, wasn't it?

Nothing left to do but shed the hideous nursing bra. In retrospect, stripping out of it probably increased her sexiness quotient. She dropped it on the ground near her blouse and fought the urge to cover herself when Antonio's heavy-lidded gaze swept her with clear appreciation.

"You might want to hurry," he muttered, hands clenched on his thighs as he looked up at her from his prone position. "I'm about to lose my mind."

"Really?" That sounded…lovely. "Am I making you crazy?"

The thought pleased her. Imagine. Caitlyn Hopewell was driving a man insane with a slow striptease. It practically made her giddy.

He groaned. "Completely. You're killing me. If you had any idea how much I want to—" He shook his head, teeth gritted. "Never mind. You take this at your pace. I'll be the one over here practicing my patience."

"No. Tell me. What do you want to do?" She fingered the clasp on her jeans, toying with it the way she imagined a more experienced woman might do. "I might let you."

"Oh, yeah?" he growled. "Lose those pants and let's rumble, my darling."

The endearment rolled through her and left a whole lot of heat and pleasure in its wake. "I like it when you talk to me like that."

"You do, huh?" Amusement curled his lips upward. "Not well enough, since you're still dressed."

"Well, you still haven't told me what you want to do." The curiosity was killing her. So she shoved off her pants, careful to take her nonsexy underwear along for the ride, and kicked them both away.

She couldn't get more naked. With the moon as the only source of light, her flaws weren't as noticeable and the lines of her postpregnancy body smoothed out. And that was when it dawned on her—that had been the whole purpose of lights-out. Was there nothing that the man missed?

Antonio worshipped her with his gaze and she let him, keeping her arms by her sides. The way he looked at her made her feel beautiful. As though she had nothing to hide.

"Now then. Tell me," she commanded, proud that her voice didn't waver. "What sorts of wicked activities do you have in store? Because I've waited a lifetime to be thoroughly ravished and I'm a little anxious to get started."

Groaning, Antonio tried to keep his faculties about him as he surveyed the very tempting woman on display before him wearing nothing but moonlight and a smile.

Blood and adrenaline pounded through his veins. He'd kept a very tight hold on his body since he'd opened the bedroom door. Caitlyn had just pushed him to the brink with a unique mix of innocence and friskiness that belied her lack of experience.

He hadn't expected it to be such a turn-on.

Or for her to systematically break down his resistance until he held on to his self-control by the barest edge. He wanted her more fiercely than he'd ever wanted anything—including his memories. His muscles strained to pounce. To possess. To claim. To relentlessly drive her to the threshold of madness the way she'd driven him.

But he couldn't because Caitlyn deserved something special for her first time. She deserved someone gentle. Restrained. Refined.

She had to make do with Antonio Cavallari instead.

"I…" He nearly swallowed his tongue as Caitlyn sauntered toward him, invitation in her eyes that he couldn't misread even in the pale light. "My intentions are to make love to you. There's nothing wicked about that."

The hard floor beneath the comforter ground into his knees, but he couldn't have moved if his life depended on it. He should have prepared better for this, changed out the furniture. Caitlyn's first experience with sex should happen in a bed, but he refused to make love to her in the same place he'd been with another woman. Whether he could remember it or not. It was a matter of principle.

"Why not? What if I want wicked?" she murmured and halted directly in front of him, then folded her legs under her to mirror his pose. Knee to knee. She pierced him with a gaze far too knowing for a woman of her innocence. "Listen to me so there's no confusion about this, Antonio. I watched you in the ring and it was brutal. But it was beautiful at the same time. Like you. It was an unsettling, thrilling experience. There's probably something wrong with me that I like the primal part of you. But I don't care."

Without hesitation, she traced the falcon tearing across his flesh, watching him as she touched him, and he sucked in a breath as his skin pulsed under her fingers.

"I want Falco," she said simply. "And Antonio. I'll only have one first time. Make it memorable. Give me all of it and don't hold back."

His iron will dissolved under the onslaught of her sensuous plea. With equal parts desperation and need, he hauled her into his arms and fell into her, into the innocence that called to him. Not to destroy, but to absorb. She was perfectly whole and exquisite and the shattered pieces of his soul cried out for her.

Hungrily, he kissed her, twining her body with his so he could feel her. His skin screamed for more of the sweet friction against hers. He palmed her heavy breasts, which filled his hands and then some. They were gorgeous, full, with huge nipples that his mouth strained to taste.

Unable to wait, he sucked one between his lips. She gasped and her back arched instantly. *Yes.* Amazingly responsive, as he'd fantasized. He moved to the other breast, and the sensation of his tongue curling around her hard nipple had him pulsing with need.

The groan ripped from his throat and he murmured her name as he eased her back against the comforter. Moonlight played with her features as she lay there, exactly as he'd envisioned, and it was almost too much to take in. The mother of his children. His savior. Soon to be lover.

He needed her. Needed to be inside her, with her, loving her. But first things first. He bent one of her legs back and knelt to swirl his tongue at her center.

She froze and made mewling sounds in her throat.

"Shh, my darling," he murmured and kissed her inner thigh. "You asked for wicked." He kissed the other and opened her legs farther. "Close your eyes and imagine me in the ring. What about it excited you?"

"You were so graceful," she murmured. "Like an apparition. But so very real and raw. It made me hot. All over."

"Like this?"

Slowly, he touched her again with the tip of his tongue. She shuddered but didn't tense up this time. He went a little farther, lapping a little harder. Her hips rolled and she sighed in pleasure.

"That's right, sweetheart. Lie still, think about me and let me taste you." He cupped her hips and tilted her up to his lips to feast.

She thrashed under his onslaught, but since her shudders brought her center closer and closer each time, he took full advantage of it instead of scolding her for doing the opposite of lying still. Honey gathered under his tongue a moment before she cried out.

Her climax went on and on and his own body throbbed in response, aching for a release in kind inside this woman.

Shaking with the effort, he managed to roll on a condom without breaking it—a minor miracle, given that he couldn't precisely remember the technique—and stretched out next to her to take her into his arms.

"Ready?" he asked hoarsely, shocked he could speak at all.

"There's more?" Since the question was laced with wry humor, he hoped that meant she was kidding.

"Oh, yes, there's more," he said fiercely. "I'm dying to show you."

She feathered a thumb across his lips, sparking sensation to the point of pain. "Show me, Antonio."

More roughly than he'd intended, he nudged a knee between her thighs and rolled, poised to thrust with all his pent-up energy. But he held back at the last second, somehow, and kissed her with every ounce of that longing instead. When she responded with a throaty moan that he felt in his groin, he couldn't wait. He pushed as slowly as he could into her center.

She wasn't on board with slow.

Her hips rose up to meet him, accepting him, encouraging him, and with a groan, he sheathed himself completely. Then forced his muscles to pause, though every fiber of his being screamed to let loose, to drive them both to completion with frenzied coupling.

He sought her gaze. "Tell me it's okay."

She nodded and let out a breath, her eyes shining as she peered up at him, hair a dark mass around her ethereal face. *She* was the apparition, a heavenly body trapped on this plane, and he'd been lucky enough to find her.

"It doesn't feel like I would have thought," she commented.

That made two of them.

Emotion he couldn't name wrenched at his heart, threatening to pull it from his chest. *Love.* He wanted it to be love, to know that he could feel such things and wasn't irreparably damaged.

But the sense he had of his previous experiences didn't match this. Not even close. This was so much bigger, so overwhelming. What if he *was* damaged? What if his memories never returned? How would he know if he was loving Caitlyn the way she deserved?

"You feel amazing," she murmured. Experimentally, she wiggled her hips. "What does it feel like to you?"

Her innocent movements set off a riptide of heat. "Let's compare notes later."

Settling her firmly under him, he began to move, rendering them both speechless. She arched against him, nails biting into his shoulders, those perfect, full breasts peaked against his torso.

Thrust for thrust, she met him, never retreating, never yielding. *More. Faster.* His body took from hers and she gave endlessly. Palming her rear, he changed the angle. Reversed the dynamic so he was doing the giving. Spiraling her higher into the heavens where she'd already taken him.

He needed to discharge, to explode. But he couldn't… not yet. He tasted blood on his lip where he'd bitten down with the effort to hold back. Animalistic sounds growled from his throat as he bent one of her legs back to go deeper still.

Exquisite pleasure rolled over him, and he needed more. Relentlessly, he rolled his hips to meet hers, and when she tightened around him with a small moan, he lost control.

Groaning as he spilled his release, he collapsed to the side, rolling her with him as he lost all feeling in his extremities.

In the aftermath, they lay together, and he gently spooned her into his body to hold her tightly. She snuggled in willingly with a small sigh of contentment.

He let her essence bleed through him as he lay with his eyes shut, absorbing her. If he never had to move from this spot, it would be too soon.

An instant later, he cursed his own selfishness. "Can I get you anything?"

What did you give a woman who had just offered up her virginity? Diamond earrings? A washcloth? She was likely bruised and raw. It wasn't as if he'd been gentle, not the way he'd pretended he was going to be.

"I'm fine, thanks. Don't you dare move." She wiggled closer to him. "Your body heat feels good against my sore muscles."

"I should have gone slower." Remorse crashed through his breastbone. He'd taken her innocence like the brute that he was. "I'm sorry I hurt you."

"Don't you dare apologize. Some of it hurt, but in a good way. It was amazing. Perfect. Beautiful. Everything I've ever dreamed of." Threading her fingers through his, she raised his hand to her lips. "Thank you for that."

Emotion clogged his throat and he swallowed against it, fighting to keep himself level.

The things she made him feel… He wished he could understand them. Could draw on his past to make sense of the swirl in his belly when he looked at her. But he couldn't.

All he knew was that Caitlyn was a miracle. Everything he'd prayed to find when he'd set off from Indonesia in search of his life.

He stroked her side and with moonlight spilling over them both, he murmured the million-dollar question. "Why me? Of all the men in the world you could have chosen for your first experience."

"I always wanted it to be you," she said slowly. "Well, not *always*. Vanessa was…rather free with her affections, even back in high school. I didn't like how broken up she always was after, and I vowed to save myself for the right man. The first moment I met you, I had this strange shock of recognition, like *there you are*."

His hand stilled. "The first moment? You mean the pink-shirt meeting?"

She nodded and her hair brushed his chin. "After that, no other man could compare. I've had a crush on you for a long time."

"Even while I was married?" It should have seemed wrong, but it thrilled him for some reason. Caitlyn had been saving herself for *him*, even through his marriage to someone else. It spoke to her constancy and devotion, and it humbled him.

"I didn't say I was a saint. I had a lot of mixed feelings about it. You know, I cried for almost two days straight when they came to tell me the plane had crashed. I thought I'd lost you forever," she whispered brokenly.

In the long pause, he gathered her in his arms and held her as close as physically possible as his heart thumped in tandem with hers.

While he'd been lost and alone, Caitlyn had been here in his house, mourning him. He'd thought no one cared. But she had. She still did.

It was a far better gift than her virginity.

Ten

The next morning, Caitlyn awoke at dawn, stiff and sore from a night sleeping on the floor entwined with Antonio. And every inch of her body felt glorious.

Antonio had kissed her soundly before sending her off to her own room, presumably to keep the rest of the household in the dark about the new relationship that had bloomed between them. She showered under the hottest stream of water she could stand, letting the water ease her aches. Her thoughts never strayed far from the sexy man down the hall.

He might even be in his own shower, naked, with water sluicing down his gorgeous body. Feeling a little scandalous, she allowed the image to play through her mind... because she could. She knew what every inch of that man's flesh looked like, thank you very much.

She'd slept with Antonio. Her sister's husband, whom she had always coveted. There was probably a special place in hell for a woman who did that. And she hated to admit that she'd loved every second of it.

When she emerged, steam had obscured the mirror. She wiped it with a towel and stared at herself in the glass. Odd. She didn't look any different than she had yesterday morning, and it was a bit of a shock to see her same face reflected back at her.

By all rights, there should be *some* external mark to account for the rite of passage she'd undertaken. What, she couldn't say. But a man had loved her thoroughly last night. He'd filled her body with his, tasted her intimately, brought her to a shuddering climax. Twice. It was an earth-shaking event worthy of distinction. Maybe she should get a tattoo to commemorate the experience.

A dove on her breast, maybe.

Silly. She was already picking out matching tattoos after sleeping with a man one night.

But it had been so incredible. Now she totally got why he'd said he planned to do it a thousand more times. Once could never be enough.

She'd just pretend he'd never been married to Vanessa. Block it out and never think about it. Vanessa was gone, and Caitlyn and Antonio deserved to move on. Together. It wasn't a crime.

At breakfast, the babies played with their bananas and Cheerios as always, Brigitte chattered up a storm as she did every morning and Caitlyn sat in her usual spot at the table. But the secret looks Antonio shot her gave everything a rosy, sensual glow, and she was very much afraid she was grinning at him like a besotted fool.

Perhaps she should be more covert if the goal was to keep their relationship on the down low.

"Caitlyn and I are going shopping today," Antonio announced out of the blue when everyone finished eating.

"We are?" Did they have some Christmas presents to

buy that she'd forgotten about? "It's two days until Christmas. The stores will be insane."

"I believe I have adequately demonstrated my ability to dispense with holiday crowds," he countered with a smirk.

"So that's your solution to everything now? Just buy out the whole store?"

"When I find something that works, I stick with it. You might consider thanking me for that." His dark gaze flickered with promise, and yesterday, such innuendo might have made her blush, but she was a worldly woman now. So she stuck her tongue out at him instead.

Brigitte watched all of this with unabashed fascination, probably interpreting the exchange in the wrong way. "Well. You two have *fun*."

Or the right way, depending on how you looked at it.

Antonio herded her into the Range Rover, and she dutifully drove, navigating through the paparazzi outside the gate. She wasn't used to all of this. The cameras had camped out there ever since the first time Antonio had gone to Falco.

As always, Antonio ignored them. Oh, his lawyer and Thomas Warren had fielded a ton of questions on Antonio's behalf, but he wasn't in a hurry to take that part of his life back. He liked his privacy, which suited Caitlyn fine.

Once they were clear of the knot of people and vans, she asked, "What are we shopping for?"

"Bedroom furniture."

She glanced at him askance and flicked her gaze back to the road immediately. "Because there's something wrong with the furniture you already have?"

"Yes. It's Vanessa's," he explained quietly, oblivious of the sword he'd just stuck through her abdomen. "Every stick of furniture in that room will be gone by the time we return. I already arranged it. Help me pick out something new."

Oh. So that was why they'd slept on the floor. He didn't

want to sleep with Caitlyn in the bed he'd shared with his wife. He'd probably considered it the height of betrayal.

Her throat burned with sudden unshed tears. "That's…"

There were no words to explain the hard twist of her heart. Vanessa had been his wife first, and there was nothing she could do to change that. After all, Antonio hadn't chosen her when he'd had the opportunity. Caitlyn was the backup sister.

And Antonio had done something unbelievably considerate in removing the remnants of his first marriage. He'd told her last night that he wanted to move on. She couldn't blame him for choices he'd made either before the crash or after.

He deserved a fresh start after the horrors he'd endured. If he wanted new bedroom furniture because the old pieces had belonged to his first wife, she'd help him redecorate once a week until he was happy. And keep her mouth shut about how hard it was on her to constantly recall that she was living her sister's life by default.

A clerk approached them the moment they stepped into the hushed store. Expensive plank flooring and discreet lighting lent to the moneyed atmosphere, and the high-end pieces on display even smelled expensive. It would be a Christmas miracle if Antonio walked out of here with a full bedroom set for less than fifty thousand dollars.

"What are you looking for today?" the salesclerk asked politely. "A new sofa to accommodate extra party guests, perhaps?"

"We're in need of new bedroom furniture," Antonio said as Caitlyn did a double take.

What was this "we" stuff?

"Absolutely, sir." The clerk eyed them both. "Can you give me an idea what style you might be looking for? Art deco, maybe? American heritage or contemporary?"

"Caitlyn, did you have a particular style in mind?" Antonio asked, and put a palm to the small of her back as if she had every right to be included in the decision. As if they were a couple shopping for furniture together.

"I, um…don't know what you'd like," she admitted, which seemed ridiculous to say when she'd not only studied him surreptitiously for years, she'd also just had sex with him. Shouldn't she know what he liked?

"I'd like something that puts a smile on your face." The look he gave her curled her toes and rendered her speechless. To the clerk, he nodded and said, "Show her everything and make sure she's given the opportunity to pick colors and such. I assume you do custom orders."

Dollar signs sprang into the clerk's eyes. "Of course. Down to the throw pillows. Please call me Judy. And you are?"

"This is Ms. Hopewell," Antonio said smoothly. "And she's the star of this show. She doesn't walk out of here without an entire bedroom set. When she's finished picking what she wants, you let me know and I'll pay for it."

"Excuse us a moment." Caitlyn pulled Antonio to the side. "What are you doing?" she whispered hotly. "I can't pick out your bedroom furniture. It's too…"

Intimate. Fast. Expensive.

"I want you to," he insisted. "After all, you're going to be using it."

She shut her eyes for a moment as she envisioned exactly what he meant by that. "But it's not going to be *mine*. I have a bedroom."

"Not anymore." Antonio's eyebrows drew together as her eyes widened. "I'm messing this up, aren't I? I should have talked to you about this at home. I want you to move into my bedroom. Permanently."

Warmth spread through her abdomen. The staff would know instantly that they were together, so maybe he *didn't* intend for their relationship to be a secret.

But what *was* their relationship? She knew he was the committed sort—it wasn't a surprise that he wanted something permanent. But it would be nice to have specifics. She'd never done this before. Was this his subtle way of asking her to be his girlfriend? Or was this the precursor to a marriage proposal?

Yes. Yes. Yes. No matter what he was asking, the answer was yes.

This definitely wasn't the time nor the place to hash this out, but she couldn't be upset. He wanted her to be a part of his life. Permanently. There was no possible way to misinterpret *that*. Who cared what label they slapped on it? Her heart flipped over and back again, unable to find the right spot in her chest now that everything she'd ever dreamed for herself had fallen in her lap.

He took her hand and squeezed it. "Help me make it a place we can be together without shadows of the past."

Her unsettled heart climbed into her throat as the sentiment crashed through her happiness. If only new furniture could actually achieve that.

She could never be rid of Vanessa's shadow. She was living her sister's life, the one Vanessa couldn't live because she'd died. A life Caitlyn never should have had, despite desperately wanting it. The enormous burden of guilt settled over her anew.

And the worst part was, she couldn't even tell Antonio how she felt, because he definitely didn't need an extra layer of guilt. He couldn't even *remember* Vanessa and it weighed on him.

This was going to go down far worse than the toy store. Picking out a forty-dollar toy for their children didn't carry a million heavy implications the way picking out furniture did.

"Please." Antonio's plea slid through her. "I need to feel as if I'm not still adrift and alone. I need you."

She shut her eyes and let Antonio bleed through her. This wasn't just about furniture. *Nothing* in their interaction was surface level. Or simple. Regardless, there was no point in acting as if there was a choice here. She lacked the strength—or the desire—to deny him anything.

"Okay." She blew out a breath and turned back to the expectant clerk. "I'm ready."

Panic ruffled her nerves. This was so far out of her realm of experience. She was shopping for furniture with a man. With Antonio.

But he was holding her hand and smiling at her as though she'd just given him the world's best Christmas present. She couldn't let her guilt or the circumstances ruin this. She couldn't let him down.

"Right this way." Judy escorted her to the left, already chattering about fabric and colors and who knew what.

At the end of the day, she'd be sleeping in Antonio's bed. Honestly, who cared what the furniture looked like when her full attention would be firmly fixed on the amazing, sensitive man lying on the next pillow?

As dawn broke through the glass wall overlooking the pounding Malibu surf, Caitlyn curled around Antonio's slumbering form and watched him breathe. The way she'd done yesterday morning. Because it could never be enough. He didn't get any less beautiful, and it was her God-given right to gawk at the man she was sleeping with, wasn't it?

His sooty lashes rested above his cheekbones and his lips pursed as if he was dreaming about kissing her. Funny, that was exactly what she'd dreamed about, too.

So she indulged them both and kissed him awake. "Merry Christmas."

His dark eyes blinked open and he smiled sleepily. "Is it already the twenty-fifth? I lost track."

"We've been busy."

Once she'd gotten over herself, the redecoration effort had consumed them both as they'd laughed and argued good-naturedly over the style and placement of the purchases. Then Antonio had gotten started on artwork, perusing gallery upon gallery until he'd found precisely what he wanted.

Late last night, they'd tossed the final teal pillow onto the couch in the sitting area and declared it done. The finished product looked nothing like the former space. Vanessa's taste had run to heavy and ornate baroque. Caitlyn had selected more simple lines and colors: a four-poster bed with simple square posts. A compact dresser in espresso-colored wood with silver pulls. Teal and dark brown accents.

It had been a magical, breathless few days. But as she'd suspected, Antonio was the best thing in the room. Every day was Christmas, as far as she was concerned.

Antonio rolled onto his side and pulled her into his arms. "Then, Merry Christmas to you, too."

She snuggled into his warm body. "We don't have to get up right away, do we?"

"Not for years and years. The kids won't know about Santa until they're, like, three or four, right?"

She loved it when he talked like that, as if they were a family who would be together forever, come what may. He hadn't mentioned the word *marriage*. But she hoped that was where they were headed.

"Ha. We'll be lucky if they aren't up at 5:00 a.m. next year, pounding down the stairs on their little toddler feet to see what Santa brought."

With a gleam in his eye that was impossible to misread, he winked. "Then, we better make good use of our one bye year."

So slowly she thought she might weep, he took her lips

in a long kiss that set off a freight train of heat through her blood.

It was so much more powerful to know what this kind of kiss led to as she fell into the sensual pleasure of his lips thoroughly claiming hers. His tongue was hot and rough and she reveled in the shock of it invading her mouth. Thrilled in it. Because while it mated with hers, it was so unbelievably arousing to recall that he'd also tasted her intimately with that same tongue.

His thigh slid between her legs, insistent and tight against her core. She moaned and arched into the pleasure as sparks exploded under his ministrations. Silently, she urged him on, riding his muscular thigh with small rolls of her hips. She needed…more. But she didn't have to tell him because he seemed to know instinctively what she wanted, as if he could read her mind.

He replaced his thigh with one strong hand and instantly, he found her sensitive bud, rolling it between his fingers as if he'd been born to touch her exactly in this way.

She gasped and her eyelids fluttered shut as waves of heat broke over her skin like the surf on the shore below their window. The man must have a deal with the devil. How else could he be so beautifully built, so incredibly successful at both of his chosen professions *and* be so *good* at making her feel like this?

Murmuring flowery Italian phrases like a prayer against her lips, he touched her intimately and pleasured her until she feared her skin would incinerate and leave her in ashes. Then he trailed his lips down her throat and set that magic mouth on one of her incredibly sensitive breasts. As soon as he curled his hard tongue around a nipple, she detonated like the Fourth of July.

The climax overwhelmed her, tensing her muscles and sending shooting stars across her vision.

"Antonio," she whispered. Or screamed. Hard to tell

when her entire body sang his name so loudly, it deafened her.

"Yes, my darling. I'm here." He rolled her to her back and covered her with his unbelievable body, resting his weight on his forearms so he wouldn't crush her.

But it was far too late to prevent that. As he positioned himself to slide into her, joy burst open inside her chest and streamed through her entire body. Oh, she'd been crushed, all right.

Crushed by the overwhelming sensations of being completely, fully in love. That desperation of wanting him from afar—that wasn't love. That was infatuation, and there was no comparison.

Antonio filled her to the hilt, and she rocked her hips to draw him deeper still, a technique she'd discovered by accident last night. And judging by his answering groan, he approved of it just as much this morning as he had last night.

She shut her eyes and savored the fullness of him as he shifted to hit her sweet spot. A sigh escaped her lips. Perfection. Was it always like this, like being touched physically and spiritually at the same time? Or did she and Antonio have a bond other people never experienced?

It was an academic question because she'd never know. This was the only man she'd ever love. The only man she'd ever be intimate with. She trusted him fully, knew he'd be there for her, steadfast and strong. Waiting for him had been worth it. She couldn't imagine being with anyone else like this, opening her body and her heart to another person in this beautiful expression of their love.

His thrusts grew more insistent, more urgent, and she bowed to meet him, taking pleasure, giving it until they came together one final time in a shuddery dual climax that left her boneless and replete.

They lay in each other's arms, silent but in perfect harmony until her muscles regained enough strength for her to move. But she didn't go very far. She pillowed her head on his shoulder and thanked whatever fates had seen fit to grant her this second chance to be with Antonio.

As he'd done yesterday morning, Antonio flipped on the wall-mounted flat-screen TV to watch the news. Habitual, he'd told her when she asked, since returning from Indonesia—to break the silence.

"You don't need that noise anymore," she said and grabbed the remote with every intention of powering it off again.

But in the split second before she hit the button, the news anchor mentioned Antonio's name.

"What are they saying?" He sat up against the headboard and focused his attention on the newscast.

"...the identity of the anonymous donor who had the entire inventory of a toy store delivered to Toys for Tots." The blonde on the screen smiled as a photo of Antonio appeared next to her head. "It will be a merry Christmas indeed for thousands of local children who have this secret Santa to thank. Antonio Cavallari made headlines recently by returning to LA after being presumed dead in a plane crash over a year ago—"

"They shouldn't have tracked down who donated those toys." Antonio frowned. "It was anonymous for a reason."

The newshounds had finally scented Antonio's story due to his generous gesture, which, as he pointed out, should have remained anonymous. He could have paraded around naked in front of Falco and generated less interest apparently, but the one thing he hadn't wanted advertised was what had garnered coverage. The nerve.

A photo of Vanessa flashed on the screen and she flipped the channel. The guilt was bad enough. She didn't need her sister staring at her from beyond the grave. "Enough of that."

But Antonio wasn't even looking at the TV. His gaze was squarely on Caitlyn. "You're very good for me, you know that?"

He tucked a lock of her hair behind her ear and then lifted the long strands from her neck to press a kiss to her throat. She shuddered as he gathered her closer, fanning the ashes of their lovemaking, which apparently hadn't fully cooled.

"I have something for you," he said, his lips sparking against her skin.

"And it's exactly what I wanted," she murmured, arching into his mouth, silently encouraging him to trail those lips down her throat.

It could never be enough. He could touch her every minute of every day, crawl inside her ten more times before they left this bed, and she'd never reach the saturation point.

He laughed and reached behind him to pull a long, flat box from the bedside dresser drawer.

Entranced by the possibilities, Caitlyn ripped off the green foil wrapping paper and lifted the lid. A silver chain lay on the velvet interior.

Antonio withdrew it from the box and held it up so she could see the silver-filigreed initial charms hanging from it. "There's an *A*, an *L* and another *A*."

"Oh," she breathed as her heart surged. "One for each of the babies."

He fingered an *A* and tilted it so the light glinted off the polished white stone set in the center. "When I was in Indonesia, I trained in a makeshift dirt ring. Oftentimes, when we sparred, we'd uncover rocks buried in the soil. I carried one in my pocket when I left in search of where I belonged. It was symbolic of what I hoped I'd find when I got to America. Myself, buried beneath the layers of damaged memories."

Speechless, she stared at him as her pulse pounded.

"I had the jeweler cut and polish my stone. Each letter holds a fragment of it." His gaze far away and troubled, he set the *A* swinging with a small tip of his finger. "If Vanessa had been carrying the babies, they would have died along with her."

True. And horrifying. She'd never thought about her decision to be their surrogate in quite that way. When Vanessa had asked her, Caitlyn had agreed because she loved her sister, but honestly, the thought of getting to carry Antonio's baby had tipped the scales. It had been a win-win in her book, but the reality had so much more positives wound up in that she couldn't feel guilty about it any longer.

He bunched the chain in his fist and drew the covers back from her naked form. She was too emotional to do anything but watch. He knelt to lay his lips on her C-section scars for an eternity, and then his dark gaze swept upward to fixate on her. "My children are a piece of me that I never would have had without you. I cannot ever repay you for what you've given me. This is but a small token."

Tears splashed down her face unchecked as Antonio leaned up to hook the chain around her neck. Everything inside swelled up and over, pouring out of her mouth.

"I love you," she choked out.

She didn't care if he didn't say it back. Didn't care if the timing was wrong. Didn't care if it was only the emotion of the moment that had dragged it out of her. It was the pure honest truth, and she couldn't have held back the tide of her feelings even with a dam the size of Asia.

His gaze flicked to hers and a wealth of emotions swam through his dark eyes. "I wish I could say the same. I'd like to. But it would be unfair."

She nodded and a few more tears splashed down on the teal comforter she'd painstakingly selected. His heart still belonged to Vanessa. It was a poetic kind of justice for her sister. And for Caitlyn, truth be told.

"It's okay. I'm not trying to pressure you. But I thought you should know how I feel."

He gathered her close and held her as if he never planned to let go. "Yet another gift you've given me without expectation of anything in return. You're an amazing woman, Caitlyn."

She laid her cheek over the falcon and listened to his heartbeat. He just needed time to get over Vanessa. She'd *help* him get over her so that strong, beautiful heart could belong to Caitlyn forever. And then she'd be complete.

"Let's go spend Christmas with our family," Caitlyn suggested, and Antonio's rumbled agreement vibrated against her cheek.

The day after Christmas, Antonio couldn't stand his own company any longer and the only solution for his foul mood was to go to Falco. Without Caitlyn.

She sent him off with a kiss and nary a backward glance, as if she really had no clue he was about to lose his mind. Seemed as if he'd done a spectacular job keeping his doubts and trepidation to himself.

He had to do something different to regain his memories. It wasn't fair to Caitlyn that she was stuck in a relationship with a man who had no concrete memories of his marriage and therefore no guideposts to help him move on.

He wanted to. Desperately. He'd hoped finally getting Caitlyn into his arms would do the trick. Instead, all he'd accomplished was to make things worse.

She was in love with him. And the way he felt about her—*wonderful and terrifying emotions* was a stellar way to describe it. When he looked at her, it was as if every star in the sky shined all at once, lighting up the darkness. *She* was his star. The only constellation in his life that would ever make sense. Because he'd done exactly what he'd set out to do. He'd created new memories, new experiences with her.

Surely this was love.

But he'd been in love with Vanessa, or so Caitlyn had told him. Why couldn't he remember her clearly? It seemed wrong to tell Caitlyn about his feelings, his fledging certainty that he was in love with her, too, to promise her any sort of future, when he'd done the same with Vanessa... only to lose all consciousness of that relationship.

What if he did that to Caitlyn one day? What if he got in the ring with Cutter again and the next blow to his head erased his memories of her?

He couldn't stand the thought.

At Falco, he sat in the chair behind his desk. It was a sleek behemoth with a front piece that went all the way to the ground, hiding his lower half from view to visitors. Why had such obscurity appealed to him? He had no idea, but Caitlyn had told him he'd selected it along with all of the other furniture in the office.

Perhaps he'd shopped for furniture with Vanessa, too, as he'd done with Caitlyn. He yearned for his relationship with Caitlyn to feel special and unique. But how would he know either way?

This frustration was useless, and nothing he'd done thus far today came close to handling his memory problems differently. So he picked up the phone and scheduled the CT scan for the following week after the holidays.

It might not help, but he couldn't live in this fog of uncertainty any longer. He'd promised Caitlyn they would talk about the future after the first of the year and he'd been entertaining the notion of taking her to someplace she'd enjoy for New Year's Eve, like Paris or Madrid. Just the two of them.

Antonio pulled the ring box from his pocket and flipped

the lid. The fifteen-karat diamond dazzled like a perfect, round star against the midnight velvet. The moment he'd seen it in the case as he'd waited for the jeweler to retrieve Caitlyn's custom-made necklace, he'd known. That was the ring he wanted on Caitlyn's finger forever, as a physical symbol that she belonged to him and he needed her. He imagined her eyes filling with all that sweet, endless emotion as she realized he was asking her to marry him.

But he couldn't ask her until he exorcised the ghost of his first wife.

He pushed away from the desk and strode outside to get some fresh air. Street sounds and the ever-present sting of smog and pollution invaded what little serenity he might have found outdoors.

A flash of red hair in his peripheral vision put a hitch in his gut. An otherworldly sense of dread overwhelmed him.

Slowly, he turned to see a woman approaching him, a quizzical, hopeful slant to her expression. Long legged, slim build, beautiful porcelain face, fall of bright red hair to her waist.

Vanessa.

Oh, God. *It was his wife.* In the flesh. A million irreconcilable images flew through his head as he stared at her. Pain knifed through his temples.

"Antonio," she whispered, her voice scratchy and trembling. She searched his gaze hungrily. "I saw the news report and couldn't believe it. I had to find you, to see you for myself."

"Vanessa," he croaked, and his throat seized up.

She recoiled as if he'd backhanded her across the face. "What is that, a joke?"

"You're supposed to be dead. Caitlyn told me they found your body."

Caitlyn. Horrified, he stared at the redhead filling his vision. Caitlyn was the mother of his children, his lover.

She lived in his house, in his heart…and there was no room for Vanessa. How could this be *possible*?

"I'm not Vanessa, Antonio. What's going on? It's me." Confusion threw her expression into shadow when he shook his head. "Shayla."

The name exploded in his head. Across his soul. *Shayla.*

Laughing, moaning, murmuring his name—dozens of memories of her scrolled through his mind. Her body twining with his. Her full breasts on unashamed display, head thrown back as she rode him, taking her pleasure as if she had done it often, as if she had a right to use his body.

And of course she *had* done it often.

Shayla. His mistress. Vanessa—his wife.

The images in his head of the redheaded woman were so jumbled and nonsensical because he'd had incomplete, fragmented memories of *two different women.*

Eleven

A swirl of nausea squeezed Antonio's stomach as his eyes shut against the shocking revelation. He couldn't look at her, couldn't take the idea that he'd been intimate with her.

He'd been carrying on an affair with this woman. Cheating on his wife with her.

It was repulsive. Wrong. Not something he'd ever have imagined himself doing.

But clearly, that hadn't always been his opinion of adultery.

Gagging against the bile rising in his throat, he turned away from Shayla's prying, too-familiar gaze.

"What's the matter?" she asked. "Aren't you happy to see me? Vanessa is gone and we can finally be together."

"I don't…" *Remember you.* But it was a lie. He remembered her all too well.

Oblivious of his consternation, she put a manicured hand on his arm. He fought the urge to shake it off because it wasn't her fault he'd forsaken his marriage vows.

His skin crawled under her fingers.

He yanked his arm away and her hand fell to her side as hurt clouded her expression.

"I'm sorry," he said roughly, as pain ice-picked through his skull. "Things are not like you assume."

She cocked her head. "I don't understand what's wrong. You're alive and it's a miracle. Why didn't you call me? I've thought you were dead for over a year. Do you have any idea what I've gone through?"

His short bark of laughter startled them both. "Shayla, I—" God, he couldn't even say her name without wanting to cut out his tongue. Swallowing, he tried again. "I have amnesia."

It was the first time he'd uttered that word out loud. And oddly, naming it, *owning* it, diminished its power. Not completely, but his spine straightened and he nodded at her stunned flinch.

"Yes, you heard correctly," he told her a bit more firmly. "The plane crash dumped me on the shore of an island in Indonesia with few memories. I only found my way home a few weeks ago."

"You don't remember me." Her expression caved in and tears shimmered in her eyes. "Of all the things… I thought we'd pick up where we left—I mean, Vanessa is dead. When I heard you'd survived the crash, I figured you—"

"I remember you," he broke in. "But I didn't until I saw you."

As he'd remembered his lawyer and Thomas. But he hadn't remembered Caitlyn. Or Rodrigo. Which led to the most important question—

Would he remember Vanessa if he saw *her*?

A perverse need to know overtook him.

"I'm sorry," he told the tearful redhead before him, determined to get home and discover what else he could extract from the sieve in his brain. "There's nothing here for you any longer. I'm not in love with you and I never will be."

She laughed bitterly. "Funny, that's almost exactly what you said before you left to go to Thailand. Except you were talking about Vanessa at the time. Didn't stop you from running off on your lovers' retreat."

The words blasted through his head, but in his voice as he said them to Shayla one night.

I'm not in love with her and I never will be. There's nothing left for me in that cold, empty house. The Malibu house. He'd meant the one he'd shared with Vanessa. The one he now shared with Caitlyn and his children.

He'd told Shayla he wasn't in love with Vanessa. Truth? It might explain why he couldn't recall what that had felt like. Or had it been something he'd told his mistress to string her along?

After all, he'd gone to Thailand with Vanessa. Had fathered children with her. All while conducting a hot-and-heavy affair with this woman.

What kind of man did such things? When he'd come to LA to find out who he was, he'd never imagined he'd discover such dishonesty and selfishness in his past. Who had he *been* before the crash?

Some aspects, like being a fighter, he didn't have to question. That was a part of him. Was being an adulterer part of him, too? A part he couldn't remove any easier than he could stop fighting? He owed it to himself, his children and Caitlyn to learn everything he could about what kind of person Antonio Cavallari had been. So he could chart a course for the kind of man he wanted to be in the future.

"I'm sorry," he repeated. "I have to go. Please don't contact me again. Our relationship, whatever it was, is over."

"Yeah." She sighed. "It has been for more than a year. I mistakenly assumed we had a second chance this time.

A real one. You were never going to divorce Vanessa, not with the baby on the way."

That resonated. Divorce wasn't something the man he *knew* he was deep inside would tolerate. "No, I wouldn't have. And turns out there were three babies. Triplets."

Her smile was small but genuine. "Congratulations. Didn't see that coming. Vanessa was smarter than I would have given her credit for. That's triple the amount of child support if you ever did divorce her. I wish I knew how she'd pulled that off."

Child support. A fight with Vanessa where that term had been launched at him like a grenade... The details slammed through his head. Shayla's name had come up. Vanessa was furious because he'd sworn he'd end things with "that woman," but he apparently hadn't. Then Vanessa had taunted him with the pregnancy, saying it was insurance. Against what?

He couldn't remember that much of the conversation.

"The triplets were an accident," he assured her. "A happy one."

She nodded and he watched her walk away, then strode to the town car so the driver could take him home, where he would get some answers to the mysteries locked in his mind, once and for all.

Once he got into the house, he disappeared into the media room to queue up episodes of the TV show Vanessa had starred in. He should have done this weeks ago. Why hadn't he?

He'd told himself it wouldn't do any good. That his memories of Vanessa were so scattered and fragmented that seeing her wouldn't help. It was a lie, one he'd convinced himself of for his own self-preservation.

Vanessa walked onto the sixty-inch screen as his pulse thundered in his throat. Slim, redheaded, with delicate features. The way she held herself, something about her demeanor, was horribly familiar…because she looked like a redheaded version of Caitlyn.

Pain knifed through his temples, throbbing in tandem with his pulse.

His memories of Shayla and Vanessa split instantly. Distinct and whole, the snippets of scenes and his interactions with each woman flooded his consciousness. He let them flow despite the enormous shock to his system, absorbing, reliving. And he didn't like the realizations that followed.

Maybe he hadn't wanted to remember either his wife or his mistress. Maybe he'd known subconsciously that he didn't deserve someone as innocent as Caitlyn and he'd suppressed his memories on purpose to avoid facing the dark choices he'd made before the crash.

Grief clawed at his throat.

He had to tell Caitlyn. She should know what kind of man he'd been. What kind of man he still was. Amnesia hadn't made him into someone different. Just someone who didn't remember his sins.

He powered off the TV and sat on the plush couch in full darkness for an eternity, hating himself. Hating his choices, hating that he couldn't remember why he'd made them. Because that was part of the key in moving toward the future—understanding the past.

The door to the media room opened and Caitlyn's dark head poked through. "Hey, I didn't know you were back, but I saw the car and—"

"Come in," he commanded unevenly. "Please."

She was here. Might as well lay it all on the line. The hordes of paparazzi hanging out at Falco had likely snapped a picture of his conversation with Shayla, and he'd rather Caitlyn hear about it from him.

She came into the room, reaching for the lamp switch. He caught her arm before she could turn it on. Dark was appropriate.

"What's wrong?" she asked, concern coating her voice.

It was a painful, unintentional echo of Shayla's question. Apparently, they could both read him well. Better than he could read himself. "I need to talk to you."

How did you approach such a subject? He hadn't dishonored *her*. But she'd likely be outraged on her sister's behalf. Regardless, she had to know the truth.

"Sure." She perched on the couch, her features barely discernible in the faint light from the still-open door. He could sense her, smell her light coconut shampoo, and his heart ached to bury himself in her, no talking, no specters of the past between them.

But he'd probably never touch her again. She deserved better than he was capable of giving her.

"I…ran into someone today. A woman. From before the crash. I…remembered her."

"That's great!" Caitlyn's sweet voice knifed through him.

"No, it's not. I was having an affair with her," he said bluntly. Harshly. But there were no punches to be pulled here, no matter how difficult it was to keep swinging.

"An affair?"

Her confusion mirrored his but must have been ten times worse because she'd only just learned of it. He'd had hours to reconcile how truly sinful he was.

"Yes. A long-standing one, apparently." Remorse nearly overwhelmed him.

She grew quiet and he wished he hadn't insisted on no lights. Was she upset? She should be. But the darkness left him only his own guilt for company.

"I don't understand," she finally said. "You and Vanessa were happy. You were in love."

"I wasn't. Happy," he clarified. "Or in love."

That was perhaps the most painful realization of all. His confusion about love stemmed wholly from not ever having been in love before. When his memories of Vanessa resurfaced, he'd recognized the truth Shayla had revealed. He hadn't loved Vanessa.

He couldn't compare how he felt now to the past because there was nothing to compare it to. His feelings for Caitlyn were unprecedented.

And he was most definitely in love with her.

Otherwise it wouldn't be breaking his heart to tell her who he was, deep down inside where he couldn't change it.

"Why didn't you get a divorce, then?" Her voice had grown faint, as if she'd drawn in on herself.

"I don't know," he admitted quietly. "Too Catholic, maybe. And there was a baby on the way. I'm still missing huge pieces of my memories of the past, pieces I might never recover."

They lapsed into silence and he ached to bridge it, but this was an unprecedented situation, too. She should be allowed to react however she wanted.

"Did Vanessa know?" Her voice cracked and he realized she was crying as she sniffled quietly.

His gut twisted, and her pain was far worse than the pain he'd caused himself. She was hurting. More than he would have anticipated. Of course he hadn't thought this would go over well, but he'd expected her to be angry, not injured. His nails dug into his palms as he struggled to keep from touching her, comforting her. He was the source of her hurt, not the solution.

"She knew." And he wished he understood the dynamics of his marriage, why Vanessa would have stayed in a marriage where her husband didn't love her and was having an affair with another woman. He didn't even remember if she'd professed to love him. "I'm sorry to drop this on you with no warning. It's not how I envisioned this going between us."

They should have been talking about the trip he'd hoped to surprise her with, the imminent marriage proposal.

"It's a lot to take in, Antonio." Her voice fractured again on the last syllable of his name. "I don't know what to say."

Frustration and grief and anguish rose up inside, riling his temper as he tried to reconcile how to get through this, how to move forward when all he wanted was to hear her say it was okay, that she still loved him. That it didn't matter who he'd been. "Say how you feel. Are you mad at me? Hurt? You want to punch me?"

"I feel as if I don't know you. Commitment isn't important to you like it is to me. I wish I'd never slept with you," she admitted on a whisper that turned his whole body cold. "I can't deal with all of this. Not right now."

She slid to her feet and left the media room with a rush of quiet sobbing.

His guiding star had left him in the dark, and he felt further away from finding himself than ever. Ironic that he'd spent so long fighting to remember and now all he wished for was the ability to forget.

Dry-eyed, Caitlyn fed the babies. It was the only accomplishment she could list for the afternoon.

She rocked Annabelle, staring blindly at the wall as she tried to quiet the storm of misery zinging through her heart. If only she could crawl into bed and shut out the world, she might figure out how to get through this.

But she couldn't. Children still needed to be fed no matter what pain had just ripped a hole in your chest. Christmas decorations still had to be put away, leaving an empty hole where the holiday cheer had been. Life went on, oblivious of how one simple phrase had destroyed her world.

I was having an affair with her.

For years, Caitlyn had envied her sister's marriage. For

years, Caitlyn had lived with her unrequited feelings for
Antonio. *For years*, she'd suffered crippling guilt over both.

And it was all a lie.

Her sister's marriage had been a sham. The strong,
beautiful commitment she'd imagined was an illusion.
The man she'd thought so steadfast and constant? An adulterer. Antonio wasn't perfect in the way she'd thought he
was, and her guilt had been all for nothing.

Nothing. That guilt certainly hadn't served to keep her
out of Antonio's bed. Oh, no, she'd hopped right into his
arms with practically no resistance. She'd given her virginity to a man who thought so little of marriage vows that
he couldn't honor them. Who thought so little of love that
he hadn't considered it a necessity when choosing a wife.

It was reprehensible.

And none of it made *sense*. The awful words pouring out of Antonio's mouth: the admission that he hadn't
been in love with Vanessa, the affair, the reasons for not
divorcing—they didn't mesh with the man she'd fallen in
love with.

She'd known Antonio for seven years. Was she really
such a bad judge of character that she could love a man
who'd treated her sister like that? How could she forgive
any of this?

She wished she could cry. But everything was too numb.

After the babies had been fed, she slumped in the rocking chair as Leon, Annabelle and Antonio Junior crawled
around on a blanket in the center of the nursery. It had
been only a couple of hours since Antonio had told her.
But it felt like a year.

"May I come in?"

Her gaze cut to the door. As if her thoughts had conjured
him, Antonio stood just inside it, his expression blank.

For an instant, her heart lurched as she drank him in.
Apparently, nothing could kill the reaction she still had

to him. A sobering realization. As was the fact that he hadn't tracked her down with some magical solution to the giant cloud over them now, as much as she might wish that such a thing existed. No, he was here because they always played with the babies before dinner. It had become a ritual all five of them enjoyed, and he would still want to spend time with his children no matter what else happened.

Life went on. And they were co-parents of small children. Forever.

"Of course you can come in," she said. "This is your house."

He winced and she almost apologized for the bitter tone. But she didn't have the energy and she wasn't all that sorry. The old Caitlyn would have apologized. The old Caitlyn always had a kind word for everyone and lived in a rosy world of rainbows and unicorns, obviously.

All that had gotten her was devastated and brokenhearted. Why hadn't someone warned her that a commitment had absolutely nothing hidden inside it to guard against being hurt? Actually, it was worse because then you had to figure out how to live with your hurt.

Antonio crouched on the blanket and handed Leon a rattle, murmuring encouraging words as his son crawled toward it. Annabelle hummed as she explored the perimeter of the blanket and Antonio Junior lay on his back in the center of the room, examining the ceiling with his unique brand of concentration.

Not so unique, actually. His father had that same ability to hone in on something and it was nearly hypnotic.

She tamped down the tide of sheer grief. Antonio wasn't who she thought he was. He hadn't been probably since the beginning. She had to get past it, forgive him and get over her disappointment so they could move on. Didn't she?

The clock on the wall ticked loudly, marking off second after interminable second. They bled into a minute, then another. The silence stretched, heavy and thick. But this was how it had to go. They'd play with the babies and eat dinner. Then what? They shared a bedroom. Would they get ready for bed and lay next to each other with the silence and the big letter *A* for *affair* creating an invisible boundary between them?

"I can't do this." She was on her feet, hands clenched in tight fists, before she fully registered moving. "It's like waiting for the executioner's ax to fall."

Antonio glanced up at her, his mouth set in a hard line. It ruined the beauty of his face. He was obviously as miserable as she was. She hated that she noticed and hated even more that she apparently still cared.

"What is? Hanging out with our kids?"

"No. This." She swirled a taut hand in the air to encompass the room at large, but she meant the two of them and the big question marks surrounding their relationship, how they moved forward, all of it. "I can't do this with you. I'm not Vanessa. I won't put up with affairs and I'm not okay with it."

She'd yearned for her sister's life and now she had it. The whole kit and caboodle. Clearly she needed to be more careful what she wished for. Yet it was such a suitable penance. She bit back hysterical laughter.

"I'm not asking you to be okay with it," he countered quietly with a glance at Annabelle who had pulled up on her crib with a loud squeal of achievement. "*I'm* not okay with it. And you should know, it wasn't affairs. Just one. I told her not to contact me anymore. I don't want anything to do with her."

Did he honestly expect any of that to make a *difference*?

"I need to move back into my own bedroom." Her throat hitched as she said the words and she wished she could take them back, but it was the smartest move for her sanity. "I can't be with you anymore, not like we were."

And there it was. She'd held this man in her arms, cradled him with her body, loved him, slept with him, tasted him. Never in a million years would she have imagined she'd be the one to call off their relationship. In the end, she'd been painfully spot on—she wasn't the right kind of woman for Antonio Cavallari.

Grimly, he crossed his arms. "What will we be like, then?"

She shook her head blindly. "Parents. Roommates. I don't know. I just know I can't sleep in that bedroom. I can't—"

A sob broke through, ending whatever she'd been about to say. Head bowed, she buried her head in her hands, squeezing her eyes shut. She sensed Antonio's presence as he approached, but he didn't touch her.

She wished he would. Wished they were still in a place where he could comfort her. But was glad he didn't. It would only confuse things.

"Caitlyn."

She blinked up at him through watery eyes.

His dark gaze zeroed in on her, overwhelming her with unvoiced conflict and soul-deep wounds. Even now, with these irreparable ruptures between them, she could read him.

"Will you fight me for custody of the children?" he asked softly.

She gasped. "What? Why in the world would I do that?"

"What kind of father could I possibly be?" Resolute and stoic, he stared her down. "I have an uncontrollable urge to decimate other men in the ring. I have amnesia. I defiled my marriage with a tasteless affair. Any judge would grant your petition to take my children and likely award you as much money as you ask for to raise them. If I were you, I would have already taken steps to remove them from my influence."

"Antonio." Her chest constricted as she searched his ravaged expression. "None of that makes you a bad father. Your children need you."

I need you.

But she bit it back. She needed the man she'd *thought* he was, the one who made her feel treasured because he'd chosen her. Because of all the people in his life he could have reached out to, he'd taken her hand and asked her to stand with him when he had gone to Falco the first time. He'd asked her to see the doctor with him. He'd been alone and frightened and he hadn't wanted anyone else but her.

Then he'd destroyed her trust by morphing into someone else. Someone who didn't respect and honor marriage the way she did. Who hadn't loved his wife.

If he couldn't love Vanessa, what hope did Caitlyn have that he could ever feel that way about her? And she wouldn't settle for anything less than a man's love. Yet, how could she trust him if he *did* say that he loved her?

It was a vicious cycle, one she couldn't find a way to break, no matter how many times she went over it in her head. All this time, she'd thought he couldn't tell her he loved her because his heart still belonged to Vanessa. The reality was…indescribable.

Antonio glanced at the babies, and all the love she knew he felt for them radiated from every pore of his being. He was capable of love. Just not loving her.

"No, I need *them*," he said. "As long as you're not going to take them from me, I can handle anything else."

It was a strange reversal of some of their earlier conversations, when she'd been terrified he'd find a way to dismiss her from her children's lives. She knew what that clawing, desperate panic felt like and it softened her. More than she'd have liked.

A harder, more cynical person might have taken the information he'd laid out and run with it, ensuring that she got exactly what he said—custody and Antonio's money. It would be a fit punishment for his crimes.

But she wasn't that person, and as she stood close enough to touch him, close enough to smell his heady masculine scent, her heart twisted.

She still loved him. Nothing he'd said to her today could erase that.

"I will never take your children from you," she promised and her voice cracked. "But I can't have a romantic relationship with you. We have to figure out a way to live together as parents and nothing else. Can we?"

He stepped back, hands at his sides and his beautiful face a mask. "I'll respect whatever decision you make."

Her heart wept over his matter-of-fact tone, as if he had no interest in fighting for her. But what would she have said if he told her no, that it was totally unacceptable to end their relationship? That he loved her and wanted her in his bed, come hell or high water?

She'd have refused.

So here they were. Parents. And nothing else.

That made her want to weep more than anything else that had happened today.

Twelve

Antonio stood outside Caitlyn's old bedroom at 1:00 a.m., hands on the wood, listening to her breathe. God, this separation was an eternal hell.

After two days of staying out of her way, he was done with it.

She was awake and lying there in despair. He could sense it. Her essence had floated down the hall to him on a whisper of misery, and he'd caught it easily because he'd been lying awake in his own bed in similar turmoil.

His headaches had grown worse since they'd been apart, and his pillow still smelled like Caitlyn even after ten washings. She haunted him, asleep or awake. Didn't matter. She was so close, yet so far, and his body never quite got used to the fact that she wasn't easily accessible any longer. He still rolled over in the night, seeking her heat and the bone-deep contentment that came with touching her.

Only to come up empty-handed and empty hearted. The

only thing in life that made sense was gone, and it hurt worse than any physical pain he'd ever endured.

The pounding in his temples wouldn't ease no matter how many rounds he went in the ring at Falco. He'd even resorted to a pain pill earlier that evening, to no avail.

The only thing that ever worked to take away his headache was Caitlyn.

He pushed the door open and stepped inside her room. She didn't move, but the quick intake of her breath told him she knew he was there.

"I can't sleep," he said inanely.

Her scent filled his head, pulsing through it with sweet memories, and it was worse than being in his lonely bed without her. This was too close. And not close enough.

It was maddening.

"I'm sorry." Her voice whispered across his skin, raising the hair. "But you can't come in here in the middle of the night."

"This is my house," he growled as his temper got the best of him. It was the wrong tactic; he knew that. But she was killing him. "I need to talk to you."

"Can't it wait?"

It was a reasonable request for one o'clock in the morning. "No, it can't. Please, Caitlyn. What can I say, what can I do? I'm sorry. I hate that I did something so inexcusable. Can't you get past it?"

"I don't think so." The quiet words cut through him. "We don't have the same views on commitment, and that's not something that I can get past. You told me you believed in forever and I believed you. Now I can't trust you, and without that, what kind of relationship would we have? I'm not like Vanessa."

Why couldn't she see that he didn't want her to be like Vanessa? At one point in time, he'd liked a certain kind of woman, clearly. But he didn't remember why and didn't want to.

He wanted Caitlyn.

And she didn't want him. Because of something he'd done a long time ago. Something he couldn't undo. Something that haunted him, something he hated about himself. He'd surgically extract whatever she objected to if he could. If it would make a difference.

But it wouldn't, and this was one fight he lacked the skill to win.

Without another word, he left her there in the dark because he couldn't stand the space between them any longer. Couldn't stand that he didn't know what to do.

He had to change her mind. She was everything to him and he needed her. Loved her.

For the first time in his life, he was pinned against the fence, strength draining away, and his opponent was too big to overcome.

But he refused to go down for the count. He needed to do something big and drastic to win her back. But what?

After a long night of tossing and turning, Caitlyn gave up at 5:00 a.m. She'd slept in this bed pre-Antonio for over a year and had never thought twice about it. A few days in paradise, also known as the bedroom down the hall, and suddenly there was no sleep to be had in this old room.

And she wasn't fooled into thinking it was the mattress. Her inability to sleep had everything to do with the black swirl of her thoughts and the cutting pain in her chest after shutting down Antonio's middle-of-the-night plea. Closing her eyes only made it worse.

Caitlyn padded to the sunroom and tried to get in the mood for Pilates before Leon woke up. But all she could think about was the first time Antonio had kissed her. He'd backed her up against a wall, literally and figuratively, in this very room, demanding she tell him about love. So she'd spilled her heart and turned the question back to him, expecting a profound tribute straight from the poetry books. An ode to his late wife about his devotion and the wonders of their marriage.

What do you know about love? she'd asked.

Nothing, he'd returned.

She'd assumed he didn't remember love and stupidly thought he was asking her to help him. But really, he'd meant he'd never loved Vanessa. How awful it must have been for her sister, to be stuck in a loveless marriage with a man who wouldn't divorce her solely because of the baby on the way. Instead, he'd forced her to put up with his infidelity.

How had Vanessa done it? How had she woken up each morning, her mind ripe with the knowledge that her husband had been intimate with another woman? Unrequited love was something Caitlyn had a special empathy for. Had her sister cried herself to sleep at night, the way Caitlyn had over the past few days? Why hadn't Vanessa told her what was going on?

Inexplicably, she wished her sister was here so she could bury her head in Vanessa's shoulder and weep out all her troubles. Which was the worst kind of juxtaposition. If Vanessa was alive, Caitlyn's troubles would be nonexistent. She'd still be laboring under the false premise that marriage, commitment, love and sex were all tied up with a big, magnificent bow.

Leon woke up early. While Caitlyn fed him, her mind wandered back to Vanessa and it suddenly hit her that her sister's possessions sat tucked away in the attic. Her sister might be gone, but Caitlyn could still surround herself with Vanessa. Maybe it would help ease Caitlyn's bruised and battered soul.

She turned the babies over to Brigitte, who bundled

them up for a ride in the triple-seated stroller, and then escaped to the attic. *Attic* might be a little grandiose of a term—it was really a small, unfinished room above the second floor, accessible by a narrow staircase next to the linen closet.

Caitlyn hadn't been in here for over a year, not since she'd moved the bulk of Vanessa's things after the plane crash. A coating of dust covered the items farthest from the entrance. The boxes near the front had been placed there recently and weren't as grimy. Shortly after Antonio had returned, Caitlyn had asked the housekeeper to pack up the rest of her sister's things.

Sitting down cross-legged, she opened the nearest un-taped box. Clothes. She pulled out one of her sister's silk blouses and held it to her cheek. The heavy, exotic perfume Vanessa had favored wafted from the fabric. All at once, Caitlyn recalled the last time she'd smelled it, when she'd been four months pregnant and had come to say goodbye before Vanessa and Antonio left for Thailand.

Tears slid down her face and she suspected the majority of them were because she missed Antonio. Not Vanessa. Apparently, her shame knew no bounds, but he'd been so lost last night. She'd wanted to tell him she wished there was a way to get past it, too. But she couldn't see it.

The clothes weren't helping. Pushing that box to the side, she dived into the next one, which was full of Vanessa's toiletries, including two small, jeweled bottles of her perfume. Caitlyn pulled them out to give to Annabelle. The perfume would likely not last that long, but the bottles were encrusted with real semiprecious stones and the pair would be a lovely keepsake for their daughter.

Perhaps the children she shared with Vanessa were actually the answer Caitlyn had been seeking about how she was supposed to find the strength to live in the same house with Antonio. Had Vanessa considered the babies a good enough reason to stay with her husband despite the emotional pain he'd caused her? Leon, Annabelle and Antonio Junior were certainly the reason why Caitlyn was still here after all. She couldn't imagine not waking up each day and seeing the faces of her kids. It was worth the sword through her heart every time she saw their father to get daily access to her children.

Maybe it had also been worth it to Vanessa to keep her family intact. Maybe that was why she hadn't pressed for a divorce and stayed with Antonio even after she found out about his affair.

Drained, Caitlyn rested her head on the box. Her weight threw it off balance and it tumbled to spill its contents into her lap.

A leather-bound book landed on top. It looked like an old-fashioned journal. Curious, Caitlyn leafed through it and recognized her sister's handwriting.

"Sept 4: Ronald doesn't think the Paramount people will consider me for the lead in *Bright Things*. The role is too opposite from Janelle. I should fire him, but he's my third agent in two years. Ugh. I really want that movie!"

Interesting. Caitlyn wouldn't have considered Vanessa the type to record her innermost thoughts, especially not in written form when her sister had been so attached to her smartphone, but here it was, in blue pen. With all of the email hacking and cloud-storage security breaches that plagued celebrities, Vanessa might have felt paper had a measure of privacy she couldn't get any other way. Feeling a little voyeuristic, Caitlyn read a few more entries at the beginning and then skipped ahead.

Wow, she hadn't realized how much Vanessa had wanted to move on from Janelle, the character she'd played on the prime-time drama *Beacon Street*. Her sister had never said anything about how trapped she'd felt.

It kind of stung to find out Vanessa hadn't confided in

Caitlyn about her career woes. Or much of anything, apparently. The journal was full of surprises. Caitlyn would have said they were pretty close before the crash, but obviously Vanessa had kept a lot of things hidden.

Antonio's name caught her eye and she paused mid–page flip.

"I told Antonio about Mark. He totally freaked out, worse than I expected. Simple solution to the problem, I told him. If he'd just stop this ridiculous nonsense about reviving his glory days in the ring, I'd agree to stop seeing Mark. Which won't be hard. He's nowhere near as good as Antonio in bed, but I had to do something to get my stupid husband's attention!"

Caitlyn went cold, then hot.

Her sister had been having an affair, too?

Dread twisted her stomach inside out as she flipped to the beginning of the entry. It was dated over two years ago. Well before Vanessa had approached Caitlyn about being a surrogate. Her sister's marriage problems had extended that far back?

She kept reading entry after entry with slick apprehension souring her mouth.

"Antonio is still really upset about Mark. He demanded I quit *Beacon Street*. I laughed. As if I'd ruin my career for him just so my darling husband didn't have to watch me on-screen with the man I'm sleeping with? Whatever."

And then a few pages later: "Antonio is so horrible. Not only is he still talking about fighting again—which I will not put up with!—he's found what he thinks is the best way to get back at me for Mark. He's having an affair with a woman who looks like me. On purpose. It's so juvenile. He's so not the type to be this vindictive. But I left him no choice, he said in that imperious voice that never fails to piss me off."

Antonio had started his affair in retaliation for Vanessa's. It didn't change how she felt about infidelity, but it changed how she felt about her sister. And her sister's views on marriage, which clearly didn't mirror Caitlyn's.

Information overload. Wave after wave of it crashed over her. So Antonio had wanted to get back in the ring even before the crash—did he remember that?

Her throat and eyes both burning uncontrollably, Caitlyn forced herself to read to the end. Without checking her strength, she threw the leather-bound confessional at the wall, unable to hold the evidence of how little she'd actually known her sister.

She'd walked into this attic hoping to find some comfort for the task ahead of her—living with a man she loved but couldn't fathom how to trust—and instead found out her sister hadn't been sitting around pining for her husband. In fact, Vanessa had had skeletons of her own in her closet.

Hot, angry tears coursed down Caitlyn's face, and she couldn't stop the flood of grief. Didn't want to. Nothing was as she'd thought. Vanessa had pushed Antonio into the arms of another woman first by forbidding him from doing something he loved and then punishing him via a romance with her costar. It didn't make Antonio's choices right, but against everything Caitlyn would have expected, she had sympathy for him nonetheless.

It was too much. She sank into a heap and wept.

She registered Antonio's presence only a moment before he gathered her into his arms, rocking her against his strong chest. Ashamed that her soul had latched on to his touch like a greedy miser being showered with gold, she clung to him as he murmured her name. She cried on his expensive shirt and he didn't even seem to notice the huge wet spot under her cheek.

His fingers tangled in her hair as he cupped her head gently, massaging with his strong fingers. Tiny needles of awareness spiked through her skin, energizing her with the power of his sweet touch, but she ignored it. He didn't speak and somehow that made it okay to just be, no words, no excuses, no reasons to shove him away yet again.

When the storm passed, she peeked up at his blank expression. "Where did you come from? I didn't think you were home."

"I just got back," he said gruffly. "I…heard you and I couldn't stay away. I know you can take care of yourself, but I needed to check on you. Don't say I should have left you alone and let you cry because that was not going to happen."

"It's okay. I'm glad you found me."

"I doubt that's true when I'm the reason you're crying."

His arms dropped away and she missed them, almost calling out for him to encompass her again with that blanket of serenity. But she didn't. There was still so much unsaid between them. So much swirling through her heart that she could hardly think.

She shook her head. "Not this time. Vanessa—" her deep breath fractured on another half sob "—was sleeping with her costar. Mark—"

"Van Allsberg." Antonio's expression wavered between outrage and bleak resignation. "I remember now. I didn't until you said his name. I almost got in the car to drive to his house and take him apart for touching my wife. How did you find out?" he asked quietly as he sat back on his heels.

"She wrote in a journal." Bitterness laced her tone involuntarily. Vanessa had been very free with information when the page was her only audience. "I read it. It was illuminating."

Caitlyn's chest hurt as she watched the pain filter through his entire body anew, as if he was experiencing it for the first time. And perhaps amnesia was like that, continually forcing Antonio to relive events he should have been able to put behind him. Distance didn't exist for him the way it did for other people, who could grow numb to the pain—or deal with it—over time.

Unwittingly, she'd forced him to do the same by jumping on the self-righteous bandwagon, lambasting him for an affair that had happened a long time ago when in reality, she'd known nothing of the difficulties in his marriage. She'd been judge, jury and executioner without all of the facts.

She stared at the exposed beams of the ceiling until she thought she could talk without crying. "Her affair was your punishment for daring to express your interest in fighting again."

"I... It was?" Frustration knitted his features into an unrecognizable state. "I thought..."

His anguish ripped through her, and before she could list the hundreds of reasons why it was a bad idea, she grabbed his hand, holding it tightly in hers as if she could communicate all her angst through that small bit of contact.

"You made mistakes, Antonio. But there were extenuating circumstances."

It didn't negate the sacredness of marriage vows, but it did throw a lot of light on how Antonio's choices had come about.

"That's no excuse," he bit out savagely. "There *is* no excuse. That's why I can't forgive myself."

That speared through her gut and left a gaping wound in its wake.

His distress wasn't faked. Cautiously, she searched his face, his body language, and the truth was there in every fiber of his being. He clearly didn't think the affair was okay now, despite having thought differently back then.

Not only had the affair happened a long time ago, she'd refused to take into account that Antonio wasn't the same person he'd been while married to her sister. As many times as she'd noted he was different, in this, she'd convicted him of being the same.

Amnesia had taken pieces of his memory, and perhaps what was left had reshaped him. Could she find a way to trust the Antonio who had returned to her from the grave and allow the old one to stay buried?

"Antonio." He didn't look at her, but she went on anyway. "You should know something. She said you talked her into going to Thailand as a way to reconnect. You wanted to try again, just the two of you."

He nodded. "I don't remember. But I'm glad that Vanessa died knowing that I was committed to her."

That gelled with the Antonio she'd always known. A man who valued commitment, who despite the rockiness of his marriage had wanted to try again. "I'm sorry I dredged up all of this pain again."

He huffed out an unamused half laugh, scrubbing his face with his free hand. "You don't have to apologize. I remember so little about Vanessa in the first place. Hell, practically everything I know is from things you've told me. So the fairy tale you painted wasn't true. That's actually easier to deal with than the reverse."

"The reverse?"

With a small smile, he stared at the dusty attic floor between them. "That Vanessa was the love of my life but I would never remember what that felt like. That I'd never be able to move on until I properly mourned our relationship. Now I know all I had with her was a dysfunctional marriage that I can put behind me. The future seems a lot brighter knowing that the best relationship of my life is yet to come."

The cloud of pain seemed to lift from his features as he spoke, and she couldn't look away from his expression. It was fresh, beautiful, hopeful.

His strength was amazing and it bolstered hers. "I like the sound of that."

He tipped up her chin and feathered a thumb across her cheek. Lovingly. She fell into his gaze, mesmerized, forgetting for a moment that things were still unsettled between them. Then it all crashed down again: the disappointment, the heartache. The sense that they'd both cleansed a lot from the past but the future still had so many question marks.

Did she have what it took to put the affair behind her, as he seemed to want her to? As he seemed to do so easily himself?

"Caitlyn," he murmured and hesitated for an eternity, his gaze playing over her face as if he couldn't make up his mind what to say. Finally, he sighed. "I'm miserable without you. Can't sleep, can't eat. I deserve this purgatory you've cast me into, but you have to know that our relationship isn't going down without a fight."

"I'm miserable, too." She bowed her head. "But part of that misery is because I don't know how I'm supposed to feel about all of this. The revelations in Vanessa's journal don't change anything. Marriage is a sacred thing. Sex is, too. I have a hard time trusting that you truly believe that. I have a hard time trusting that if you and I fall into a rough spot in the future, you won't console yourself with another woman."

It was the old adage: once a cheater, always a cheater. Except she'd never thought she'd be wondering how true it was. People could and did change all the time, especially when presented with the best kind of motivation. Just look at her—she'd never envisioned being a mother, and it had taken a huge mind-set change to prepare for it.

He winced and nodded. "I deserve that, too. So that's why I went to Falco this morning and spent hours locked in a room with Thomas Warren and the other executives to hash out the details required to sell Falco Fight Club."

"You...what?" She couldn't catch her breath.

"I want it gone." Grimly, he sliced the air with a flat palm. "It's a brutal, bloody sport. I've got kids now, and limiting their exposure to MMA is always in the back of my mind. But that's not the reason I want to sell."

Sell. The word reverberated in her heart and nearly made her sick.

"Antonio! You can't sell Falco." It would be akin to her announcing she wanted to sell one of the babies. It was lunacy. "That place is a part of you. I watched you fight. You love it. It's as if you were born to be in the ring."

"Exactly. I sign everyone's paychecks. Who's going to tell me no if I say I want to get back into rotation? As long as I own Falco, I have a guaranteed path into the ring."

"You're not making any sense. All of that sounds like a *good* thing. If you want to get in the ring again, I won't stop you. I'll support it," she countered fiercely. "I'm not Vanessa."

Caitlyn would never be so daft as to forbid Antonio to return to the ring if that was what he wanted. Love didn't bind a man's wings and then selfishly expect him to fall in line.

"No, you're not." He knelt on one knee and cupped her face in his hands, holding her steady as he treated her to a beautiful, tender smile. "That's why I'm selling. I want to show you that I can stop fighting. Don't you see? If I can shut off such a deep-seated piece of my soul, I can also remove the part that believed infidelity was okay."

Her eyelids flew shut as she processed that. "Why would you do that just for me?"

"It wasn't just for you. I need to prove it to myself, too." His smile faltered. "As hard as it's been to live without you, it's been even harder to live with myself, knowing that I have the capacity to do something so wrong. This is the only way I can come to you again and ask you to reconsider being with me. How else could you believe me when I say I'd never have an affair again? I needed to prove in a concrete way that I love you."

Stricken, she stared at him as tears spilled over and splashed down her face.

He'd done this for her, as a gesture to show that he loved her. That she could give him another chance and she could trust him because he'd truly changed.

And he *had* changed. She'd recognized that from the very beginning.

He wasn't the same Antonio. It was blatantly, wonderfully obvious that he'd become someone else. Someone better, stronger, who knew the meaning of love to a far greater degree than she did.

He'd fought the demon of amnesia to find his family and fought to regain a foothold in his life. Antonio had been nothing but brutally honest with Caitlyn from day one, and just as he'd been honest about his affair, she could trust that he was telling the truth that he'd never do that to her. Perhaps she should look within for the root of her issues.

She'd feared for a long time that she wasn't woman enough, strong enough or just plain *enough* for a powerful, complex man like Antonio. Because she wasn't Vanessa and couldn't be like her sister.

But the dynamic between Caitlyn and Antonio would never follow the same path as his first marriage because her relationship with Antonio had no parallel to the one he'd had with her sister. He loved *Caitlyn*, enough to do something crazy like sell his company, which he'd never have considered for Vanessa.

No, she wasn't Vanessa, who had no clue how to love a man like Antonio. Caitlyn did.

Antonio was a fighter. And so was she.

"No," she said firmly. "I refuse to stand by and let you do this. It's not necessary."

"Then, what can I do, Caitlyn?" Frustrated, he started to drop his hands, but she snatched them back and threw her arms around him.

"You can love me." His embrace tightened and she melted into it as all her reservations vanished. "Forever. That's what I want."

She loved Antonio, and forgiveness was a part of that. She wouldn't withhold it a moment longer.

He murmured her name, his lips in her hair as he shifted her more deeply in his lap. "You've already got that. You should ask for the moon because I would give it to you."

"You're more than enough. You're all I've ever wanted."

Antonio stood with her in his arms and navigated the narrow stairway from the attic with all the grace and finesse she'd come to expect from such a magnificent man.

Caitlyn silently said goodbye to her sister and left the past in the dusty attic where it belonged. She had the family of her dreams and she'd never let it go again.

Epilogue

The announcer took the mic and announced, "And by unanimous decision, the winner is Antonio Cavallari!"

With his name buzzing in his ears, Antonio raised his aching hands to the roaring crowd in a classic fighter's victory pose, but his gaze only sought one face—Caitlyn's. The lights of the packed arena blinded him, as did the trickle of blood from his eyebrow, but he ignored it all until he located her in her usual ringside spot.

His wife of six months shot him that sexy, sleepy smile that had replaced her maidenly blush. Sometimes he missed that blush, but not very often, because she backed up the smile with abandon behind closed doors. He grinned back. He couldn't wait to get her alone later. But it would have to wait because a hundred people wanted a piece of the new welterweight champion.

After an hour of interviews, in which he was asked over and over again the secret to revitalizing his career, and then showering through the pain of his cuts and bruises and Thomas Warren's incessant chatter about another champion coming out of Falco, Antonio finally threaded through the animated crowd to press up against Caitlyn's back.

Exactly where he wanted to be.

She leaned into him, and he slipped his arms around her. The silk of her blue dress felt like heaven under his battered hands, but her skin would feel even better, and he let all his desire for her surge through his veins because she could take it. Later, she would beg for him to love her, meet him in his urgency. Because she was his missing piece, and without her, he'd still be wandering through the confusion inside his head, trying to figure out where he belonged.

"Congratulations," she murmured and turned her head to press a kiss to his throat. "How does it feel to be the king of the comeback?"

"Feels as if it's been too long since you were naked," he grumbled in her ear, careful not to say it too loudly when Brigitte was only a few feet away with the babies.

The au pair had one hand on the three-seated stroller, expertly splitting her attention between her charges and the young featherweight fighter engaging her in conversation. Matteo Long was a rising star in Antonio's empire, and his children's caregiver could do worse.

Caitlyn had continually insisted the kids should be immersed in their father's world so they could learn for themselves the artistry and discipline of Antonio's passion. The fact that she truly understood what made him tick was yet another reason he loved his wife completely.

And his love for her and his children had finally gotten him into a doctor's office to get that CT scan. That had led to more tests and procedures that had eventually uncovered the medical reason for Antonio's headaches—and a solution. He rarely had them these days, which was a blessing for an athlete going after a title.

His private detective hadn't turned up evidence of other survivors from the plane crash. So Antonio had let that quest go—his own amazing story was enough.

Turning in his arms, Caitlyn fingered the chain around her neck where she wore his wedding band while he was in the ring and undid the clasp. Encircling the band, she slid it on his finger and said, "Till death do us part."

It was a ritual they performed often, reminiscent of their wedding ceremony. A tactile reminder of their love, commitment and marriage vows. He'd insisted on it.

Not that he needed any reminders. He still hadn't fully regained his memories from before the crash and had accepted that he likely never would. Odd flashes came to him at strange times, but it didn't matter what his brain resurfaced.

Caitlyn was the only woman he could never forget.

* * * * *

HOLIDAY BABY
SCANDAL

JULES BENNETT

To all the readers who've asked about Ryker...
you're welcome!

One

With one hand clutching the forgotten cuff links and one hand firmly over her still-flat stomach, Laney pulled in a deep breath and willed courage to make an appearance.

She was an O'Shea, damn it. She didn't back down in the face of fear. Fear was nothing but a lie. A bold-faced lie capable of defeating most people. Laney wasn't most people.

She'd come this far, all she had to do was knock…and make a life-changing confession to a man she'd been in love with since she was old enough to notice boys. Forget the fact he'd been ten years older. Age meant about as much to her as fear did.

Tears clogged her throat as emotions threatened to overwhelm her. Whatever his reaction, she owed him the truth. But if he rejected her, the pain would slice deep.

Laney pushed aside the hurt, the fear and the nausea, and pounded on Ryker Barrett's front door.

No turning back now.

Ryker had been part of her life since she was a child. He'd worked for her father, was best friends with her brothers. Her family had taken him in when his own had turned him away. He was mysterious, intriguing and frustrating.

And for the past five weeks he'd been pretending nothing had happened. He gave no hint that he even recalled tearing her Chanel dress from her body before holding her against her hotel room wall and bringing her every desire to life.

Nope. It was business as usual. When she'd had to feed him information via email or text for O'Shea's auctions, he'd never given any indication that their one heated night had made an impact on his life whatsoever. Was he that emotionally detached?

Well, he was about to sustain one hell of an impact. He may try to ignore her, but there was no way he could ignore the consequences of their night.

The door swung open and the entire speech she'd rehearsed all morning vanished from her mind. Ryker stood before her wearing only a pair of running shorts, a tatted chest and glorious muscle tone.

She'd never seen him this way. The man who traveled the globe in designer suits, the man who donned a leather jacket and worn jeans to blend in when necessary, had never presented himself in such a beautiful, natural manner. He should do this more often.

Casual as you please, Ryker rested a forearm on the edge of the door and quirked a brow as if she'd disturbed him. Yeah, well, he deserved to be put out. She'd been fighting her feelings for him for years.

Rage bubbled from within as she slapped his cuff links against his bare chest and pushed past him. In all the years she'd known him, Laney had never come to his house in Boston. When they met, it was always on neutral ground, usually at the O'Shea family home her brother Braden now lived in.

As infuriating as Ryker could be, Laney was the first to admit that her family would crumble without him. He may be the "enforcer," the guy who kept them protected and took the brunt of any backlash they ever faced, but he could easily cut ties and leave. This billionaire never threw his money around like most men she knew. Loyalty meant much more to Ryker than finances ever would… one of the many reasons she was drawn to him.

The door closed at her back. Laney shut her eyes and tried to forget the intensity of their complicated relationship, tried to ignore the way her body instantly responded to this man. She was here for one reason. And the fact that he worked for her family, was practically *part* of her family, wasn't making this confession any easier.

"If you're here regarding the painting in L.A. that you emailed me about last week, I've already—"

Laney whirled. "I'm not here about work."

Crossing his arms over his broad chest, Ryker widened his stance and gave a brief nod. "I can't believe it took you this long to come to me."

Laney's heart kicked up. So he knew she would bring up that night, and he'd what? Been waiting on her? Jerk. Uncaring, unfeeling, stupid, sexy jerk. Why couldn't he put a shirt on? She was trying to keep her anger going, but lust was creeping into the mix.

"You could've come to me," she threw back. "Or, I don't know, actually talked to me when we were exchanging work information."

The O'Sheas were a force all their own, known around the globe for their prestigious auction houses. Laney had ignored the whispered "mafia" or "mob" rumors her entire life. She knew full well what her family was, and she was a proud member. They remained on the right side of the law thanks to the connections her late father had made and the ones her brother Braden, who was now in charge, and her other brother Mac continued to work at.

And Ryker Barrett, other than starring in her every fantasy for years, was the family's right-hand man, security detail and any other job they needed him for. He did the dirty work and lay low, staying out of the limelight and behind the scenes.

Laney waited for him to say something, anything, but he stood there staring at her, which only made her nerves worse. How could he have so much power over her? She was an O'Shea, for crying out loud, and he was just standing there.

Standing there looking all half-naked, sexy and perfect.

Focus, Laney.

Ryker held up the cuff links. "Was this all?"

Laney narrowed her eyes. "Am I interrupting something?"

Or someone? It hadn't even occurred to her that he may be entertaining. A sick feeling in the pit of her stomach grew, and she hated the spear of jealousy that ripped through her.

"Yeah, my morning session with the punching bag."

Which explained those perfectly sculpted arms, shoulders and pecs, though Laney figured he used a punching bag as a means of releasing his emotions rather than to stay in shape. Ryker was the epitome of keeping to himself and never letting anyone get too close. So what did that say about that night they shared? Clearly he'd thrown all of his rules out the window because they'd been as close as two people could get.

Nausea pushed its way to the front of the line, bypassing her worry, her fear. Laney closed her eyes, waiting to see if she needed to find the bathroom or take a seat and let the wave pass. *Please, please, just pass.* Of all times to appear vulnerable, this was not the one.

"Listen, I get you want to discuss what happened," he began, oblivious to her current state. "I take the blame. I shouldn't have followed you into your room and—"

"Ripped my clothes off?" she finished, holding a hand to her stomach and glaring across the room at him. "I'm not sorry it happened. I've been waiting on you to notice I'm not just Mac and Braden's little sister. I've fantasized about you ripping my clothes off, and I don't even mind that you ruined my favorite dress. So, I'm not sorry a bit. I'm only sorry about how you treated me after."

Other than the muscles ticking in his stubbled jaw, Ryker showed no emotion.

"This wasn't just some one-night stand," she argued.

"It was."

Okay. That hurt—the truth often did—but still. They were more, so much more, than a quick, albeit amazing, romp.

"How dare you act like I was just some random stranger?" she yelled, throwing her arms out wide. "I've known you almost my whole life. You think it's okay to have sex with me and—"

He moved in a flash, gripped her shoulders and hauled her against his bare chest. "No, I didn't think it was okay, but I couldn't stop. Damn it, Laney."

Ryker released her and took a step back, letting her go as if she'd burned him. "I couldn't stop," he whispered.

She had to get out of here. The last time they'd been alone his control had snapped, and he was barely hanging on by a thread now that she was in his living room, on his turf.

He'd purposely been avoiding her since their one-night stand, only communicating through texts for stuff related to O'Shea's. They'd been working together for the past several years. He could admit that when she came on board, his job had become so much easier. With her being able to dig deeper, to infiltrate systems he never could've…she was invaluable. Laney's computer hacking skills were eerily good. If she ever worked with the wrong crowd, she could be dangerous. Granted, some considered the O'Sheas the wrong crowd, but whatever. He couldn't do his job without her, so avoiding her altogether wasn't an option.

The torture of working so close together was worth it, though. Even the slightest communication with Laney kept him going. He shouldn't enjoy the pain of being so near, unable to fulfill his every desire, but he chalked up his masochistic tendencies to his less than stellar childhood.

When he wasn't on assignment, he typically would hide out at his home in London or take a trip to some random destination just because he could and had no ties. When he was in Boston, he was too tempted to give in to his desires for his best friends' and bosses' little sister.

When Laney started to reach for him, Ryker held up a hand. "No." If she touched him, this whole distance thing would crumble. He'd been playing with fire when he'd grabbed her a second ago…but damn if she didn't feel good against him.

This had to stop. He owed it to the family who saved him from a living hell. For years he'd ached for her, watched from afar as she grew into a breathtaking woman who managed to slip beneath his defenses. When she'd dated other men, it had nearly gutted him, but what right did he have to say anything?

She was the mafia princess, and he was the family… problem solver. He'd been involved with a lot of dark deeds before her father passed away and left the family business to Braden. Now they were all on the path to being legitimate. But legitimacy didn't change what he'd done in the past. And no matter that his bank account had more zeroes than any one person would need, that didn't change the fact he wasn't worthy of Laney. Not only was she the daughter of one of Boston's most powerful men, but she'd never made it a secret she wanted a large family, complete with babies and pets. He opted for lovers in other states and countries, to keep things physical and void of all emotions.

To put things simply, they were on opposite ends of this warped world. Since Patrick's death months ago, Braden and Mac protected her, and rightfully so, from the harsh realities their family faced each day. Actually, Laney's protection had also been part of Ryker's job.

Not that he needed the money or the job. But he owed the O'Sheas. Anything they asked for, he would provide or die trying. And it was all of that watching over Laney that had damn near done him in.

Blowing out a breath, he shook his head and faced her, but froze. Laney had stepped back and was leaning against the wall. Her closed eyes, her long, slow breaths had him narrowing the distance between them.

"Laney?" He was near enough to touch her, but kept his hands to himself. See? He could do it. He'd just be right here in case she needed something…like his hands on her.

With shaky fingers, he shoved her hair away from her face. Her lids fluttered open, but a sheen of sweat had popped up over her forehead. Was she that nervous about being here?

"I know you don't want me here, but I have to tell you something."

She pushed from the wall, swaying slightly.

Now he didn't resist contact. Ryker grabbed her around the waist and held her against him. "Are you all right?"

"Let me go."

Those vibrant green eyes came up to meet his. The punch to his gut instantly forced him back to that night, to her pinned between his body and the wall. She'd panted his name as she'd clung to his back. Never had he experienced anything so…perfect. And he didn't deserve one second of her affection. Mac and Braden would kick his ass if they knew… Well, they'd try, anyway. He could handle himself in a fight, but he deserved at least a punch to the face over the way he'd seduced Laney like she was just another woman he'd met on one of his trips. Laney was nothing like those other women, and he needed to remember that.

Ryker dropped his hands but didn't step back. He couldn't, not when she still seemed so unsteady and his body was wound so tightly. She was a drug, his drug. They were bad for each other for too many reasons, yet he wanted more.

"I'm pregnant."

Ryker stilled. Had she just...

What the hell? He hadn't heard her right. No way. When they'd been in Miami, he hadn't planned on having sex with her after the party at the new O'Shea's location, but she'd assured him she was on birth control. So, no. He hadn't heard right.

But Laney continued to stare up at him, and Ryker waited for her to say something else, anything else, because there was no way in hell...

"I'm sorry." Laney leaned her head back against the wall and shut her eyes once more. "I didn't know how else to say it. I mean, there's really no good lead-in to something like this."

Pregnant. As in, a baby. Their baby.

Ryker turned away as dread consumed him. How the hell had he allowed something like this to even be a possibility? A child was definitely not something he ever wanted in his life. No damn way would he purposely bring an innocent baby into this world. Into his darkness.

"You said you were on birth control."

He didn't mean for the words to come out as an accusation, but he was confused, damn it. And angry. Angry at himself, because had he kept that control of his in line, Laney wouldn't be dropping this bomb.

"I was." She pulled in a breath and squared her shoulders. "I had to switch the one I was on and started a new one the week before Miami. I don't know if that's why it happened. I just don't know..."

He remembered so clearly her tugging his shirt over

his head and telling him she was on birth control, that she had just had a physical and was clean. He knew full well he hadn't been with anyone for a while, and he'd never gone without protection. So in their frantic state of shedding clothes and getting to the good stuff, they'd had a two-second conversation about contraception.

So here they were. Laney was expecting his child and he was…screwed. Literally.

Bracing his hands on the antique table behind the sofa, Ryker dropped his head. He'd kept his hands, and all his other parts, to himself this whole time. Out of respect for the family who took him in and saved his life, Ryker hadn't given in to the one desire he'd had for years. Until Miami, damn it. How would he ever make things right with the O'Sheas?

Patrick had taken Ryker in at the age of twelve when Ryker had stood up for Braden and Mac on the playground, and the boys had become best friends. Ryker had instantly become like family, but he'd never thought of Laney as a sister. At the time, he'd ignored her because she was so much younger. But by the time she graduated high school, Ryker was deep in the family business, and more than aware that his dirty hands should never touch the sophisticated Laney O'Shea.

When her computer hacking skills were made apparent, Ryker knew she'd be an asset. He'd just had no idea how difficult it would be to work with her. He could afford to hire anyone to do the behind-the-screen work, but he trusted only her.

Braden and Mac were going to kill him. They would kill him and bury his body, and no one would ever know…and he deserved nothing less.

Damn it. Ryker blew out a breath. This was how he

repaid the family who trusted him, who was loyal to him when no one else cared?

"This isn't your fault."

Her soft voice washed over him, and he let out a curt laugh. "No? Am I the one who pushed his way into your room, tore that dress off and demanded you wrap your legs around me? Or was that another man?"

He threw her a glance just in time to see her flinch. Great. Now he was being an ass. All of this was on him. Laney didn't deserve his anger—she was just as innocent as the child.

His gaze dropped to her flat stomach, and fear engulfed him. Images of his biological father flooded his mind, and Ryker vowed that second to never be that man. Never would he lay a hand on his child, never would he choose the next fix over putting food on the table.

Ryker's childhood may be a sad cliché, but that was life and all too often kids were mistreated while other adults turned a blind eye to the abuse.

Ryker looked down. Random scars covered his knuckles, his forearms. His life was made up of more ugly than anything else, yet this beautiful, vibrant woman stood here giving him something so precious and all he wanted to do was…

Hell. What did he want to do? He never wanted Braden or Mac to find out about the night he'd spent with their baby sister. Not that he was afraid of them. He could handle anything thrown his way—almost anything.

They trusted Ryker to keep the family safe, to keep all threats away. Wasn't that why he'd been ordered to follow her back to her hotel that night? Because there had been a threat against her?

For years he'd kept asshats away from her. A few

months ago he'd had to use physical force and pull some major strings to get her ex out of her life. The man had made a menace of himself and had started harassing Laney. He hadn't told Laney what happened, and he never would, but he knew she wondered. Wondered if Ryker had done something sinister. And maybe that was for the best. Maybe she wouldn't get those stars in her eyes like she'd had when they were intimate in Miami.

Pushing off the table, Ryker ran a hand down his face. Stubble rustled beneath his palm, and he honestly had no idea what to do next. He'd never faced something this life-altering, this damn scary.

"I don't expect anything from you." Laney stood straight, apparently feeling better. Her coloring was back. "But I wasn't going to keep this a secret, either. I know you don't want anything to do with me—"

"Stop saying that," he growled. "You have no idea what I want."

She tipped up her head, quirked a brow, as if issuing a silent challenge. "Enlighten me."

If only things were that easy. If only their relationship was about sex and nothing else. *If only* was the story of his entire messed-up life.

"I will be here for this child," he told her, turning to face her fully. "I'll keep you protected."

"You've been looking out for me for years."

He took a step forward. "Not like this. If you think I was protective before, you haven't seen anything."

Laney rolled her eyes. "Don't do this. Don't be overbearing. If I hadn't gotten pregnant, I know you would've gone on to ignore me on a personal level. That night we spent together wasn't supposed to happen, but we were on that path for so long, it was inevitable."

He hated when she was right. Hated even more that every night since then, he'd had to replay it over and over in his mind because he would never be that close to her again. And she'd ruined him for any other woman.

"I can take care of the baby and myself just fine." She glared back. "But I don't want my brothers to know just yet. I'm not ready."

As much as he hated hiding from anything that threatened him, he was in total agreement. Braden and Mac would find out soon enough, but for now, just no. First, he and Laney had to grasp this news themselves.

Ryker took another step until the gap between them was closed. "Let's get something straight now. I will take care of you and our baby. You need anything, I'm providing it. You won't shut me out. If I have to haul you off to my home in London and watch you personally, I will."

Laney snorted. "Really? Now you choose to let me in?"

"I don't have a choice," he muttered.

And maybe he never had…not where Laney was concerned.

So how the hell did he even attempt to keep his loyalty to this family when he'd betrayed them? And how was he going to be closer to Laney than ever before and keep his hands off her?

Ryker Barrett had lived through some rough times, but he had a feeling he was entering a whole new level of hell.

Two

How cute was he, thinking he could be all protective and overbearing? Poor Ryker. He clearly forgot he was dealing with an O'Shea. She may be the baby sister, she may be the one everyone loved to keep safely tucked away behind the computer, but she knew more than they'd ever realize. She wasn't naive, and she wasn't blind.

And going to London? Not an option. She was working on something right here in Boston that was so near to her heart, she refused to walk away. Pregnant or not, she'd see this project come to fruition.

Once she'd left Ryker's house earlier, she headed home, changed her clothes and went for a run. Her doctor had informed her that keeping up with her regular exercise routine was perfectly fine. She needed to release some pent-up energy and blow off steam anyway. Perhaps she should've joined Ryker in his punching bag workout. Although she feared he'd have pissed her off and she'd have ended up socking him in the face to knock some sense into that thick head of his.

Why did she have to be attracted to such a stubborn, frustrating man? Why did she still have to feel how amazing he was weeks after their encounter? The imprint of his powerful touch would be with her forever. Laney had always wondered if the reality of being with Ryker would measure up to the fantasy…and it was better. So much better than anything she could have dreamed up.

But now that she was pregnant, she wasn't going to use the child as an excuse to get closer to him. She wasn't a pathetic, desperate woman. She may have loved Ryker for as long as she could remember, but she would never use an innocent child to get a man.

She'd worried about telling him, though. Worried because she knew enough of his childhood to figure out he probably had no dreams of becoming a father. Ryker never spoke of his birth family—his family had become the O'Sheas the instant Mac and Braden brought him home after school one day. All she knew was that his first twelve years had been hell, and nothing any child should have to go through.

Ryker may be ten years older than her, but that didn't make him out of her reach. By the time she'd been old enough to notice boys, she'd had eyes for only one man. Oh, she'd dated, but nobody had captured her attention like Ryker. And for years he'd ignored her.

Then one night, as if the dam had broken, he'd quite literally torn off her clothes. Never had Laney been so thrilled, so relieved to finally have a dream become reality. But no dream could've ever prepared her for the experience Ryker gave her.

Laney pulled her damp hair into a loose topknot. Now that she'd exercised and showered, she was ready to get some work done. Her brothers were so close to finding their family's missing heirlooms, and she so wanted to be the one to crack the mystery.

For years, decades actually, their family had been searching for nine missing scrolls. The precious documents dated back to the sixteenth century, when one of their ancestors, an Irish monk, transcribed some of William Shakespeare's work. The scrolls had been handed down from generation to generation.

But when the Great Depression robbed so many people of their normal lives, the O'Shea family lost their home and everything inside. The home actually ended up falling into the possession of Zara Perkins's family, which was how Zara and Braden met. Braden had thought that cozying up to the pretty event coordinator and getting inside her house would help in their search. Little did Braden know he'd fall in love.

The scrolls weren't found, so now the search continued. And Laney would love nothing more than to be the one to find the missing treasure. Her entire life she'd been sheltered, kept at an arm's length from the dangers of the family business. If her father and brothers hadn't needed her mad computer skills, she had no doubt they wouldn't have told her a single thing.

Well, if she found these scrolls, they'd have to acknowledge just how much she brought to the table and how she wasn't afraid to get her hands dirty. Family meant everything, and, now more than ever, she was determined to take a stronger role in the business. Proving to her brothers, to Ryker, that she could keep up with them wasn't going to be a problem. She was an

O'Shea. Determination was ingrained in every fiber of her being.

Laney pulled up her email and slid a hand over her flat stomach. This baby would be so hardheaded and strong. There was no other option, considering the genes.

Scrolling through messages, Laney tried to forget Ryker and his demanding ways. But it was those demanding ways that had rocked her entire world at a hotel in Miami.

Maybe she could distract herself with some online Christmas shopping. Maybe that would take her mind off Ryker and the fact she now carried his child. Laney couldn't help but wonder how her overbearing brothers would react to this news.

Dread filled her stomach. How would Zara take the pregnancy? She and Braden had miscarried a child several months ago. Were they trying for another one? Laney hated to pry, but she also didn't want to seem insensitive. Especially if they tried and were unsuccessful.

Oh, they'd be happy about the baby, but privately would they be hurt? Laney loved Zara like a sister and didn't want to cause her any more grief.

With Mac and Jenna planning a wedding, Laney seriously hesitated to say anything to anybody. There wouldn't be a perfect time, but at least she could wait for a better time.

Laney clicked on an email she'd been waiting on. Her offer had been accepted. Finally. She'd been wanting this news for over a week, and the timing was perfect. One more step closer to her goal of revamping an old, run-down building in Boston's south side... Ryker's old neighborhood.

She'd set these plans in motion before Miami. Over

the years, she'd heard Ryker talk about unfortunate kids, never of his own childhood, but she knew his worry stemmed from where he'd come from. So Laney wanted to help. She hated the idea of kids feeling like there was no hope, no one there who really cared about their future.

Her father had instilled in her that commitment. To help the unfortunate. When he'd taken in Ryker, he'd done so without another thought. If more people reached out like her father had, maybe this world would be a bit brighter.

She was keeping the project a secret because she wasn't in it for the praise or the recognition. And she definitely wasn't out to make the O'Shea name look better in the community, which was what many would think if they knew she was involved.

Laney starred the email and laid her phone on the desk in her office before taking a seat. It had gotten so dark since she'd finished her run. She longed for summer and sunshine, where she didn't have to worry about getting back in time before sunset. She also wondered if running alone was the smartest choice. She always had done it by herself to clear her head and think, but now that she was pregnant, she felt more vulnerable.

From the time she was little, her father had taught her to always be aware of her surroundings. But now she should take a few more precautions. Even though she lived in Boston and the streets were bustling with people, she might want to consider using her treadmill or finding a jogging partner.

A laugh escaped her as she thought of Ryker. She couldn't quite imagine the brooding man throwing on a pair of sneakers and running. No, he was more of a boxer type, a guy who lifted heavy weights, or did pull-ups with one arm. He was all strength, all power.

And the thought of all of that excellent muscle tone had Laney attempting to focus on something else. Anything.

Christmas shopping. Right. That's what she'd been planning to do. Why go to the stores and fight all the crazies when she could go braless at home and have everything delivered right to her door...wrapped even.

Online shopping was glorious.

She also had a few final touches to put on the O'Shea's holiday party they were having for the staff at Braden's house in two weeks. The annual event had grown even more since Mac had opened satellite offices in Miami and Atlanta.

Still, Laney loved working on the party and Zara was a professional coordinator, so her sister-in-law had done the majority of the work this year. Laney just needed to order the centerpieces she and Zara had agreed on.

She'd just opened a new browser to search for a dress to wear to the party when her doorbell rang. Glancing quickly at the monitors, she saw Ryker's hulking frame. He kept his head down, shoulders hunched against the brisk December air. He never came to her house...just like she had never gone to his. He'd followed her home before to make sure she was safe, but he'd never popped in of his own accord.

Who knew it would take a pregnancy to get him to come for a visit?

Pushing away from her desk, Laney headed toward the front door. Darkness had set in and snow swirled around, bright flakes catching in the streetlights.

Laney flicked the lock on her door and opened it, immediately stepping back so Ryker could come in out of the cold.

Without a word he strode inside. Those heavy black boots were quite the contrast to her bare feet with polished pink toes. And that was barely the beginning of all the ways they differed.

Laney closed out the cold and set the dead bolt. Crossing her arms over her chest, she faced the man she'd been half in love with since she was a teen.

"This is a surprise," she told him. "Did you come to talk or is something wrong?"

"I need to head out of town."

Laney nodded. His rushing out of town was nothing new. He did so many things for the family. The O'Sheas had gone global with their famous auction houses. Ryker sometimes traveled to obtain relics or random pieces for a specific auction. He'd been known to procure heirlooms that had been stolen. Some may look at him as a modern-day Robin Hood since he returned items to their right owner.

He also was known to go to his home in London for a quick escape, but he was always a text or call away. He put her family first above all else.

"I'm leaving in the morning, and I'll be gone a few days."

Laney tipped up her head. "You never tell me when you're going out of town unless you need my computer skills to pull up the blueprint of a building. If that's what you—"

"I'm not here for the blueprint."

The way those black-as-night eyes held her in place had her shivering. Why did she let him have such power over her? He had more power in one stare than most guys did in a kiss. And she'd dated some great kissers.

"Then why are you here?" She was proud of her strong tone but worried about what his answer would be.

"Are you feeling okay?" he asked, his eyes dropping to her stomach, then back up. "I didn't ask earlier. Or, hell, maybe I did. It's all still kind of a blur."

So he was here about the pregnancy. She should've known he wouldn't stay too far from her. He'd always been protective in that overbearing, bouncer kind of way.

"If you're going to hover, don't waste your time."

She didn't want to sound ungrateful, but she didn't want a babysitter. She wanted him, damn it. She wanted him to see her as a woman. As the woman he'd let down his guard with several weeks ago.

Up until then, she'd always thought he saw her as Mac and Braden's little sister. Someone he helped when necessary, but who was more family than anything.

"If I want to hover, I damn well will," he growled. "You're having my child. You're part of a very well-known family, and it's my job to protect you."

That was the crux of the entire problem. The slice to her heart shouldn't surprise her. Did she honestly think that after they'd had sex he'd come around? That when he knew about the baby he'd profess his undying love to her? No, but she'd at least hoped for him to treat her like…hell. Was it too much to ask for him to act like he cared about her as more than his friends' baby sister?

"I don't want to be your job."

Laney turned before he could see the hurt on her face. Heading back toward her office, she couldn't care less if he let himself out or if he followed. Trying to capture

Ryker's attention for so long was exhausting. She sure as hell didn't want it now due to a job or a baby. She wanted him to look at her for her. Nothing else.

Apparently that was too much to ask. With his traveling schedule, he probably did hookups and one-night stands. She'd never seen him in any type of a relationship or even heard him mention seeing someone. Laney thought she may take way too much delight in that, but whatever.

Just as she reached the threshold of her office, a hand clamped around her arm and spun her.

"Don't walk away from me."

Laney raised her brows. "You're not in charge of me, no matter what my brothers tell you to do. I can get along just fine without being coddled."

"Would you quit acting like you're so put out? Your brothers care about you and only want you safe."

Laney jerked free of his hold but kept her eyes on his. "And what about you, Ryker? Do you care about me?"

"Of course I do."

Laney swallowed. "As a brother?"

The muscles along the stubbled jaw ticked. "I'm not doing this, Laney. I'm not hashing out my feelings or letting you get inside my head."

Of course he wouldn't. Ryker would never let anyone in because he was made of steel. She'd never seen him show emotion, other than frustration and anger. But he never talked about what drove him to those feelings. The clenching of the muscles in his perfectly squared jaw indicated he was angry. Other than that, he played his cards seriously close to his chest.

"Whatever." She waved a hand in the air. "I'm feeling fine. There. Now you've checked up on me, and you can go on your way, guilt-free. This all could've been done in a text."

"Maybe," he agreed. "But if you were feeling bad you'd lie, and I wanted to see for myself."

Laney went for broke. "I think we both know between the two of us who would lie about how they feel."

When he remained still, silent, Laney was done. They were getting nowhere, and she wasn't in the mood to play games or whatever the hell else he wanted.

"I won't keep you out of the baby's life, but I don't want your attention just because I'm pregnant. I've waited for years for you to notice me. I thought Miami was something, but I was clearly mistaken, since you ignored me until you knew I was having your child."

All of that was so hard to admit, but at this point what did she have to lose? She wasn't one to hide her feelings, which only made Ryker squirm. Good. He deserved it.

The second she jerked the door open, a burst of cold air rushed in. "If you're done here…"

Laney turned and stared out at the blowing flakes. She didn't want to look at him, not when she still craved him. Putting up some type of emotional barrier was the only way she'd survive this.

Heavy boots moved across her hardwood floor. Ryker stopped right in front of her but kept his gaze out the open door. Laney stared at his black, leather-clad shoulder. The smell of his jacket, the familiar woodsy cologne and the unmistakable scent that she only associated with Ryker assaulted her senses. Why did he have to be the one to hold her emotionally captive?

"I've noticed you," he whispered as he remained rooted inches from her. "I've noticed too much for too long."

Laney's breath caught in her throat.

"But Miami won't happen again." Turning, he locked those dark eyes on her. "I'll check on you while I'm away."

And then he was gone. Shoulders hunched against the blowing snow, head down, Ryker walked off her porch and down the walk toward his car. Despite shivering, Laney waited until he was in the SUV with the engine running before she closed the door…but not before she caught him looking back at her.

Just that glance from a distance was enough to have her stomach doing flops, her heart pounding.

Ryker may be checking on her because of the baby, something she couldn't be upset about, but his telling words gave her hope. He'd noticed her. And from the way he seemed to be angry about it, he'd clearly been fighting with himself over the fact for a while now.

Laney leaned back against her door and wrapped her arms around her abdomen. She had no idea what was going to happen now that she and Ryker were on this journey, but one thing was perfectly clear. They were in this together, whether he liked it or not.

Three

"I don't like this."

Ryker's cell phone lay on the console as he watched the house across the street. With Braden on speaker, Ryker could focus on who was coming and going.

"I'm not a fan myself, but I think there's something here," Ryker replied.

This was his first interaction with Braden since Ryker discovered Laney was expecting. The guilt of his betrayal weighed heavily on his chest. The O'Sheas had been everything to him over the years, and he'd purposely kept his distance from Laney because he knew what would happen if he touched her. Just one touch, that's all it would've taken at any given time for him to snap.

But she'd mouthed off at the party and between her sass and that body-hugging dress, his self-control had finally expired.

Damn, the woman could tempt a saint…not that he

was anywhere near that holy. But he'd completely lost it in Miami. Years of pent-up frustration, the fact she'd been receiving threats and not sharing that information, and the way she'd looked in that short black dress had been the combination for his undoing.

"How long are you going to wait?" Braden's low tone cut through the memories.

Ryker rubbed the penny between his thumb and index finger, hating the way he carried the damn thing around like some good-luck charm. He was pathetic for even still having it, but the reminder of where he came from always needed to be front and center.

"I've seen a member of the DeLuca family go in, but nothing else."

The DeLuca family was known for organized crime. Thugs, actually. They didn't even compare to the O'Sheas, though Ryker thought some members of law enforcement would lump the two families in the same category…or prison cell.

"What activity has Laney uncovered?" Braden asked.

Ryker raked a hand down his face. "She's seen some email chatter with several family members discussing moving a package. When she dug a little deeper, she found they have an old trunk in the basement that contains some documents. But we have no clue what they are."

Ryker didn't know how the coveted scrolls would've ended up hours away from where they were last seen or how they were in a basement belonging to an organized crime family, but this was the strongest lead they'd had in a while. Ryker had followed every tip that had popped up. He'd been to London twice, Mexico, Paris and several US states.

When Patrick passed several months ago, he had one dying request. He wanted the scrolls found and returned to the O'Shea family. He'd tried for years to recover them but to no avail. Ryker fully intended to finish the job... it was the least he could do for the people to whom he owed his life.

"Damn, Laney is calling me," Braden stated. "Keep me posted no matter what happens or what time it is."

Laney was calling? Was she okay? Did something happen?

Every time he'd thought of her since Miami, all he could think about was the way she came apart in his arms. She'd been so responsive, so passionate. Now when he thought of her, all he could think was that she was carrying his child. His. Child.

The words didn't seem real even in his own mind. How the hell was he going to take care of a baby? What did he know? His father had only taught him how to get high, get laid and steal. The essentials of every childhood according to dear ole Dad.

Ryker kept his eyes on the house, but his mind wasn't on the job. Damn. This was why he never got involved with anyone. His loyalties were with Braden and Mac now. And by default, as their baby sister, Laney. If he was worrying about anyone, especially a woman, he wouldn't be able to concentrate on the task at hand. And the task sure as hell wasn't Laney.

She'd called Braden, not Ryker. That shouldn't bother him, but it did. There was no denying that he wanted to be the one she called on when she needed anything. But he couldn't be that deep in her life and keep his distance at the same time.

His mind went into overdrive. If something was going

on with the baby, she wouldn't have called Braden, that much Ryker was sure of.

Ryker disconnected the call. The penny was heavy in his hand. Over the years, he'd tried to tell himself that the souvenir from the best day of his life was ridiculous and childish to keep. Yet each day he left his house, he grabbed his keys and the penny and shoved them in his pocket. He couldn't seem to let go of his past.

Story of his life.

After another hour of waiting, which brought the grand total up to six, Ryker decided to call it a night. Laney would let him know if more activity came through her. She'd managed to tap into several areas: emails, private messages on social media, a cell phone.

Ryker always marveled at how crazy brilliant she was. She was seriously the brains behind the operation when it came to research and hunting down people. For years, she'd managed to find anything online, while Ryker did the grunt work. They were a team in a sense, but he never wanted to look at things that way. If he did, then he'd have to admit there was a relationship. And even when their dealings had been platonic, he couldn't analyze things too deeply when it came to Laney.

The woman could make a man forget everything else in this ugly world. She had beauty, grace and a stubborn streak he couldn't help but admire.

And now she was having his baby.

Pulling himself up straighter in his seat, Ryker brought the engine of his SUV to life. Snow covered the streets and showed no sign of stopping soon. December in New York was just as brutal and unpredictable as in Boston.

Cranking up the heat, he maneuvered through the

streets toward the hotel. Another cold hotel. He always booked a suite. Mostly because growing up he'd lived in a one-room dump of an apartment. Now that he could afford to stay anywhere or buy anything he wanted, he fully intended to take advantage.

But he'd never look at another hotel the same after Miami. Laney changed everything.

He couldn't even wrap his mind around the fact he was going to be a father. What the hell did he know? His own father had used him as a punching bag when he was awake and only half drunk. Ryker never wanted marriage, kids, the minivan experience. He was just fine with the job he had. Though Braden and Mac would never tell him this was a job, to them he was simply a brother, a best friend.

Which made this pregnancy so much harder to comprehend. He couldn't come to grips with how he should deal with it, so how the hell could he figure out how to tell them?

Laney was such an innocent. They'd worked for years to keep her safe, to keep her behind the scenes. Ryker had made enemies all over the globe. Now that Laney was pregnant, he would have to be twice as diligent about keeping those he cared about safe.

Yeah, he cared about her. Too much. Being ten years older than her, he'd not paid much attention when he first came to the O'Sheas as a teen. Then he'd been out of the house mostly doing grunt work and earning his way in the family, so he didn't have to go back to his former hellhole.

By the time he'd started coming around the house more often, Laney was a teen herself and he was a bastard for looking at her twice. If Patrick O'Shea had ever thought Ryker was eyeing his daughter, Ryker doubted he'd still be here.

But Ryker had respected the man more than anyone. Patrick had shown him what a true father figure was. Patrick had cared for his children, put them first and kept them protected at all costs. He had demanded loyalty, and there was nothing Ryker had wanted to give him more.

Which was one of the main reasons he wanted to be the one to uncover the scrolls. Patrick was gone, but Ryker still wanted to do this one final job for the only real father he'd ever known.

And all the more reason Ryker needed to keep his hands to himself where Laney was concerned. Patrick had been extremely protective and cautious when Laney wanted to date certain men. There were guys who wanted to date her simply for her last name or because they thought they could get into the family and wanted to use her as a warped version of a job interview.

Ryker had done neither of those things. He'd just gone straight to taking her against a wall and getting her pregnant like a loser.

One thing was for sure. He may not be father material, but he wasn't about to ignore his responsibilities. If he had his way, he'd whisk Laney and their baby away and tuck them safely in his home in London...or he'd buy a damn private island. Anything to keep them safe.

He had the funds, that wasn't the problem. No, the problem came in the form of a beautiful, stubborn, Irish goddess who would rather argue with him than listen to reason.

Ryker pulled into a parking spot right outside the window to his room. Always on the ground floor, always near an exit.

Fear overwhelmed him for the first time in years. Not for himself but for Laney and their unborn child.

When he got back to Boston, they were going to have to talk. He couldn't outrun her any longer. He may not want a relationship with her, or anyone else for that matter, but he'd make damn sure she was taken care of... regardless of the cost to his own heart.

Most would say he didn't have a heart. Ryker would have to agree. But Laney made him feel, and he could see the train wreck coming. Someone was going to get hurt.

When Laney had called her brother because her Christmas decorations were too heavy for her to lift, she hadn't even realized the time of night. But here he was hauling box after box into her living room.

"Why do you have so much stuff to put up for only one month?" he growled as he sat the last box beside her sofa.

"So you can enjoy it when you come to visit." Laney smiled and patted his cheek. "Just think, in about four weeks you can come back and take this all back up to my attic."

"I'll hire someone. Hell, just leave it up all year long. I won't judge."

Laney pulled the lid off one box and stared down at the contents. Christmas decorations were her crack. She loved everything about them. The lights, the glass ornaments that belonged to her mother, the garland she strung over her mantel and down her staircase. Everything was so magical, so perfect, and it made her remember how amazing her childhood had been. A house full of family and laughter, the parties they'd thrown in the O'Shea ballroom.

Tears pricked her eyes. She wanted that for her baby.

She wanted her child to know the meaning of family gatherings. There was nothing more valuable to Laney than her family. She needed them now more than ever, but she had no idea how to tell them a little O'Shea was about to join their ranks.

She wasn't afraid of how they'd react to the baby; her brothers would welcome another O'Shea. But how would they treat Ryker? He was such a staple in their family, and he was so much more to Braden and Mac than just an employee. He was…everything.

Laney sighed and blinked back tears.

"Hey, you okay?" Braden stood beside her, bending to look her in the eye. "Oh, damn. Please don't cry. I'll help take them down later, I swear."

Why was it that the strongest of men couldn't handle a little water?

"I'm fine," she assured him, waving a hand. "It's late and I'm tired. That's all."

His dark brows raised in disbelief. "And you opted to start decorating now?"

"I've got a lot on my mind." Wasn't that an understatement. "I'll work on this until I think I can fall asleep."

Crossing his arms over his chest, Braden straightened and pinned her with his eyes. "Is there a problem I need to know about?"

Laney picked up an ornament and began to peel away its bubble wrap. "Just worrying about my brothers. Nothing new."

That wasn't a total lie. She always worried about them. Their business kept them busy, traveling, sneaking around. Thankfully they had enough law enforcement in their back pocket to keep them out of the hot seat, but still. Laney always worried something would happen. There were worse fates than being arrested.

"We're all fine." Braden took the ornament from her and waited until she turned her attention toward him. "I'm asking about you. Are you still receiving threats? I'd hoped after Shane—"

"Stop worrying about me."

She didn't want to talk about her emails or Shane. Ryker had taken it upon himself to…handle the problem of Shane when he'd attempted to abduct Laney from in front of her home in Beacon Hill. Shane had been the bane of her family's existence for years, but he'd crossed the line when he'd harassed Braden's wife, Zara. When he'd tried to grab Laney, Ryker had had enough.

And Laney knew the way Ryker had managed the situation had been an issue between him and Braden. Since Braden had taken over the family business after their father passed, he'd been adamant about going legitimate, and that included how they took care of their enemies. Ryker insisted that ending their old practices so suddenly would make them look weak and invite retribution.

Laney was still unsure what happened to her ex, but she was fine about being kept in the dark regarding that.

"Why don't you get back home to your bride?" Laney suggested. "It's late. I'm just going to sit here and tear up a little over Mom's things."

Braden looked as if he wanted to say more. That intense stare could make even the most seasoned criminal break, but Laney wasn't caving. She'd grown up around strong-willed alphas her entire life. Not much fazed her.

"If you have any issues, you call me or Ryker immediately."

Laney nodded, though if she had an issue she'd deal with it herself. She wasn't a helpless female.

Once she hugged her loving, overprotective brother good-night, she reset her alarm and glanced around at the mess. The tree sat completely naked in the corner near the fireplace where she always put it. She wasn't even sure at this point if she had any working lights. She tried to buy new ones each year, but, well, this year had been a bit exceptional and her mind had been elsewhere.

Laney found the box with her garland and decided to work on the staircase. That would be simple enough and keep her mind occupied for a few minutes.

She'd barely started when her thoughts drifted to Ryker. There was always a level of fear anytime she knew he was working. But the not knowing was frustrating. She knew the lead he was working on, she'd supplied him with the intel, but she didn't like how he insisted on going out alone. He always stayed just detached enough to be in the know but keep to himself. Damn frustrating man.

Laney carefully wrapped the banister, fluffing the greenery as she went. This time next year she'd be playing Santa and buying the baby's first Christmas things— tacky bibs and ridiculous ornaments would be welcome here.

What would her world be like with a child? Laney smiled. As scared as she was to tell her brothers, as worried as she was about what this meant for her and Ryker, there was no way Laney would change one single thing about Miami. This baby would never question how much he or she was loved, and the first person to call this pregnancy a mistake would be throat punched.

The thought of Ryker holding a baby was nearly

laughable. She'd never seen his softer side, though she knew he had one. He cared for her, even if he opted to show it in Neanderthal-type ways.

Those whispered words before he left kept playing through her mind. She wished he'd stayed so they could talk, but he was prone to run rather than discuss his feelings. Well, he couldn't hide from her forever. Eventually they had to talk about the future and their baby.

Laney's cell chimed from the living room. She hurried down the stairs and carefully maneuvered the minefield of boxes. She found her phone on the coffee table next to a wreath that was in desperate need of fluffing. Because of the time of night, she figured the text would be important.

And she was right.

Ryker's name lit up her screen, and she swiped her phone to read the message.

Nothing new tonight. Anything come through on your end?

Work. It was always work with him. A sliver of disappointment speared through her as she replied.

Nothing. I'll keep you posted.

Her thumb hovered over the Send button. She wanted to make this more personal. She wanted to say…something. But Ryker was all work. What would he say if she asked personal questions or called him out on what he'd confessed to her earlier? Could he talk about his feelings when he wasn't looking her in the face? She understood that. She totally got how people were more apt to open up when they could hide behind an electronic device.

She hit Send but immediately started typing another message.

Earlier when you said you think about me, why were you angry about it?

Laney sent the message before she could change her mind. She wanted to know. She deserved to know, but the screen seemed to mock her as no reply came. She waited several minutes, but still nothing.

Fine. She wasn't going to beg. Yes, she would give anything to get inside that head of his, but she didn't want to have to beat the information out of him.

The second she laid her phone down, it chimed once again. Laney stared at the screen. She almost didn't want to read the message, but she hadn't been raised to give into any fear.

Because it isn't right.

Laney resisted the urge to roll her eyes as she contemplated her reply. There was so much to be said, it was too much to text and should be said face-to-face.

But he wasn't completely closing her out, so she went for it.

Whatever you feel can't be helped. Why fight it?

Laney jumped when her phone rang. The cell bounced from her hand and onto the sofa, hit a box and landed on the floor. She snatched it up, thankful the screen wasn't cracked, and she was a bit surprised to see Ryker's name.

"I didn't think you'd actually talk to me," she answered.

"You wouldn't leave me alone until I did."

Laney smiled. Just that gruff tone had her nerves calming. Ryker could always make her feel safe, at ease. Even though they argued and got on each other's nerves, he was her comfort zone. Banter was their normal. Normal was so vanilla. What she and Ryker had, well…that was more Rocky Road.

"Where are you now?" she asked, scooting a box over and taking a seat on her couch.

"Hotel."

"Plenty of time to talk, then."

Ryker's heavy sigh resounded through the line. "I'm not in a chatty mood."

"Have you ever been?"

"What do you think?"

Laney toed the disorderly wreath aside and propped her socked feet on the coffee table. "Maybe it's time you stop fighting whatever you're feeling and just go with it."

The laugh that escaped him was void of any humor. "Life isn't that easy."

"It's your life, isn't it? Make it that easy."

"You think I enjoy pushing my level of self-control?" he asked, his voice gravelly, as if fighting back anger. "I have a responsibility to your brothers. I have a responsibility to you." He let out a deep sigh. "To our baby."

Laney's heart clenched. Closing her eyes, she dropped her head back on the cushion and focused on not botching this. Ryker was so much more to her than she could even put into words, but he may never comprehend that.

"You have a responsibility to yourself," she said softly. "You owe my family nothing. I know you think you—"

"I owe your family everything. And I've betrayed them."

His last words came out on a strangled breath. Laney stilled. Did he honestly believe that? Was he that torn up over the baby that he truly felt he'd gone against her brothers? Why did everything have to come back to his sense of loyalty to her family? They trusted him, they knew him better than anyone else and they might be angry, but they would still love him.

Tears pricked her eyes, and she cursed her stupid pregnancy hormones. Tears had no place here. She was fighting for what she wanted, what Ryker wanted. Hell, what they deserved.

"If that's how you feel, then there's nothing I can say. If you don't want anyone to know this baby is yours, we don't have to say anything. I can just say I'm not involved with the father and not tell my brothers any name at all." Though it would kill her. Pain like nothing before speared through her at the thought of Ryker not being involved. "I can't make you want—"

"That's the whole problem," he yelled. "I want, damn it. Too much. But I'll never turn my back on you or this baby."

Laney picked at the hem of her T-shirt and swallowed a lump of remorse. "Right. Responsibilities."

"Laney—"

"It's late. I'll let you go."

She ended the call, dropping the phone into her lap as she battled back tears. Why did he have to be so noble, yet so ignorant at the same time? Why did he feel that he had to sacrifice his own happiness in order to fulfill some past debt? Ryker had more than proved himself to this family.

At least he hadn't agreed to being left out of the baby's life. That would've gutted her. But he still only saw her as a responsibility, and Laney feared she'd never be more in his life.

Four

"We need to get inside that house."

Braden nodded in agreement. "How soon can you get back? I don't want them moving that trunk."

Ryker leaned back on the leather sofa in Braden's study. He'd left New York after staying an extra day longer than planned, and had driven straight to Braden's house. He hadn't called or texted Laney after their talk on the phone. He'd revealed too much, she'd gotten too close to the raw emotions…emotions he feared he couldn't hide forever.

Damn it. He hadn't even been aware of suppressing them, so how the hell did he continue to hide them?

"I can go as soon as I get the blueprint."

Braden came to his feet. "Great. Laney is due here anytime."

The blueprint was a pathetic excuse to see her again.

He could've gotten it the other day when she offered, she could've also emailed it. But, he wanted to see her, touch her, consume her. But reality was cold and harsh. He'd had her once, and that would have to stay with him forever because he couldn't let his guard down again.

He'd not only betrayed Braden and Mac by slashing right through their trust, but he'd let Laney down, as well. He should've had more control in Miami, should've walked her to her room and kept going once he knew she was safe. How could he have let his all-consuming need for her change their entire lives?

"Ryker?"

Jerking his attention back to Braden, Ryker stood. "Lost in thought. What were you saying?"

"Laney just pulled in."

Ryker glanced to the monitors and saw Laney stepping from her car. While it had stopped snowing, the ground was blanketed in several inches. Braden's drive and walk had been cleared though.

He tried not to watch as she pulled her coat tighter around her waist or how her long, dark hair blew in the breeze. He didn't have to concentrate too hard to still feel that hair over his body. Ryker clenched his fists and ordered himself to get control before she stepped inside. This would be the first time the three of them would be together since he'd found out about the pregnancy. He couldn't give anything away. He couldn't—

On the screen, Laney slipped and went down. Ryker tore out of the study, down the hall and through the foyer. He whipped open the door, oblivious to the wind and the bitter air. Laney had a gloved hand on the bumper of her car and was pushing herself up.

"Stop." Ryker slid his arms around her waist. "Lean into me."

Laney pushed her hair away from her face and looked up at him. "I'm fine. Embarrassed, but fine."

Ryker didn't let her go as she came fully to her feet. "Is she okay?"

Ryker glanced over his shoulder to Braden who was coming toward them. "I think so."

Laney tried to push off Ryker, but winced. "Okay. Just give me a second."

His hands flattened over her stomach as his heart sank. "Laney?"

Her eyes held his. "It's my ankle. Just sore. I'm okay."

How did she know? Could she be sure the baby was okay? Ryker didn't know how hard she fell. Hell, he didn't know anything about pregnancies or babies, but seeing her go down had nearly stopped his heart.

Scooping her up in his arms, and careful to avoid random ice patches, he stalked past Braden and into the house. Zara rushed in from the kitchen, her dark hair flying around her shoulders.

"What happened? Laney?"

"I'm okay." Laney waved a hand. "Just slipped outside and my ankle is sore. Ryker is being overbearing as usual."

Considering he'd been that way with her for years, this wasn't out of the ordinary. He didn't give a damn if it was. Seeing Laney go down like that had ripped something open inside him. In the brief seconds it took him to get outside, all he could think of was their baby. How the hell was he going to handle parenting?

"I'll get some ice," Zara told them.

Ryker gently laid Laney on the chaise in the formal

living room. Her hand slid against the side of his neck as she let go. Even though she had gloves on, just that simple touch took him back to Miami when she'd—

No. That was then. A mistake. He couldn't live in the past. He'd vowed to move on and that's exactly what he had to do if he wanted to get their intimacy out of his life.

Unfortunately, Laney had imbedded herself into his soul…and he thought he'd sold that to the devil a long time ago.

But he felt her. When she looked at him, he swore he felt her. That delicate touch, the tender gaze. She was hurting now, and he needed to focus.

"I'll call our doctor," Ryker stated.

Laney immediately started to shake her head. "I just went down wrong. I'm fine. I didn't fall hard."

"Let's get your boot off and look at your ankle." Braden went to unzip her boot. "Can you move it at all?"

She wiggled her foot, and Ryker watched her face for any sign of discomfort. When her bright eyes flashed up to his, he had to tell himself not to look away. She could draw him in so easily…and she knew the power she possessed.

"It's a little swollen," Braden commented. "I'd say you're fine. Just stay off it for a while."

Laney smirked. Freakin' smirked at him like a child who'd been playing parents against each other. Ryker narrowed his eyes. "I'm calling the doctor anyway just to be safe."

Before he could slide his cell from his pocket, Laney laid a hand on his wrist. "I'm fine." Her eyes bore into his, completely serious now. "I promise. I'd know if I needed to be seen."

She didn't look away, her grip tightened. Ryker blew

out a breath he wasn't aware he'd been holding. Of course she would get a doctor here if she thought she needed one. Laney loved this baby and wouldn't make poor choices. Still, for his peace of mind, he'd feel better if she was seen.

"Relax," she whispered, her eyes darting toward her brother.

Yeah. Relax.

Ryker took a step back and glanced down at her ankle. He needed to get a grip. Being cautious and protective was one thing, but acting like a hovering boyfriend was—

Seriously? How had that word even popped into his head? He wasn't her damn boyfriend. This wasn't junior high. But she was right. If he didn't get a grip, Braden would wonder what was going on, and that wasn't a topic he wanted to dive headfirst into right now.

"Here you go." Zara came back in and placed an ice pack wrapped in a towel over Laney's ankle. "Let's put a pillow under you to keep it propped up."

Ryker stayed back as Braden and Zara got Laney situated. He wanted to scoop her up and take her back to his house where he could take care of her. He wanted her tucked away behind his state-of-the-art security system where she'd be safe at all times. But none of that was possible. She'd never be at his house on personal terms. He'd never see her in his bed.

Ryker reached into his pocket, his fingertips brushing over the penny. The reminder he wasn't cut out for family life.

"Do you feel like working?" Braden asked. "I hate to ask, but time is of the essence."

Laney shifted on the sofa. "I can work. My laptop is

out in the car, though. I was walking to the passenger side to get it when I fell."

"I'll get it."

Ryker needed more cool air. He needed to get his heart rate back to normal and to chill out. Laney had had to talk him down, and that had never happened. Damn it.

She may not want a doctor, but one thing was certain. When they left here, he'd be driving her. Whether they went to her house or his, that was her choice, but they'd be leaving together.

Laney concentrated on digging up the layout of the house Ryker needed to get into. Her ankle throbbed more than she wanted to admit, but she was absolutely certain nothing else was hurt. The baby was fine. If she even thought for a second that something could be wrong, she'd have a doctor here. But she honestly hadn't fallen that hard, just turned her ankle on the sliver of ice she hadn't seen.

Zara and Braden were in the study. Her brother had told her to yell when she found something because he was helping his wife work on finalizing the company party.

Laney's sister-in-law was a top-notch events coordinator and in high demand. The way Braden supported her business was adorable. He was proud of his wife, and their love was evident whenever they were around each other.

The miscarriage they'd suffered a few months ago had only forged their bond even deeper. But Laney still couldn't bring herself to tell them about her own condition.

"Will you stop brooding?" Laney's fingers flew over the keys, but Ryker's presence was wearing on her nerves.

"I'm waiting."

She glanced over to him and raised her brows. "You're leaning in the corner with your arms crossed, and you've been staring for twenty minutes. That's brooding. I can actually hear your frustration."

When he pushed from the wall and strode over to her, Laney realized she'd poked the bear. Fine. At least he was showing emotion.

Ryker loomed over her, hands on his narrow hips. "How much longer until you have something?"

"I'm downloading the blueprints now."

"Good. Then we're leaving."

Laney jerked back. "Excuse me?"

He leaned down, pinning her with those coal-black eyes. "You heard me. I'm driving. The destination is up to you."

O-kay. The clenched jaw and the no-nonsense tone told her he wasn't giving her an option.

"Fine. We're going to my house. I have things I need to get done."

Ryker shoved his hands in his pockets. "Not with that ankle. You're relaxing, and if I even think you're trying to put weight on it, I'll have the doctor at your house so fast you won't know what hit you."

Laney believed him. He didn't take chances with her on a good day, but add in a pregnancy and a fall, and Ryker was dead serious.

"Oh, don't worry." She offered him her sweetest smile. "I plan on letting you do all the work."

Poor guy. He had no idea he was about to be covered head to toe in glittery garland, lights and delicate glass ornaments. She'd most certainly have her phone at the ready to snap some pictures of Ryker decorating her house.

"Oh, here we go." She glanced back at her screen, surveyed the pages that had downloaded and quickly emailed them to Braden and Ryker. "All done."

Ryker stalked from the room. There was no other word to describe his movements. He was angry, most likely with himself, or maybe with her. Whatever. He was about to be doused in Christmas happiness. He wanted to order her around and demand he leave with her? Fine.

Laney hesitated for a second but quickly pulled up her emails. Nothing new on the property in Southie. She'd had some contractors survey the building so she could get some quotes. After she signed the paperwork next week, the place would officially be hers and she could get to work. She seriously wanted the place open by spring so kids could come and play when the weather got nicer.

Opening the community center in Ryker's old neighborhood was perfect. She couldn't wait to have children filling the place. Children who may not have an exemplary home life and just needed a break.

Laney wondered where Ryker would be today if someone had intervened and helped him earlier than her father had. Would he still be part of their lives? Would he still be as hard, as jaded as he was now? He'd made it a point to be her personal security detail from the time she was a teenager. Was that because no one had protected him?

Laney's heart clenched. Had his worry for her led to whatever happened to her ex?

No. She wouldn't believe that Ryker would do anything to him beyond a few harassing calls and texts. Ryker could be over the top at times when it came to people he cared about, but she truly hoped he hadn't done anything rash.

Laney swallowed as she closed her laptop. Ryker cared about her. Beyond their intense night together, he'd admitted as much…and he didn't mean the sibling type of caring, either.

Ryker may think he'd been keeping her safe, but she always had his back, too. She held the reins with the intel coming in, and she chose what to feed him and what to keep to herself.

Laney would be even more diligent now that he was going to be a father. There might be times she made sure he didn't get a case because of the danger it posed to him, and she'd deal with the backlash from her brothers. Ryker needed someone to look after him; he was long overdue for it, actually. And Laney was just the woman for the job.

Five

The second Ryker stepped into Laney's house, he froze. He'd been duped. He glanced at her, only to see a smirk on her beautiful face. Now she mocked him.

Why did he find himself so attracted to her again? Oh, yeah. She was sexy as hell, and she took charge. A perfectly lethal combination to his senses. If he were ever considering a relationship, those were the qualities he'd look for. But a relationship with Laney was not only risky, it was suicide.

"Don't even tell me I'm decorating."

Laney leaned on him because she wouldn't let him carry her, yet she was limping slightly. Stubborn woman.

"I can do it, but you'll just get all grouchy and make me sit down."

Ryker reset her alarm system, still wishing he'd ignored her request and gone to his own house. After escorting her over to her sofa with an attached chaise, he got her settled and pulled off her boots. He grabbed one of her fluffy yellow throw pillows and set it beneath her ankle.

"Still sore?" he asked, glancing down at her, trying to ignore how perfect she looked all laid out.

"It's fine."

Ryker crossed his arms over his chest and sighed. "You've said that at least five times since it happened, which means it's anything but fine."

Laney tipped her head back on the cushion, her hair falling around her shoulders. Try as he might, he couldn't help but recall how all those strands felt on his bare skin. A memory he prayed never diminished. He needed that to keep him going, especially since he'd never have her again.

"Stop hovering. My ankle is fine, the baby is fine." She laced her fingers over her abdomen. "Do you want to put the lights on the tree or would you prefer to decorate the mantel?"

Ryker narrowed his eyes. Testing his patience was a surefire way to get him to take her back to his house. Did he look like a damn interior designer?

"Maybe you didn't notice, but I don't do Christmas."

"I always buy you a gift. In fact, you're the first person I buy for."

Yeah, and he'd kept every single one of them. He always felt like a fool for not buying her something, but what would he get her? What was an appropriate gift for a woman he wanted but couldn't have? So he never did gifts...for anyone.

"You don't have to buy me gifts," he growled. He'd rather put up lights than get into this uncomfortable topic.

Laney shifted on the chaise and patted the spot beside her. "You're staring down at me like I'm a bug on your shoe. So, either sit down, get to work or leave."

Ryker loved how she always spoke her mind. Except when she kept revealing her feelings for him. Nothing good could come from her making an impossible situation even more difficult.

And if he sat next to her, he'd want to touch her. Touching would lead to what they both truly wanted, and he refused to betray this family again by giving into his selfish desires.

Ryker turned and grabbed a box. "What's in here?"

From the corner of his eye, he saw Laney's shoulders fall, her eyes close. He'd hurt her. He couldn't sit close to her. Didn't she get that? She had to understand this wasn't about them. There was so much more to it than just a man and a woman who were attracted to each other. So he'd have to keep his distance…as much as possible, no matter how much he wanted her.

"That's the ornaments," she told him. "I have a bag of lights I just purchased. It's on the steps. There's also a bag from All Seasons there, but be careful because I just bought the cutest Nutcracker there."

Fine. He'd put the damn lights on the tree. He'd decorate her house to put a smile on her face. He knew full well how much Laney loved Christmas. She used to go to her parents' house, which was now Braden and Zara's, and cook an elaborate dinner on Christmas Eve. She'd pass out gifts she'd bought and wrapped in thick, sparkly paper. Most likely she'd hand tied her own bows, too. Laney's face would light up as she sat and watched her family open their gifts. Ryker was always so mesmerized, so humbled he got to experience Christmas with them.

Damn it. They were his family. The only family he'd truly considered his own—the only one that mattered.

He'd just reached the steps and spotted the bag when Laney's soft voice stopped him.

"I know you don't want to be here."

Ryker glanced over his shoulder. Those bright green eyes locked him in place from across the room.

"I never said that."

Smiling, she said, "You didn't have to. You regret sleeping with me. Probably feel trapped because I'm pregnant. And I'm positive you think you betrayed my brothers. But please, don't patronize me or pity me. I'm fine on my own, Ryker."

When she held her ground and didn't glance away, he ignored the bag and started back toward Laney. She was a strong woman, what man wouldn't find that a complete turn on? She was everything he'd want in a woman, but she was the little sister of his employers, his best friends. She was off limits. And he'd ignored that unwritten rule.

Taking a seat on the edge of the chaise, he faced her. "I don't regret sleeping with you. I've tried, but I can't even lie to myself."

She reached out, tracing his scarred knuckles with her fingertip. "That's something, at least."

"I don't feel trapped," he went on. "I feel sorry for you, for this baby. I know nothing, Laney. The most impressionable years of my childhood were spent in hell. I couldn't begin to tell you what a baby needs. I don't even know how to help you adjust to this. I'm not made to be in a relationship or to be a parent. But that doesn't mean I'm turning my back on you guys. It just means…"

Ryker shook his head and turned away so he didn't have to look her in the eye. Apparently she was the stronger of the two. "It means you deserve better, and this is what you've got."

He barely heard her shift before her fingers threaded through his hair. "There's nobody better than you, Ryker. You're a fighter, you're noble and you're loyal. I know you'd do anything to keep me and this baby safe. What makes you think I'm so unlucky?"

Reaching up, he gripped her wrist, but didn't pull her hand away as he turned to meet her questioning gaze. "Because you deserve a man you can share your life with. You're the type who wants a family, who wants that big Christmas morning celebration with chaos and Santa stories. I can't give you that."

Laney smoothed his hair from his forehead. He should stop her. He should remove her hand, but he was such a selfish bastard. One more touch. He just needed one more and then he'd get up.

"Have I asked you for anything? You're already family. Just because we're having a baby doesn't mean you have to marry me."

Just the thought of marriage had him trembling. He traveled too much, took too many risks to bring a wife into the mix.

Laney's hand fell to her lap. "I didn't realize you were so put off by the thought of marriage. Glad I didn't propose."

She'd tried to make light of the situation, but the hurt in her tone gave her away.

"Laney—"

"So, if you want to bring me that sack of lights, I can

get them out of the boxes, and you can put them on the tree."

He stared at her another minute, to which her response was to stare right back, as if daring him to turn the topic back around. Ryker didn't necessarily want to get into a verbal sparring match with her, so he nodded and went to get the bag.

He'd thought Christmas decorating was torture, but seeing Laney hurt, knowing he'd caused her feelings to be crushed, was even worse. He was going to have to learn how to make her smile again or…what? It wasn't as if he could remove himself from her life. He worked for her family, and she was having his baby.

For once in his life, Ryker had no idea what the hell to do. He'd lived on the streets, he'd fought for his next meal and he'd taken risks that not even Mac or Braden knew about. But the shaky ground he stood on with Laney was the scariest thing he'd ever had to face.

Laney wasn't sure what was more amusing, Ryker cursing at the tangle of lights that had somehow wrapped itself around his shoulders, or Spike and Rapture continually getting into the tree and swatting at Ryker's hand.

Poor cats. They thought Ryker wanted to play each time he reached for another branch. Most of the time her cats kept to themselves, ignored her completely. But the excitement of the tree and the boxes had brought them out of hiding.

Laney realized she had completely forgotten about the pain in her ankle. The entertainment in her living room was more than enough to keep her distracted.

But part of her couldn't help but drift to the "what-if" state. The scenario right now with Ryker decorating,

Laney pregnant, resting on the chaise, the fire roaring and the cats playing, it was like a scene from a Christmas card.

Laney couldn't lie to herself. She wanted that Christmas card. She wanted to have a family like the one she'd grown up in. The O'Sheas were Irish—they knew how to do family gatherings. She had always dreamed of having her own home, having a husband and children. She'd never seen her future any differently.

Perhaps she was going about her plan in the wrong order, but she still had every hope of having children and a husband.

So, how would Ryker fit into this mix? He wasn't exactly the type of man she'd envisioned when she'd been doing her daydreaming. She'd never thought of being with a man who had scarred knuckles, tattoos, constant scruff along his jawline and an attitude that matched that of her cocky brothers.

Still, Ryker was absolutely everything that got her excited. He turned her on and made her want more—and not just physically. Ryker always made her feel safe, even if he drove her out of her mind.

Perhaps that's why she was so drawn to him. He didn't back down, he didn't care what her last name was and he matched her wits.

Laney stared across the room as Ryker reached toward the top of the tree for the last section of lights. So what if she was admiring the way his T-shirt rode up when he reached or the way his worn jeans covered his backside.

"Why are you staring?"

Laney blinked, realizing Ryker had glanced over his shoulder. Oops. Oh, well, it wouldn't be the last time she'd be caught ogling.

"I've never had a hotter decorator," she told him with a smile. "Next you can start on the ornaments."

Ryker turned. Hands propped on his hips, he shook his head. "This isn't going to work. Whatever is in your mind, get it out."

Laney shifted on the chaise to prop her elbow on the arm. Resting her chin in her hand, she raised her brows. "I don't know what you're talking about."

"The innocent act also doesn't work on me."

Laney laughed. "No? Offering to strip my clothes seemed to work."

Ryker's stony expression told her he didn't find her nearly as amusing as she found herself.

"Listen, we're going to have to learn to get along," she told him. "We can't always be griping at each other. You need to relax."

"Relax? You think I'll ever relax, especially now that you're having my child?"

Laney shrugged. "Shouldn't I be the one freaking out? I mean, I'm carrying the baby."

Ryker raked a hand over his jaw, the bristling of his stubble against his palm doing nothing to douse the desire she had for him. She recalled exactly what the coarse hair felt like on her heated skin. She'd give anything to feel it all over again.

"Are you that worried about my brothers?" she asked. "I mean, once they find out about the baby, they'll get used to the idea of us being together."

"We aren't together."

Laney met his dark gaze. "We could be."

Laying it all out there was ridiculous. Her hint was about as subtle as a two-by-four to the head, but she wanted him to see that they could at least try to be more.

"No, we can't." Glancing around the room, he located a box marked Ornaments and pulled off the lid. "You know why and I'm not going to discuss this every time we're together. I already told you I'd support you and our baby."

"I don't want your money." Laney swung her legs over the side of the chaise and pushed off, using the arm of the sofa for support. "I want you to stop dancing around this attraction. We already know we're compatible between the sheets."

"Sit down before you hurt yourself." In three strides he'd reached her and was ushering her back down. "I hope you don't care how the ornaments are put up because I've never done this before."

Laney didn't budge, but it was difficult to hold her ground when he was pushing her and she was putting her weight on one foot.

"Why are you so stubborn?" she demanded, then waited until he looked her in the eyes. "Seriously. Can't you just tell me why you won't even consider giving this a chance?"

His fingers curled around her shoulders. "Because you see something in me, in us, that isn't there."

"I see potential. I see a man who wants something and never goes after it. He's too busy working his ass off for everyone around him."

The muscles in his jaw clenched. "That's enough, Laney."

"Is it?" she threw back. "Because I don't think it's near enough. I think you need someone to tell you just what the—"

His mouth slammed onto hers. For a split second she was stunned, then she was thrilled. Finally. He was finally taking what he wanted.

Those hands moved from her shoulders at once. One went to the small of her back, pulling her closer to his body. The other crept up beneath her hair, fisting it and jerking her head just where he wanted it.

Laney held on to his biceps to steady herself. A full-on attack like this required a bit of warning. She supposed her warning had been his intense gaze, the way he stalked across the room toward her. The way he'd torn her dress weeks ago.

Ryker broke the kiss, his forehead resting against hers. "You have to stop."

Excuse me? "You kissed me."

"To shut you up," he growled. "I can't keep fighting this with you. You push and push until I snap."

"Maybe I push so you can see what it is you're missing."

Ryker pulled in a deep breath and took a step back. His arms dropped to his sides. "Believe me, I know what I'm missing."

If she'd ever met a more frustrating man, she couldn't recall. "What would you do if I quit pushing?" she countered. "Maybe one day I'll give up, move on. What would you do then?"

Six

Ryker shoved his hand in his pockets, a futile attempt at reaching for her. There was nothing he wanted more than to take her and rip those clothes off and make use of that sofa.

The penny in his pocket mocked him, reminding him of where he came from, of who he actually was. If he were a better man, a man who could offer Laney and their baby something of worth, he wouldn't think twice about taking her up on her offer.

"I won't wait on you forever," she whispered. "I feel like I've already waited most of my life. We had one night and you flipped out. And that was before you found out about the baby."

Ryker didn't know what to say. He didn't do feelings, and he sure as hell didn't discuss them. Laney was right, though. He'd flipped out after their night together.

Never in his life had he ever felt something so perfect—he didn't deserve perfect. In the midst of betraying the only family he'd ever loved, he'd found a dose of happiness he never knew he was longing for.

"I think we're done here." Laney eased herself back onto the chaise. Clearly she'd taken his silence as rejection. "I'm tired. Set the alarm on your way out."

"You think I'd leave when you're this upset?"

Laney's bright green eyes misted. "I'm not upset. I'm exhausted. I've beat my head against the proverbial wall for too long, and now I have a child who needs my attention. I have to look out for myself now, and if you can't see what we could be, then we have nothing left to discuss."

Getting shut out was not what he wanted, damn it, but he couldn't let himself in, either. There was no right answer, but there was an answer that would keep Laney and their baby safe.

"We need to tell Mac and Braden soon." Ryker ignored the pain in his chest. Pain was just a by-product of doing the right thing for those he cared about. "I'll do anything for you and our baby, Laney, but I can't be that perfect man in your life. You know why."

She kept her focus on her lap where her hands were folded. "I know you're a coward, so maybe you're not the man I want."

Her harsh words gutted him. The idea of her being with anyone else made him want to hit the faceless bastard. How could Ryker let her go so easily?

Because she was an O'Shea. Her father had taken Ryker in when he'd been on the verge of going down a path of complete destruction. Respecting Patrick, keeping his relationships with Mac and Braden, that's what

Ryker needed to do. He'd built his entire life around working for them, taking risks to keep them safe and going through hell in keeping his distance from Laney.

He'd failed. His penance would be to let her go.

"Let me at least help you to—"

"I don't need your help." Laney held up a hand, her lips thinned in anger, though her eyes still held unshed tears. "Since you won't take a chance, then I have nothing left to say to you right now. I'll let you know when my doctor's appointment is, and I'll fill you in on work. Other than that, we're done."

Swallowing, Ryker nodded. "I'm going back to New York since you got me the blueprints of the DeLuca property. I don't know when I'll be back, but shouldn't be more than a couple of days."

When she said nothing, Ryker moved around the coffee table and the storage boxes. He grabbed his coat off the hook by the front door and had just jerked the leather over his shoulders when her soft voice stopped him.

"Be careful."

With his back to her, Ryker closed his eyes.

"I may be angry with you, but I still care and I want you safe," she went on. "Your baby is counting on you to be here."

His baby. Words he never thought would come to mean so much to him.

"I can take care of myself." He opened the door and typed in the alarm code.

He thought he heard her mutter, "That's what scares me," before he closed the door, but he didn't stop to ask. The bitter cold whipped around him. Ryker pulled his jacket tighter around his shoulders and made his way off her porch and toward his SUV. Walking away from

Laney was the hardest thing he'd ever done. Before Miami, he'd always thought not knowing what being intimate with her felt like was the worst thing, but he'd been wrong. Because now he knew. Now he was fully aware of how perfect they were, how compatible they were. Now he had to live with the knowledge that he'd never have something that amazing in his life.

As Ryker slid behind the wheel of his car, he cursed himself. In the long run, this was the right answer. He'd been teetering on the wrong side of the law for so long, and he should finally feel good about a decision he was making.

So why did he feel like hell?

"It's a trap." Laney gripped her phone and tried not to panic as she left Ryker a voicemail. The third in as many hours. "Don't go inside. It's all been a setup."

She stood in Braden's office, staring out the massive wall of windows that overlooked a snow-blanketed backyard. She'd come here after her first call and several texts had gone unanswered. It was late, too late to be worrying about Ryker and this damn job. She should be at home asleep. Ryker should be safe in his hotel room. But she'd been given intel that the DeLuca home was going to be empty around eight in the evening, and Ryker had been given the green light to go in, check the trunk in the basement and get out before they arrived back sometime around midnight.

It was now one in the morning, and nobody had heard a word.

"Find out something, damn it." Braden's frustration level was just as high as hers as he shouted into his cell. "Call me back."

Laney turned to face her brother. "Anything?"

"I called one of our FBI guys in that area, and he's looking into where Ryker is."

Which meant they still knew nothing. Laney tamped down her fear because Ryker had been in sticky situations before. For years she worried each time he went out, but he'd always come back. On occasion he'd dodge the topic of why he had new scrapes or bruises, or a run-in with the law, but he always returned.

All Laney could think of was how they'd left things last night. Why had she told him that she was done? If he came back right now and told her he wanted to give things a shot, she'd be right there with him. He was it for her.

Laney smoothed her hand down the front of her tunic and over her flat stomach. She needed to remain calm for the baby. Ryker was okay…he had to be.

"He'll be fine," Braden assured her. "It's Ryker. You know he's probably somewhere laying low. Most likely he's hiding in that house with his phone on silent and dodging the DeLucas. You know he loves a challenge."

Laney jerked the leather chair from behind the desk and sank into it. "You're not helping. It's all my fault for giving him that information."

"Laney, you were going on a lead. That's all."

Exhaustion had long since set in. She hadn't slept well after Ryker had left last night. Then today she'd been searching for the root of her troublesome emails that had been sent a couple months ago when she'd gotten another bit of information on the DeLuca property. She'd instantly noticed something was wrong when the chatter turned to humorous banter about a setup. She'd almost gotten sick. After her texts to Ryker went unanswered, she called. And called.

She hadn't suffered much morning sickness yet, but the constant state of I-need-a-nap was ever-present. This situation with the DeLucas wasn't helping. All the worrying, all the fear. She wanted to believe the best because she wasn't sure she could handle it if Ryker got hurt...or worse.

Laney crossed her arms on the desk, making them a pillow for her head. Strong hands came to rub her shoulders.

"Relax," Braden told her. "Any minute he'll walk through the door and get angry because you're worrying."

Yeah, that was so like Ryker. She wished for that scenario more than anything.

"I swear, when you two aren't at each other's throats, you're both worrywarts."

Laney couldn't respond. She was too busy enjoying the massage and trying to wrap her mind around how she'd survive if something happened to Ryker.

Oh, she'd live and get along, but she'd be empty. Her child would be fatherless. She couldn't imagine anything scarier. Ryker had been in her life for so long, she truly didn't know how to exist without him.

When Braden's cell chimed, Laney jerked her head up and turned to stare as he answered.

"Yeah?"

Her brother's hard jaw, set mouth and grip on the phone weren't helping her nerves, but that was just typical Braden. As head of the family now, he was all business, all the time. Mac, their more carefree brother, was still down in Miami with his fiancée, Jenna. Those two

had danced around their attraction for years…which reminded Laney of another stubborn couple she knew.

"Where is he now?"

Laney jerked to her feet, hanging on each and every
word, watching to see if Braden's expression changed.
Was Ryker okay? She wanted answers. Right. Now.

"I'll be waiting."

Braden pocketed his phone. "He's fine," he assured
her. "But he was arrested. After some strings were pulled
in the right direction, my contact with the Bureau managed to get him released. Ryker is being escorted by my
acquaintance. I'm going to meet them just outside the
city in a few hours."

Laney gripped the desk for support. "I'm going with
you."

Braden put a hand on her arm. "You're going home.
He's fine and it's late."

When she started to protest, Braden shook his head.
"No, Laney. I don't know what's gotten into you. This
is Ryker. You know he's fine. He'll be annoying you by
morning, I'm sure."

What had gotten into her? Well, the father of her baby
had been arrested, though the charges wouldn't stick
because of their connections. He'd been set up in a trap
that could've gone so much worse than what it had been.

How could she do this? How could she keep letting
herself get all worked up over a man who kept pushing
her away?

Finally Laney nodded. "Will you text me once you see
him? Just to let me know he's really okay?"

After she grabbed her purse and keys, Braden kissed
her cheek. "I will. Now go home and get some sleep."

Laney wouldn't sleep until she knew for sure. And

a text from Braden wasn't good enough. She wanted to see with her own eyes.

As she let herself out of her childhood home in Beacon Hill, Laney knew just where to go.

Seven

The last thirty-six hours had been a bitch. Ryker wanted nothing more than to get into his home and crawl between the sheets of his king-size bed. So much could've gone wrong in New York, but he refused to dwell on that. All he could concentrate on was the fact that he'd failed. One more dead end.

No scrolls. He hadn't even gotten to the mysterious damn trunk in the basement before he'd been caught off guard and cuffed.

Punching in his security code, Ryker let himself in. The sun was bright and promising a new day…and he was thankful for thick blinds. He hadn't slept since he left Boston. He sure as hell hadn't been able to relax when he'd been taken into custody. Not that he'd been worried. This wasn't his first run-in with the law, but he didn't have time for all this nonsense.

As soon as he stepped through his door and closed it behind his back, Ryker took in the sight before him. Without turning, he reached over his shoulder and reset the alarm. He wasn't about to take his eyes off the sleeping beauty perfectly placed on his leather sofa.

Laney wasn't quite lying down. She had her feet curled up to the side, her hands were tucked under her face, which rested on the arm of the couch. She looked so fragile, so small. But he knew she was neither. There was a vibrancy, a strength in her that terrified him. She feared nothing. He'd never found a woman who was willing to verbally spar with him like Laney. She wasn't afraid to throw back anything he dished out. She was absolutely perfect.

And she was the most beautiful sight he'd seen in days.

Ryker released the grip on his bag until it thunked onto the hardwood floor. He shed his coat and hung it up. She still didn't stir. Pregnancy was taking its toll on her. It wasn't like his Laney to be tired all the time.

Ryker froze. *His Laney?* Not in this lifetime. She'd never be completely his. But he was on a slippery slope and wasn't going to be able to hold on much longer. He'd told her before he was selfish, he'd proved that in Miami. But there was going to come a point when he wouldn't be able to turn her away.

Laney stirred, blinked until she focused on him, then jerked awake. The tousled hair, the slight crease on her cheek from where she'd lain, the flawless face void of any makeup staring back at him…maybe that time had come.

He started forward as Laney swung her legs off the side of the couch and stood. "I'm sorry. I didn't mean to fall asleep," she stated, tugging her long shirt in place over her leggings. "I just wanted to wait until you got home so I could see you were safe."

Something stirred inside him. Something primal. No one had ever waited to see if he was okay. Nobody had ever gone to the trouble of checking up on him. Oh, Mac and Braden checked in, but they were friends, brothers.

Laney was...special.

"I didn't think you'd mind if I used your code."

She'd only been to his house once, but every O'Shea had his code for emergency purposes and he had theirs. This was clearly an emergency for her. That primal feeling turned into a warmth he didn't want to recognize.

"But now that I can see for myself you're okay, I'll just go." She was adorable when she was nervous. "I'm sure you're tired and need to rest."

Ryker moved closer as she rambled, his eyes never coming off that lip she was biting. She'd been scared—for him. More scared than he'd ever seen her—for him. She was the most beautiful sight, and after the hellish past day and a half, he needed something beautiful in his life. He needed Laney.

"After we left things, and then we couldn't get in touch with you—"

His mouth slid over hers, cutting off her words. His arms wrapped around her waist, jerking her flush against his body.

Finally.

He felt like he'd waited forever to have her in his home, in his arms again. There were countless reasons why he shouldn't have been doing this, why he should've let her walk out that door.

But he needed this. He needed her, and he hadn't realized how much until he'd walked in and seen her curled up on his couch.

Laney melted against him, her fingers threading through the hair at his nape. Her mouth opened to his instantly, and Ryker didn't hesitate to take everything he wanted from her.

He wanted to devour her, wanted to take her into his bedroom and lay her flat out on his bed, taking his time the way he should've in Miami.

Laney was in his home, and this was one fantasy he'd had for way too long. No way in hell was he turning her away. He needed this. They needed this.

Before common sense or those red flags could wave too high, Ryker secured his hold around her waist, never breaking away from her lush mouth. He lifted her up, arousal bursting through him when she wrapped her legs around his waist.

"I didn't think you wanted me," she murmured against his lips.

Ryker spun and headed toward his bedroom. The sleep he'd needed moments ago was no longer on his radar.

"I never said that. Ever."

Laney nipped at his lips. "You push me away."

Ryker stopped, pulled away and looked into those engaging eyes. "Do you feel me pushing you away now?"

Her hips tipped against his as her ankles locked behind his back. "I wouldn't let you at this point. But what about tomorrow? Next week? What then, Ryker?"

On a sigh, he closed his eyes and rested his forehead against hers. "Right now, Laney. Let's concentrate on right now."

She hesitated a second longer than he was comfortable

with, but finally nodded. "I'm going to want answers, Ryker. I'm going to want to talk, not fight, about us."

About us. Those words terrified him and thrilled him at the same time. He'd worry about that conversation later. Right now he had the only woman he'd ever wanted in his bed actually here. He sure as hell wasn't going to talk, not when his emotions were raw. He had Laney and that was enough.

The second he crossed the threshold to his master suite, he hit the panel on the wall to close the blinds, encasing his room in darkness—much like the way he lived his life. Laney was the brightest spot he'd ever had, and he didn't need anyone to tell him he didn't deserve her, or their baby.

But heaven help him, he wanted both.

Laney tucked her face into the crook of his neck, her warm breath tickling him as he led her to his bed in the middle of the room. Easing down, he laid her on his rumpled sheets. He hadn't made a bed in…well, ever.

As much as he wanted to follow her down, he pulled back because he had a driving need to see her splayed out. He'd never brought another woman into his house, into his bed. If he thought too hard about this moment, he may let fear consume him, but he latched on to his need for Laney and shoved all else aside.

Her long shirt pulled against her breasts, her hair fanned out on his navy sheets and her eyes held so much desire, he didn't know if he was going to be able to take his time.

"If you are reconsidering, I'm going to kill you myself."

Ryker couldn't help but laugh. He reached behind his back and jerked his T-shirt over his head, flinging it across the room. Her eyes raked over his chest, his abs, lower. Pure male pride surged through him. He kept in shape and had never cared what anyone thought of him, not even his lovers, but he wanted Laney to care. He wanted her to…hell, he didn't know. There was nothing of worth in him, yet she wanted him. He was humbled and proud at the same time.

Laney sat up on the bed, pulling her shirt over her head as she went. Ryker was rendered speechless at the sight of her in a pale pink bra that did little to contain her full breasts. And when she reached behind her to unfasten it, staring up at him with those wide eyes, Ryker's control snapped.

With a need he couldn't identify, Ryker reached down and gripped the top of her leggings and panties. In one jerk he had them off and flung over his shoulder.

Laney lay back on his bed, a smug grin on her face. Ryker couldn't get his jeans unfastened fast enough.

"You think you've got me where you want me?" he asked, remembering he still needed to get his damn boots off.

She lifted one bare shoulder. "I've got you where you want to be."

No truer words were ever spoken.

After freeing himself from everything, he placed a knee on the bed beside her hip. Laney trailed her fingertips up his bare leg, sending shivers through him. Damn shivers. He was trying to keep some semblance of control here, but one touch from her and he was powerless.

Ryker glanced to her flat belly, worry lacing through him. He glanced up to see her smiling.

"It's fine," she assured him. "I promise."

He was clueless when it came to pregnancies or babies. Hell, he couldn't even deal with his own emotions, let alone care for another person. What was he thinking? Why was he letting his desire for Laney cloud his judgment?

"Hey." She reached for him, her fingers wrapping around his biceps. "Don't. Wherever you just went, come back. We'll deal with it later."

The war he'd battled with himself for years had no place right now. He couldn't deny her, couldn't deny himself. She was right. Whatever they needed to deal with could wait.

Laney eased her legs apart, tugging on him until he settled right where he needed to be. With his hands on either side of her head, he lowered onto his forearms so his hands could be free. He smoothed her hair away from her face, letting his fingers linger on her smooth skin.

"My scarred hands don't belong on you," he whispered, the words spilling from him before he could stop himself.

"I don't want anybody else's hands on my body," she purred, arching into him. "You're perfect."

Perfect. A word never associated with him before, let alone said aloud. Laney closed her eyes, blowing out a slow, shuddering breath. Ryker slid his body against hers, finally taking the time to appreciate how incredibly they fit together.

Laney flattened her palms against his back, urging him even closer. Her knees came up on either side of his hips as she let out a soft sigh. He couldn't take his eyes off her as he watched her arousal consume her. She could easily become a drug that kept him addicted forever.

But forever wasn't in his vocabulary. Forever wasn't a word for a man with his lifestyle.

"Tell me if I hurt you," he muttered. "I mean, with the baby...damn. I just don't—"

She leaned up, capturing his lips. "We're both fine."

Ryker captured her hips once more and rolled them over so she was straddling him and he was on his back. She sat straight up, her hands resting on his abdomen.

"I like this view better." He could look at it forever.

Damn that word for creeping into the bedroom again and making him want things he had no business wanting.

"You're letting me have control?" she asked, quirking her brow.

Ryker reached between them, rubbing his fingertip against her most sensitive part. Laney gasped, throwing her head back.

"I'm still in control, baby. Always."

Laney shifted, and in seconds settled over him, joining them, and Ryker's eyes nearly rolled back in his head. She was a vixen and she damn well knew it.

Her hips shifted, slowly. Too slow. Agonizingly slow. Enough.

Ryker gripped her hips between his hands and held her in place as he slammed into her at a feverish pace.

Laney's fingers curled into his bare skin, her nails biting into him. Perfect. This was what he'd missed. Her passion, her need for him that stirred something so deep within his chest, he refused to analyze it.

Laney tossed her head, her hair flying to cover part of her face. She clenched her eyes shut as her knees tightened against his sides. Ryker held his palm over her stomach a second before curling his fingers back around her side.

Mine.

The word slammed into him as Laney cried out her

release, and there was no stopping his now. Ryker's entire body trembled as he let go, Laney's pants only urging him on. He locked his eyes on her, shocked to find something in hers. Something much more than desire, much more than passion.

Damn it. Laney had love in her eyes. Love for a bastard who didn't deserve her, who'd betrayed her brothers. Love for a man who'd been told he was unlovable for the first twelve years of his life.

Ryker shut his eyes. He couldn't face this now. Not when he'd told her they'd talk later, not when he was feeling too damn exposed, and not when he knew there was no forever for them.

Eight

Monday morning had Laney heading to O'Shea's, the actual office in downtown Boston. Apparently there were some computer issues Braden needed fixed ASAP, per an employee's plea. Braden had told her this was top priority in an early-morning text.

Laney had only met the newest employee a handful of times, but based on what she'd seen of her and how she'd corresponded with her via emails and texts, Viviana was exactly the type of professional, poised person the business needed. The woman had been with them for nearly a year now and was proving to be an extremely loyal, trustworthy team member. She fit right in with the O'Shea family.

Laney let herself into the old building, which had been renovated into something of grand beauty back in the fifties. A few modern touches had been added to keep the ambiance up-to-date, and for security purposes, but overall, the building had been restored to its original grandeur. The old etched windows were kept, as well as the intricate trim and crown moldings. Scarred hardwood floors had been buffed and refinished to a dark, sparkling shine.

They wanted potential clients to feel at home. Because that's what O'Shea's was all about. Family.

Shaking off the cold, Laney turned and smiled at Viviana. The striking beauty was around the same age as Laney's brothers, but she could easily still be carded. She had glossy black hair, almost as if she had some Native American heritage. Her dark eyes and skin only showcased how gorgeous she was naturally.

"I nearly froze just walking in from my car," Laney stated, tugging off her gloves.

"Maybe I'll ask for a transfer to Mac's store in Miami," Viviana joked, her painted red lips parting in a stunning smile. "Just during the winter months. Boston can be brutal."

Laney nodded in agreement, recalling the snowstorm nearly a year ago when Braden and Zara ended up trapped together. Of course, if not for that storm, Zara may not be in the family now.

Laney couldn't imagine being trapped with Ryker. Actually, if their encounter two days ago was any indicator, their private time would be absolutely glorious. Maybe being trapped together would do them some good. Then he couldn't run away from what they shared and he'd have to listen to reason.

But Laney knew if they were alone, their clothes would be off and that would be the end of talking.

"We love you too much here to let you go," Laney replied, heading toward the back office. "Braden said the new program was giving you fits?"

Laney glanced at the framed images lining the walls. Ancestors in front of the store, some of her grandfather and father at the auction podium, another of her great-grandfather at his desk in the backroom…the same desk she was heading toward.

Viviana fell into step beside her. "I tried to go back through some records to find a piece we auctioned last spring in London, but the program shows a blank, like nothing was entered until two months ago."

Two months ago Laney had installed a simpler program; she'd put all the history of their auctions on there for easy access. Something was definitely wrong.

"Let me take a look." Laney moved into the spacious office and circled the antique desk her great-grandfather had found at an estate sale in Spain. This piece was part of O'Shea's history, passed down through generations. "Do you have any clients coming in this morning?"

Viviana crossed her arms over her plum suit jacket and shook her head. "Not today. I was hoping to get some pieces logged in to the system. We've already received quite a few framed pieces of artwork and several items from a recent estate sale Mac handled in Naples."

Laney settled into her comfort zone behind the screen. She pulled up the system she'd created and saw everything was up-to-date from the time she'd installed it. Then when she tried to retrieve backdated records, the files were completely empty. That was impossible. Everything should have been in chronological order just like she'd programmed.

"If you want to work, you can still get into the system

to add new items. You just can't go back." Laney didn't look up as she continued going from screen to screen to see what happened. All of her codes were still as they should be. "I'll let you know if I need you."

Laney's cell chimed from her purse, which was on the leather club chair beside the door. "Would you care to grab that for me?" she asked without looking up.

Scrolling down the screen, Laney dissected each and every entry she'd made. Nothing was off, but—

Wait. She scrolled back up. That couldn't be possible. She stared at the screen again.

"Something wrong?" Viviana asked.

Laney leaned closer to the computer, sure she was mistaken. But she didn't want to say anything to anyone until she could research things further. Braden would explode when he found out about the security breach. Still, she wanted to double-and triple-check everything before she went to him with this. There was no need to alarm anyone if she was misreading everything…but the odds of her being wrong were pretty much nil.

Her stomach turned. Who would hack into her system? Who had the balls big enough to go up against the O'Shea clan? How the hell had anyone gotten through all the security she'd installed?

The answer was simple. They weren't hacked. This was an inside job.

"Laney?"

Fury raged through her as she turned to look at Viviana, who held out Laney's phone. "You sure everything is okay?" she asked.

Laney nodded. "I think I've found the problem, but it's going to take some time to fix. I'm going to take this laptop with me. Can you use one of the others?"

Viviana's eyes widened for a second before she glanced around the office. "Of course. Is there anything I can do?"

Be on the lookout for the enemy?

"No. I've got it handled." Laney looked at her phone, still in Viviana's hand. "Oh, thanks."

She saw Ryker's name on the screen and opened the text. She'd left him sleeping the other night because she knew if she'd actually stayed, she'd want to spend every night there.

She had to make Ryker realize he wanted this. Perhaps if she wasn't so available, he'd ache for her the way she did for him. She wanted him so needy for her, so desperate to have her in his life, he'd ignore his demons and take a chance. She wasn't playing a game, she was simply opening his eyes to what they had.

Pulling up his message, she read:

We need to talk. Meet at Braden's now.

Laney closed the program and shut the laptop. "I need to go. Call me if you have any more issues, no matter how minor."

Viviana nodded and scooted back, and Laney headed toward the office door. "Of course."

Laney tossed her phone back into her bag. Pulling on her wrap coat, she knotted the ties before grabbing the laptop and sliding it into the side of her bag, as well.

"There haven't been any strange calls or emails, even from regular clients?" Laney asked as she slid the bag onto her forearm.

Viviana shifted, her head tipped as she glanced at the floor. "I can't recall any. It's pretty black and white here," she told Laney, looking back up. "You think someone has been messing with the system?"

"I think it's a possibility, and I want you to keep your eyes and ears open. Call me, not Braden or Mac, if you notice anything odd."

She'd figure out what was going on in the meantime.

"Of course," Viviana stated.

Laney headed through the main part of their office area and back out into the swirling snow. The streetlights lining each side of the street were decorated with simple, elegant evergreen wreaths with bright, cheery red bows. The garlands twisting around the poles ran from the wreath to the base. The city was battling the snowfall by keeping the sidewalks salted, the streets cleared. Laney absolutely loved her hometown of Beacon Hill and never wanted to be anywhere else.

As she climbed behind the wheel of her car, she wondered what Ryker wanted. Did he actually love Boston like she did, or did he love the lifestyle he led of traveling, going from one adventure to the next? Would he slow down, take fewer risks now that he was going to be a father?

Knowing Ryker…no. He would think he could do it all, as if he were invincible.

She headed toward her childhood home and pulled in behind Ryker's SUV. Large, menacing, just like the man himself. That whole dark, mysterious persona he oozed was so damn sexy, but there was infinitely more to Ryker. The layers that made up that man were tightly woven together, but she wasn't giving up on removing each one until she uncovered the very heart of him.

Grabbing her bag from the passenger seat, she got out of the car, careful where she stepped this time. Watching the ground before her gray boots, she started when a pair of black boots came into view.

"Easy." Ryker gripped her arms to steady her. "I came to make sure you didn't fall again."

Laney's heart flipped. She didn't want to keep sliding further in love with him, but there was no way to stop. Regardless of the baby, Laney loved Ryker. She'd love him even if they'd never kissed or slept together. Nothing could ever diminish her feelings for him.

"Well, startling me is not the way to go about helping."

Ryker took the bag from her arm and slid his other arm around her waist. "I wouldn't let you fall. Ever."

"If you keep tossing gallant gestures my way, I'm going to think you're trying to get all romantic."

Those dark eyes locked onto hers. "I don't do romance, Laney. I do reality."

Laney rolled her eyes. The reality was that she loved him, and he could ignore it all he wanted, but he had feelings for her, too. She wasn't offended by his words, not when his actions were booming louder than ever. Laney was optimistic that Ryker would come around… the question was how long would she give him before she finally told him how she truly felt? If she pulled out the cringe-worthy *L* word at this point, he'd sprint back into his steel shell and never come out again.

Ryker was vulnerable, not something she'd ever say to him or he'd ever admit, but the truth was glaring them both in the face. The don't-give-a-damn attitude, the rough exterior he offered to the world, wasn't who she saw. She looked beneath all of that and found the man he truly was…a kind, gentle and generous man with so much to give, one capable of so much love. It was a man he probably wasn't even aware existed. Or one he was battling to keep inside.

Regardless, Laney was about to rip his mask off and shove him in front of a mirror.

"Ankle okay today?" he asked.

"Just tender, but nothing I can't put weight on."

His arm didn't leave her waist, which was fine with her. She wanted his hands on her, and clearly he wanted them to be there.

"We have a problem."

Laney froze on the sidewalk, jerking her gaze up to his. "What?"

After the security breach, she didn't need more bad news. Dread curled in her stomach.

"We had a call from one of our contacts with the Bureau." Ryker ushered her toward the steps. "Let's get you inside. It's too cold out here."

"No." Laney placed a gloved hand on his chest. "First tell me what he wanted."

Ryker clenched his jaw. "Apparently someone is feeding them information. Intel only someone in our organization would know. They've discovered some pieces of art that are in our computer system, that only we have the log for. And I know you put those in like any other items we obtain legally, but they have a list of our back auctions."

Laney pulled in a breath, the air so cold her lungs burned. "This isn't a coincidence," she murmured.

Ryker's grip on her tightened. "What?"

"I have something on my laptop to show you guys. Let's get inside."

She could pull up any company document on a family computer, but she was most comfortable working with her own. She knew what documents and files to access right from the start. Time was of the essence.

As she turned, everything seemed to shift all at once. She tilted, thankfully against a firm, hard chest.

"Easy," Ryker told her, his arm around her waist tightening. "What happened?"

Laney held a hand to her head, shutting her eyes. "Just got a bit dizzy, that's all."

Before Laney could say another word, her world tilted again as she was swept up into Ryker's arms. "Put me down. I can walk."

"And I can carry you and your bag, so be quiet."

There it was. That emotion he held so hidden within him, one he didn't seem to recognize. If she thought for a second he didn't want her, she'd let it go. But when she saw a need in him, a need that matched her own, she couldn't ignore the facts...or let the best thing in her life slip right by because she was afraid to take a chance.

Laney wrapped her arms around his neck, nestling her face against the heat of his. She closed her eyes, relishing this pivotal moment. The baby would not be a tool in this path she was on to show Ryker how much she loved him, and that's not what this moment was about. Right now, he cared about her.He wasn't about to let her fall or get hurt. Laney only prayed by the time this was all said and done, that would still be the case.

She also refused to let him fall. She'd do anything to keep the man she loved safe. She was an O'Shea. The fact she was a female made no difference because she was brought up to be strong, fierce and resilient. Nothing could stop her from staking her claim.

"What happened?" Braden's worried tone brought her out of her thoughts. "Did she fall again?"

Ryker brushed by Braden and into the warmth of the house. "No. She started getting dizzy."

Ryker eased her down because it wasn't as if he could hold her forever. Shame that. Plus, if she clung to him too long, Braden would get the idea something was going on. Which reminded her that they were going to have to tell her brothers soon. Their unknown reactions terrified her.

"I'm fine," she assured them both, offering a smile. "See? Standing on my own two feet."

"Did you eat breakfast?" Braden asked, his brows still drawn together in worry. "Go sit in the living room, and I'll bring you something."

"No, no." She waved a hand, then opened the ties on her coat. "I ate. I must've just moved too fast, and with all that's going on with work, I'm just stressed."

Oops. Wrong choice of words. Ryker's eyes darkened, narrowed. His lips thinned.

"You'll be taking it easy. I'll make sure of it."

He delivered the threat in that low, sexy tone of his that left no room for argument. Laney merely nodded because now she was facing down two of the most alpha men she knew.

"Have a seat anyway," Braden told her, gesturing toward the living room.

Laney headed into the room that screamed Christmas: from the sparkly garland draped over the mantel, to the twelve-foot-tall noble fir standing proudly in front of the old windows, to the various candle stands, berries and other festive decor.

Quite the opposite of Ryker's house. Not one sprig of evergreen was to be seen there. A testament to what he came from. The child who didn't do Christmas had

turned into a man who didn't, and it was one of the sad-
dest things Laney had ever seen.

She took a seat on the high wing-back chair her mother
had fallen in love with at an estate sale when she and
Laney's father had first gotten married. Patrick O'Shea
had never been able to say no to his wife. Their love,
though cut too short in Laney's opinion, was something
Laney wanted. That love, the family, the bond was what
Laney dreamed of. And they weren't little girl dreams.
She was going into this situation with Ryker knowing
full well she could get hurt, but the chance of a love and
family of her own was worth the risk.

Weren't O'Sheas built on all the risks they'd taken?
A challenge was never avoided, but met head-on. And
conquered.

"Ryker told me you had a call from the Bureau," she
started, not wanting to waste any time. "I don't know
what all you found out, but Viviana's problem at the office was the system's backlog. I was looking into that
when I got Ryker's text."

Ryker leaned one broad shoulder against the mantel, crossing his arms over his chest. "Tell me what you
found."

Braden remained standing as well, right by the leather
sofa across from her. The tension in the room was palpable.

"When I go into the records, there is nothing showing from before I changed systems," she explained. "Everything should be in the files I added by year and then
broke down into months. Before October, there is nothing."

"Define nothing," Braden said between gritted teeth.

Laney faced him, staring into eyes exactly like her

own, exactly like their father's. "Not one document is on there. Don't worry, I have backups of everything at home. I'm not sloppy, Braden."

"I never said you were, but what the hell is going on and what does this have to do with my call from the Feds?"

"When I first started digging to see what happened, it appeared someone hacked into our system. But that would be virtually impossible."

There was no easy way to deliver such a statement, so she went for it.

"The only way someone could access the system is if they work for us. My security is so tight—"

"Not tight enough," Braden growled.

Laney straightened her back, squared her shoulders.

"Chill, Braden." Ryker's warning couldn't be ignored. "Respect."

Braden turned his attention across the room. "She's my sister, I can damn well say what I want."

"No, you can't." Ryker's sneer even made Laney shiver. "She's the best programmer I've ever met, and I know some shady bastards."

Even though she could've handled herself, and her brother was justifiably angry, Ryker's quick defense warmed her. He'd always protected her, but he'd never spoken back to Braden in such a manner.

"Who the hell are you to tell me?" Braden countered. "We may be facing a real issue here, not to mention the scrolls are who knows where. But the Feds are on our back and our system was hacked? Doesn't take a genius to figure out we have a mole."

The idea horrified Laney. They were so careful about who they hired. The background checks were extensive,

their training and "babysitting" period was just as metic-
ulous. Now the question was how did they narrow their
search down to one office? They had branches all over
the globe. Their main one, of course, was in Boston, and
a year ago one opened in Miami and in Atlanta.

Could the traitor be one of the employees down South?

"We need to warn Mac," she stated, thinking aloud.
"He needs to start scouring his crew while we look at
ours. We clearly should start with our US locations. I
doubt the threat is coming from overseas. That wouldn't
make any sense."

Braden nodded. "I agree. What I want to know is how
someone fractured your system."

Laney rubbed her forehead, wondering the same
thing. Closing her eyes, she willed the slight dizziness
to pass. Maybe she should get some orange juice or something in her stomach.

"I'm going to figure that out." Laney eased back in
the chair, rested her elbow on the arm and opened her
eyes. "I took one of the laptops from the office, and I
plan on looking through its history. I'll do the same for
the rest of them."

Braden's hardened gaze held hers. "I love you, Laney.
I'm not doubting you. I'm shocked, actually. We've never
had this kind of breach before, and the last thing I need
is the Feds sniffing around."

Since Braden had taken over after their father's passing, the O'Sheas had been moving into more legitimate
territory—which meant staying off the radar of the law.
To her full knowledge, they'd been so careful. Minus
Ryker and Shane's incident, there wasn't anything that
she knew of that would cause this level of scrutiny…well,
she still didn't know what happened to her ex.

What a mess. Having the Feds involved did not bode well for the O'Sheas.

"I promise you, there won't be a problem. I'll get this fixed, and we'll find out who the snitch is."

She risked a glance at Ryker, who looked even more menacing than usual. Those dark lashes fanned out over coal-like eyes, his hard-set jaw was clenched, his arms were crossed over that impossibly broad chest. Ryker was pissed, and she only prayed she could get to the bottom of this betrayal before he took matters into his own hands.

Nine

Laney had just grabbed a bottle of water when her front door slammed. Because she lived in an old brownstone, she didn't have that whole open-concept thing going on. She liked her rooms cozy and blocked off into designated areas.

"Hello?" she called as she made her way to the front of her house.

She wasn't too concerned about an intruder, considering she had alarms, cameras and an insane security system she knew her brother and Ryker had paid quite a bit for. They'd insisted on making sure she was safe the second she moved out of the O'Shea mansion.

The bottle crinkled in her hand as she stopped in the entryway to her living room.

"What are you doing here?"

Without taking his eyes off her, Ryker jerked out of

his leather jacket and tossed it onto the couch. "I'm making sure you're okay, and then I'm helping you get to the bottom of this damn mess."

Nerves stirred in her stomach. He was here because he cared, and he was here for work. Their worlds collided on so many levels, there was no way she could find separation.

"I'm fine."

"You were dizzy earlier, then you weren't feeling well when you were talking with Braden."

Laney twisted the cap on her bottle of water and took a drink. He hadn't made a move to come in any farther, but clearly he was staying since he'd taken off his coat. This was becoming a habit…one she would gladly build on.

"I was feeling a little light-headed while we were talking. It passed."

"You're not driving anymore."

Laney screwed the lid back on and cocked her head, sure she'd heard wrong. "Excuse me?"

Now he moved, like a panther to its prey. He crossed to her until they stood toe to toe, causing her to tip her head back to meet his intense, heavy-lidded gaze.

"You heard me."

"I did," she agreed. "I'm giving you the chance to choose different words."

A hint of a smile danced around those kissable lips. "I'm not backing down on this, Laney. Until your dizzy spells pass, I'll be your chauffeur."

Even though she knew he wouldn't back down, Laney waited a minute to see if he wanted to add anything…or retract such a ridiculous statement.

Finally, when he said nothing, Laney stepped around him and headed toward the corner of the sectional she'd been cozied up in. Well, as cozy as one could be while working on discovering who hacked into her family's computer system. Clearly the O'Sheas were smarter than to have all of their skeletons exposed for anyone to see. But there were items, especially in the past when her father was at the helm, that could be looked at twice. Some may find their "mysterious" auction pieces to be a red flag, considering the majority of them had been reported stolen.

Laney eased back into the curve of the couch and picked up the laptop she'd laid to the side.

"Glaring at me and using this whole silent predator vibe definitely will not change my mind," she told him without looking at him. She typed in the password for the laptop. "So, did you want anything else? Or are you ready to move on to work?"

Laney had just pulled up the system, but before she could go any further, a delicate pewter ornament appeared between her and the screen. Jerking her eyes up to his, she gasped.

"What is that?" She looked back to the ornament. "I mean, I know what it is, but—"

Well, damn. There she went, tearing up. She hated all these pregnancy-induced crying jags.

She reached out to take the likeness of a woman wrapping her arms around her swollen belly. The simple pewter ornament would look absolutely perfect on her white-and-silver tree. She clutched it against her chest.

But when she looked back up, Ryker glanced away, shoving his hands in his pockets. "I wasn't sure what to get. I mean, I didn't set out to get anything, but I was passing by that Christmas shop near the office."

"All Seasons."

He nodded. "Yeah. I knew you liked that place since you mention it every year."

Her favorite little shop because they literally transformed their store into a completely different place depending on the season. She could spend a fortune in there…and she had. A fact he well knew because he'd taken her there a few times when he felt she was in danger of being in public alone. Of course he'd kept his brooding self out front or waiting in the car at the curb.

"They have a tree in the window that reminded me of yours, and it caught my eye," he went on. He looked at his feet, the wall, the tree…anywhere but at her. "Then I saw this and…"

How adorable was he, being all nervous? This was definitely a side of Ryker Barrett she'd never seen before. Laney set the laptop aside and came to her feet. Tears flooded her eyes as she held tight to this precious gift.

She slid her arms around his neck, tucking her face against his. "This might be the sweetest thing anyone has ever got me."

Slowly he returned her embrace, and Laney wanted to sink into him. "You deserve more," he whispered into her ear.

She knew he wasn't talking monetary items. Ryker could buy her an island and a private jet to get there if he wanted. There was a fear in Ryker that allowed him to touch her, yet not get too emotionally involved. He felt he didn't deserve her, but she was just getting started in proving him wrong. He was everything she deserved.

"This doesn't mean you're driving me," she muttered.

Ryker laughed. The vibrating sensation bounced off her chest. "We'll talk about that later."

There wasn't going to be a later for that particular

topic, but he'd find out soon enough. They didn't have time to argue.

Laney pulled back, kissed him briefly, then shifted from his hold. Crossing the room to the tree, she hung her ornament right in the center, then stepped back to look at how perfectly it fit.

"I love it," she said, turning. "You didn't have to get me a gift, but it's my new favorite decoration."

Ryker nodded, which was about as much of a reaction as she was going to get from him.

"Now, we need to get to work because whoever is fighting us has chosen the wrong family to mess with."

Before she could settle back onto the couch, Ryker's arm snaked out and wrapped around her waist, pulling her against his hard chest. He closed the space between them, covering her mouth with his. Heat, instant and all-consuming, swept over her as she wrapped her arms around his neck.

All too willingly, she opened to him. He eased her back slightly, keeping his hold on her tight, protective. Laney threaded her fingers through his hair, wishing they didn't have to work, wishing they could go to her bedroom and use this kiss as a stepping-stone to something much more erotic and satisfying.

When he pulled back, nipping at her lips, Laney waited for him to say something…anything.

"I'm not complaining," she started when he remained silent. "But what's going on between us? You keep me in your bed the other day, you buy me the sweetest gift ever and now you kiss me like your next breath depended on it."

Ryker's hands slid to her hips where he held her still. "I have no idea," he stated on a sigh. "I can't put a label on this. I only know I did want you in my bed all day, I knew you had to have that ornament and just now my next breath did depend on kissing you."

Laney stared into his dark eyes, eyes that had terrified many enemies. Eyes she'd fallen in love with when she'd been only a teen. She'd seen him come and go many times while she'd been in high school. While her friends were out at the malls or movies with other boys, Laney was home waiting on Ryker to show for a meeting with her father. She'd get a glimpse of him as he'd come into the house. When she was lucky, he'd turn his gaze toward her, meet her with that intense stare for a half second before moving on to the study.

That split second had been worth skipping a night out with her friends.

"Don't fight whatever is happening," she told him. "And don't be afraid of it."

Ryker grunted. "I'm not afraid of anything, Laney. I think you know that."

Again, she wasn't going to argue. They didn't have the time. But he was so terrified of his feelings, he refused to even acknowledge them. Or perhaps he didn't even know they existed.

She eased back into her seat, set her water bottle on the cushion next to her and pulled the laptop back into her lap. Ryker grabbed the large ottoman from the accent chair and pushed it in front of her.

"Put your feet up."

Laney waited a second, but he merely raised a brow and continued to glare. Okay, no point in arguing. Propping her feet up, she started pecking at the keys. Ryker stood.

"It's going to be a while, maybe even days. Might as well have a seat."

"We don't have days."

Laney prayed she would find something that would lead them in the right direction. "You think I don't know that, Ryker?" She didn't even bother to spare him a glance as she worked. Time was of the essence—the only reason she didn't pursue that kiss. "I'm an O'Shea, a glaring fact my brothers and you often forget. I know what's at stake."

Laney ignored the silence as she scrolled through code after code. Let Ryker process her words because it was rather ridiculous how they attempted to keep her sheltered at all times, but expected her to twinkle her nose at the first sign of a computer problem. She wasn't naive; she knew exactly what her family did, what they stood for. She also knew Braden was doing his best to make sure they kept their reputation impeccable within the auction world while cleaning up their act on the legal side. Well, as much as it could be cleaned up. She knew Ryker had done things at her father's request...

She shut her eyes, forcing away any mental images. A shudder rippled through her.

"Laney?"

Instantly he was at her side. Sure. Now he chose to take a seat.

"I'm fine," she assured him. "Just a chill."

More like a clench to her heart. That was the part of her family's past she preferred to keep under wraps. She knew were justifiable reasons for their actions, she even knew there were times it was self-defense. She'd been fifteen years old when she'd overheard a twenty-five-year-old Ryker describing a trip to Sydney to her father. Ryker had been telling Patrick about a guard who'd attacked him with a knife. Laney recalled standing on the landing of the house, curled up on the floor and holding on to the banisters in the dark. At that moment, she'd realized how dangerous Ryker's job truly was and what he put on the line for her family.

"I don't know how the hell you comprehend all that," Ryker muttered.

Laney kept scrolling, slowly, looking for any hint as to how their security had been breached. She knew the threat was on the inside. Which meant if she had to access every employee's computer, she damn well would.

Her mind kept returning to the timing. The newest stores had been opened a year ago in Miami and Atlanta. The Boston office had been around since the beginning. Where was the mole more likely to be?

Laney didn't know how long she searched. Losing track of time was an occupational hazard. Her stomach growled, and she waited for Ryker to make some snarky comment, but when he remained silent, she glanced over. The man was out. Head tipped back on the cushion, face totally relaxed. Laney wasn't sure she'd ever seen him this peaceful, this calm.

When Ryker was in work mode, which was nearly every time she saw him, he was hard, intense, focused. When they were intimate, well…he was exactly the same way.

Laney's hands went lax on the keyboard as she studied his facial features. His brows weren't drawn in, his mouth was parted just slightly, as if waiting for a lover's kiss, black lashes fanned over his cheeks. She could study him forever.

Forever. If she even said that word to him he'd build yet another wall to protect himself.

Without tearing her eyes away from him, Laney slid the computer off her lap and onto the cushion beside her. She tipped her head back on the cushion as well, needing just another minute of this. One more minute of nothing but Laney and Ryker. There was no outside world, there was no issue with work and there was no fear of telling her brothers that she was expecting Ryker's baby.

Given how fiercely he protected her, Laney knew he would be an amazing father. He doubted himself, but she'd be right there showing him how perfect he was. She wasn't experienced at being a mother, but she knew love. Between her love and his protection, their child would have everything.

Laney bit her lip to keep from tumbling into that emotional roller coaster that seemed to accompany pregnancy. She shifted her thoughts to what their baby would look like. Dark hair for sure since they both had black hair. But would the eyes be green or coal-like? Would Ryker's strong jawline get passed down?

Suddenly those coal-black eyes were fixed on hers. "How long are you going to stare at me?"

Ten

"You scared me to death," she scolded him, swatting his arm. He lifted his lids and couldn't help but smile.

Ryker had known the second Laney had stopped working. He'd heard her stomach growl and was about to say something, when he'd felt her shift. The sudden awareness of her eyes on him had him holding still. He'd felt the slightest dip in the cushion next to his head, and he wondered what she'd been thinking.

Then he'd worried where her thoughts were. He knew Laney had dreams of a big family. She had that innocence about her that would cling to romance and love. She had hope. He'd lost that when he'd been in diapers.

"Find anything?"

Laney kept resting her head on the cushion next to his. "Nothing new. We've already established that it was an inside job. Braden doesn't like hearing that one of his employees is a mole, but we have to find out who it is before they cause more damage."

Rage burned in his gut. There wouldn't be a hole deep enough for this bastard to hide.

"Don't." Laney's hand slid up his forearm. "I'm furious, too, but don't let it ruin this moment. I just want a minute more of no threats, just us."

Us.

"We're always threatened." Unable to resist, Ryker flipped his hand over and shifted to lace their fingers together. "The authorities who aren't on our side are always looking for things to pin on us. On me."

Laney closed her eyes. Ryker hated this. Hated wanting her with an ache that was indescribable. Hated that he couldn't have her fully because of who he was. Hated most of all that he was the one who put worry into that beautiful life of hers.

"I can't stand the thought of you being hurt, being a target." She met his gaze once again. The fear in those eyes gutted him. "I've known for years how much you put at stake, but now it's different."

"The baby—"

"And me." She leaned forward, resting her forehead against his. "Before the baby, before Miami. I started falling for you."

He'd known. Hell, he'd known for years, but hearing her say the words seemed so official and real. He couldn't have her committing herself to him. There was no future for them as a couple, only as parents to this innocent child. That's all they could share.

But, damn it, he couldn't hurt her. He couldn't reject this gift she'd just presented. Laney was everything perfect and pure in his life. She was that place in his mind he went to when he was on assignment and the world around him turned ugly. She'd been his salvation for so long…but telling her that would only give her false hope.

"I know you don't want to hear those words." She eased back, leaving Ryker feeling cold. "But I can't lie to you."

He didn't know what to say, so like a complete moron, he said nothing. Laney shoved her hair away from her face and turned to get her laptop, instantly diving back into her work. The moment was gone.

Ryker reached over, gripping her hand beneath his. Her fingers stilled on the keys. She kept her eyes on the screen, her throat bobbed as she swallowed. Nerves were getting to her, he needed to at least reassure her…what? What the hell could he say? Ryker had no idea, all he knew was he wanted that helpless look gone.

"I'm out of my element here, Laney." He decided to go with honesty. "You've been part of my life for so long, but—"

"I know," she whispered.

How could she know when he didn't know himself?

"No, you don't." Damn it, he needed to make her understand. "You can't possibly know what I feel. You have no clue what those words mean to me."

Her head dropped as she pulled in a deep breath. "I know you better than you think," she said quietly.

Silence settled heavily around them. Ryker had never been this close to a woman. He'd had lovers, mostly when he traveled and needed a stress reliever. The possibility of a serious relationship had never entered his mind. It had no place in his life.

"I know who you are," she went on, still not looking his way. "I've known all along."

Now she did turn, those vibrant green eyes piercing him right to his soul. Until now he hadn't even been aware he had one.

"I know full well why you're trying to keep me at a distance. I'm not backing down, Ryker. You need to know that I intend to fight for what I want, and I want you."

Laney's words should have terrified him. But damn if her fire wasn't the sexiest thing he'd ever seen.

"I'll consider myself warned."

Her eyes narrowed. "If we weren't in so deep with this traitor mess, I'd show you right now how much I love you. That will have to wait."

Ryker's body stirred. He'd never put his work second to anything or anyone before...but right at this moment he was seriously considering doing just that.

"Get that look out of your eyes." She laughed. "How about I keep working and you go see what you can find in the kitchen?"

Ryker came to his feet. "Because I'm all for equal rights, I'll cook for you. But I expect you to open doors for me and buy me flowers."

Laney laughed, the exact response he was hoping for. He couldn't handle tension...not with her.

"That wasn't sexist at all," she said, grabbing a throw pillow and smacking him.

That smile lighting up her face never failed to warm him in spots only she could touch. Guilt slammed through him. There was no way in hell Braden and Mac were going to allow their baby sister to have a relationship with Ryker, even if he thought he could risk it. No, Laney's brothers were looking out for her, and they would be justified by telling her *hell no* when it came to Ryker.

Baby or not, the O'Shea brothers wouldn't budge in

this area. They'd had him follow Laney's boyfriends over the years. Ryker had investigated worthless jerks, and he'd scared off the ones who posed any threat to Laney or the O'Sheas in general. Each time he'd had to intervene, Ryker had selfishly felt relieved that Laney wasn't going to be with some jerk any longer.

Now here he was taking that role…and Mac and Braden were going to have to be the ones to talk some sense into Laney because he sure as hell had no willpower where she was concerned.

And she was wrong. This baby did change everything. Ryker knew he'd never be the same again.

Dinner consisted of chips, salsa and, surprisingly, a taco salad. Apparently Ryker's favorite food was Mexican, and he'd made it happen. She hadn't known those ingredients were in her kitchen, but Ryker had worked a miracle and produced something amazing.

Hours later, Laney's eyes were crossing. She closed the laptop and glanced across to Ryker, who was on his phone, leaning against her newly decorated mantel.

"I'm waving the white flag," she told him around a yawn.

He straightened, shoving his cell in his pocket. "It's nearly one in the morning. You need to sleep."

"What about you? You need sleep, too."

Looking at him in her living room, all dark and menacing, he actually seemed to fit. Amid the sparkling tree, the garland, the Nutcrackers and especially the new ornament, Ryker worked perfectly in her living room, in her life. He'd been a sport and had hung the rest of her ornaments and even added the newly fluffed wreath to her front door. He did draw the line sprinkling the iridescent glitter across the silver and white decor on her mantel..

But he'd stayed. He'd brought her living room to life with Christmas, made dinner and put the empty storage boxes back in her attic. There was something to be said about a man who put his woman's needs first. And she was his woman. He'd figure that out on his own soon enough.

Ready to make good on that promise to fight for what she wanted, Laney set the laptop to the side and came to her feet.

"You need sleep, too," she repeated, slowly closing the space between them. "It would be ridiculous to go out in this weather."

His half-lidded perusal of her body from head to toe and back up sent shivers racing over her, through her. The man's stare was nearly as potent as his touch. She practically felt him when he licked his lips as if she were a buffet. And he could devour her anytime he wanted.

"I'm not afraid of snow," he told her.

Taking a risk that the hunger in his eyes was his weakness, Laney gripped the hem of her shirt and pulled it over her head, tossing the garment to the side. His eyes remained fixed on her, exactly where she wanted them.

"But why take the chance?" she asked, reaching around to unhook her bra.

In a flash, Ryker reached out, wrapping those strong hands around her upper arms. For a second she feared he was going to stop her. Then she focused on his face. Clenched jaw, thin lips, desire staring back at her.

"You want me to stay?" he growled. "Then I'll be the one doing this."

He tore away her bra, jerked down her pants and panties. She had to hold on to those broad shoulders as he yanked the material over her feet. Standing bare before him sent another thrill through her. He stood back up, his hands roaming up the sides of her body, over the dip in her waist, cupping her breasts. His thumbs brushed against their peaks.

Laney couldn't help but lean into his touch. But then his hands moved back down. His hands covered her stomach.

"No matter what happens with us, this is all that matters. I'll do everything to protect our baby."

Laney nodded. There was so much uncertainty between them, but the baby's security was top priority. Until the arrival of their child, Laney would show him just how much she loved him, how much he deserved to be loved.

"If that means you have to move to my house in London, then you'll do it." She started to say something, but his hard eyes stopped her. "I'm serious, Laney. We don't know what we're dealing with, and I'll be damned if I take a chance with our baby."

Fear fueled his words. She knew this unknown threat had him as worried as the rest of them. Now was not the time to bang her chest and be all independent. They were a team.

"I promise," she whispered as she went up onto her toes to slide her lips over his. "Anything you want."

Ryker's hands shifted to her backside. Pulling her flush against his fully clothed body, he growled. "I want to take you up those stairs and keep you locked in your bedroom naked for the next week."

Oh, if only…

"But all I can promise is right now."

He kept saying that. All of these "right now" moments were adding up. Did he notice? He would. One day he'd wake up to the fact they were it for each other. Laney dared her brothers to even try to stop her happiness.

"Then show me," she muttered a split second before his mouth came crashing down onto hers.

He lifted her with ease, carrying her toward the staircase as his lips demanded everything from her...and promised so much more. As if she weighed nothing at all, he took the four steps onto the landing. Just when she expected to feel him turn and head the rest of the way up, he stopped. Laney tore her mouth away, ready to ask him what he was doing, but she found herself being eased onto the built-in, cushioned bench.

She tipped her head back to peer up at him, the soft light from the lamp in the living room casting a perfect yellow rim around his frame. She had no idea what he intended to do, but he reached behind his neck and jerked his T-shirt over his head. After he tossed it behind him, he quickly rid himself of his black boots, sending them back down the steps with a heavy thunk.

Laney couldn't take her eyes off that impressive chest. Spattered with dark hair, a scar over his left pec and a tattoo of a menacing dragon over his right, Ryker was all man...and he was still stripping.

"This is the best show I've ever been to."

The snap to his jeans popped open, he drew the zipper down, all without taking his eyes from hers. "I don't want to hear about the time you and your friends went to Poppycocks."

Laney gasped. "You know about that?"

"Baby, I know everything about you, and I sure as hell am not getting into this now, nor are we discussing the fact I had to do damage control with your father and tell him you were at the mall."

Laney bit her lip to keep from laughing because Ryker clearly didn't find the humor in her sneaking into a male strip club when she was only seventeen. Those fake IDs she'd made for herself and her friends as a joke had come in handy.

Laney opted to keep her mouth shut and enjoy the view as Ryker ridded himself of the rest of his clothes. Unable to keep her hands still, she reached out. She needed to touch him, explore him. Every time they were together her ache for him grew.

Ryker took her hands before she could touch him. Jerking her to her feet, he tugged her until she fell against him.

"I'm calling the shots here. No touching."

Laney quirked a brow. "Then this night is a total bust if I can't put my hands on you."

Strong arms banded around her waist, and instantly she was lifted once again. Laney wrapped her legs around him as he continued up to the second story.

"I'll tell you when you can touch me," he ordered. "I'm going to lay you down and do this right. We're always in a hurry."

Laney rested her head against his shoulder. "Does this mean you're staying all night?"

He reached the double doors to her bedroom and shouldered them open. Looking down into her eyes, Ryker nodded. "I'm staying. Saying no to you is becoming impossible. I don't know what the hell that means, but for now, I'm staying."

Laney knew exactly what that meant. It meant Ryker was hers, and he was finally, *finally* coming around.

Eleven

Ryker rolled over in bed. The canopy with white sheers draped all around the posts was definitely not his bed. This was Laney's world, a world she'd graciously let him into.

No. Scratch that. A world she'd woven him into, and he was getting to the point where he wasn't sure if he ever wanted to leave. It would be the smart thing to do, but he had needs, damn it…and he wasn't just talking physical.

He had no clue what time it was, but the sun wasn't up yet. The soft glow from Laney's phone had him squinting to see what she was looking at.

Baby furniture. Something twisted in his gut. All this time he'd been worried about their safety, about how he'd handle Mac and Braden. The reality was this child would need things. Probably lots of things he had no damn clue about. But he'd learn. He refused to be a deadbeat dad like his had been. Ryker would go out of his way to make sure his child, and the mother of his child, was comfortable and wanted for nothing.

Ryker slid an arm around Laney's waist, flattening his palm on her stomach. "I'll buy whatever you want," he murmured, nuzzling the side of her neck.

The warmth of her body penetrated him, never failing to warm areas that had been iced over for years.

"I can get the things for the nursery." She scrolled through a variety of white cribs. "I really want yellow and white, no matter the sex. I can always add accent pieces once we find out what we're having."

Ryker swallowed. This was a conversation he never, ever thought he'd be having...especially with his best friends', his *employers'*, little sister.

"Do you care what we have?" Laney turned her head slightly to look at him.

Ryker eased back. "I hadn't thought about it, actually."

Blowing out a soft breath, she turned back toward her phone. "No, I'd say you haven't. This isn't something that excites most men, and when you weren't wanting a baby at all—"

Ryker lifted enough to roll her beneath him until she was on her back and staring up at him. He rested his hands on either side of her head.

"A baby may not have been on my radar before now, but that doesn't mean even for a second that I'm not excited about this life, Laney."

Her face lit up. Her brows rose, a smile spread on her lips. "You're excited?"

Hell. He hadn't realized he was excited until he'd said the words aloud.

"I am. I'm scared as hell, though. I haven't thought

about the sex because it doesn't matter to me." Ryker kissed her softly. "All that matters is you two are safe, healthy, happy. That's my goal here, Laney."

Cupping the side of his face, she stared back at him. Her brows were drawn in, the happiness in her face vanished.

"I'm scared for you," she murmured. "When Braden and Mac—"

He silenced her with his lips. "I'm not worried about them."

"They won't like this." She blinked as moisture gathered in her eyes. "They'll blame you, and I've been half in love with you my whole life, and Miami was—"

"Amazing." He nipped at her lips, her chin, along her jawline. "Miami had been coming for a long time. There was no way I could've avoided you forever."

The screen on her phone went dim, plunging the room into darkness. He settled perfectly between her spread thighs.

"I can resist many things in this world, but you're not one of them." He ran his lips along the side of her neck as she arched her body against his. "I'm only human, Laney. And I can only ignore my body for so long. I've told you before, I'm a selfish bastard."

"No, you're not. You're one of the most giving people I know." Her arms and legs encircled him as he slid into her. "You know this is more than just the baby and chemistry between us, right?" she asked.

Ryker stilled for a second before moving his hips slowly. "I can admit that, yes. But beyond that, let's just—"

"I know. Concentrate on now." She returned his thrust

with a quicker pace. "I'm all for what's happening right now."

But they would get back to this topic later, he knew.

Ryker framed her face between his hands again and covered her mouth with his. He'd never wanted to take his time like this, never wanted to enjoy the process of getting to the climax. Fast and frantic had been just fine with him. Slow, passionate...that meant getting more emotionally involved.

And God help him, he had plunged headfirst into this...whatever this was...with Laney.

Her nails bit into his back. She opened her mouth fully for him, completely taking him in every way she could. There was a fire, a burning for her that hadn't been there before. The all-consuming need he'd had in the past was nothing compared to right here, right now. She was taking him and wrapping him into her perfect world where she believed such things as love actually existed.

Ryker tore his mouth from hers, ran his lips down her neck, to one perfect breast. Her hands came up to his head, as if to hold him in place. Her soft gasps only fueled him further to make sure she had everything she wanted.

"Ryker..."

He eased back, then pushed forward hard. Once, twice. Her entire body shuddered beneath his. It was almost too much to bear as Laney cried out his name, arched beneath him and came undone all around him.

And it was all Ryker needed to follow her over the edge.

The papers for the new property had been signed a few days ago, the contractor had been hired and Laney couldn't wait to get her hands dirty and dig into the process of renovating the old, neglected building in Southie.

Right now, though, she was having a difficult time breathing in the damn dress she'd purchased for O'Shea's annual Christmas party. She'd thought it was fine in the store, but, the overflowing cleavage and the slight pull of the emerald green satin at her waist gave her pause. She hadn't noticed her midsection getting any larger, she was only eight weeks pregnant now, but something had happened overnight because she was seriously worried about popping that side zipper.

"Being so gorgeous and built like that should make me hate you."

Laney spun to see Jenna, her arm looped through Mac's. Crossing the ballroom, Laney threw her arms out wide.

"I'm so glad you guys made it in." She hugged her brother before turning to Jenna, taking in the gorgeous red dress that highlighted her curves. "Like you're one to talk. You look stunning."

Jenna had a voluptuous figure, not model-thin like some women felt they needed to be. Jenna was a beautiful woman and looked even more striking now that she was in love. Mac, Laney's globe-trotting playboy brother, had finally been tamed by his best friend when he had to pose as her fiancé. Laney would've given anything to see the moment her brother realized Jenna was the one. She had seen this coming for years and couldn't be happier for the two of them.

"I was worried the snow would delay you all getting here."

Mac shrugged. "I checked the area before I took off."

Her brother doubled as a pilot. "I was confident we'd be safe. If not, we could've gone into DC and rented a car."

"He'll fly in almost anything," Jenna joked. "He's had me white-knuckling it more than once, but he assures me he has everything under control."

Mac's pilot's license came in handy since he hated Boston winters and was now living it up in Miami.

"Next year I vote we move this party to my house," he suggested. "Too damn cold up here."

"Are you complaining already?" Braden stepped into the room, Zara by his side. He slapped Mac's shoulder. "You haven't been in town an hour and already a hater."

Laney noticed Zara scanning the room and tuned out her brothers' banter. "I came a little early and made sure all the centerpieces were set up like we'd discussed. I hope you like them."

Her sister-in-law smiled. "They're beautiful."

"You're beautiful," Laney countered. "That gold dress is perfect on you."

"I think we all look amazing." Zara continued to look around, her brows drawn in a frown. "Is Ryker here? I thought he told Braden he'd be here early."

Laney's heart quickened. It had been several days since he spent the night in her bed. He'd gone out of town on business to acquire some authentic pieces for the spring auction. He'd only gone to Toronto, then to Chicago, but she hated not knowing he was in town. Not that she ever felt at risk, but she definitely felt safer knowing he was around.

"He's in the study," Braden stated. "He...had to take a call."

A call? Why had Braden hesitated? Laney knew Ryker's personal life was technically none of her business, but she still wanted to know what was going on. And if Braden had been in the study with Ryker, then the call was most likely business…in which case she still wanted to know.

"The room looks amazing," Jenna said as she pulled away from Mac's side and started walking around. "The lights, the tables, all of it looks magical. You all really know how to treat your employees."

"Loyalty deserves to be rewarded," Mac stated simply. "And O'Shea's wouldn't throw a cheap party."

"Neither would I," Zara chimed in. "I totally use you all to boost my own company."

Braden smiled, leaned down to kiss his wife on the head. "You do an incredible job. You don't need us."

Her brothers had found two amazing women to share their lives with. Laney wanted to tell them all about the pregnancy, but she wasn't ready. Beyond the fact that she worried how they'd treat Ryker, Laney wanted to tell Zara privately so she didn't have to absorb the news around others. Zara would most likely be elated, but Laney didn't want to take any chances. The miscarriage was still fresh, but did that loss and ache ever really go away?

Laney prayed she never had to find out.

She pulled in a breath, as much as her dress would allow. "I'll be right back."

She wasn't going to make up an excuse to leave the room. The guests weren't due to arrive for another hour, so her presence wasn't needed at the moment.

The foursome continued talking as the caterers entered through the side doors to set up the food tables in the back of the room. Laney saw her chance to slip out. She headed toward the wide, curved staircase and made her way up to the study. Nobody would think twice about her and Ryker talking.

Once she reached the landing, she glanced over her shoulder to see that she was still alone. She didn't hear Ryker on the phone as she approached the study, then she realized the door was closed. Laney turned the knob slowly as she pushed the door open a crack. When she peeked inside, she didn't see Ryker on the phone at all. His hands were on the desk, his back to the door, his head bowed.

Opening the door wider, Laney let herself in. Her heels were quiet on the carpet, but the shift in the full skirt of her dress pulled Ryker straight up. He spun and froze. Laney stilled, as well.

She'd seen him in a tux before, but something about seeing him now that she knew him so intimately…damn, he was one sexy man. His all-black tux played up the menacing male he was on a daily basis, but the expensive cut screamed money and class. Ryker was every type of fantasy man wrapped into one delicious package.

And something was troubling him. His tight face, clenched jaw and worried eyes stared back at her.

"What's wrong?"

Shaking his head, he pushed off the desk and walked toward her. "Nothing now that you showed up wearing this killer dress."

As much as her ego appreciated his approval, she wasn't letting his compliments distract her from digging deeper.

"Tell me." She stepped back when he stood right before her. Touching him now would get them nowhere… except naked, which was a bad idea, considering her family was downstairs. "Something happened."

Raking a hand over the back of his neck, Ryker blew out a sigh. "Nothing for you to worry about."

When he reached for her, Laney held up her hands. "No. You're not blowing me off. I do worry, Ryker. It's what happens when you care about someone."

"It's just work, nothing I can't handle." He moved lightning-fast and wrapped his arms around her, pulling her body flush with his. "You didn't tell me you'd look so damn sexy tonight. I'm going to have a hard time keeping my hands to myself."

Laney wanted his hands all over her, but she also wanted to know what he was hiding from her.

"You better keep your hands off. If we expose ourselves here, you and my brothers will have a fight and that's not the atmosphere we want for this party."

"I'll just have mental foreplay until I can get you back to my bed tonight."

Laney lifted a brow. "Your bed?"

He slid one fingertip up her arm, across her collarbone and down to the V of her plunging neckline. "My bed. Where you belong."

Laney could barely process the meaning of those words for all the delicious tingles shooting through her. Finally, he was coming around and admitting he wanted her. They were making progress and she was going to continue to build on this, to show him exactly what they could be together.

Ryker's eyes held hers, so much desire and passion staring back at her. She couldn't get to his house soon enough.

The click of the door had Ryker easing his hand away and crossing his arms over his chest. Laney took a step back.

"Everything okay?"

Laney kept her back to Mac, who'd just come in. Her eyes stayed on Ryker, who was looking over her head.

"Yeah. Laney was just following up on an email she sent me earlier."

When Ryker moved around her, Laney turned in time to see the one-armed man hug between the two.

"I hear we got the Feds on us now." Mac shoved his hands in his pockets and rocked back on his heels. "If you all need me here, let me know. I doubt the source is coming from down South."

Laney shook her head. "I disagree. I think the timing is too coincidental, since you opened two new stores and now we have a mole."

"We can't rule out anything yet," Ryker, the voice of calm and reason, interjected. "I'll pursue every angle, and Laney will dig deeper to get to the bottom of this. She's been losing sleep over it."

Mac's eyes darted to her. "You can't take on all of this by yourself."

Guilt hit her hard. "I set up the system, I did background checks on every employee. By default, the blame comes back to me."

"We don't work that way," Ryker told her, his gaze hard. "We're a team. Remember?"

The burn in her throat, the prickling sensation in her eyes came out of nowhere. Now was not the time to cry. But damn him for reminding her of that fact.

"He's right," Mac agreed, oblivious. "We're all in this together, and we'll get out of it together. We just have to pool our efforts like we always do."

Laney pulled in a shaky breath and nodded. "You're right. I still feel responsible, but I will get to the bottom of this. I just need more time with the computers to eliminate our main office as the source of the snitch."

"Not tonight," Ryker told her. "Tonight we're all taking a few hours off and not worrying about work. We have enough Feds in our pocket to hold them off for a bit."

Between the Feds and worrying about the baby and when to drop that bombshell, and trying to analyze Ryker's sudden change of heart about sleeping with her, Laney had a headache. No surprise there.

She rubbed her forehead and closed her eyes for a moment. The guys continued to talk, and she willed the oncoming migraine to cease. Maybe it would help if she ate something. The caterer they'd hired was the best in the area. Laney's mouth watered at the thought of the filet mignon on the menu, and the chocolate fountain and fresh fruit sounded amazing, too.

"Laney?"

Ryker's worried tone had her opening her eyes, offering a smile. But the smile was moot when she started to sway.

Instantly Ryker took one of her arms and Mac had the other.

"You all right?" Mac asked.

Laney nodded. "Just getting a headache. No big deal."

She glanced between her brother's worried expression and Ryker's questioning gaze. She knew where Ryker's mind was, but she couldn't reveal too much here.

"I'm fine, I swear. I just need to eat, that's all."

Ryker's grip on her elbow tightened. "Then let's go downstairs and get you something."

Nodding, Laney pulled from both strong holds. "I can take care of myself. I'll just go into the kitchen and grab some crackers to hold me over."

"No, you'll eat more because when guests arrive, you'll be talking, and you'll forget to get a plate for yourself."

Laney stared at Ryker and he glared right back. While the whole protective thing was cute and sexy, she couldn't stay around him during this party. Their guests—her family—would be on to them in a second. Laney saw how Zara and Jenna stared at their men, and Laney knew for a fact she had that same love-swept gleam in her eye.

"I'll grab some fruit or something, too," she assured him. "I'm fine."

Without waiting for another argument, she turned from the guys and headed out of the room. Once in the hallway, Laney leaned against the wall, held a hand to her stomach and took a moment to relax. She needed to stay focused on finding who was betraying her family, but she couldn't neglect her body. This baby was everything to her. She'd wanted a family of her own since she could remember, and she'd been given this gift. It might not be how she had pictured things would fall in line, but did life ever really work that way?

Laney pushed off the wall and headed downstairs. She needed to get a hold of herself and put on her game face. This night had to be about the company and her family. And discovering the traitor in their midst.

Twelve

Ryker moved about the room, never straying too far from Laney. That damn dress was going to be the death of him. He wasn't sure if he wanted her to leave it on later when they were alone or if he wanted to peel it off of her. Those curves, the breasts that threatened to spill out and the fact she was carrying his baby were a lethal combination.

"You think our betrayer is here?"

Ryker gripped his glass of bourbon and nodded to Braden. "Yeah, I do. I think the bastard wants to keep close, thinking if they didn't show up, we'd see it as a red flag. They'll act like the doting, perfect employee."

"Damn it." Braden took a sip of whatever he was drinking, *Scotch by the smell of it*, Ryker thought, and let out a sigh. "I knew they'd be here. When I find out who I opened up my home to, my family to, they will be sorry they ever crossed us."

Ryker scanned the room. Laughter, chatter, hugs, everything seemed like a regular O'Shea's Christmas party. Women wore glamorous gowns and the men wore their finest suits. The tradition had been started decades ago. Before the O'Shea clan had taken him in, he never would've dreamed this was where he'd end up. A boy from a broken home with a deadbeat, druggie father had turned into a billionaire by simply being loyal and valuing what family was all about.

And Ryker would do it again even without all the money.

Zara joined them, swirling her glass of wine. "I'd say this party is another success."

Braden nodded. "Of course it is. I married the best event coordinator in the world."

Ryker listened, but his eyes were on Laney. She was chatting with Viviana and whoever her date was. Some guy with a beard and an expensive suit. Ryker had never seen the man before, but he'd met Viviana and knew the family trusted her. Laney hugged the woman and turned, her gaze catching Ryker's. His heart kicked up as she made her way across the floor. The way her body shifted, the way that dress hugged her until mid-thigh then flared out, those creamy shoulders exposed…he was going to have to think of something else because Laney was seriously killing him. And from the smirk on her face, she damn well knew it.

"Feeling better?" Braden asked when Laney stood before them. "Mac said you'd gotten dizzy or something earlier."

"I'm fine."

"You're not taking care of yourself," Braden added.

"This is the second time this has happened recently. Have you been to the doctor?"

Laney nodded. "I have, and I promise I'm perfectly healthy."

Ryker hated this. Hated lying to the only people he truly cared about.

"Have you tried this white wine?" Zara asked Laney. "It's the best I've ever had. I already asked the caterer the name, and I'm going to order it for my next event."

Laney shook her head. "Wow, it must be good."

"Let me get you a glass," Zara stated.

Ryker froze at the same time Laney's eyes widened. "Um, no. I'm just going to have some water for now."

Zara's brows drew in. "Are you sure?"

"Positive."

Ryker needed to move this conversation in a different direction. Laney was uncomfortable, and that was the last thing she needed.

"Braden, are you—"

"Oh, Laney." Zara's words cut him off. "Are you... are you pregnant?"

The last word was whispered, and Ryker gritted his teeth. He scrambled for a defense, but he couldn't outright lie. It wasn't as if they could keep the baby a secret forever. Damn it, he wanted, needed to come to Laney's aid here, he just had no idea how.

"Laney?" Braden jerked his attention to his sister. "Are you?"

The party went on around them, but the silence surrounded their little group, blocking everything else out. Ryker opened his mouth, not sure what he was about to say, but Laney's one word response cut him off.

"Yes."

"Oh, honey." Zara stepped forward and hugged Laney. "I'm sorry. I just blurted that out because I recognized the symptoms. I shouldn't have said anything."

Laney returned the embrace. "It's okay. I was waiting to tell you all. I wasn't sure how you'd take the news."

Zara leaned back. "I'm happy for you if you're happy. Braden and I are confident we'll have children, so don't worry about me."

Laney's smile widened as she turned her attention to Braden. "Well, do you have something you want to say?"

"Who's the father?"

His low, anger-filled tone cut right through Ryker. To Laney's credit, she didn't even flick a glance his way as she continued to smile.

"Right now we're just keeping things low-key. I'm not ready to say who the father is just yet."

Part of Ryker was proud of her response, honest but still keeping their secret. The other part of him, the bigger part of him, hated the fact he was kept out of the equation. He wanted to be part of this child's life from the start. Not hidden in the background.

And he sure as hell didn't want Laney defending him. That wasn't how this was going to work. He may not know where the hell they were headed, but he wasn't going to hide behind a pregnant woman.

"I'm the father."

He ignored Laney's gasp and concentrated on Braden...who slowly turned his eyes to Ryker.

"You're lying," he stated in a low, threatening tone. "You'd never do that to me."

Laney reached forward, putting her hand on Braden's arm. "Don't. Not here."

Braden shrugged her off. "I will kill you myself."

Ryker clenched his fists. "You can try."

"No bloodshed." Laney stepped between them, her back to Ryker. "Now is not the time to discuss this."

Zara tugged on Braden's arm. "She's right. You need to step back, and we can all talk after the party."

Braden's hard eyes never wavered from Ryker's. This was his brother and he'd betrayed him. Ryker didn't blame Braden for wanting to kill him. Whatever Braden, and Mac, threw his way, Ryker knew he deserved every bit of it. But the worst part, the scariest part, was the possibility that he'd no longer be part of the family.

Braden shifted his attention to Laney. "What the hell were you thinking?"

"My personal life is none of your business," she spat.

"What is going on?" Mac moved to the group, Jenna right on his heels. "You all are causing a scene."

"Laney's pregnant and Ryker is the father." Braden delivered the blow to Mac in a disgusted tone, but never took his eyes from his sister. "She was just about to explain what the hell she was thinking."

"I wasn't about to explain anything to anyone," Laney said, lowering her voice. "I don't owe any of you a defense. And I sure as hell am not getting into this here."

When she turned away, Braden reached out and snagged her arm. Ryker saw red.

"Get your hand off her," he gritted out. "Or I won't care what type of scene we cause."

Braden's anger was palpable. Ryker would gladly take the brunt of his rage, but he refused to have Laney shoulder the blame.

"This isn't the place," Mac stated. Ryker glanced to him, but was met with equally angry eyes. "But we are going to talk when this party is over."

Ryker nodded in agreement. Laney jerked free of Braden's grip and gracefully walked away. She wasn't going to cause any more of a scene than necessary, and he applauded her for her poise and determination. Ryker, on the other hand, was ready to throw his fist through a wall.

"Come on, Braden. You have a party to host." Zara wrapped her arm through his. "Getting angry isn't going to change a thing."

Braden remained still for several moments before being led away. Ryker turned to Mac and Jenna.

"You want to say something now?"

Mac's jaw clenched. "Later. I'll have plenty to say later."

"What your sister and I do is none of your concern."

Mac's sneer indicated otherwise. "You got my sister pregnant. I'd say every bit of this is our business, *brother*."

The parting shot did the damage Mac had intended. He walked away, leaving Ryker feeling even more like a bastard than he already did. He'd never thought he was good enough for Laney—and her brothers had just hit that point home.

There was no certainty how things were going to go down, but Ryker vowed to keep Laney safe. He'd told her he wouldn't let her get hurt, and he damn well meant it.

Oh, he wasn't concerned her brothers would physically harm her. No way in hell would they do that. But words could cause more damage than any actions, and tensions were running high.

Ryker felt for the souvenir penny inside his pocket, the reminder he needed right now. Family was everything to him, and he'd slashed right through that shroud of trust.

Now he had to pick up the pieces and make some vain attempt to put them all back together.

Laney's nerves were shot. She didn't have the energy to argue with her brothers, and she was furious at Ryker for dropping their bombshell the way he had. She'd had things covered, she was trying to keep him out of the hot seat until her brothers had a chance to process the pregnancy.

And she could think of so many other times that would've been more appropriate.

The caterers were gone, the room now a skeleton of a beautiful Christmas party. The employees had all mingled, chatting about the upcoming spring auction, the biggest one of the year. Laney had tried to zero in on who she thought could be capable of betrayal, but after the intense scene with her brothers and Ryker, she had lost focus.

"I'm so, so sorry, Laney."

Laney turned toward the doorway to the ballroom leading off the foyer. Zara had her hands clasped in front of her as she worried her bottom lip.

"None of this is your fault." Laney moved toward her sister-in-law and let out a sigh. "I have no idea where the guys went, but I hope Ryker is still alive."

Zara nodded. "Braden and Mac are outside, and I saw Ryker go up to the study. Jenna is finishing up in the kitchen, but I wanted to slip out and see you without the others."

Tears pricked Laney's eyes. "I was so worried how you'd take the news. I didn't want to bring back all of those memories."

Zara reached out, taking Laney's hands in hers. "The

memories are always there. The hurt will never go away, I imagine. We are trying to have another, and my doctor says he sees no reason why we can't get pregnant again. Don't worry about me, Laney. This is a special time for you and Ryker."

Laney blinked back the burn and moisture. "I don't know what Braden and Mac are going to do. I mean, they're all like brothers, they're best friends. Ryker needs them in his life. He had no one before coming here. He—"

"You love him," Zara said softly.

There was no denying the truth. "Yes."

"Then fight for this. Your brothers are in a state of shock, and most of their anger stems from getting caught off guard. Make them see how much you care for Ryker. Does he feel the same way?"

And wasn't that the question? How did Ryker feel? The man was so closed off. She knew full well how he felt about their physical relationship, and she was almost positive he had feelings for her, but she wanted him to say it. To admit how he felt and stop hiding from everything.

"It's okay." Zara squeezed Laney's hands. "Go on upstairs. Your brothers will be up shortly, I'm sure."

Laney wrapped her arms around Zara. "I'm so glad you're in our lives."

Returning the embrace, Zara whispered, "Me, too."

Pulling herself together, Laney made her way upstairs. She wasn't ready for this talk, didn't think she'd ever be. She knew going in that harsh words were going to be exchanged, some things that could never be taken back. But she wouldn't let her brothers blame Ryker. That was an issue she refused to back down on.

When she eased open the study door, she saw Ryker

across the room, facing the floor-to-ceiling windows behind the desk. With his hands in his pockets, he looked
as if he didn't have a care in the world. Laney knew different. He carried everything on his shoulders.

She closed the door at her back, and the click had
Ryker glancing over his shoulder.

"You need to leave," he told her, turning back to look
out the window. "I've got this."

Yeah, carrying the entire weight, as if this pregnancy
was one-sided.

"We're a team, remember?"

She moved across the floor, nerves swirling in her
stomach. If he shut her out now, Laney didn't know how
she'd handle his silence.

"Why didn't you let me manage things earlier?" she
asked as she came to stand beside him. When he didn't
look at her, Laney's heart sank just a bit more.

"I don't want you to think I was keeping your name
from them for any reason other than it wasn't the time
or place to get into this."

Ryker whirled, eyes blazing with fury. "I'm not hiding behind a woman. You think I was just going to stand
there and let Braden speculate? How would that have
worked out for either of us when he did find out the
truth? If we'd let that go, his rage would've been worse."

Once again, Ryker was the voice of reason. Plus, it
wasn't his style to let a woman take the fall, especially
her. She should've known he wouldn't stand by while she
made excuses and skirted around the truth.

"I just want to go home with you and be done here,"
she whispered.

"I'm not sure that's the best idea right now."

Laney froze. "What? Don't even tell me you're letting them come between us already."

He turned back to stare out at the dark night, illuminated only by the glow from the patio lights below. "I've told you before there is no 'us.' Their reaction should have told you that."

Laney crossed her arms over her chest. "And we're not going to fight them on this?"

The muscles in his jaw clenched. His silence might as well have been shouted through a bullhorn.

The door to the study opened, then slammed. Laney glanced up to see her brothers. Furious over Ryker's stance, Laney had had more than enough.

"If you're going to come in here and beat your chests over how you're supposed to protect me and Ryker knew better, save it." Laney glared across the room as her brothers started in her direction. "I'm expecting a baby. We didn't plan it, but your anger won't change a thing."

Mac stopped behind the leather couch and rested his hands over the back. "Maybe not, but we're still pissed. We're family, Laney. Ryker crossed the line."

Laney rolled her eyes. "I assure you, he didn't make the baby himself."

"So what now?" Braden asked, his eyes on Ryker. "What do you plan to do with my sister?"

Laney stilled, her back turned to Ryker as she waited on his response.

"I plan on helping her raise our baby and continuing to keep her safe. This changes nothing."

Laney's heart broke. Cracked right in two, then splintered into shards on the ground. She wasn't going to beg anymore. She'd tried to show him how perfect they'd be together, but clearly he wanted to keep that bit of distance in place so he could hold together the only family he'd ever known. She understood his fear, admired him for clinging to what he'd built, but to throw away her love was the last straw.

Laney turned to face Ryker. "You're right. This changes nothing. We're going to have a baby, but that's all."

Those dark eyes stared back at her. Lips thinned, jaw clenched, he was seething. Laney continued to stare, tipping up her chin in defiance. If he wanted to expand, then he needed to do so now. If he wanted to come to her "rescue" like he always had in the past, he needed to say what he felt. Why did have to be so set on doing the right thing? He was human, and they were attracted to each other. He'd showed her with his actions that he cared. Why was he choosing her brothers over her—again?

"We have too many problems going on right now for you two to be at odds," Mac cut into her thoughts. "Laney, are you feeling okay? Are you sure you can keep working?"

Throwing her arms in the air, she spun. "For heaven's sake, I'm pregnant, not terminal. I've had a few dizzy spells, but that's all normal."

Braden ran a hand over the back of his neck and glanced toward the ceiling. Laney waited for the backlash.

"Don't take this out on Ryker—"

"Stop, Laney."

She glanced over her shoulder. Ryker had turned from the window. His dark eyes held her in place, and she wanted to say so much more. She wanted to beat some sense into him until he relaxed his moral compass. He was so damn worried about getting shut out, he was literally letting her slip away.

"I'll handle my end," he told her.

His end? So they were on separate sides?

"Yeah, I guess you can." She swallowed the hurt, ignoring the threat of tears. She had no time for tears, she was too angry. "I'm going home. I'm tired, I've had a long day."

Gathering the skirt of her gown in one hand, she marched toward the door.

"Laney."

Ryker's voice stopped her.

"I'll drive you home."

Letting out a humorless laugh, Laney turned. "Like hell you will. I can handle this myself."

Throwing his words right back at him should've made her feel marginally better, but she only felt empty. She shot a glance to each of her brothers.

"If I come across any new leads on the mole, I'll let you know."

She couldn't be in this room another second, and at this point she didn't care what they did to one another. They were all morons. Laney wondered how the hell she'd been cursed to be surrounded by idiots. Not one of them was thinking beyond this moment. Her brothers weren't looking to the future, to a new generation of O'Sheas, and Ryker was being so damn stubborn, she was getting another headache thinking about it.

By the time she got home, all Laney wanted to do was soak in a bubble bath and think about her precious baby. Designing a nursery in her head was exactly what she needed to relax. No work, no men, just sweet little baby thoughts.

Thirteen

Ryker's eye throbbed. He'd deserved the single punch to the face…hell, he had expected so much more. Braden had delivered the blow, and Ryker hadn't even attempted a block.

How could he fault them for being protective of Laney? Ryker had done several interventions on her behalf when she'd been with men who weren't appropriate. He expected nothing less from Braden and Mac.

But Ryker had hurt her. He'd lied when he said the baby changed nothing. This baby changed everything. He'd been void of emotion for so long, something uncomfortable kept shifting in his chest, and he was scared as hell. Not that he'd ever admit such a thing aloud. He'd meant what he said when he'd told her there was no "us." Even so, he couldn't seem to stay away.

Though it was late, Ryker found himself standing outside Laney's house. It was time for damage control. He didn't text her first, nor was he about to knock. He knew O'Sheas hurt deeply and wanted to be left alone.

Too damn bad.

Ryker let himself in, punched in her security code and locked the dead bolt behind him. The Christmas tree lit up in the corner drew his attention to the pewter ornament hanging front and center. She'd genuinely been surprised and happy when he'd given that to her. He'd never seen her smile like that, at least not directed his way. He wanted to see that again. He needed to know he hadn't damaged something inside her.

Damn it. He raked a hand through his hair. He knew more than most how deeply harsh words sliced, and once they were out, there was no way to take them back.

"What do you want?"

Ryker glanced up the staircase. Laney stood on the landing, belting her robe, her damp hair lying across one shoulder.

He remained where he was, though everything inside him demanded he rush up the stairs, grab her and beg for forgiveness. Pride wouldn't let him…the same damn pride that was making her hurt.

Why did he have to be such a bastard? Why didn't he have normal feelings like everyone else? He'd been fine with his callous ways…until Laney.

"I came to apologize, though I doubt you'll accept it."

Crossing her arms over her chest, she nodded. "You're right. Which brother hit you?"

"Braden."

"Neanderthals," she muttered before starting down the steps. "I should get you some ice."

Ryker paused. "You're going to play nurse after what happened?"

Laney reached the landing, her hand braced on the newel post. "Braden had no right to hit you because we slept together. That's none of his business. But don't mistake the bag of ice as my forgiveness."

Even when she was pissed, Laney wanted to help. She managed to do things to him, things he never thought possible. She made him feel as if he actually had a heart. Problem was, he had no idea what the hell to do with it.

When she reached the bottom step, Ryker pivoted just enough to block her. With her up just those few inches, she was at eye level and right where he wanted her to be.

"Don't make this more difficult," she whispered, biting her bottom lip. "I'm tired, Ryker. You said enough earlier."

Jasmine. She'd used some form of Jasmine soap or shampoo, or whatever other potion women used. And she smelled absolutely delicious.

"I didn't mean those words the way they came out," he told her, clenching his fists. He wanted to reach for her, was desperate to touch her, but he didn't want his other eye blackened. He may be desperate, but he wasn't stupid.

"Yet you waited until we were alone to tell me that." She quirked a brow. "Your apology is accepted, but the damage is done. Do you want ice or not?"

"No."

"Fine. Then let yourself out and reset the alarm. I'm going to bed."

Before she could turn, Ryker placed his hand over hers on the post. "I'm lost, Laney. I have no idea what the hell I'm doing."

Her hand relaxed beneath his, giving him a minor

hope she wasn't ready to shut him out. If there was ever a time to spill his thoughts, it was now.

"I can't lose any of you," he went on. "Do you understand that? You're all I have. Braden and Mac are my brothers. I have no idea where this is leading between you and me, but I have to have some stability. I know you think I'm some superhuman, unfeeling bastard right now, but I feel…too much."

Laney's eyes closed, and Ryker had no idea what she was thinking. Everything was new to him. He'd been infatuated with her for so long, but never thought anything would come of it. Yet, here they were, expecting a baby and trying to wade through this mess he'd made.

And she loved him. Words he could never, ever forget.

"I can't do this with you." Her misty eyes landed on his, touching him right to his soul. "You know how I feel and when you do this push-pull. I have no idea how to react. I get that this family is yours, I completely understand you can't lose us. But are you willing to ignore everything between you and me?"

The hurt in her tone destroyed him. Ryker couldn't stand another second, he had to offer some comfort, but he knew the comfort was mostly for himself.

Taking her face between his hands, he stared directly into those vibrant green eyes. How could she pierce him so deeply? Nobody had ever even come close to touching him the way Laney had. But if he risked everything, *everything*, and they fell apart, it would kill him.

He eased forward, resting his forehead against hers and pulling in a deep breath. "I need time."

"I've given you most of my life," she whispered. The direct punch hit its mark.

"I'm new here, Laney. I can't mess this up, for you, for our baby. Just…don't give up on me."

Silence settled heavily around them, and Ryker hated the vulnerability he was showing. But this was Laney, and he was starting to see exactly what it would take to keep her waiting until he figured out his jumbled emotions.

She didn't say anything, didn't touch him in return. Ryker knew he wasn't done baring his soul. Stepping away from her, because he couldn't slice himself wide open *and* touch her, he started pacing her living room.

"I had the sad, clichéd childhood," he began, ignoring that instant burn to his chest when he thought about those first twelve years. "My father was a user, a manwhore, a worthless piece of trash who never should've been allowed to keep a child. I witnessed more by the time I was five years old than most people see or hear in a lifetime."

Ryker stopped in front of the mantel, catching Laney's gaze in the large mirror hanging above the greenery. "He'd leave me alone for days. I stole food to eat, I got myself ready for school, I picked fights on the playground so I could go to the principal's office."

Bracing his hands on the mantel, Ryker lowered his head. "I just wanted any contact with a male adult. I didn't care if it was negative. They'd try to call my dad, but of course he never answered. Half the time our phone bill wasn't paid anyway. So I'd stay in the office and finish my schoolwork, which was what I wanted. I wanted to be left alone to do my thing."

Pushing off the mantel, he started pacing again. He'd never let his backstory spill out like that. But now that he'd started, he wasn't about to stop. Laney deserved this part of him, she deserved it all, but this is all he could give for now.

"When I saw your brothers in a fight, I was all too eager to jump in. My dad had been gone for nearly a week, and I was pissed. I needed to take my aggression out on someone."

"How did nobody notice this for twelve years?" Laney's quiet question broke through his thoughts.

"People are so wrapped up in their own lives." He shrugged and reached for the ornament he'd given her. He rubbed his thumb over the roundness of the silhouette's belly before letting it go to sway against the branches. "I was so skeptical about meeting Patrick, but the second I saw him, I knew he was one of the good guys."

Laney let out a soft laugh. "Only a select few would lump him into that category, but I agree. He was the best."

"From the second I came to stay with you guys, then started working with your brothers, I felt like I had a place, a real home. Braden and Mac treated me like family. You were so young at first, I ignored you. But once you got to be a teenager, I was looking at you in ways that I shouldn't. Had your dad had even the slightest idea of what my thoughts were, he would've killed me himself."

"You never looked at me twice," she stated.

Ryker threw a glance over his shoulder, just in time to see one of her cats dart up the steps and disappear. "I looked. I fantasized. My penance for lusting after you was to watch you grow into a beautiful woman, to see other bastards on your arm. Then when we saw how eerily good you were with computers, I realized my penance had just begun."

He moved to the wide window in the front of the

house. Staring out onto the darkened night, with only a street lamp lighting a portion of the view, Ryker was forced to look at his own reflection. Fitting, considering he barely recognized the man who was spouting off his life story.

Slipping his hand into a pocket, he pulled out the penny. "I have been just fine keeping my distance from you. I mean, I wanted you, but I knew you were on another level, and nothing between us could ever happen. I've never forgotten where I came from, no matter how much money I have in my account or how many houses I own."

When he turned, he found her exactly as she'd been moments ago. Standing on that bottom step, her hand on the post, her eyes never wavering from him.

Holding up the pathetic piece of metal, Ryker walked forward. "I keep this ridiculous reminder in my pocket of what I came from. I've had this with me every single day since I was ten years old."

He stood only a few feet away, but held the penny out for her. Laney took it, examined it.

"This is one of those flattened pennies with your name on it." She brought her eyes back to his. "What's this from?"

"My dad was actually sober for a few hours one time." How sad was it that Ryker could pinpoint the exact hours his dad had gone without a drink or a fix? "There was a carnival outside the city, and he took me. He got this with my name on it, maybe because he felt he owed me something. I have no clue why, but this was the only thing he'd ever bought for me. This was the only time in my childhood he'd actually taken me anywhere."

Laney's eyes filled as she clutched the penny in her hand. "Are you worried about being a father?"

"Hell, yes, I am." Ryker rubbed the back of his neck, glancing to the floor before going on. "What do I have to fall back on? What part of my past says I'm ready to help raise another human being? I won't leave either of you, but I'm scared as hell, Laney."

"You're not afraid," she countered, her voice softening. "You're refusing to accept what already is. You have all of these wonderful emotions inside you. I know you care for me, I know you care for this baby. If you'd let yourself relax, you'd see there's so much more than fear. Fear is a lie. If my father showed you nothing else, he showed you that."

"There can't be animosity between your brothers and me, or them and you. There can't be. This family needs to be unified, and I swore to your father we'd find those scrolls, we'd keep this family going. I promised, Laney."

Still clutching the penny, she crossed her arms and nodded. "And we'll continue to do just that. My brothers aren't part of what you and I have going on. You need to understand that because if you don't, then we have nothing."

"If I were Braden, I would've killed someone like me."

Laney's hard stare held him in place. Damn, when she got that look, she was every bit Patrick O'Shea's daughter. She meant business—and she was sexy as hell.

"Braden's not going to harm you. Well, other than the black eye."

"You're aware of the man I am, what I've done to keep your family safe."

Laney nodded. "I'm not naive."

"You never ask me, you never look at me as if you disapprove."

Laney shrugged. "I know my father had his reasons.

I know Braden wants no more violence and that you had to take care of Shane because he tried to hurt me." She swallowed, bit her lip and pushed on. "And I know when my ex disappeared—"

"I didn't kill him. I couldn't. I sent him away with a fat check and a promise that if he returned, he would be finished."

"I thought you…"

Ryker nodded. "I know what you thought. I let you think that because I was trying to keep some wall between us, but it didn't work."

Laney blinked, glanced around the room as if trying to process what he'd just said. "I'm glad you didn't hurt him, but why didn't you? You hated him."

Hate was such a mild term for the man who'd verbally abused Laney. The guy was lucky he was still drawing breath in his lungs.

"I didn't want you to look at me like I was a monster."

"I could never look at you that way."

Ryker took a step forward. "I couldn't take the chance."

Laney uncrossed her arms, handed the penny back to him and pulled in a breath. Ryker shoved the memento back into his pocket.

"How much did Braden give you to send Shane away?"

"He didn't give me the money."

Her perfectly arched brows drew in as she tipped her head. "You used your money?"

"I'd have paid him every last dime I had to leave. I didn't want to have his blood on my hands, and I wanted him out of your life."

Laney pushed her hair over her shoulder and clutched

the V of her robe. She'd looked so damn gorgeous earlier in that red ball gown. She'd nearly stopped his heart and was the envy of every woman there; she was also most likely most guys' fantasy tonight.

But right now, she stood before him, void of all makeup, wearing nothing but her silk robe and smelling like everything he didn't deserve.

"Don't shut me out," he murmured. "I need time, and I know it's not fair to ask, but…just don't push me away, even when I'm being a selfish bastard."

It seemed as if an eternity passed as he waited for her to say something. Instead, she reached out, took his hand and turned to go up the steps.

"Laney."

She stopped but didn't look back at him. Ryker moved up to where she stood, lifted her in his arms and carried her the rest of the way.

"This is more," he told her. "Just let me catch up."

When she laid her head on his shoulder, Ryker knew he was breaking ground on learning how to live with a heart that actually feels. Now if he could only figure out a way to make sure she didn't get hurt…and prove to Braden and Mac that he wasn't just messing around with their baby sister.

Fourteen

Laney was no closer to finding the traitor than she had been three days ago. Her family was counting on her. Their reputation, their...everything hinged on her finding the person who dared go against them. Until they knew who was behind the leak to the Feds, they were each taking turns manning the main office. Laney still wasn't convinced this was where everything went down; the clues the internet was giving her could be deceiving.

Mac and Jenna had decided to stick around through the holidays and definitely until this mess was cleared up.

Working in the office of her ancestors, Laney started looking at keystrokes with a program she'd downloaded. Every laptop in the office had to be checked. They had eight. The Boston office had to be ruled out first. Even though the new offices seemed coincidental in timing, if someone were going to attack, they may do it from close range where they could keep an eye on most of the key players.

Laney reached for another cracker. Normally she'd scold anyone for eating around their computers, but time was of the essence and her little one demanded some food.

"Anything?"

Laney didn't spare Braden a glance as he stepped into the office. "Not yet."

"How are you feeling?"

She hadn't seen him in three days, since the night of the party. He'd texted her to talk work and ask if she was feeling okay, but that was it. Ryker's name wasn't mentioned, and Laney was perfectly fine with that. The more her brothers stayed out of her personal business, the better.

"Hungry. I'm either tired or hungry. It's a cycle."

"Zara is out running errands. I'll have her bring you something."

Laney shook her head. "No need. I practically packed my kitchen in my bag because I knew I'd be here all day and evening."

Braden took a seat across from her. "You can't work yourself to death. You're expecting. I know how tired Zara was."

Her fingertips stilled on the keyboard as she glanced over the screen. "I'm sorry if this hurts you."

Braden shook his head. "You being pregnant isn't what bothers me."

Laney tried to keep the anger at bay. If they were all going to move forward, they had to stay levelheaded and remain calm. And after Ryker had spent the night simply holding her, Laney had a newfound hope that things would work out. They had to.

"You don't want to hear this, but Ryker and I aren't just fooling around."

Braden crossed his ankle over his knee and curled his hands over the sides of the chair. "No, I don't want to hear that my best friend, a guy I call my brother, is taking advantage of my sister. It doesn't sit well with me."

"You think that's what this is? That he's some sex-crazed maniac and I'm his poor, unsuspecting victim?" Laney shook her head and reached for another buttery cracker. "You have no clue, then. I love him."

"Damn it, Laney." Braden jerked forward in his seat, his hard stare holding her. "You're going to get hurt. A guy like Ryker doesn't do relationships. Have you ever wondered why he hasn't had a woman around us? That's not his style."

"It wasn't your style, either, until you got trapped with Zara. Now look at you."

That narrowed gaze didn't intimidate her. She took a bite of her cracker. "If you're done throwing your unwanted opinions around, I have work to do."

Braden came to his feet and blew out a breath. "You're going to get hurt," he repeated, his tone softer now.

"I'm a big girl."

She refused to look at him, refused to give him the power over her, because he had no say in how she handled her emotions or what she did with Ryker.

When he stormed out, Laney let out a breath. *That went well.*

Her cell chimed, but she ignored it. Braden was here, so if there was anything pressing going on, he'd know. The more she looked over this laptop, the more she was convinced it was clean. She'd just shut it down when her cell chimed once again.

Leaning over, she dug into her purse and fished it out of the side pocket. Giddiness burst through her when her contractor's name appeared.

She swiped her finger over the screen to open the message.

Inspections all passed. Moving forward on reworking the electrical.

Finally. Some good news. With the initial building inspections passed, she could push forward and hopefully come in ahead of her original spring opening.

After Ryker had shared his story with her the other night, she was even more determined to raise awareness for children who didn't have a proper home life.

She may not be able to help them all, but if she even helped one, then that was one less child who would doubt his or her self-worth. These kids needed to know someone cared about them, genuinely cared, because that was the struggle with Ryker right now. He didn't know what to do with the love she offered.

Laney sent off a quick reply that she'd be by tomorrow to discuss lighting and a few other questions she had regarding the kitchen area and the rec room.

She was making headway with the project, and possibly with Braden since he didn't seem so full of rage. Now if she could only figure out this puzzle of who was betraying her family. She didn't feel a bit sorry for the person on the other end of this investigation. Whoever had gone against the O'Sheas deserved everything they had coming.

* * *

Ryker had a sinking feeling, and he never ignored his instincts.

As he pulled in front of O'Shea's, he killed the engine and let his mind process all the intel that had come in regarding the scrolls. There were obvious dead ends, so he dismissed those immediately. But there was something eating away at his mind. It only made sense for the works to be fairly close. They were last known to be in Zara's home, or the home that the O'Sheas had lost in the Great Depression. If they had gotten out, word would've traveled.

Braden had searched, Ryker had searched. There wasn't a square inch of that house that had gone uncovered. But Ryker couldn't help but wonder if he'd missed something.

Zara's house sat empty now, well, save for her grandmother's things, because Zara had moved in with Braden. But Ryker wanted to go back in. He refused to give up. He'd been all over the damn globe on hunches, on veiled hints, but nothing had turned up. Frustration and failure were bitter pills to swallow, so he was going back to the point of origin, starting at square one. Because he was fresh out of leads.

Now more than ever, he needed to find those heirlooms. He needed to prove his family loyalties.

He stepped from his SUV, pulling his leather coat tighter to ward off the bitter chill. As soon as he stepped into O'Shea's, Braden's glare greeted him.

"Your eye looks better," he commented before looking back down at a stack of folders on his antique desk.

Ryker didn't take the bait. His eye still hurt like a bitch, but he had no right to complain.

"I want to get back into Zara's house," he said instead.

He moved farther into the spacious lobby area, complete with a Christmas tree that Laney no doubt had a hand in putting up. It had the same damn glittery nonsense she'd wanted him to put in her house.

"That resource is exhausted if you're referring to the scrolls." Braden dropped his pen and eased back in his leather seat. "Why do you need back in?"

Ryker shoved his hands in his pockets. "There's something we're missing."

"You're wasting your time."

"It's my time to waste." He refused to back down on this. "You know I'll just go in regardless. I'm merely telling you for courtesy."

Braden slowly came to his feet. Ryker didn't move, didn't bother to get out of the way when Braden came around the desk and stood toe to toe with him.

"Oh for pity's sake. If this is another pissing contest, count me out."

Ryker caught a glimpse of Laney in the doorway to the back office. Her hair was tied up in a loose knot, and her outfit consisted of an oversize gray sweater, black leggings and brown boots. She looked so young. Granted, she was ten years younger, but the simple outfit had her appearing almost innocent. His heart slammed against his chest as he took in the sight.

He offered her a smile. "I'm just letting your brother know of my plans for the evening."

Rolling her eyes, she moved toward them. "Braden, I think I found something. If you can stop being a bully for two seconds and come look?"

She'd barely gotten the words out before Braden and Ryker were in motion. Once in the office, Laney settled back into the seat, and Braden took one side of her chair while Ryker took the other.

"I found an encrypted email. I had to dig, and the person tried to delete it, but here it is."

"Open it."

Laney shook her head. "I can't. That's the problem. But the subject is damning and it's from the general computer at the main office."

She pointed to the bold header: BACKLOG

"And look at the time and date." She pointed to the screen—it was as soon as the new system was in place. Hours after it had been implemented, in fact. Then they had clearly sent the email and quickly covered their tracks.

The mole was good, but Laney was better. This was the break they'd needed.

"Bastards." Braden slammed his hand on the desk, making Laney jump.

"It's a start," she said, attempting to console him, but there was no calming him. This meant war for whoever did this. "The email wasn't from our internal system, and the account is fake. I just have to dig to find who set it up."

"You can do it." Ryker placed a hand on her shoulder and squeezed. "We all know you can. We're just frustrated and need to get this sorted out before the Feds find something incriminating."

Braden threw up his arms. "They have our sales records. If they search through each and every item, they're going to find questionable pieces."

Feeling a surge of loyalty and protectiveness, Laney glanced up at her brother. "If they searched each piece, they would have speculation at best. I have nothing in the program that indicates where the pieces came from. All of that is stored at my house, in a safe that even you two couldn't crack."

"I'd shoot it." Ryker straightened. "So, you're going to work on this, and I'm going to go back to Zara's tonight. Are you staying with her, Braden?"

Laney leaned back in her seat, looking up at the two men who seemed to be having some sort of staring showdown. She crossed her arms and waited for the testosterone to come down a notch.

"I'm not leaving her alone in her state," Braden replied. "You go. I'll make sure she's fine."

"With all this going on, I think it's safest if she's with one of us at all times."

Braden nodded. "That we can agree on."

Laney jerked to her feet, sending her chair flying back and crashing into the wall. "*She* is right here. And *she* can take care of herself."

They both stared at her as if she'd lost her mind. "I'm serious," she went on. "I don't need a babysitter, and nobody has threatened us with physical harm."

"You're pregnant," Braden growled. "You're automatically vulnerable."

Laney turned to face her brother fully. "You know I'm capable of taking care of myself. Stay all you want, but when I leave, I won't be needing a shadow."

Braden glanced over her shoulder toward Ryker. "Will you tell her? Maybe she'll listen to you."

"She won't listen to me. I ignore her wishes when it comes to things like this anyway."

Yeah, which was how he'd ended up tearing her dress off in a Miami hotel room. He'd been worried for her safety…and then she'd been plastered against the wall, panting his name.

Ryker took her arm, urging her to look at him. Laney shifted her attention. "What?"

"Just listen. For once. I'll be back later. Go to my place. I'll meet you there."

Braden practically growled behind Laney. "Can you two not talk like this?"

"Leave the room," Laney spouted over her shoulder. "I'll go home. If you want to come there, you can. I have too much to do."

Ryker nodded. "I'll try not to be too late."

Once he was gone, Laney glanced back at her over-bearing babysitter. "You know your hovering and child-ish attitude aren't going to make my feelings for him go away."

"I've thought about this. I don't like feeling betrayed, but there's so much more at stake. I want you both to real-ize what's at stake if you fall out. We need him, Laney."

"You think I'm not aware of that? I can't help who I fall in love with, Braden."

He blew out a breath and pulled her into his arms. "Damn it, Laney. I love you both and don't want either of you hurt—even if I'm still pissed at him."

Laney sank into his embrace. "I don't think it's me you have to worry about."

Fifteen

Ryker searched the obvious hiding places at the former O'Shea home once more: closets, cabinets, old trunks. He made his way to the secret tunnel Zara had showed them. The space was rather small and had no shelves, just a chair in the corner. The tunnel could be accessed at one end from an opening at the kitchen and at the other end from the long hallway. Ryker knew if those scrolls were still here, they'd likely be someplace "hidden" like this where no one would think to look.

He ran his hands over the walls. He'd never thought to look for another secret passage. Who knew what surprises this house had concealed? He covered every square inch of the walls, then worked on the baseboards, the floorboards. The tunnel was clean.

He'd been there for five hours and had covered the basement and main floor. There wasn't a loose floorboard to be found. As he went up to the second floor, the steps creaked, groaning against his weight. He froze. Old steps were bound to crackle and settle, but he'd never explored the stairs. Hadn't even crossed his mind—until now.

Ryker went back down the steps and started there. He knocked on the boards, curious if any were loose or sounded different from the others. He tapped each post on the banister, as well. He'd nearly made it to the top when, two steps from the second-floor landing, he hit pay dirt.

He'd been excited before on other hunts only to be deflated when nothing happened. But he was damn well going to devote every bit of energy he had to fulfilling Patrick's dying wish. Ryker owed him at least that—especially because he hadn't been able to stay away from Laney. That was a debt he'd never be able to repay.

Wrapping his fingers around the outside edge of the wood, Ryker gave a slight tug. The wood creaked as it started to give way. The banister that rested in that particular step splintered. Ryker jerked it out, tossed it down the steps…he'd pay to have it repaired later.

His heart accelerated as he gave the board another pull. Finally it ripped free from the step. He eased down another stair and pulled out the minuscule flashlight he'd shoved into his pocket before coming here.

Bending to get a good view, his chest clenched as he spotted something inside. No way could this be the scrolls. The odds that they'd been right under their noses the entire time was pretty nonexistent. Yet something had brought him back to the old house.

Ryker slid the end of the flashlight between his teeth,

then, using both hands, he reached into the space and tugged out a metal box.

Sinking back onto the step, his back against the wall, he stared at the box as if it held every answer he'd ever wanted. Was this them? He wanted to rip into this box to see, but at the same time he wanted to wait, to hold on to the hope he felt right at this moment. If these were the missing scrolls, Ryker had just accomplished what no one else had been able to.

Zara couldn't have known about this hiding spot in the steps or she would've told them. Which made him wonder if her grandmother even knew.

He set the flashlight aside and pulled the lock-pick kit from his jacket pocket. The box was definitely an antique, turn of the twentieth century, if he was guessing right. He'd been working with and acquiring for the O'Sheas long enough to know antiques. This box may be the one the O'Sheas had used before the scrolls had gone missing.

Carefully he went to work on the old, rusted lock. The box was long but not very wide. Ryker wondered if the scrolls could even fit in something this size. Suddenly the lock clicked and the lid flopped open. Most old locks were harder to pick. Clearly this was meant to be.

"Damn," he muttered. There were tubes inside the box. Nine tubes to be exact. Nine tubes that possibly held the nine scrolls.

Ryker couldn't get into one of the tubes fast enough. He'd barely pried the lid off one when his cell went off.

He ignored it. Nothing was more important than this right here. He didn't want to pull anything out, because if these were the scrolls, they'd be beyond delicate. But once the lid sprang free, he grabbed the light again and angled it inside the cylinder.

This was it. He'd found them. Finally.

There were no words, there was nothing but a sense of accomplishment unlike anything he'd ever known. He'd done it. After years, decades of hunting, Ryker had been the one to find the heirlooms so important to the O'Shea family.

Quickly, but with care, he put everything back into the box.

Glancing at his watch, he realized he'd been at Zara's longer than he first thought. It was late, dark, but there was no way he could let this moment pass. He had to let everyone know.

He sent off a quick text to Mac, Braden and Laney, telling them all to meet at Braden's. Mac should already be there, since that's where he was staying, and Laney…well, who knew where she would be. He hoped at Braden's so she could be safe, but knowing her, she went home and was up to her chin in jasmine-scented bubbles.

Ryker had procured many pieces over the years. He'd traveled all over the world. He'd learned languages, used disguises, made enemies all in the name of loyalty and love for this family.

And he was finally coming home with the one true gift he'd always longed to deliver.

"How the hell had we missed this?" Braden asked.

Laney couldn't take her eyes off the tubes. Nine of them lay on Braden's desk. And they were all there to witness this important moment in the O'Shea family history: Mac, Jenna, Braden, Zara, Laney—and Ryker.

She'd never in her life seen him so excited. The pride on his face… Laney couldn't put into words the transformation.

She'd had news to share with them about some antiques at an old estate not far outside the city that they needed to acquire, but that could definitely wait. This moment had been a long time coming. Decades. And here they all were gathered around her father's old desk. Laney couldn't help but feel as if he were here in spirit.

Tears pricked her eyes, but she blinked them away.

"I never even knew that step was loose, let alone came apart," Zara stated. Shock laced her voice as she, too, continued to stare. "I'm sure my grandmother didn't either or she would've told me. She was only a baby when she went to live there."

"Dad was adamant that there were no hidden areas," Braden chimed in. "We knew of the small tunnel that led into the kitchen, but nothing like this."

Braden turned his attention to Ryker and slapped a hand onto his shoulder. "You did it."

Ryker nodded, not saying a word. He may have appeared to have it all together in that typical Ryker fashion, but Laney knew that inside, he was trying hard to keep his emotions in check.

"I had to," Ryker finally murmured, his eyes fixed on the layout. "I owe you all—"

"Nothing," Braden confirmed. "I know I was pissed at you for the whole Shane incident—and I won't even get into Laney—but I see why you took matters into your own hands this time. If you do it again, though, I'll kill you."

Ryker's mouth twitched, but he merely nodded.

"But this is something I honestly never thought would

happen in my lifetime." Braden's voice grew thick with emotions. "Dad would be so damn proud of you."

A tear trickled down Laney's cheek. Zara wrapped her arm around Laney's shoulders, giving silent support. They were all feeling years' worth of frustration, hope, determination, all rolled into this moment. So many leads, so many cities... Ryker had single-handedly trekked all over the globe in an attempt to bring these home where they belonged.

"We need to get these in the safe," Mac chimed in. "Nobody can know they're here, and the security should probably be bumped up."

"I'm already on it." Work mode, that's what Laney could concentrate on. She swiped her damp cheek. "I have an alarm you can put on just the safe. It's sensitive but necessary."

Braden nodded. "Great. How are you doing on the search for our mole?"

"It's got to be one of the employees at the main office." A sick feeling settled in her stomach at the thought of anyone doing this to her family. "That narrows it down to six. Viviana is the newest employee, but I almost feel she's too obvious. Maybe whoever is doing this is using the timing of her coming on board."

Braden carefully capped the narrow tubes and placed them all back into the shallow box. "Keep everyone working on a regular schedule."

"What?" Mac questioned.

"Keep the enemies close," Ryker added. "Now that we know it was one of them, Laney can keep an eye on everything they're doing on our system."

"And they won't have a clue," she added with a smile.

"This is my favorite part of work. Oh, also freezing assets. I do enjoy knowing our enemies are broke."

Jenna laughed. "I'm so glad I'm on your good side."

Laney couldn't help but widen her smile. "You're safe. The DeLucas on the other hand…"

"What did you do?" Braden asked, his hand resting on the now-locked box.

With a shrug and a surge of pride, Laney met the questioning gazes of her brothers and Ryker. "Merely closed some credit cards, possibly drained their off-shore bank account."

Ryker's eyes widened, his nod of approval giving her another burst of excitement. No way was she going to let them get away with the petty little game they played with Ryker. Braden said no more violence, fine. She didn't get involved with that part anyway. But she could sure as hell ruin someone's life. Hard to keep being a jerk when you were broke and powerless.

"I swear, you scare me sometimes," Braden added. He came around Ryker and gave her a brotherly hug. "Just be careful. I know you make sure things can't be traced back to you, but I still worry. Especially now that you're pregnant."

Laney patted his back, meeting Ryker's gaze over Braden's shoulder. "I'm fine. The only time I'd ever been in physical danger was with Shane."

And thanks to Ryker, Shane was a nonissue.

Laney stepped back, smoothing her sweater over her torso. "Since we're talking work, I have a house out in Bradenton that has several antiques that could be of interest. The owner actually called me today asking if we could come look and discuss adding them to the spring show. I'll give you a heads-up. The price they're wanting is a bit over what I would estimate. But I haven't seen them."

"I'll go." Ryker shoved his hands in his pockets. Laney wondered if that penny was still there after his emotional purging session the other night. "Now that the scrolls have been found, I won't be so tied up and consumed with them. I'll do something normal for a change."

Laney held her breath while Mac and Braden stared at Ryker. After all that had happened—her pregnancy, finding the scrolls—Laney prayed her brothers kept Ryker in their brotherhood.

"You do that," Braden finally said. "Good change of pace for you, and it's only thirty minutes away."

Laney let out the breath she'd been holding. "I'll let them know you'll be there the day after tomorrow."

"All this excitement has me exhausted." Zara circled the group until she came to stand next to Braden. The look she gave her husband implied that she was more than ready for their company to leave. "Ryker, thank you, and please don't think a thing about tearing up the staircase."

Shifting in his stance, Ryker rubbed a hand over the back of his neck. "I'll fix it, you have my word."

"I'm going to head on home," Laney told them all. "I'm pretty tired, and it's way past my bedtime."

She gave her brothers a hug, said her farewells to Jenna and Zara, and when she turned to Ryker, there was no mistaking that hard look he gave her.

"Fine. You'll drive me home, and I'll get my car tomorrow. You don't even have to say it."

"Just to make sure she's safe," Mac chimed in.

Laney whirled. "Not now. We've had a good night. Let's not get into another pissing contest. His eye still hasn't healed."

"I can speak for myself," Ryker added. "I'll take her home, and from that point it's nobody's business."

Braden opened his mouth, but Zara elbowed him in the side. "You love them both. Let them figure out their own relationship."

Braden kept his eyes on Ryker, but Ryker only let out a slight grunt. "I get it," he said, holding his hands up. "If I hurt her, you'll bury me, nobody will find me. You all are the only ones who would look anyway."

Laney placed her hand on Ryker's arm. "Braden and Mac will get over it. We're having a baby. Let's focus on that for now."

She couldn't help but borrow his earlier verbiage. Everything that was happening between her and Ryker was going minute by minute. That's the only way her brothers could take it, as well. Besides, how could she tell them what was going on, where she and Ryker were headed, when she didn't know the answers herself?

Silence surrounded them, and Laney was beyond done with all this veiled testosterone tossing.

"Get her home safely," Braden finally said before Laney could open her mouth.

"That's what he's done for years." She had to remind them of how loyal Ryker truly was. And wasn't that ridiculous? He'd been around for decades and had proven himself over and over. "Ryker isn't the one who betrayed you. Remember that."

Laney marched from the room. Still thrilled about the scrolls, she tried not to let her brothers' archaic attitude ruin her mood. She didn't care where Ryker took her, his house or hers. She intended to show him just how thankful she was about his discovery.

Sixteen

Whether it was due to the euphoric state of finding the missing scrolls or the fact that he held Laney until she fell asleep, Ryker didn't know, but he'd been unable to relax in her bed. Last night, after they'd left Braden's house, Ryker had every intention of going to his place, but Laney had nearly crawled in his lap in the car, suggesting they go to her house because it was closer. Who was he to argue?

Now he wished he were anywhere else. As he sat in the middle of one of the spare bedrooms, Ryker glanced at all the pieces to this crib. How did all of these damn pieces go together? The picture on the large box in the corner showed what he should end up with, but he'd never built a crib before. Hell, he'd never built anything. His hands had always been used in other not-so-innocent ways.

Ryker glared at the directions, trying to make sense of the pathetic diagrams. Why the hell didn't the company just send someone to assemble the damn thing when you ordered it?

He'd known she'd been looking at furniture, but until he'd walked past the spare bedroom this morning on his way to get coffee, he'd had no idea she'd actually bought a crib. He couldn't sleep and didn't want to wake Laney, so he figured he'd give it his best shot.

He'd stood in the doorway so long just staring. It had never occurred to him where the nursery would be—her house or his. Both? This was where things started to get even murkier. He didn't want to concentrate on all the reasons this path he was on could go wrong.

Yet he couldn't help himself. The level of comfort he was settling into with Laney was hinting at something so much more. He'd spent nights in her bed, the selfish jerk that he was. Ryker just couldn't tear himself away. He'd mentally pushed Laney away for so long, for so many reasons—his childhood was crap and didn't know how to do a relationship, her father had trusted Ryker to always do the right thing, Laney was ten years younger. The list went on and on, pounding away at Ryker's mind.

Frustrated at his insecurities, he pulled over two of the long boards and a pack of screws. That took no time to put together. Perhaps this wouldn't be such a pain and he could have it done by the time Laney woke up.

The sun hadn't even come up yet, so hopefully she'd sleep a little longer. She needed it. Their baby needed it.

Maybe if this crib got assembled, and didn't fall apart, he'd take her out to pick out something else she wanted. He hadn't gotten her a Christmas present. Hell, what would he even get her? She was all sparkles and grace, and he was a wolf in an Italian suit when his leathers wouldn't suffice.

Their worlds may have collided and run parallel for the past several years, but that didn't mean they were on the same playing field.

By the time Ryker got to the sides of the antique, white sleigh-style crib, he was ready to chuck the entire thing out the window and buy her one already assembled.

"I was going to have someone come in and do that for me."

Ryker jerked around. Laney stood in the doorway, her silk robe knotted around her still-narrow waist, her dark hair tousled all around her shoulders. A lump settled heavily in Ryker's throat. How could he take the mob princess and attempt to fit into her world? Not physically, but mentally. He was a damn mess inside, and he didn't need to pay anyone to tell him that.

"Why aren't you asleep?" he asked before turning back to the mayhem that posed as a baby bed.

He wasn't sure how long he'd been in here, but he needed a break. Ryker came to his feet, brushing his hands on the boxer briefs he'd slept in.

"The bed was lonely," she told him, raking her bedroom eyes over his nearly bare body.

Her smoldering looks never failed to make his body stir. The need for her had never been in question. If all of this was physical, if she wasn't Patrick O'Shea's daughter, hell, if she were anybody else, none of this would be in question.

"What's that look about?" She tipped her head to the side and crossed to him. "You found the scrolls, but you still look as if the weight of the world is on your shoulders."

Maybe because it was. The baby, the need to want Laney in his life more... Ryker wasn't even getting into how Braden and Mac still didn't approve. That he could handle. It was the rest of it he wasn't sure of.

"Ryker?"

He closed his eyes and willed his demons to stand down, but they were rearing their ugly heads even harsher than usual.

"We need to take some time—"

"What? Are you seriously going to tell me you need time?" Laney crossed her arms over her chest. "Don't be clichéd, Ryker. I already told you I was waiting for you, that I'd be here for you."

At least one of them was strong right now.

He ran his hands through his hair, his eyes burning from lack of sleep. "I can't get this damn thing together."

"The crib?" Her brows drew in. "This isn't a big deal."

It was everything.

"Do you know my father threw a glass table at me when I was seven?" he asked, needing her to understand. He ran a fingertip along the scar on his chest. "A piece ricocheted off the wall and hit me here. That wasn't the only time he lost his temper, Laney."

"And you think this is going to change how I look at you? Because you're nothing like him."

With a snort, Ryker shook his head. "I'm exactly like him. You do know what I've done for your family for years, right? When you were learning to write cursive in school, I was already doing all the dirty work."

Her eyes narrowed. In a move he didn't predict, she reached up, planted her palms on his bare chest and gave him a shove.

"If you're going to be a coward and worry about losing

your temper with me or our baby, then get out. I won't wait around for you when you're acting like this. I know the man inside, but clearly you have yet to meet him."

Her rage shattered him. "Are you willing to take the chance? I've never done the traditional family thing, and I have one good memory of the first twelve years of my life. That's all."

"Then you should be more determined to make memories with your child."

Could he? Was that even in him? He had no clue what children wanted. All he knew was what Laney deserved.

If you love it, set it free.

He stared at her, willing his feet to move, to go into her bedroom and get his things so he could leave. But the pink in her cheeks, the hurt in her eyes and the grim line of her mouth were hard to ignore.

"You have to know I'm distancing myself for the sake of you and the baby." He wanted to reach out and touch her. To let her know he did care, too much, but he had to get inside his own head and sort things out. "I need to know you're safe. That's been my role for so many years, but now I need to know you're safe from me."

"Safe from you? Then stop hurting me," she cried, tears filling her eyes. "You can walk out that door anytime, but don't think it's revolving. You know I love you, damn it, you love me, too. I can see it. You wouldn't be so hell-bent on pushing me away otherwise."

Now he did reach for her, taking her hands in his, holding tight when she tried to jerk away. "There's so much inside me that I need to deal with. Everything hit me so hard all at once…"

Damn it. He shook his head, glancing down to their joined hands. "Your father, your brothers have been the only family I've ever loved. But there's still that demon inside me that is the twelve-year-old boy who wasn't given love and security. I need to get that under control before it controls me."

"It's already controlling you." Now when Laney pulled, he let her go. "You have shut yourself off from real feelings for so long you have no idea how to handle them. You found the scrolls, fulfilled your promise to my father, and now you have all this space in your mind that is filling back up with doubts."

She was so dead-on. There was nothing she hadn't hit directly.

Pulling the V of her robe tighter, she glanced away. "Just go, Ryker. You want to. You want to run and hide and be secluded from anything that threatens you to step outside of your comfort zone."

Damn it, she was his comfort zone. He just knew if he stayed in that space too long, he'd end up destroying it if he didn't get a handle on his past.

"For now, this is for the best." He leaned down to kiss her on the head, but she stepped away, her eyes blazing at him.

Swallowing back his emotions, he moved around her and went back to her bedroom to get dressed. He only prayed he was making the right decision because he wanted Laney, wanted their baby. But he couldn't pull them into his world when he couldn't even handle living in it himself.

So maybe going back to Southie wasn't the best of ideas. But Ryker figured if he wanted to rid himself of the past, he'd need to tackle it headfirst.

So here he stood outside his old apartment building.

The place looked even more run-down than he remembered, and he hadn't thought that was possible. The gutter hung off one side, the wooden steps were bowed, the railing half gone. There was no way this could be deemed livable because if this was the outside, he didn't want to know what the inside looked like.

Snow swirled around him. The house next to the apartments wasn't faring much better, but someone had attempted to brighten it up with a strand of multicolored lights draped around the doorway.

Shoving his hands into the pockets of his jeans, Ryker stared back at the door that led to his dilapidated apartment. For the first twelve years of his life, he'd called this place home. He hadn't known anything different. Much like so many of the kids in this area. Granted, some kids had a happy home life because money wasn't the key to happiness. Having a home that was falling apart was definitely not the same as having an addict father who didn't give a damn.

The penny in his pocket brushed the tip of his fingers. Ryker honestly had no clue where his father was now; he didn't much care, either. Most likely the man had killed himself with all the chemicals he put into his system.

Ryker had actually shed tears after Patrick's death, but felt absolutely nothing when he thought of his biological father.

This place did nothing but bring back memories Ryker hated reliving.

He turned, heading down the street. He'd parked a block away, needing the brisk walk. Keeping his head low to ward off the chill, he headed back to his SUV, which stuck out like the proverbial sore thumb. When he was a kid, if this big, black vehicle had come through, Ryker would've thought it was the president himself.

He'd just stepped off the curb and crossed the street when he noticed movement out of the corner of his eye.

"Mr. Barrett?"

Ryker glanced toward the old building that had sat vacant for several years. It used to be a store of sorts, then a restaurant, and he'd just assumed it would be torn down.

"I thought that was you."

Ryker eyed the man who was unlocking the door to the building. After getting closer, Ryker could see it was Mr. Pauley, a popular contractor around the Boston area. The O'Sheas had used him a few times in the past. The truck behind Ryker's vehicle bore the familiar emblem from Mr. Pauley's company.

"How are you doing, Mr. Pauley?" Ryker called.

"Good. Good. Did you come by to check on the property?"

Confused, Ryker stopped by his car. "Excuse me?"

"Miss O'Shea said she'd be by today." He tugged the door open and held it with his foot as he shoved his keys back into his coat pocket. "I figured since you were here, she sent you."

Miss O'Shea? Laney? What the hell was going on?

Ryker was an O'Shea by default, so there was no questioning why the contractor would think such a thing. Everyone around the area knew full well who the infamous family was, and who Ryker associated with and now called family.

Deciding to play along and figure out what Laney was up to—though after this morning he had no right—Ryker headed toward the open door. Once the two were inside, Ryker glanced around. The place was empty, save for the cobwebs that could only have come from tarantulas, some old boxes and some loose flooring.

"As I told Miss O'Shea the other day, I'm reworking the electrical." Mr. Pauley walked through the space and kept talking as if Ryker knew exactly what was going on. "I'm not sure about the kitchen. I may need to rewire some things in there, especially for the appliances she's wanting to use. This building is definitely not up to par for the two ovens she's suggested."

What the hell was Laney going to do with a building in Southie? Ryker continued following the middle-aged man toward what he assumed was the kitchen.

"She's got in mind she needs to crank out several meals a day. I admire her gumption, but this is going to take a lot of money to keep going."

Glancing at the cracked countertops, a rusted refrigerator, a sink that used to be white, Ryker started spinning ideas in his head. And all of them revolved around the perfectly generous Laney.

"But if anyone can help these kids it's her. Patrick was determined to save people." Mr. Pauley glanced back to Ryker with a side grin. "Anyway, this outside wall would be the best location for the ovens, but the wiring is all off. It can be run here. It's just going to cost more than the initial estimate I gave her. Same with the ventilation. Not much more, but—"

"I'll cover it."

His head was spinning, his mind racing over what could have possibly gotten into Laney's big heart that made her want to do this.

Damn the emotions she forced out of him. She wasn't even here and he was facing things he didn't want to. He was feeling so much...and he wasn't as afraid as he used to be. She'd come into his old neighborhood, she was renovating this old building to help kids...just like he used to be.

But he'd told her about his sordid childhood only days ago. There was no way she could've set things in motion that fast—no matter what her last name was.

Something twisted in Ryker's chest, some foreign emotion he almost didn't want to put a name to. The weight of this newfound feeling seemed to awaken something so deep within him, Ryker wondered how long he'd suppressed everything that was bursting through him now.

His entire life.

Ryker tried to focus back on what Mr. Pauley was saying as he pointed and gestured toward various parts of the spacious area that would become Laney's ideal kitchen.

Whatever Laney wanted, he was completely on board.

Seventeen

For the second time in as many weeks, Ryker had made a purchase at All Seasons. Now he stood outside Laney's house feeling like a fool. Perhaps this wasn't the way to go about things. Maybe he'd blown his chance when he flipped out over the crib and let all those doubts ruin what they had going on.

Since he left yesterday morning, she'd only texted him once, and that was to remind him of the home in Bradenton. He hadn't gone yet; there were more pressing matters to attend to.

For the first time in his life since becoming part of the O'Shea family, he was putting work on hold.

Because he didn't feel like he deserved to walk right in using his key, he rang the bell and gripped the shopping sack in his hand.

He didn't wait long before the door swung open. Laney

didn't say anything, and he waited for her to slam the door in his face. To his surprise, and relief, she stepped back and gestured for him to come in.

The warmth of her home instantly surrounded him. She had a fire in the fireplace, her tree sparkled with all the lights he'd put on it. This was home, a perfect home for their child to be raised in.

"Did you get to the estate?" she asked, brushing past him and heading back toward the kitchen.

"This is more important."

Laney stopped in her tracks, just as she hit the hallway off the living room. Her shoulders lifted as she drew in a breath and let out a deep sigh. When she turned, Ryker didn't waste any time moving toward her. He was done running, done hurting her, hurting them.

"I brought something for you." He extended the sack, smiling when her eyes caught the name on the side. "You can open it now."

She quirked a brow, kept her eyes on his and reached for the bag. Laney fisted the handles and stepped aside, sinking into the oversize chair. With the bag in her lap, she pulled out the tissue paper. Ryker shoved his hands in his pockets, waiting for her reaction, hoping he'd gone the right route in winning her back.

When she gasped and pulled out a white-and-gold stocking, her eyes immediately filled. That was a good sign…wasn't it?

"There's more." He nodded toward the bag and rocked back on his heels.

She pulled out another stocking, then another. Tissue paper lay all around her, the stockings on her lap as she stared down. Ryker couldn't see her expression for her hair curtaining her face.

Unable to stand the silence, he squatted in front of her.

"I don't have a fireplace," he started, reaching for one of the stockings. "I was hoping we could hang these here."

When she tipped her head to look at him, one tear slid down her cheek. "You put my name on one and yours on the other."

Ryker lay the smaller stocking over the larger ones. "And this will be for our baby. We can have the name put on once we know it."

"How did you...this...I don't even know what to say."

Speechless and in tears. Ryker was taking all of this as a very good sign. But he also knew Laney wouldn't be so quick to let him fully in. He'd been so back and forth, he needed to lay it all on the line and explain to her just what he wanted. Holding back was no longer an option.

"I hope you don't mind. I made a few adjustments to your plans with Mr. Pauley."

Laney's eyes widened as she sat up straighter. Her mouth formed a perfect O, and she continued to stare.

"I went back to my neighborhood, thinking maybe I could settle those demons once and for all." Before he would've gotten up to pace or avoided looking at her face, but he reached for her hands instead. "Mr. Pauley thought I was there to meet with him since you mentioned going by today."

"I...I called him a little bit ago but got his voicemail."

Ryker squeezed her hands. "Why did you start this project, Laney?"

"I wanted to make a difference for some kids." She glanced down at their hands, a soft smile adorning her mouth. "I started this before you ever told me the full story of your childhood. I'd heard enough over the years and always wanted to do something of my own. When I thought about what you went through, I would get so upset. I thought opening a place for kids to come after school would be ideal. They can get help with homework, we can feed them. In the summer, they can play basketball, interact with other kids and hopefully stay out of trouble."

She kept talking until Ryker put his finger over her lips. "You humble me, Laney O'Shea. Those kids are going to love this, love you."

Reaching out, he tipped up her chin with his finger and thumb. "Not as much as I love you."

The catch in her breath had Ryker easing forward, closing the space between them as he covered her mouth with his. He stole only a minor taste, promising himself more later.

"I do love you, Laney. Maybe I always have, but I was damn scared of it." She laughed, her eyes sparkling with more unshed tears as he pushed on. "You knew it, and I'm sorry it took me so long to catch up. But I have this past that sometimes threatens to strangle me and I... I'm working on it, but I can't work on my own. I need you, Laney."

She threw her arms around his neck, crushing the stockings and tissue between them. "I don't want you leaning on anyone else. Because I need you, too."

"I want to be here, with you." He eased back but didn't let go. "Your house is warm, it's perfect for our baby, for us. Our family."

"You want to move in here?" she asked, her eyes widening. "My brothers—"

"Aren't welcome. This is about you, me and our baby. Your brothers have an issue, they can take it up with me. I love you, Laney. I've never loved another woman. I want to be a team with you. All of the things I worried exposing you to, you've understood all along."

Laney's hands framed his face as her eyes searched his. "All of this came from you discovering my project?"

"The project just opened my eyes," he told her. "But why didn't you tell me?"

Laney shrugged, nibbling on her lip. "I didn't tell anyone. I told you I wanted something just for me. I'll tell the guys later, but I didn't do this so you all would be proud. I'm doing it for the kids."

Ryker settled his hands on her belly. "You're going to be the best mother. I can't wait to be a family with you."

Laney rested her forehead against his. "We're already a family."

Epilogue

"And who are you again?"

Ryker wasn't about to let just anyone into Braden's home. They were in the middle of a celebration. After a month of tiptoeing around the fact he and Laney were living together, the brothers had finally come to realize that Ryker and Laney were a done deal.

But it wasn't so much their relationship they were celebrating. Zara was pregnant again, and Mac and Jenna were closing in on their wedding date. There was plenty to be happy about...except this visitor at their door.

"I'm an investigator. Jack Carson."

Investigator. More like a nosey jerk with too much time on his hands.

"And what do you want?" Ryker asked, curling his fingers around the edge of the door and blocking the narrow opening with his body. "We have attorneys, so if you have an issue—"

"There's been a fire at the home of Mr. and Mrs. Parker in Bradenton."

Ryker froze. "A fire?" He'd just talked to them two days ago. They were still haggling over prices for their antiques. The young couple with a new baby had inherited the estate and all its contents, and they were hoping to earn some money by selling the larger pieces.

"You seem stunned by the news," Carson stated. "You wouldn't know anything about the fire, would you?"

Shocked, Ryker bristled. "How the hell would I know about it since you just told me? Are they all right?"

The investigator's eyes narrowed. "They were killed. Only the baby survived because the nursery was in the back of the house."

Ryker's gut clenched. The thought of an innocent baby without a mother and father was crippling.

"I hate to hear that," he said honestly. "Why are you here telling me this?"

Braden came up behind Ryker and eased the door wider. "Something wrong?"

Ryker nodded to the unwanted guest. "This is Jack something-or-other. Claims he's a PI."

"What's he want?"

Jack went on to explain the fire while Ryker studied the man. There was something about him that was familiar. Despite the expensive suit, the flashy SUV, the man smelled like a cop. But cops didn't make this kind of money, neither did the Feds. This guy was definitely suspicious...and ballsy for showing up here.

"That's terrible," Braden replied once Jack was done with the story. "I'm not sure where we fit in."

"We're just trying to find who set this fire because it appears to be a cover-up." Jack's assessing eyes kept shifting between Ryker and Braden. "There was a robbery, and most of the antiques were wiped out. The couple actually died from gunshot wounds."

Ryker remained still. "Why don't you quit dancing around the reason you're here and just spit it out."

"The O'Sheas had been talking with this couple, correct? About taking some of these antiques to auction?"

Ryker narrowed his eyes. "Our business is none of your concern."

"It is when there are two dead bodies."

Braden took a step onto the porch. Jack instantly backed up, but merely crossed his arms as if he was bored.

"Get the hell off my property," Braden growled. "If you have a problem, take it up with our attorneys. We don't talk to random strangers accusing us of something we know nothing about."

Braden took a step closer, and Ryker wondered if he'd have to step between these two.

Nah. It was nice seeing Braden get so fired up.

"What cop sent you?" Braden asked.

Jack remained silent and tipped his head. The cocky bastard was seriously getting on Ryker's nerves. Having had enough of this nuisance, Ryker stepped onto the porch and wedged a shoulder between the two.

"While this is fun and all, we actually have lives to get back to," Ryker told Jack. "So you're here of your own accord? No Fed or cop sent you? Then get your nosey ass off the property."

Clenching his fists at his side, Ryker tried to compose himself. But if this guy didn't budge soon, he wasn't going to be responsible for his actions.

Finally, Jack nodded and walked back to his car as if he'd been here for a flippin' Sunday brunch. Arrogance was a hideous trait to witness.

Once the guy was gone, Ryker turned to go back inside, but Braden hadn't budged. He was still staring at the spot where Jack's SUV had been parked.

"Don't let him get to you," Ryker stated. "It's a shame about that couple, but they can't pin any of that on us when we didn't do it."

Braden shook his head. "Did you see his eyes?"

"What?"

Braden looked to Ryker. "That guy. Did you look at his eyes? They seemed so familiar."

Ryker agreed. A shiver crept up his back. He didn't like when he got this feeling. Things never ended well.

"I don't think he was a PI." Braden ran a hand over the back of his neck and started heading toward the house. "We'll talk to Mac later, but for now keep this little visit between us."

Ryker fell into step beside him. "We need to watch our backs. Who knows who the hell this guy is."

It was hard for Ryker to put the mysterious man out of his mind, but when he walked into the house and Laney met him in the hallway, he found himself smiling. She had the slightest baby belly, only visible when she wore something tight. Today she had on a body-hugging dress with tights and boots. She was so damn sexy.

"I wondered where you went," she told him. "Who was at the door?"

Braden moved on into the living room, leaving Ryker and Laney in the foyer. "Nobody important," he replied.

They hadn't discovered the mole, yet, but it was only a

matter of time. Ryker wasn't giving up on bringing down the culprit who was hellbent on destroying the only family he'd ever known.

Laney's arms looped around his neck. "If you're done celebrating here, I'm ready to go home and celebrate privately."

Ryker whispered in her ear exactly what they would be doing in private, and Laney melted against him.

This was his woman, his forever family. They'd been his all along…all he'd had to do was reach out and claim them.

* * * * *

LET'S TALK

Romance

For exclusive extracts, competitions
and special offers, find us online:

- facebook.com/millsandboon
- @MillsandBoon
- @MillsandBoonUK

Get in touch on 01413 063232

For all the latest titles coming soon, visit
millsandboon.co.uk/nextmonth